W9-AOO-428

STAR WARS®

THE ORIGINAL TRILOGY

A GRAPHIC NOVEL

Disney • LUCASFILM PRESS

Los Angeles · New York

Printed in the United States of America

First Edition, March 2016

1 3 5 7 9 10 8 6 4 2

Library of Congress Control Number on file

FAC-034274-16015

ISBN 978-1-4847-3784-2

Visit the official *Star Wars* website at: www.starwars.com.

CONTENTS

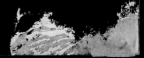

STAR WARS®

A NEW HOPE

A LONG TIME AGO
IN A GALAXY FAR, FAR AWAY. . . .

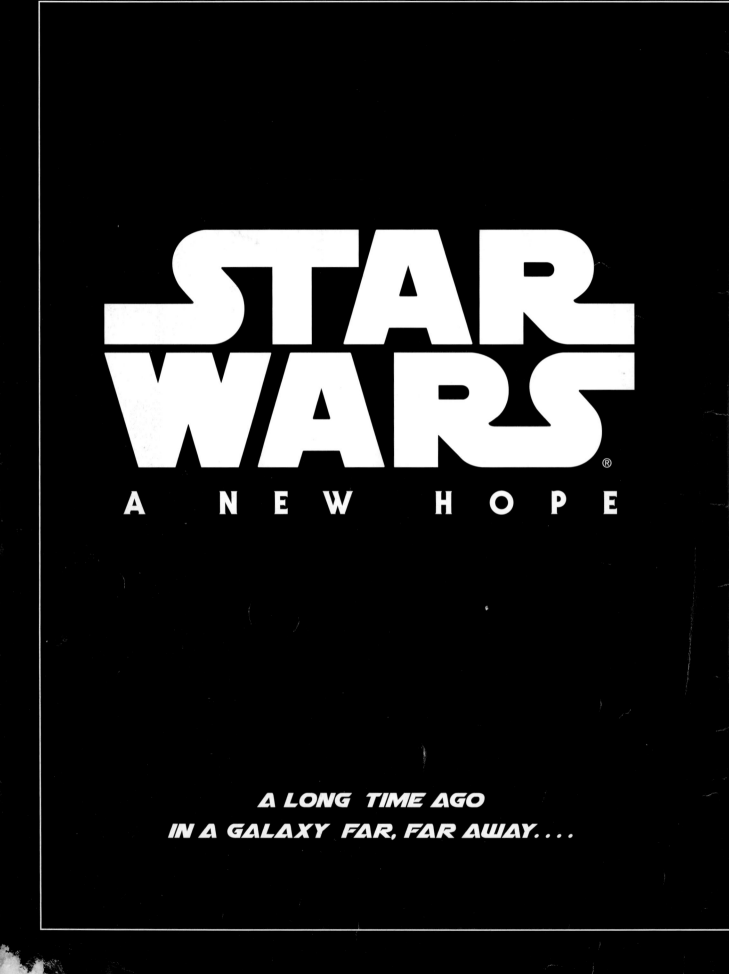

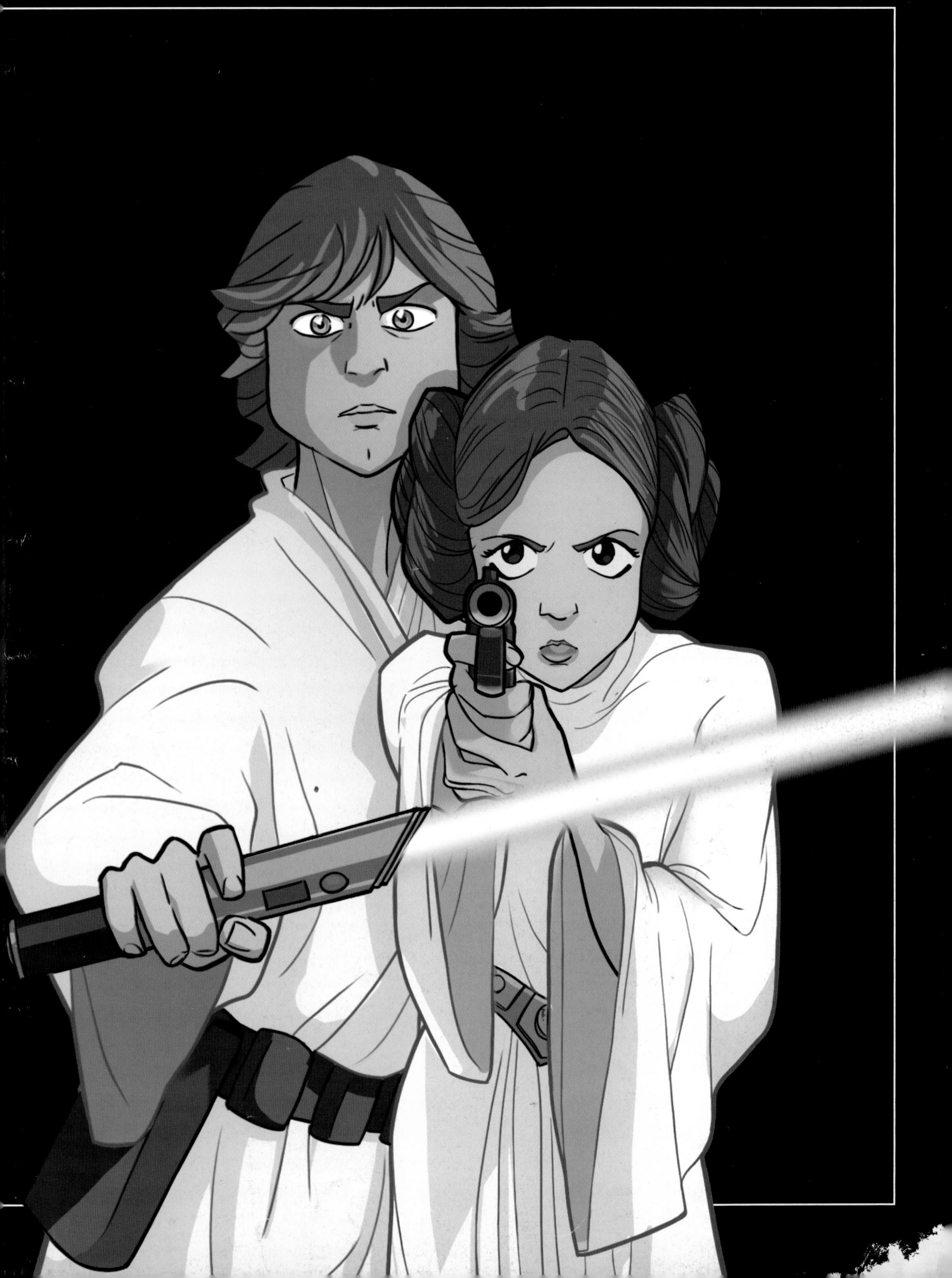

Episode IV
A NEW HOPE

It is a period of civil war.
Rebel spaceships, striking
from a hidden base, have won
their first victory against
the evil Galactic Empire.

During the battle, Rebel
spies managed to steal secret
plans to the Empire's
ultimate weapon, the DEATH
STAR, an armored space
station with enough power
to destroy an entire planet.

Pursued by the Empire's
sinister agents, Princess
Leia races home aboard her
starship, custodian of the
stolen plans that can save her
people and restore
freedom to the galaxy. . . .

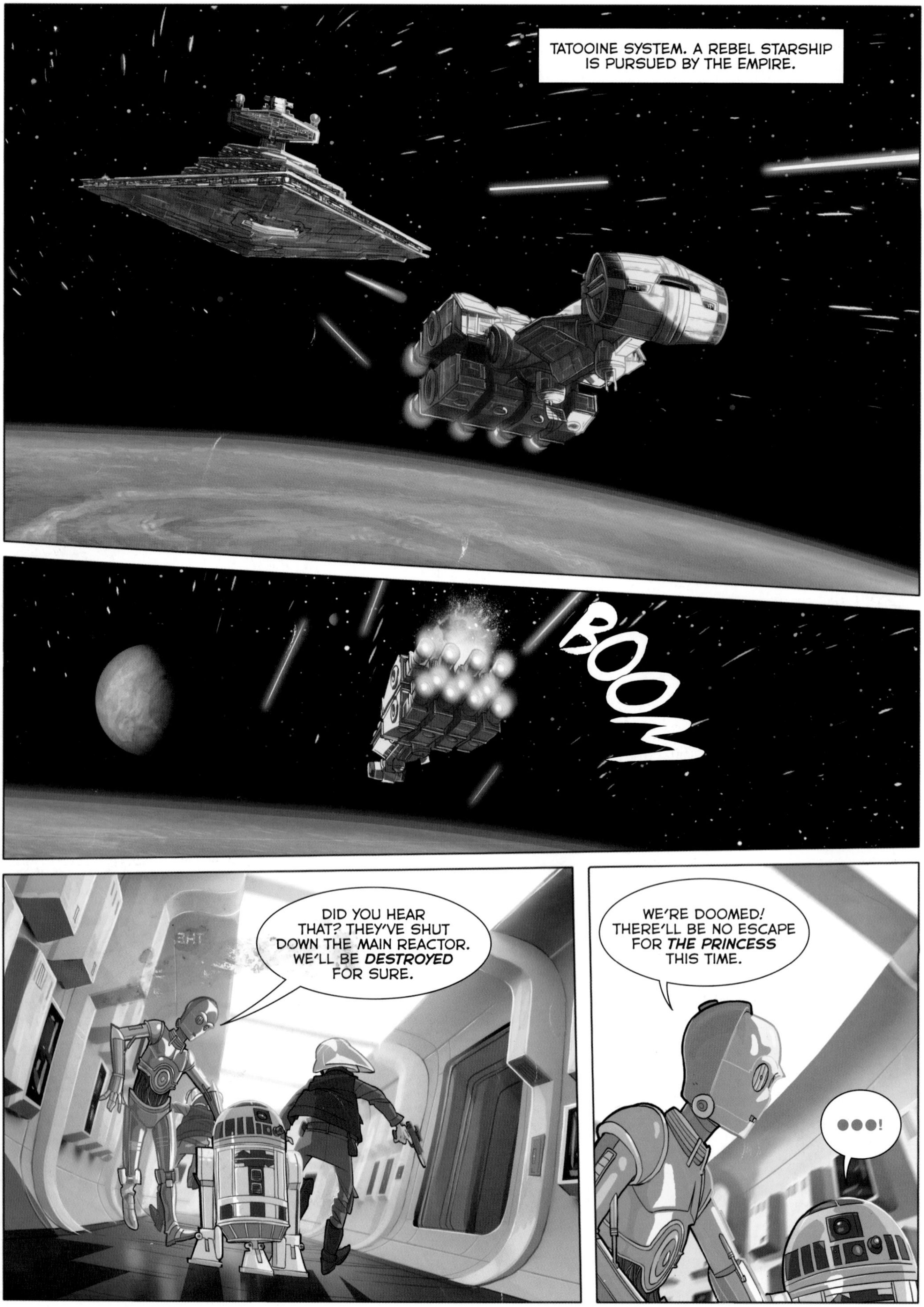
TATOOINE SYSTEM. A REBEL STARSHIP IS PURSUED BY THE EMPIRE.
BOOM
DID YOU HEAR THAT? THEY'VE SHUT DOWN THE MAIN REACTOR. WE'LL BE *DESTROYED* FOR SURE.
WE'RE DOOMED! THERE'LL BE NO ESCAPE FOR ***THE PRINCESS*** THIS TIME.
●●●!

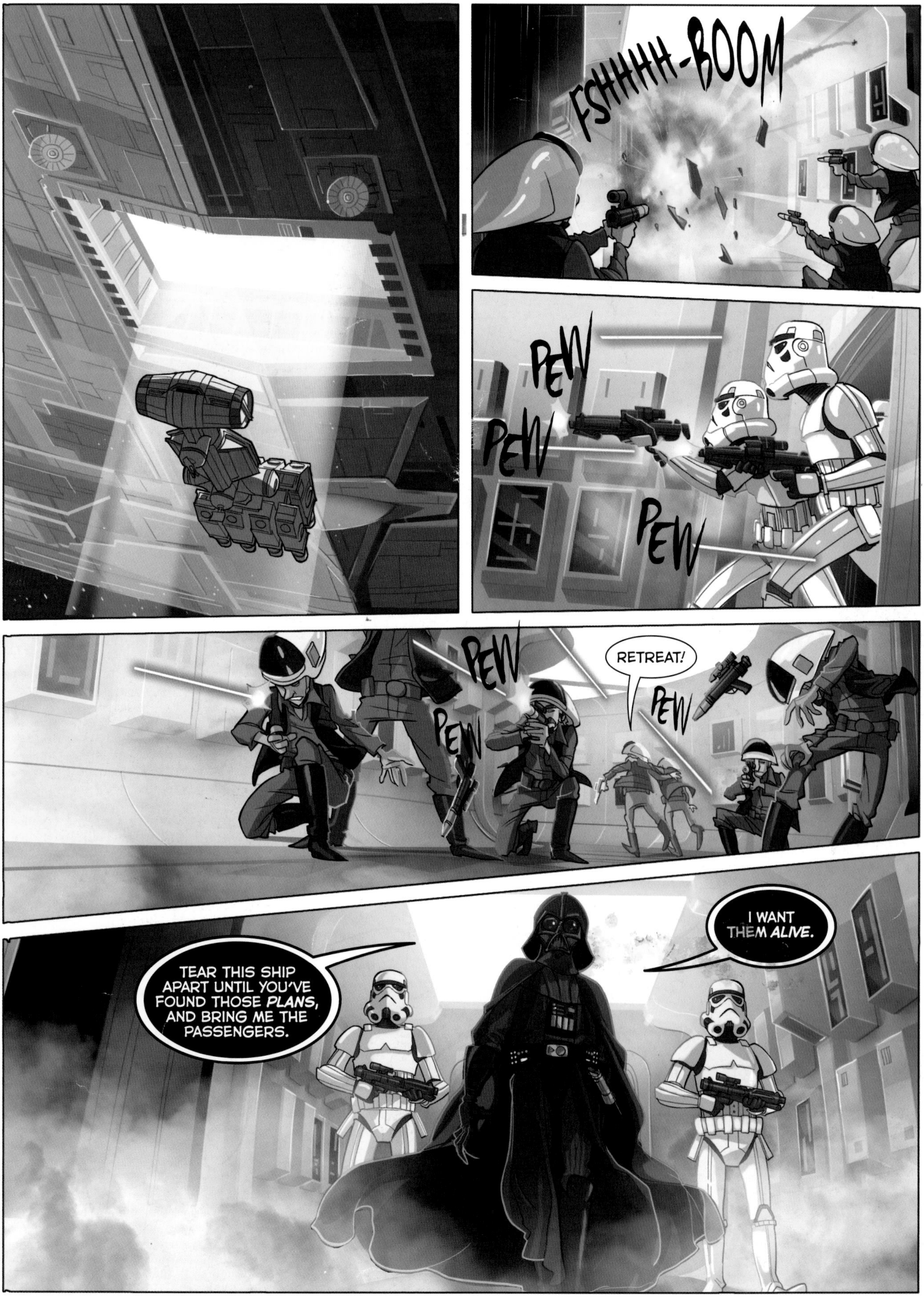
FSHHHH-BOOM
PEW
PEW
PEW
PEW
PEW
RETREAT!
PEW
TEAR THIS SHIP APART UNTIL YOU'VE FOUND THOSE *PLANS*, AND BRING ME THE PASSENGERS.
I WANT THEM *ALIVE*.

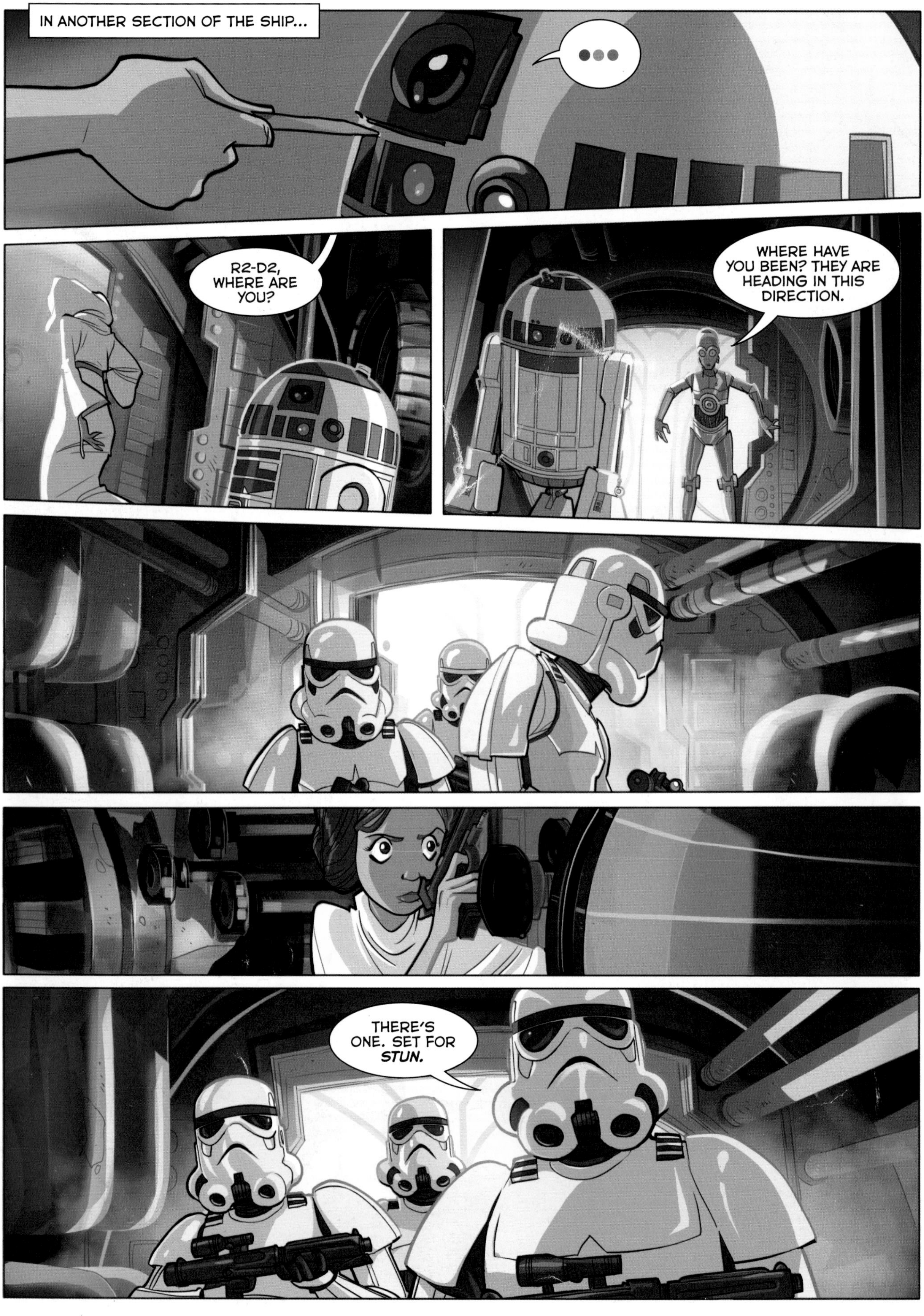
IN ANOTHER SECTION OF THE SHIP...
•••
R2-D2, WHERE ARE YOU?
WHERE HAVE YOU BEEN? THEY ARE HEADING IN THIS DIRECTION.
THERE'S ONE. SET FOR STUN.

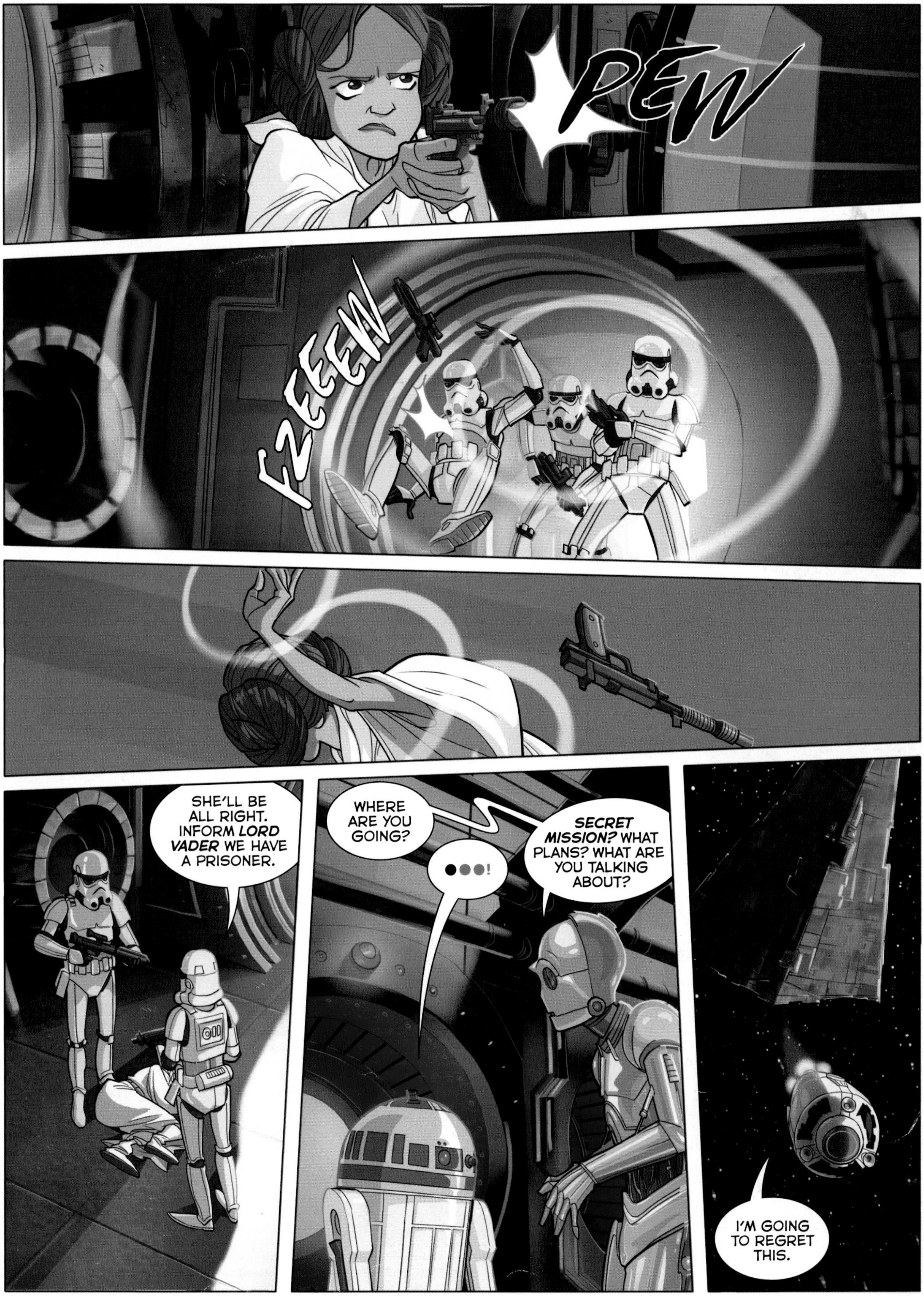
PEW
FZEEEW
SHE'LL BE ALL RIGHT. INFORM LORD VADER WE HAVE A PRISONER.
WHERE ARE YOU GOING?
SECRET MISSION? WHAT PLANS? WHAT ARE YOU TALKING ABOUT?
●●●!
I'M GOING TO REGRET THIS.

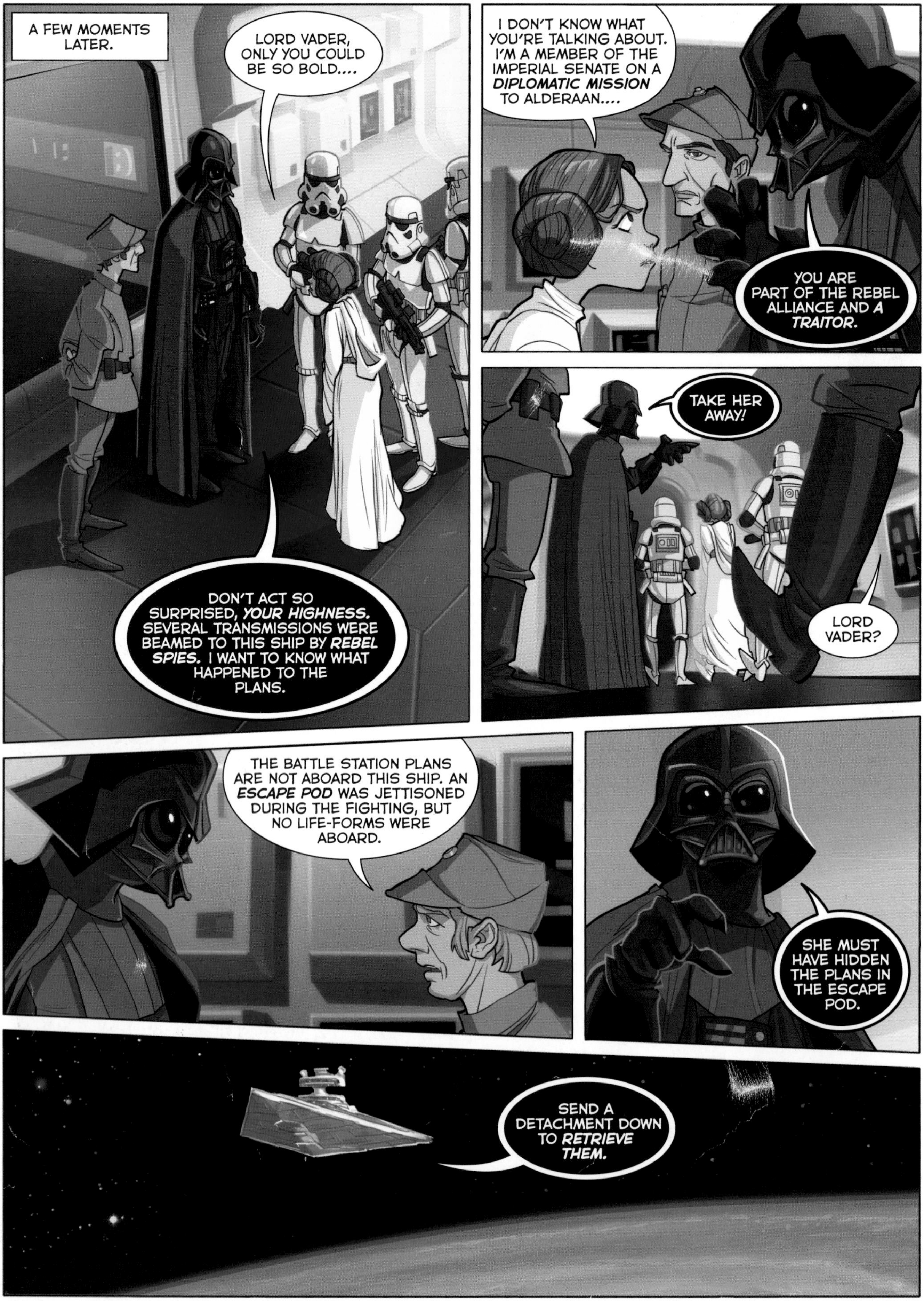
A FEW MOMENTS LATER.
LORD VADER, ONLY YOU COULD BE SO BOLD....
DON'T ACT SO SURPRISED, *YOUR HIGHNESS.* SEVERAL TRANSMISSIONS WERE BEAMED TO THIS SHIP BY *REBEL SPIES.* I WANT TO KNOW WHAT HAPPENED TO THE PLANS.
I DON'T KNOW WHAT YOU'RE TALKING ABOUT. I'M A MEMBER OF THE IMPERIAL SENATE ON A *DIPLOMATIC MISSION* TO ALDERAAN....
YOU ARE PART OF THE REBEL ALLIANCE AND *A TRAITOR.*
TAKE HER AWAY!
LORD VADER?
THE BATTLE STATION PLANS ARE NOT ABOARD THIS SHIP. AN *ESCAPE POD* WAS JETTISONED DURING THE FIGHTING, BUT NO LIFE-FORMS WERE ABOARD.
SHE MUST HAVE HIDDEN THE PLANS IN THE ESCAPE POD.
SEND A DETACHMENT DOWN TO *RETRIEVE THEM.*

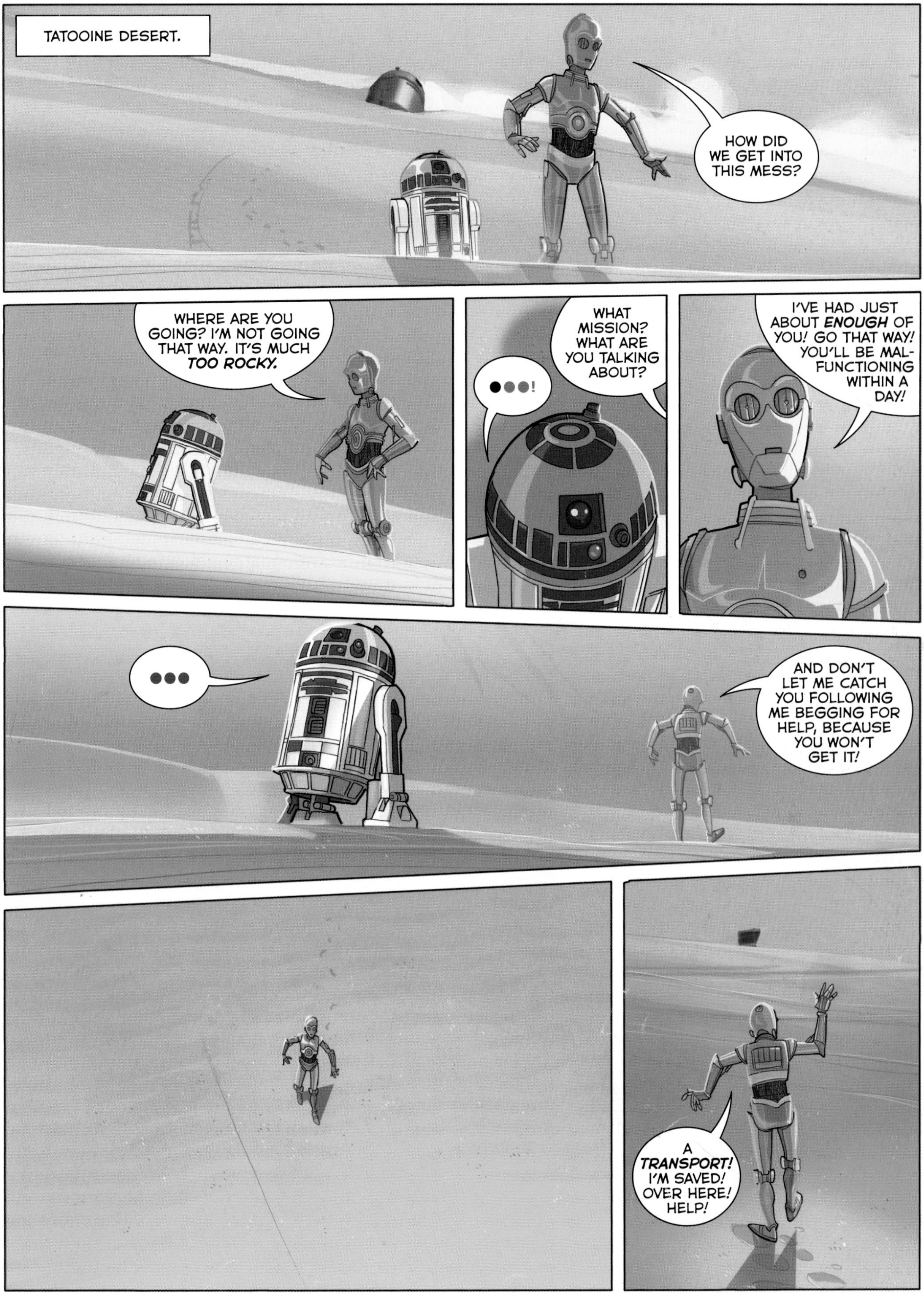
TATOOINE DESERT.
HOW DID WE GET INTO THIS MESS?
WHERE ARE YOU GOING? I'M NOT GOING THAT WAY. IT'S MUCH *TOO ROCKY.*
•••!
WHAT MISSION? WHAT ARE YOU TALKING ABOUT?
I'VE HAD JUST ABOUT *ENOUGH* OF YOU! GO THAT WAY! YOU'LL BE MAL-FUNCTIONING WITHIN A DAY!
•••
AND DON'T LET ME CATCH YOU FOLLOWING ME BEGGING FOR HELP, BECAUSE YOU WON'T GET IT!
A *TRANSPORT!* I'M SAVED! OVER HERE! HELP!

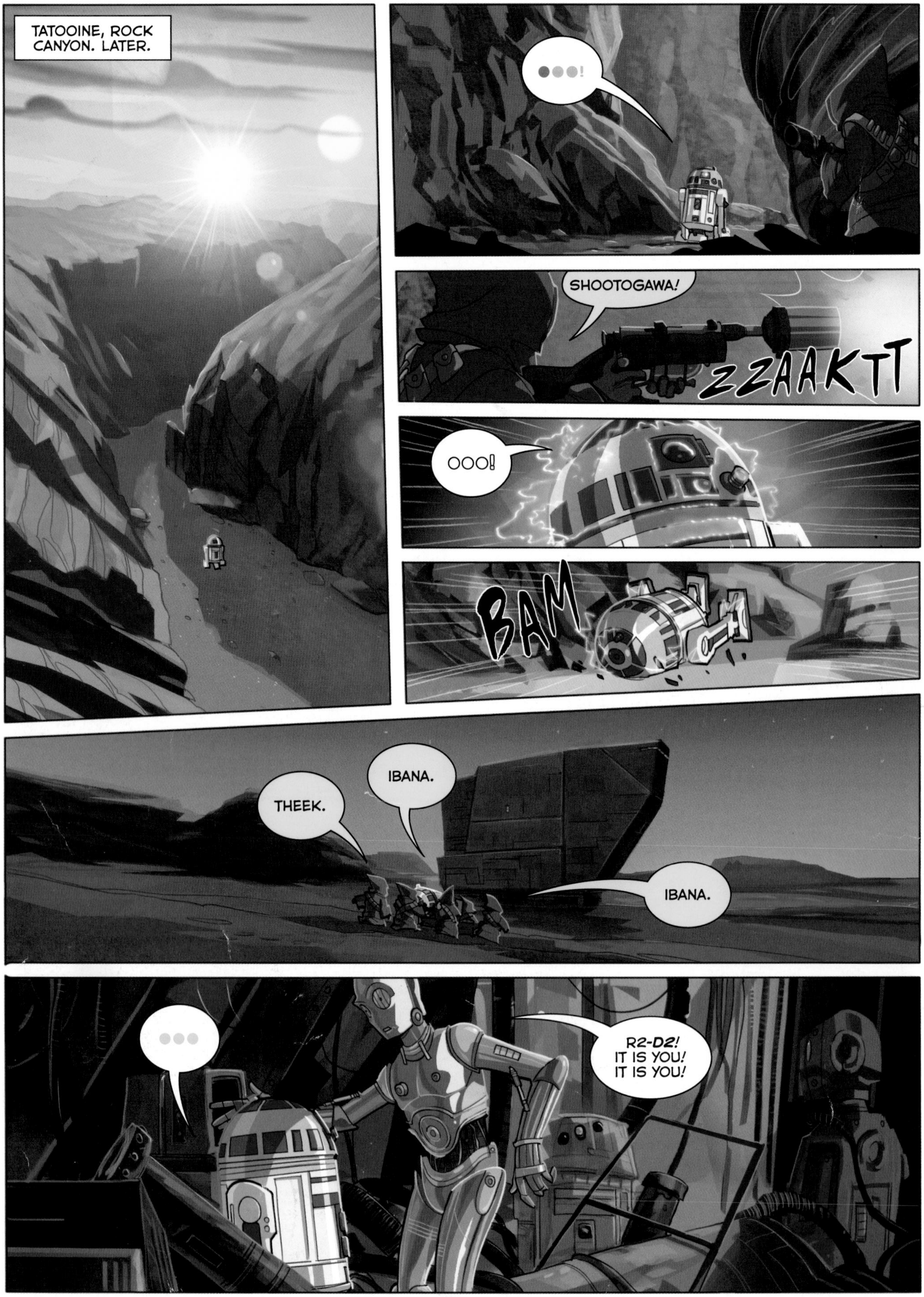
TATOOINE, ROCK CANYON. LATER.
!
SHOOTOGAWA!
ZZAAKTT
OOO!
BAM
THEEK.
IBANA.
IBANA.
R2-D2! IT IS YOU! IT IS YOU!

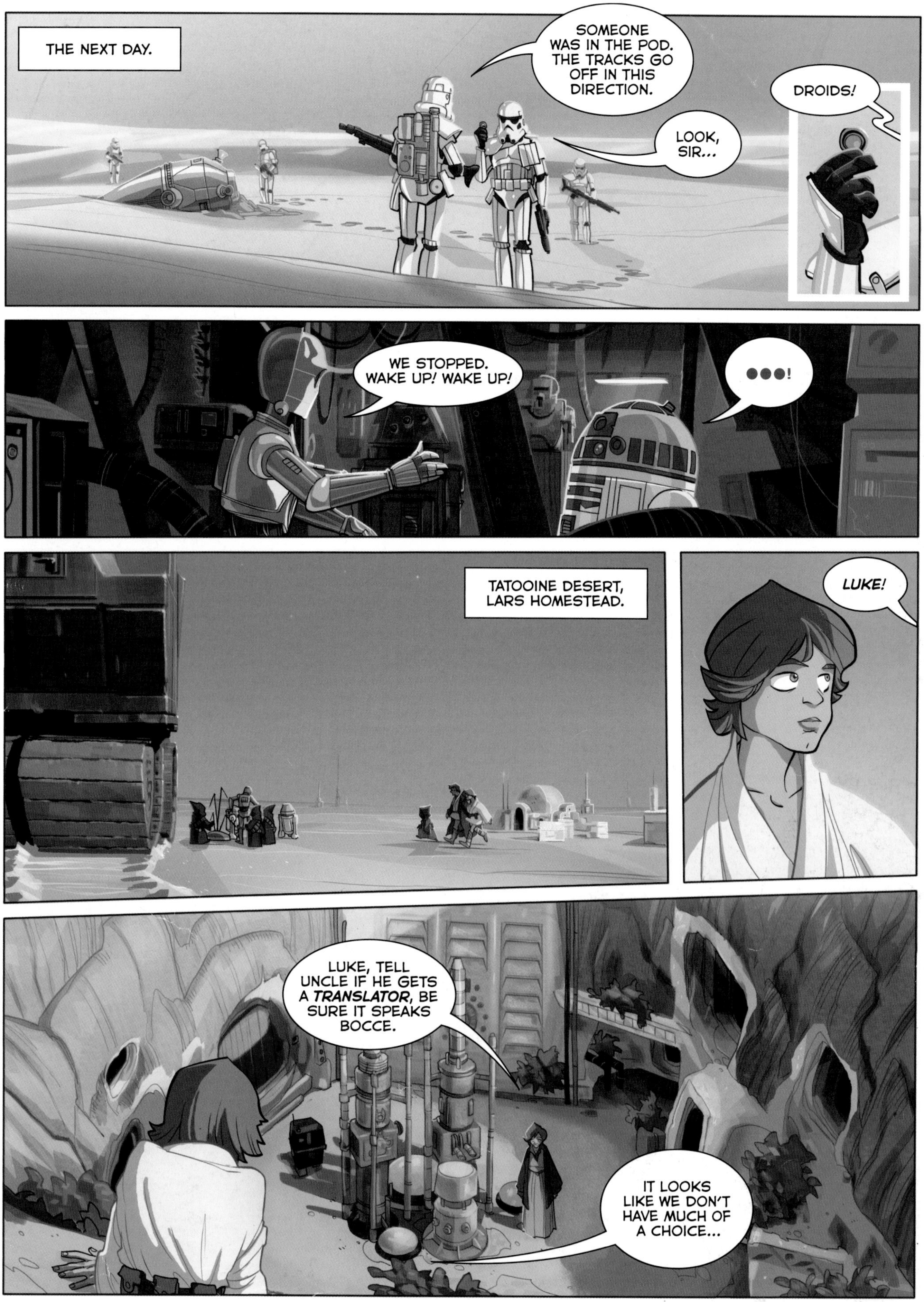
THE NEXT DAY.
SOMEONE WAS IN THE POD. THE TRACKS GO OFF IN THIS DIRECTION.
LOOK, SIR...
DROIDS!
WE STOPPED. WAKE UP! WAKE UP!
●●●!
TATOOINE DESERT, LARS HOMESTEAD.
LUKE!
LUKE, TELL UNCLE IF HE GETS A TRANSLATOR, BE SURE IT SPEAKS BOCCE.
IT LOOKS LIKE WE DON'T HAVE MUCH OF A CHOICE...

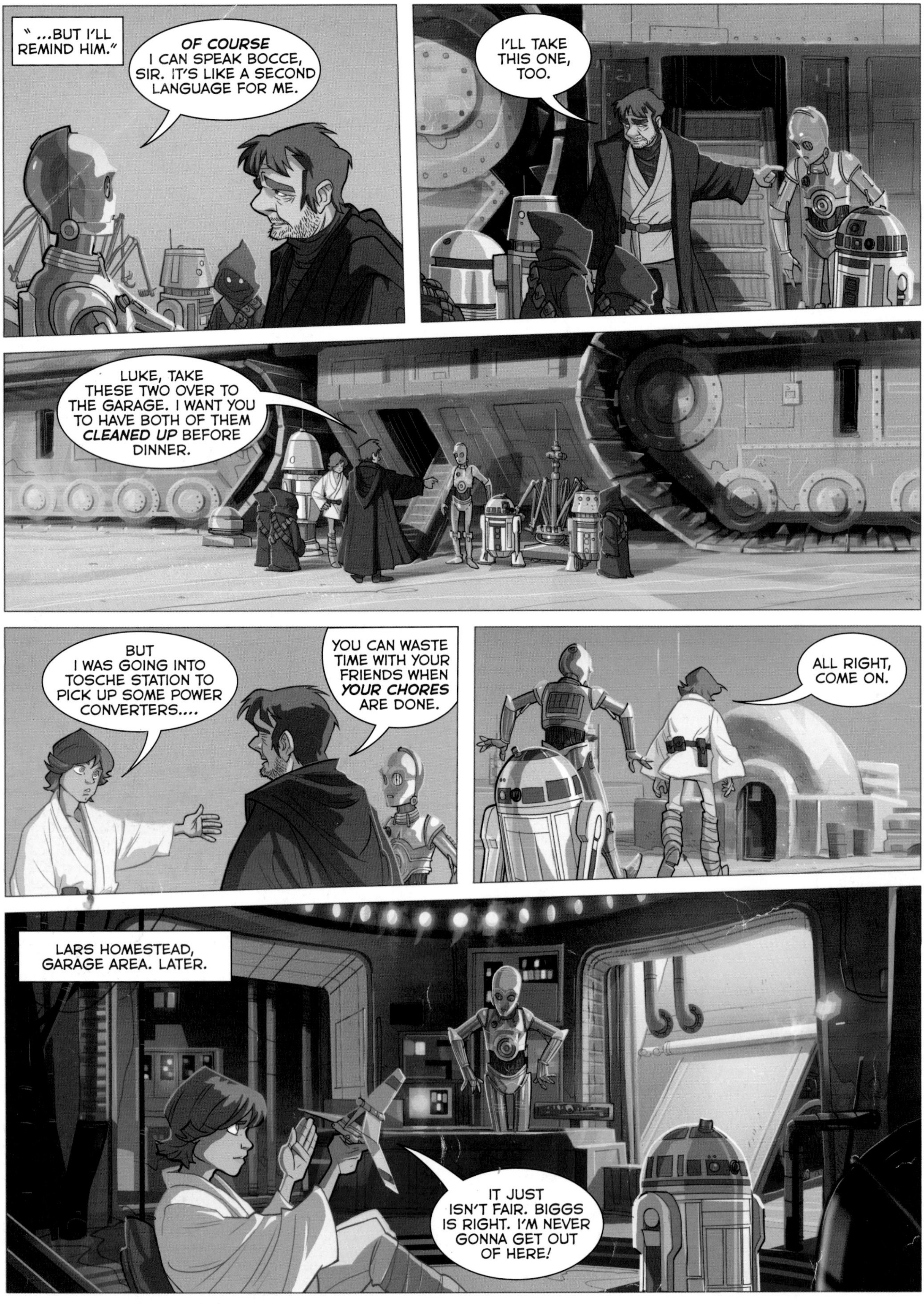
"...BUT I'LL REMIND HIM."
OF COURSE I CAN SPEAK BOCCE, SIR. IT'S LIKE A SECOND LANGUAGE FOR ME.
I'LL TAKE THIS ONE, TOO.
LUKE, TAKE THESE TWO OVER TO THE GARAGE. I WANT YOU TO HAVE BOTH OF THEM CLEANED UP BEFORE DINNER.
BUT I WAS GOING INTO TOSCHE STATION TO PICK UP SOME POWER CONVERTERS....
YOU CAN WASTE TIME WITH YOUR FRIENDS WHEN YOUR CHORES ARE DONE.
ALL RIGHT, COME ON.
LARS HOMESTEAD, GARAGE AREA. LATER.
IT JUST ISN'T FAIR. BIGGS IS RIGHT. I'M NEVER GONNA GET OUT OF HERE!

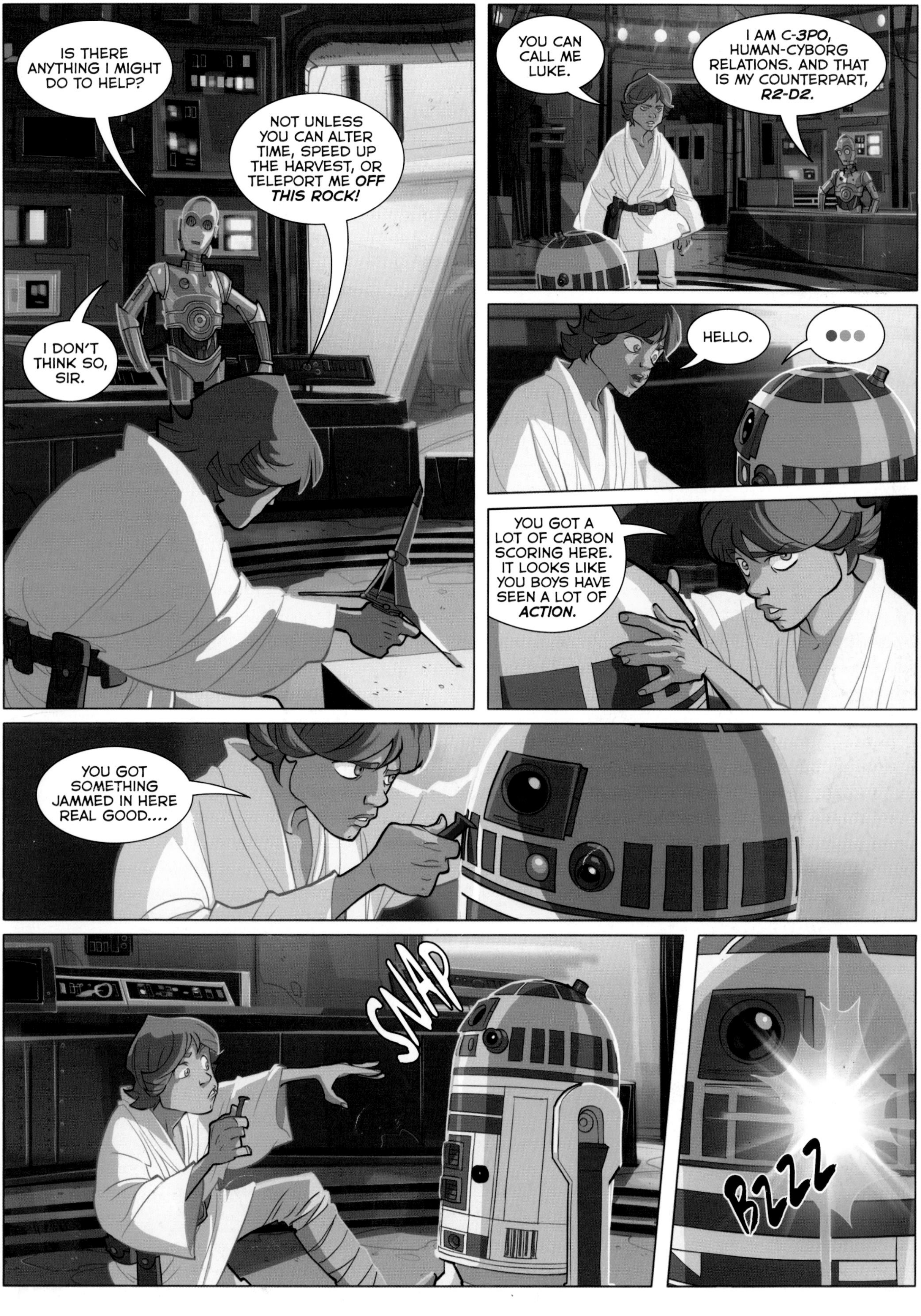
IS THERE ANYTHING I MIGHT DO TO HELP?
NOT UNLESS YOU CAN ALTER TIME, SPEED UP THE HARVEST, OR TELEPORT ME *OFF THIS ROCK!*
I DON'T THINK SO, SIR.
YOU CAN CALL ME LUKE.
I AM *C-3PO*, HUMAN-CYBORG RELATIONS. AND THAT IS MY COUNTERPART, *R2-D2.*
HELLO.
YOU GOT A LOT OF CARBON SCORING HERE. IT LOOKS LIKE YOU BOYS HAVE SEEN A LOT OF *ACTION.*
YOU GOT SOMETHING JAMMED IN HERE REAL GOOD....
SNAP
BZZZ

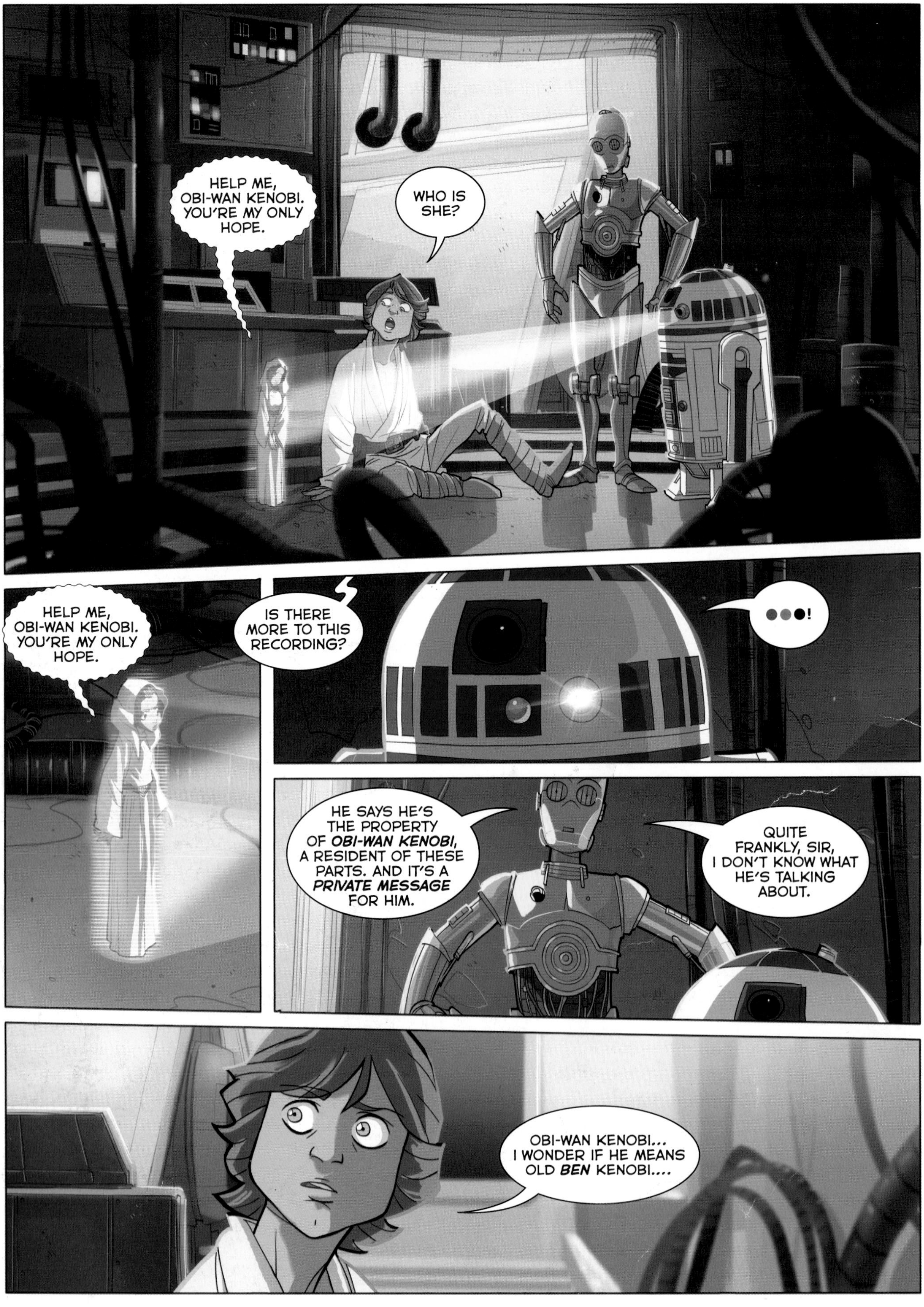
HELP ME, OBI-WAN KENOBI. YOU'RE MY ONLY HOPE.
WHO IS SHE?
HELP ME, OBI-WAN KENOBI. YOU'RE MY ONLY HOPE.
IS THERE MORE TO THIS RECORDING?
•••!
HE SAYS HE'S THE PROPERTY OF *OBI-WAN KENOBI*, A RESIDENT OF THESE PARTS. AND IT'S A *PRIVATE MESSAGE* FOR HIM.
QUITE FRANKLY, SIR, I DON'T KNOW WHAT HE'S TALKING ABOUT.
OBI-WAN KENOBI... I WONDER IF HE MEANS OLD *BEN* KENOBI....

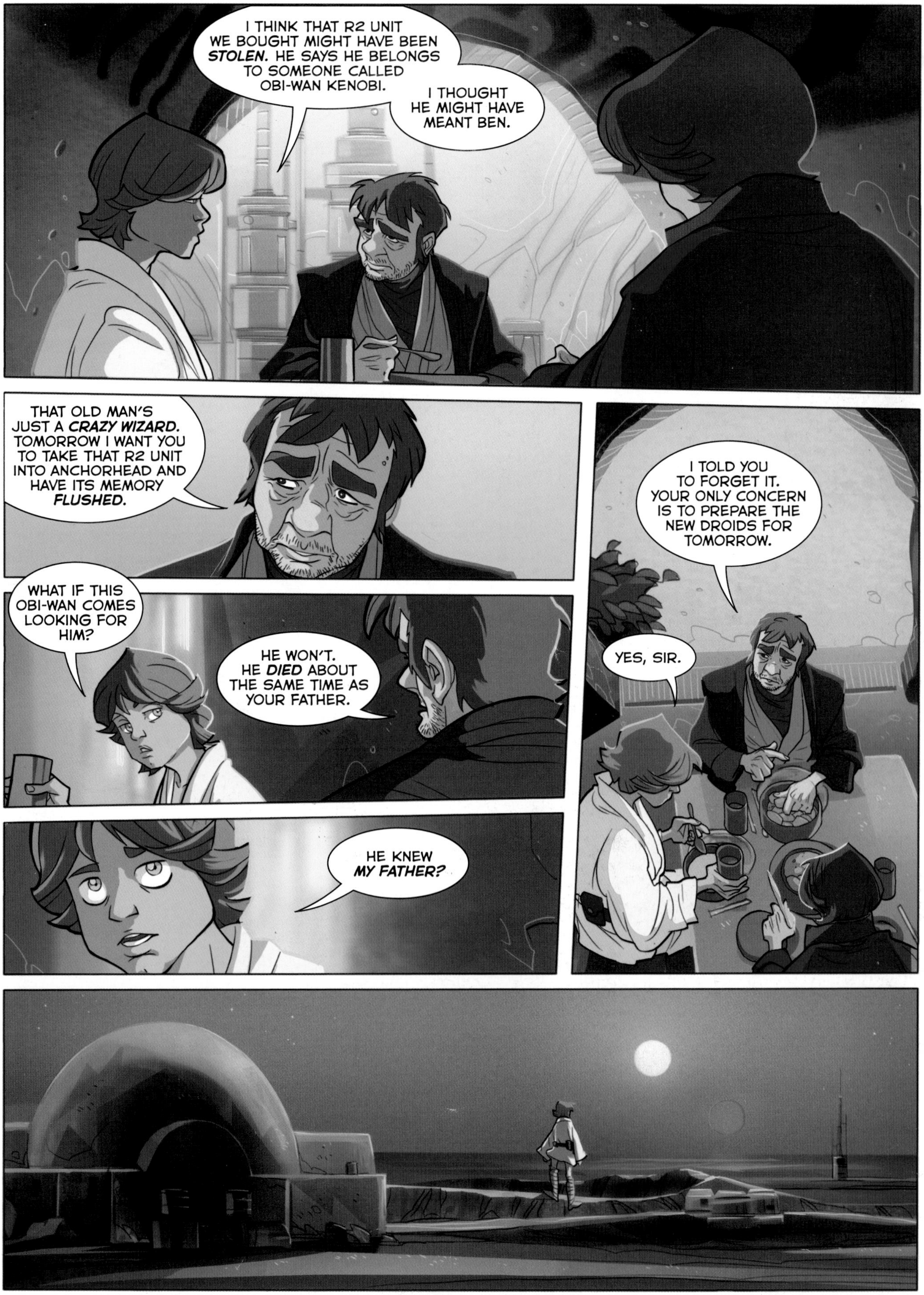
I THINK THAT R2 UNIT WE BOUGHT MIGHT HAVE BEEN STOLEN. HE SAYS HE BELONGS TO SOMEONE CALLED OBI-WAN KENOBI.
I THOUGHT HE MIGHT HAVE MEANT BEN.
THAT OLD MAN'S JUST A CRAZY WIZARD. TOMORROW I WANT YOU TO TAKE THAT R2 UNIT INTO ANCHORHEAD AND HAVE ITS MEMORY FLUSHED.
WHAT IF THIS OBI-WAN COMES LOOKING FOR HIM?
HE WON'T. HE DIED ABOUT THE SAME TIME AS YOUR FATHER.
HE KNEW MY FATHER?
I TOLD YOU TO FORGET IT. YOUR ONLY CONCERN IS TO PREPARE THE NEW DROIDS FOR TOMORROW.
YES, SIR.

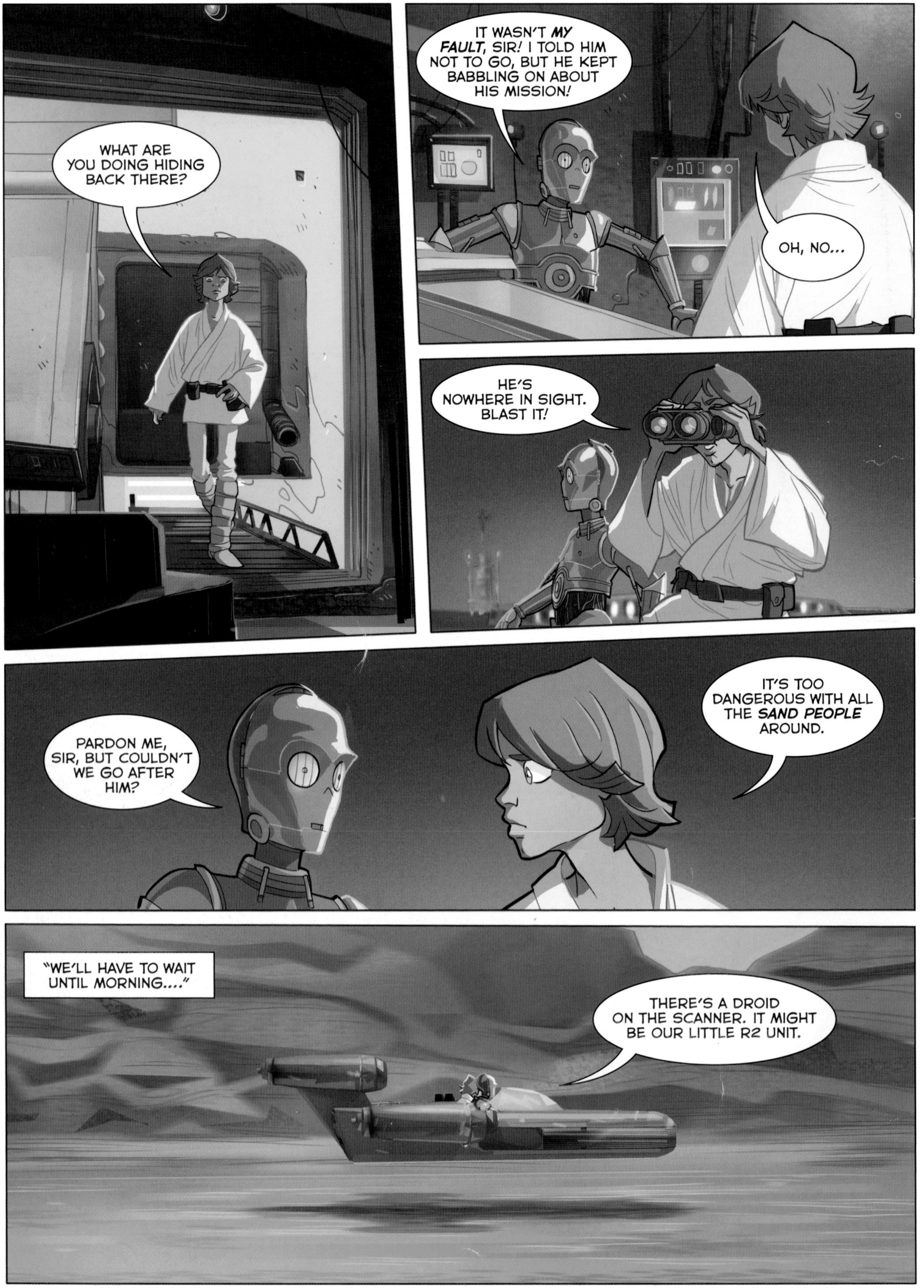
WHAT ARE YOU DOING HIDING BACK THERE?
IT WASN'T *MY FAULT*, SIR! I TOLD HIM NOT TO GO, BUT HE KEPT BABBLING ON ABOUT HIS MISSION!
OH, NO...
HE'S NOWHERE IN SIGHT. BLAST IT!
PARDON ME, SIR, BUT COULDN'T WE GO AFTER HIM?
IT'S TOO DANGEROUS WITH ALL THE *SAND PEOPLE* AROUND.
"WE'LL HAVE TO WAIT UNTIL MORNING...."
THERE'S A DROID ON THE SCANNER. IT MIGHT BE OUR LITTLE R2 UNIT.

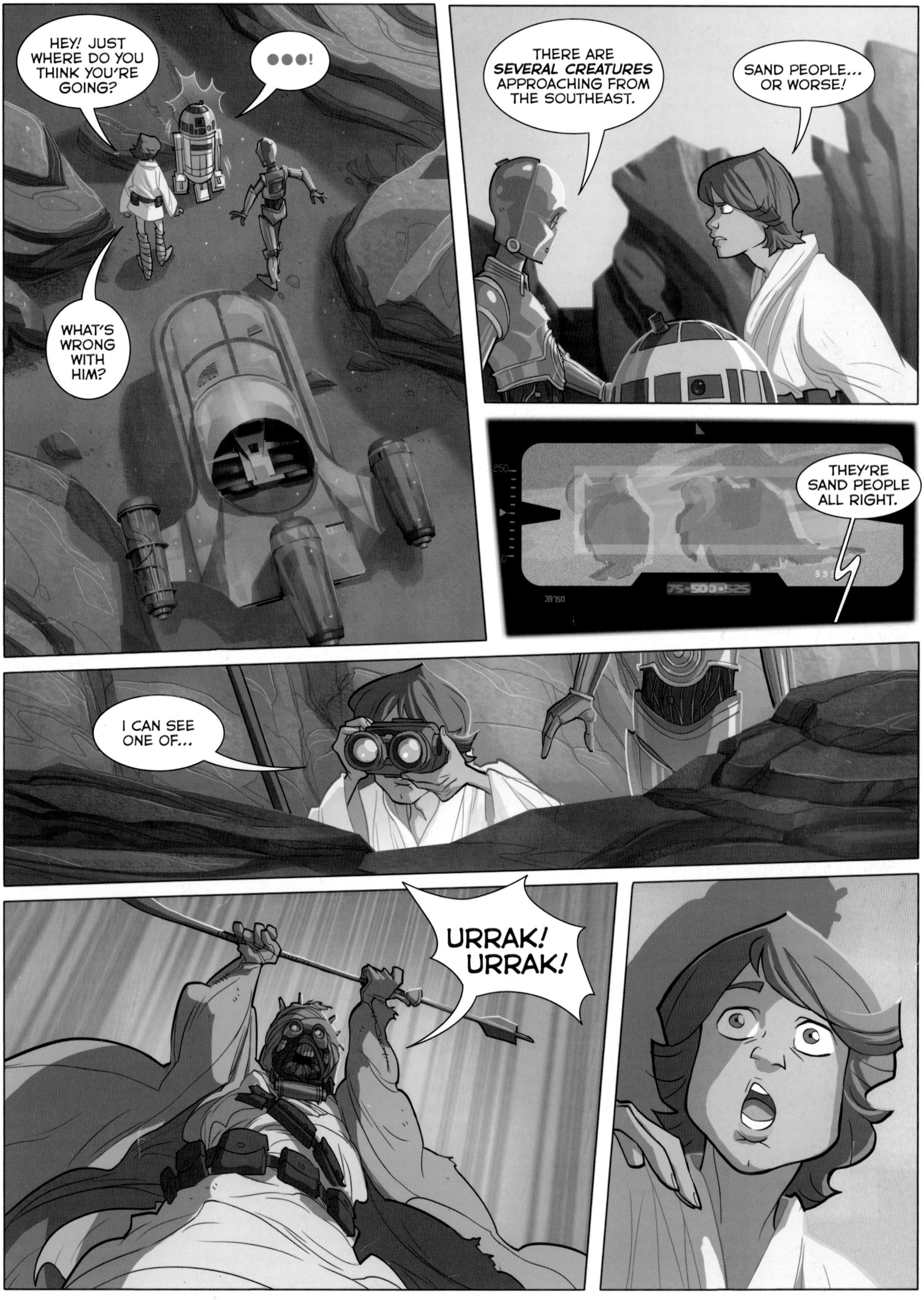

HEY! JUST WHERE DO YOU THINK YOU'RE GOING?
●●●!
WHAT'S WRONG WITH HIM?
THERE ARE SEVERAL CREATURES APPROACHING FROM THE SOUTHEAST.
SAND PEOPLE... OR WORSE!
THEY'RE SAND PEOPLE ALL RIGHT.
I CAN SEE ONE OF...
URRAK! URRAK!

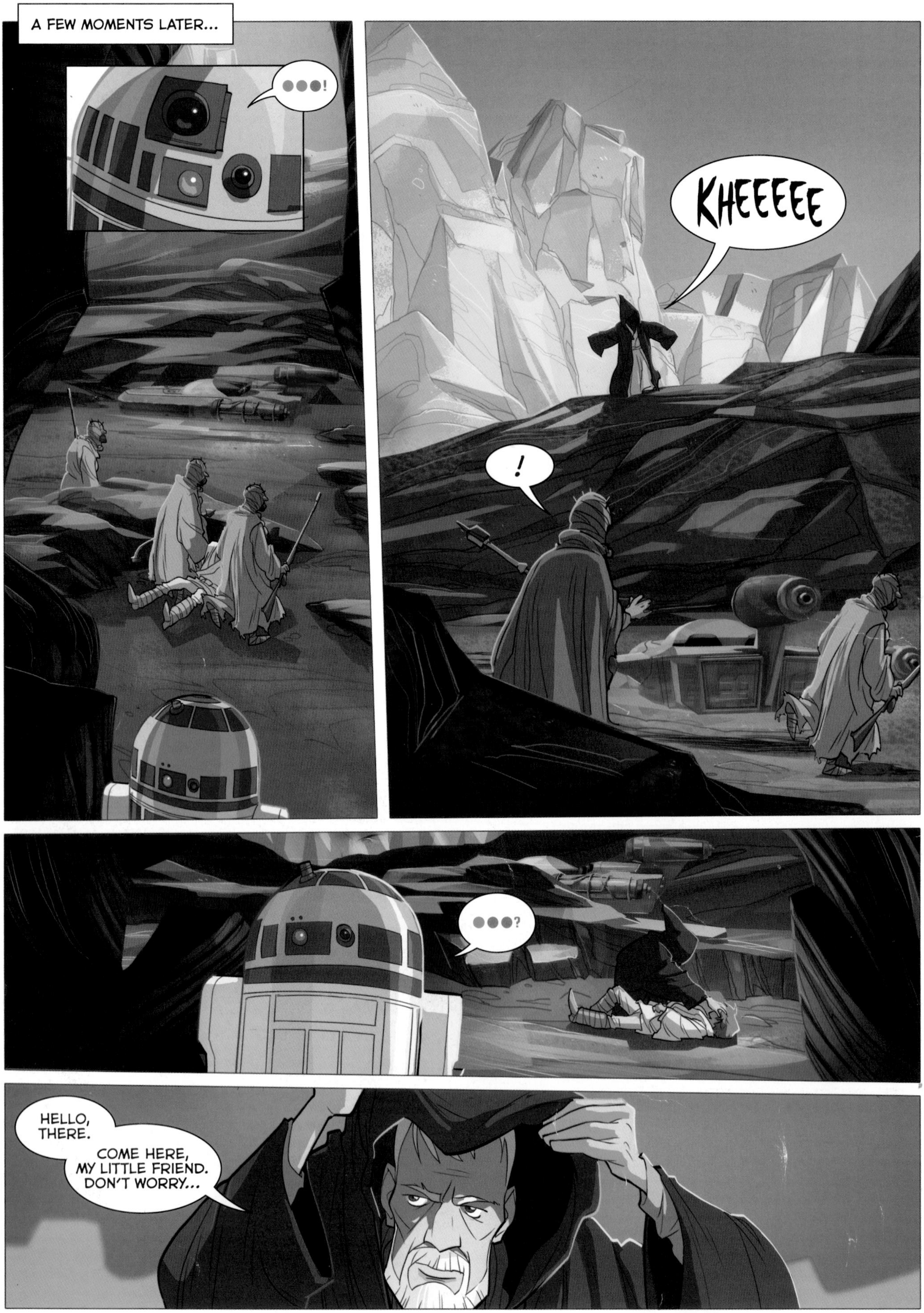
A FEW MOMENTS LATER...
●●●!
KHEEEEE
!
●●●?
HELLO, THERE.
COME HERE, MY LITTLE FRIEND. DON'T WORRY...

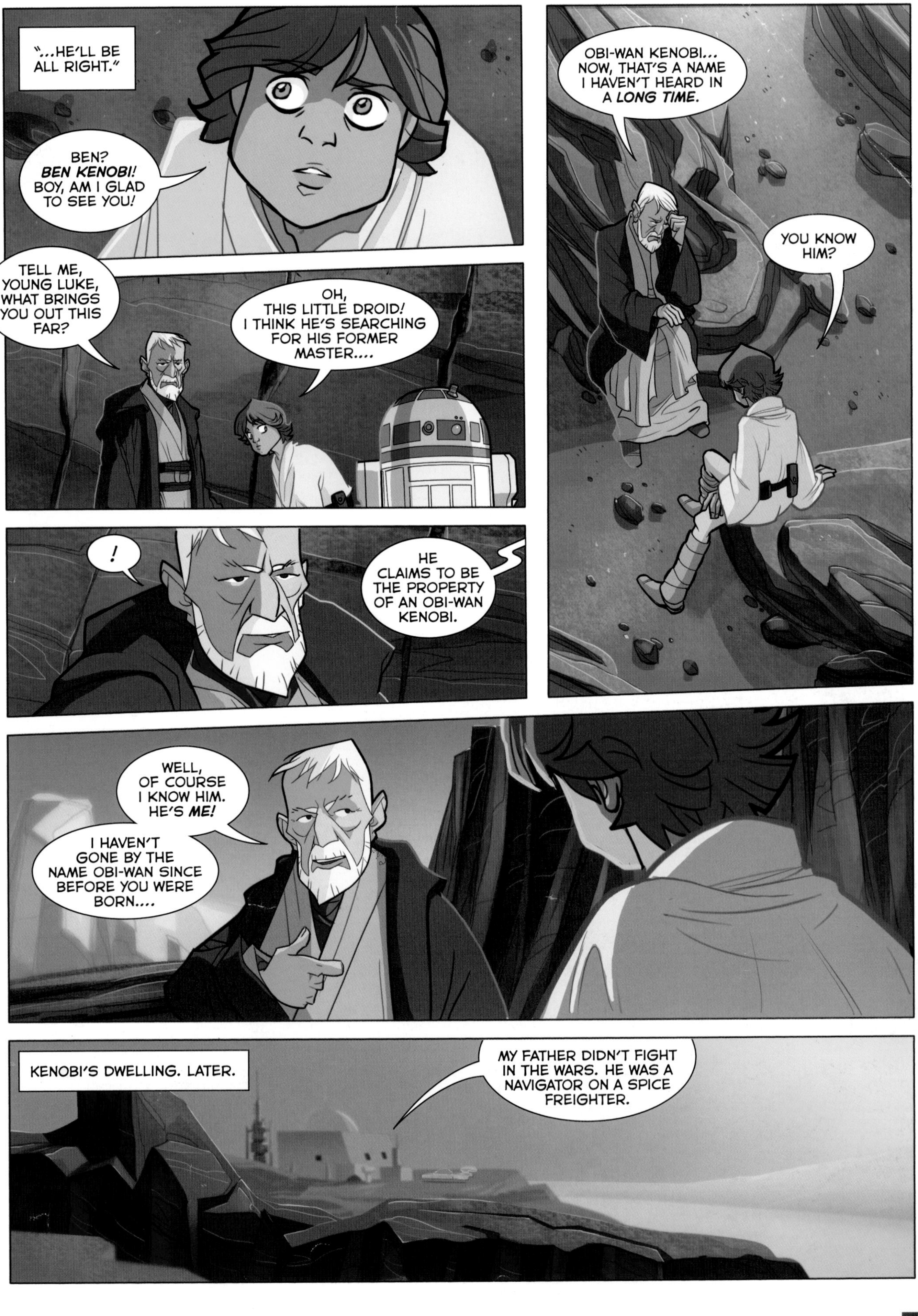
"...HE'LL BE ALL RIGHT."
BEN? **BEN KENOBI!** BOY, AM I GLAD TO SEE YOU!
OBI-WAN KENOBI... NOW, THAT'S A NAME I HAVEN'T HEARD IN A ***LONG TIME.***
TELL ME, YOUNG LUKE, WHAT BRINGS YOU OUT THIS FAR?
OH, THIS LITTLE DROID! I THINK HE'S SEARCHING FOR HIS FORMER MASTER....
YOU KNOW HIM?
!
HE CLAIMS TO BE THE PROPERTY OF AN OBI-WAN KENOBI.
WELL, OF COURSE I KNOW HIM. HE'S ***ME!***
I HAVEN'T GONE BY THE NAME OBI-WAN SINCE BEFORE YOU WERE BORN....
KENOBI'S DWELLING. LATER.
MY FATHER DIDN'T FIGHT IN THE WARS. HE WAS A NAVIGATOR ON A SPICE FREIGHTER.

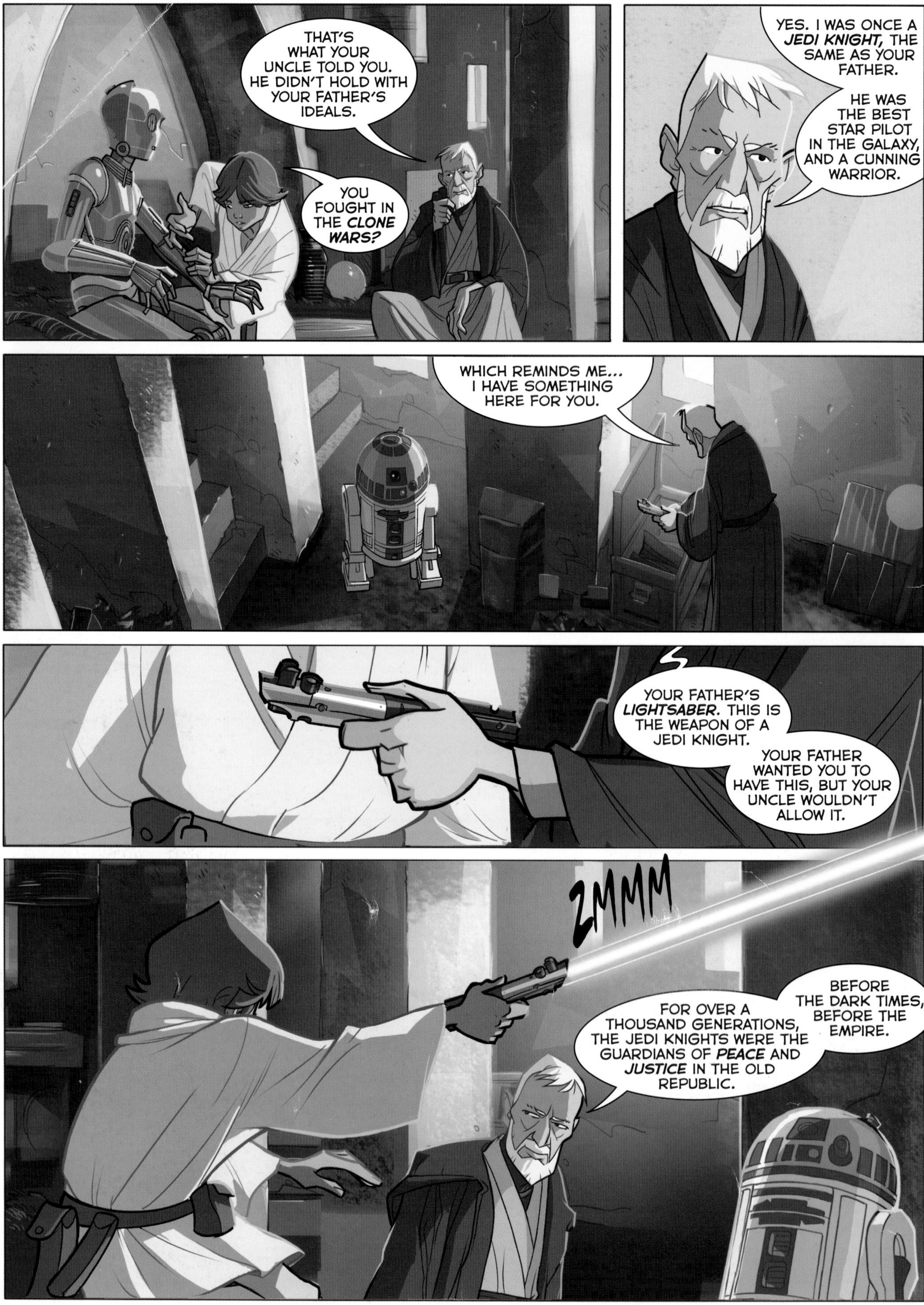
THAT'S WHAT YOUR UNCLE TOLD YOU. HE DIDN'T HOLD WITH YOUR FATHER'S IDEALS.
YOU FOUGHT IN THE **CLONE WARS?**
YES. I WAS ONCE A ***JEDI KNIGHT,*** THE SAME AS YOUR FATHER.
HE WAS THE BEST STAR PILOT IN THE GALAXY, AND A CUNNING WARRIOR.
WHICH REMINDS ME... I HAVE SOMETHING HERE FOR YOU.
YOUR FATHER'S ***LIGHTSABER.*** THIS IS THE WEAPON OF A JEDI KNIGHT.
YOUR FATHER WANTED YOU TO HAVE THIS, BUT YOUR UNCLE WOULDN'T ALLOW IT.
ZMMM
FOR OVER A THOUSAND GENERATIONS, THE JEDI KNIGHTS WERE THE GUARDIANS OF *PEACE* AND *JUSTICE* IN THE OLD REPUBLIC.
BEFORE THE DARK TIMES, BEFORE THE EMPIRE.

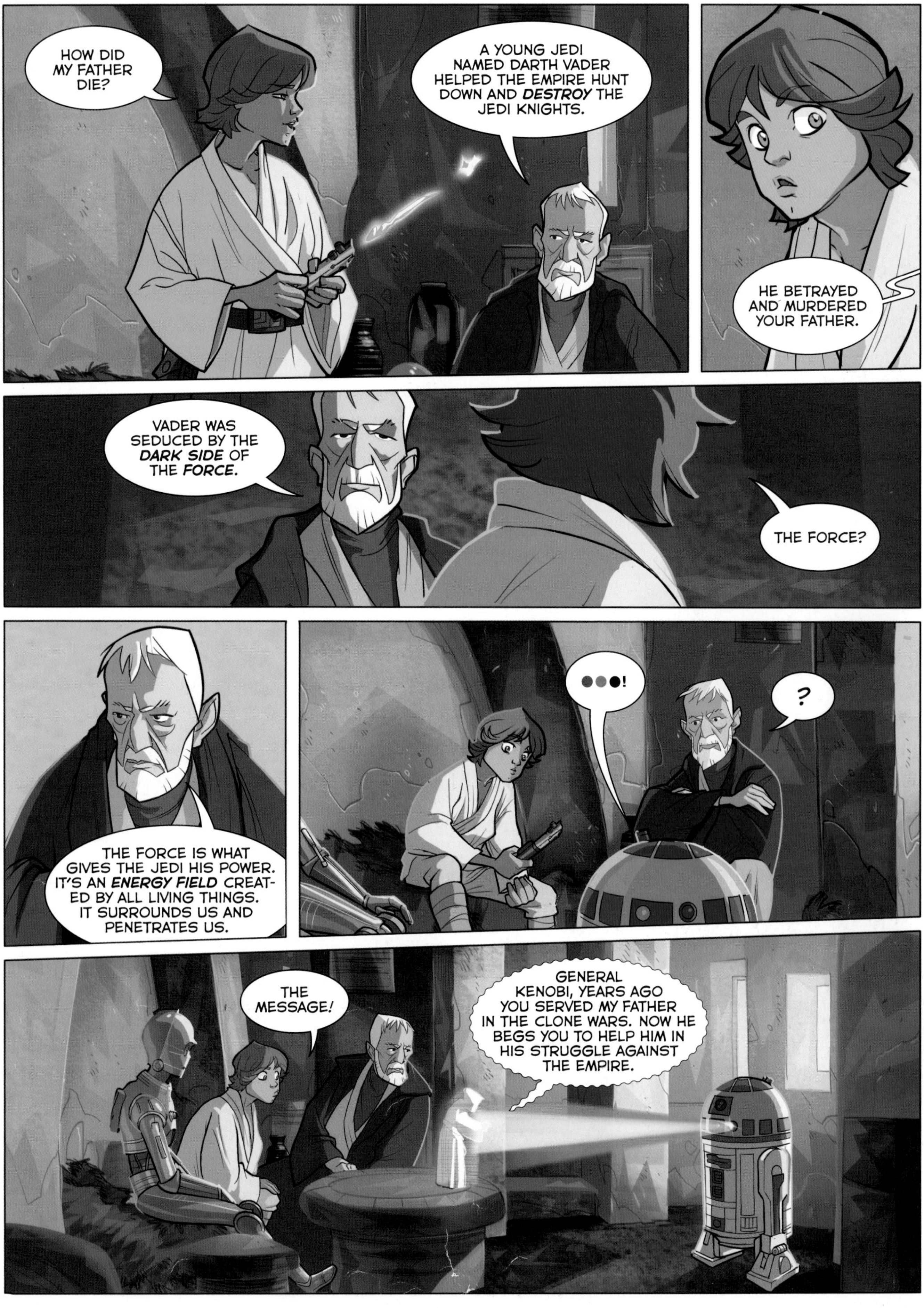
HOW DID MY FATHER DIE?
A YOUNG JEDI NAMED DARTH VADER HELPED THE EMPIRE HUNT DOWN AND *DESTROY* THE JEDI KNIGHTS.
HE BETRAYED AND MURDERED YOUR FATHER.
VADER WAS SEDUCED BY THE ***DARK SIDE*** OF THE ***FORCE***.
THE FORCE?
THE FORCE IS WHAT GIVES THE JEDI HIS POWER. IT'S AN ***ENERGY FIELD*** CREATED BY ALL LIVING THINGS. IT SURROUNDS US AND PENETRATES US.
!
?
THE MESSAGE!
GENERAL KENOBI, YEARS AGO YOU SERVED MY FATHER IN THE CLONE WARS. NOW HE BEGS YOU TO HELP HIM IN HIS STRUGGLE AGAINST THE EMPIRE.

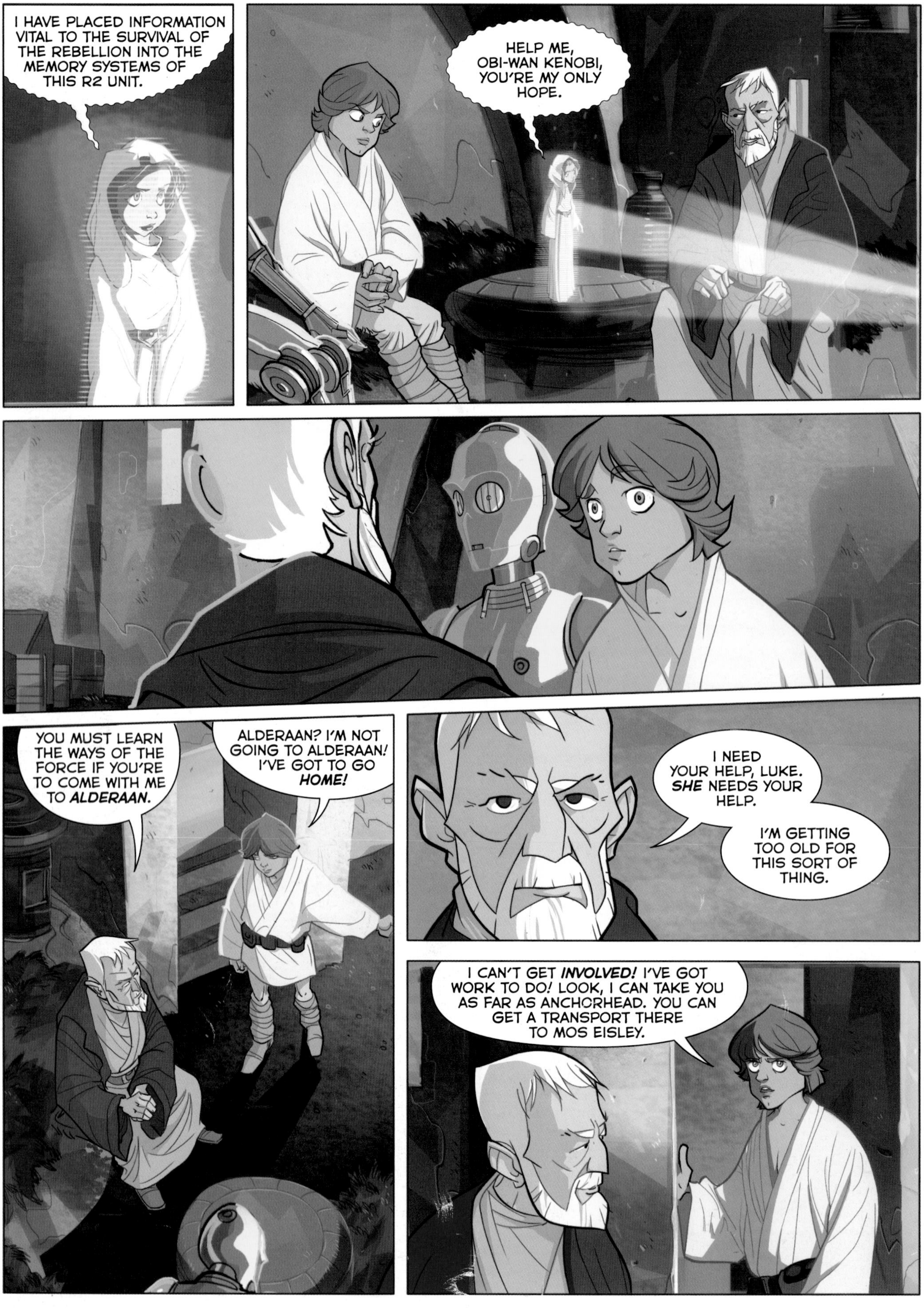
I HAVE PLACED INFORMATION VITAL TO THE SURVIVAL OF THE REBELLION INTO THE MEMORY SYSTEMS OF THIS R2 UNIT.
HELP ME, OBI-WAN KENOBI, YOU'RE MY ONLY HOPE.
YOU MUST LEARN THE WAYS OF THE FORCE IF YOU'RE TO COME WITH ME TO ALDERAAN.
ALDERAAN? I'M NOT GOING TO ALDERAAN! I'VE GOT TO GO HOME!
I NEED YOUR HELP, LUKE. SHE NEEDS YOUR HELP.
I'M GETTING TOO OLD FOR THIS SORT OF THING.
I CAN'T GET INVOLVED! I'VE GOT WORK TO DO! LOOK, I CAN TAKE YOU AS FAR AS ANCHORHEAD. YOU CAN GET A TRANSPORT THERE TO MOS EISLEY.

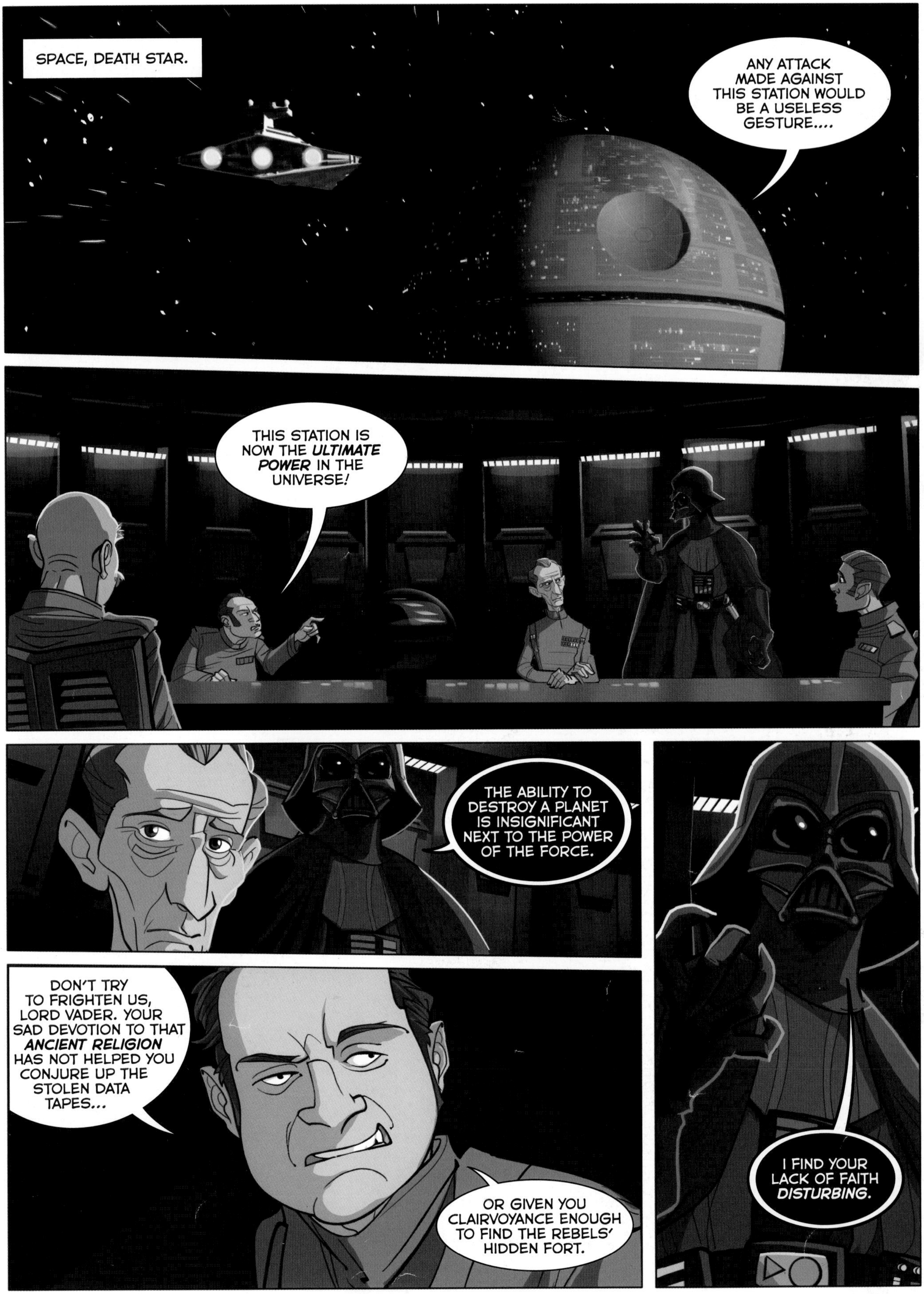

SPACE, DEATH STAR.
ANY ATTACK MADE AGAINST THIS STATION WOULD BE A USELESS GESTURE....
THIS STATION IS NOW THE ULTIMATE POWER IN THE UNIVERSE!
THE ABILITY TO DESTROY A PLANET IS INSIGNIFICANT NEXT TO THE POWER OF THE FORCE.
DON'T TRY TO FRIGHTEN US, LORD VADER. YOUR SAD DEVOTION TO THAT ANCIENT RELIGION HAS NOT HELPED YOU CONJURE UP THE STOLEN DATA TAPES...
OR GIVEN YOU CLAIRVOYANCE ENOUGH TO FIND THE REBELS' HIDDEN FORT.
I FIND YOUR LACK OF FAITH DISTURBING.

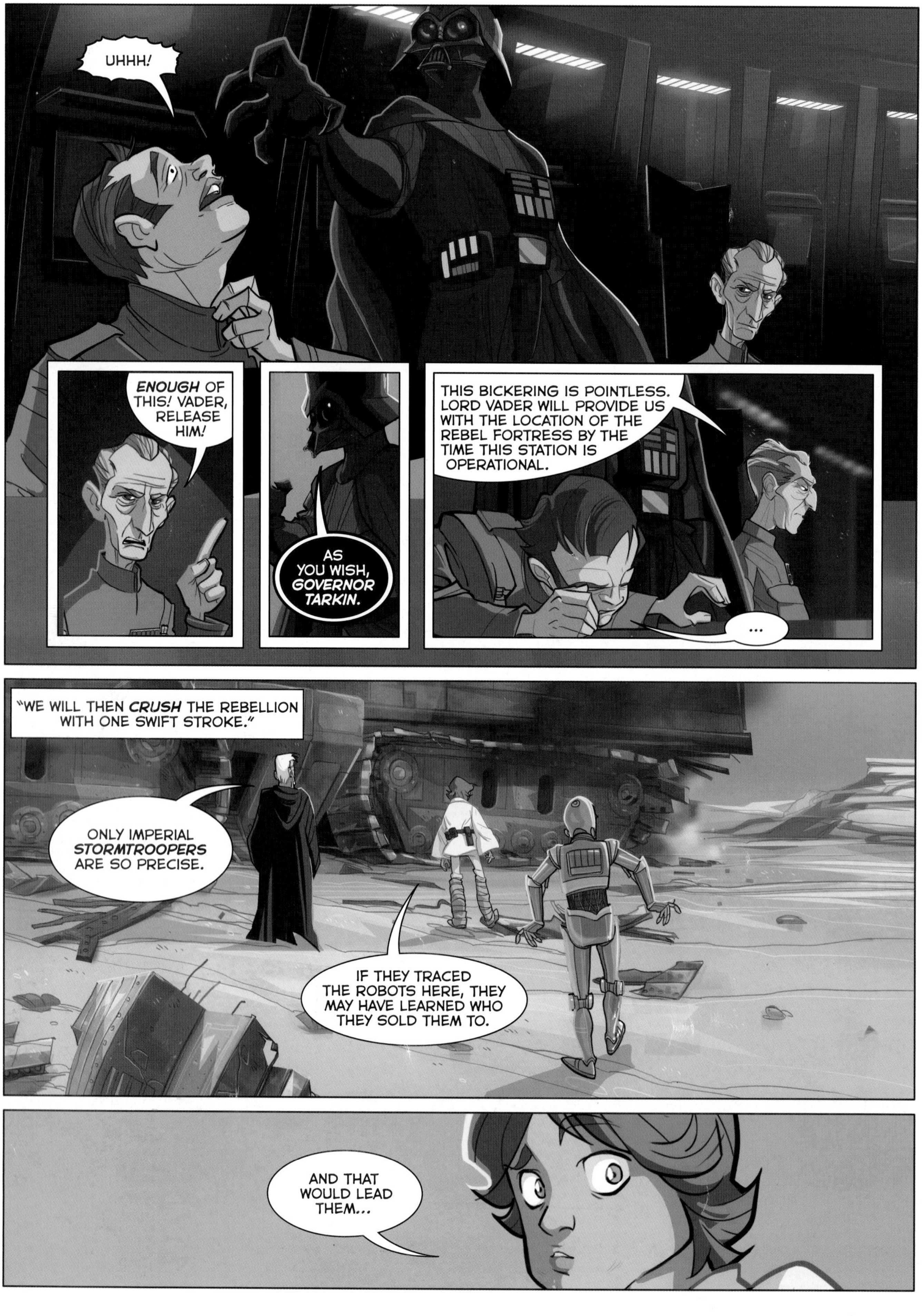
UHHH!
ENOUGH OF THIS! VADER, RELEASE HIM!
AS YOU WISH, GOVERNOR TARKIN.
THIS BICKERING IS POINTLESS. LORD VADER WILL PROVIDE US WITH THE LOCATION OF THE REBEL FORTRESS BY THE TIME THIS STATION IS OPERATIONAL.
...
"WE WILL THEN CRUSH THE REBELLION WITH ONE SWIFT STROKE."
ONLY IMPERIAL STORMTROOPERS ARE SO PRECISE.
IF THEY TRACED THE ROBOTS HERE, THEY MAY HAVE LEARNED WHO THEY SOLD THEM TO.
AND THAT WOULD LEAD THEM...

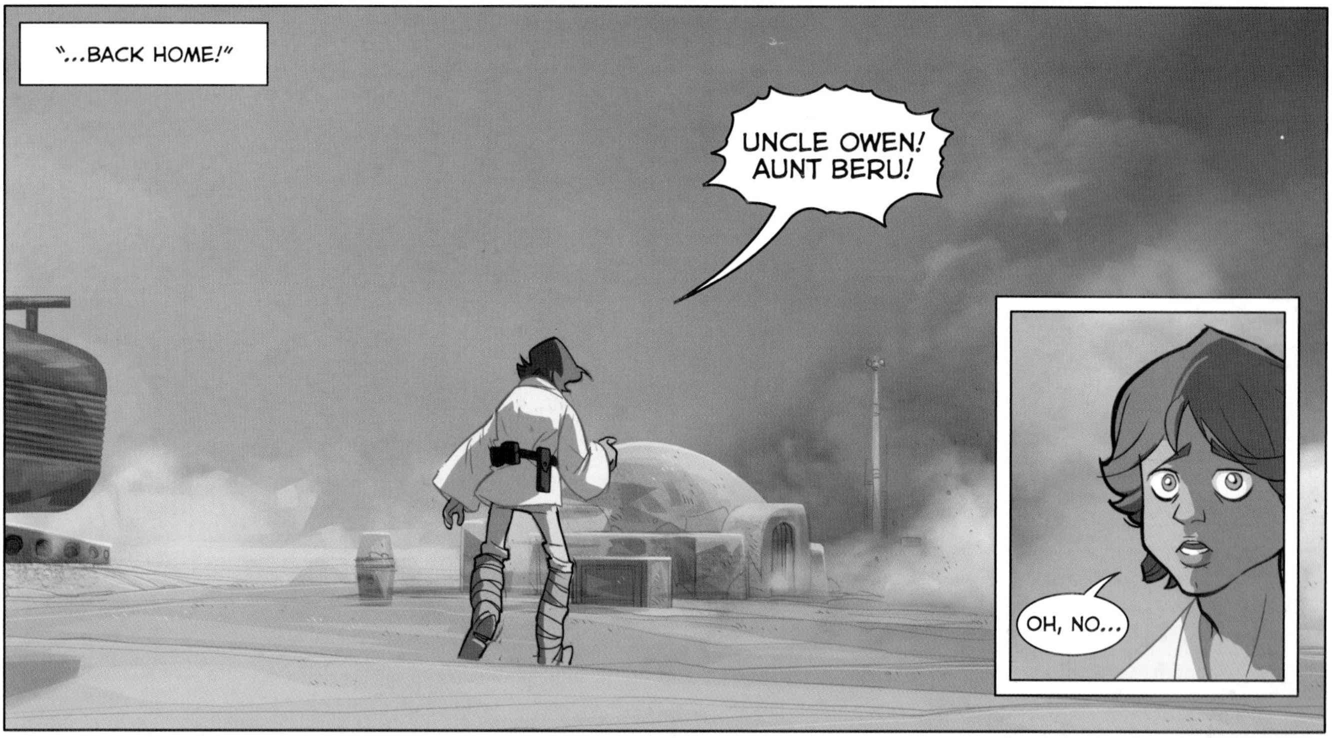
"...BACK HOME!"
UNCLE OWEN! AUNT BERU!
OH, NO...

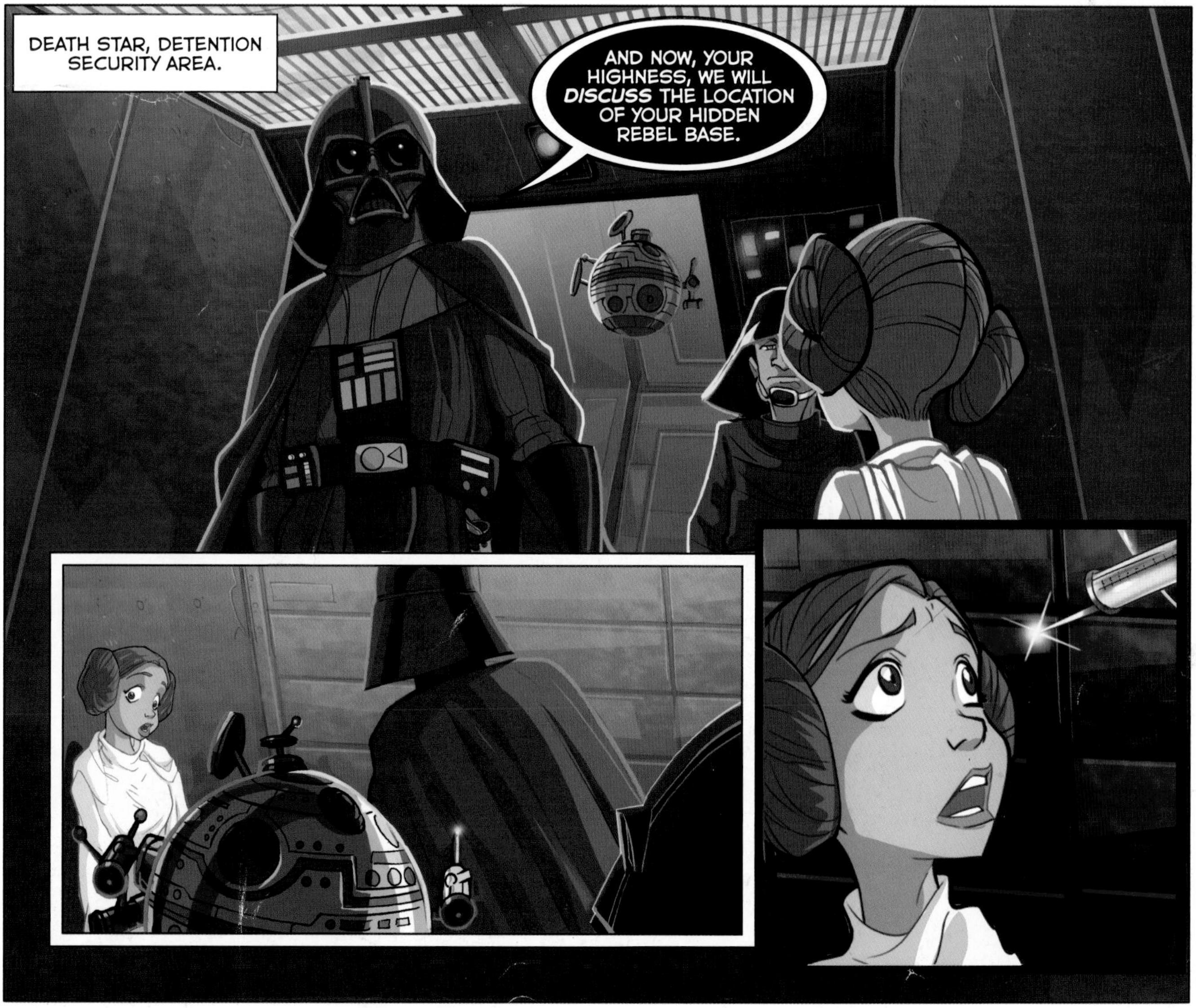
DEATH STAR, DETENTION SECURITY AREA.
AND NOW, YOUR HIGHNESS, WE WILL *DISCUSS* THE LOCATION OF YOUR HIDDEN REBEL BASE.

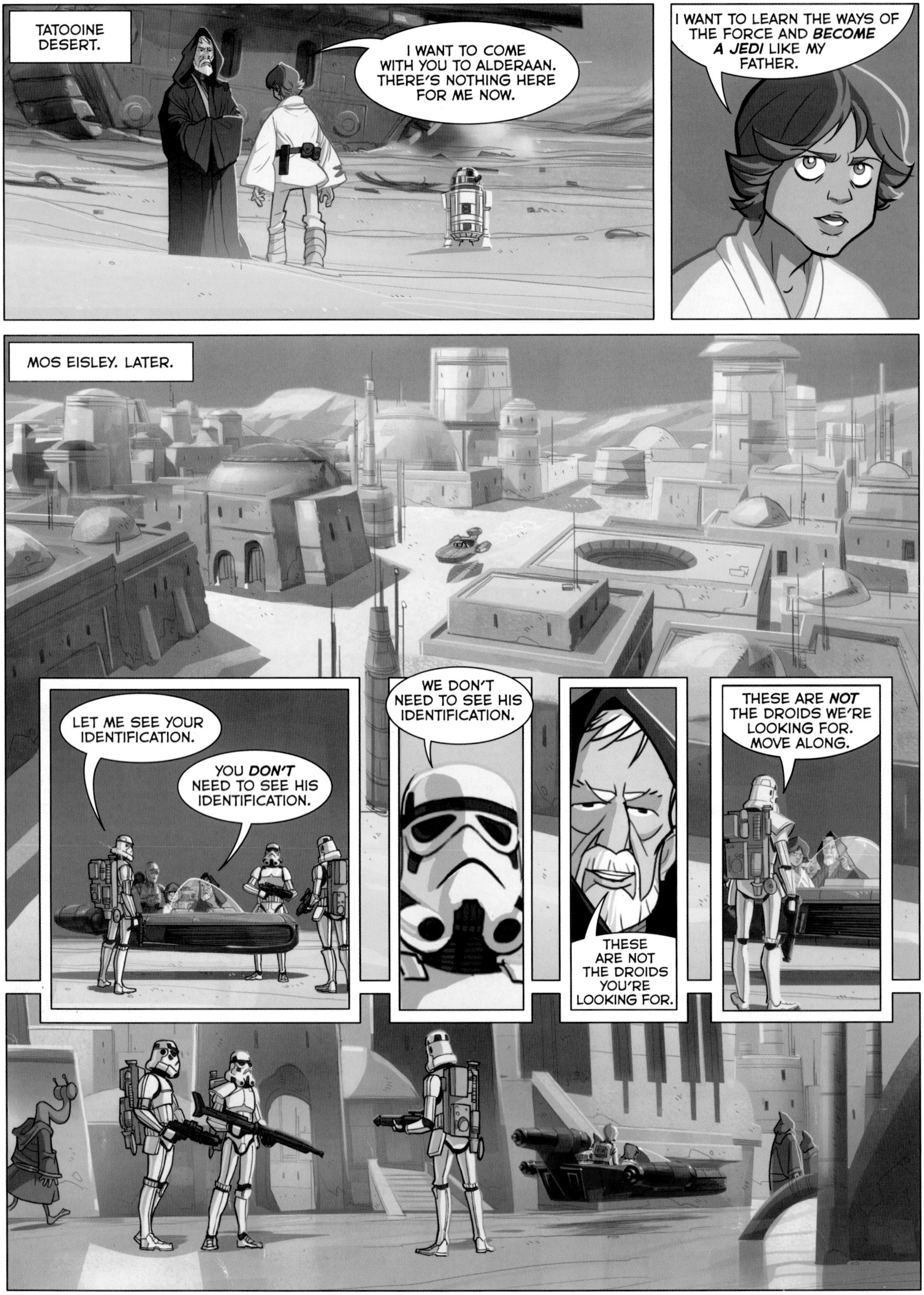
TATOOINE DESERT.
I WANT TO COME WITH YOU TO ALDERAAN. THERE'S NOTHING HERE FOR ME NOW.
I WANT TO LEARN THE WAYS OF THE FORCE AND BECOME A JEDI LIKE MY FATHER.
MOS EISLEY. LATER.
LET ME SEE YOUR IDENTIFICATION.
YOU DON'T NEED TO SEE HIS IDENTIFICATION.
WE DON'T NEED TO SEE HIS IDENTIFICATION.
THESE ARE NOT THE DROIDS YOU'RE LOOKING FOR.
THESE ARE NOT THE DROIDS WE'RE LOOKING FOR. MOVE ALONG.

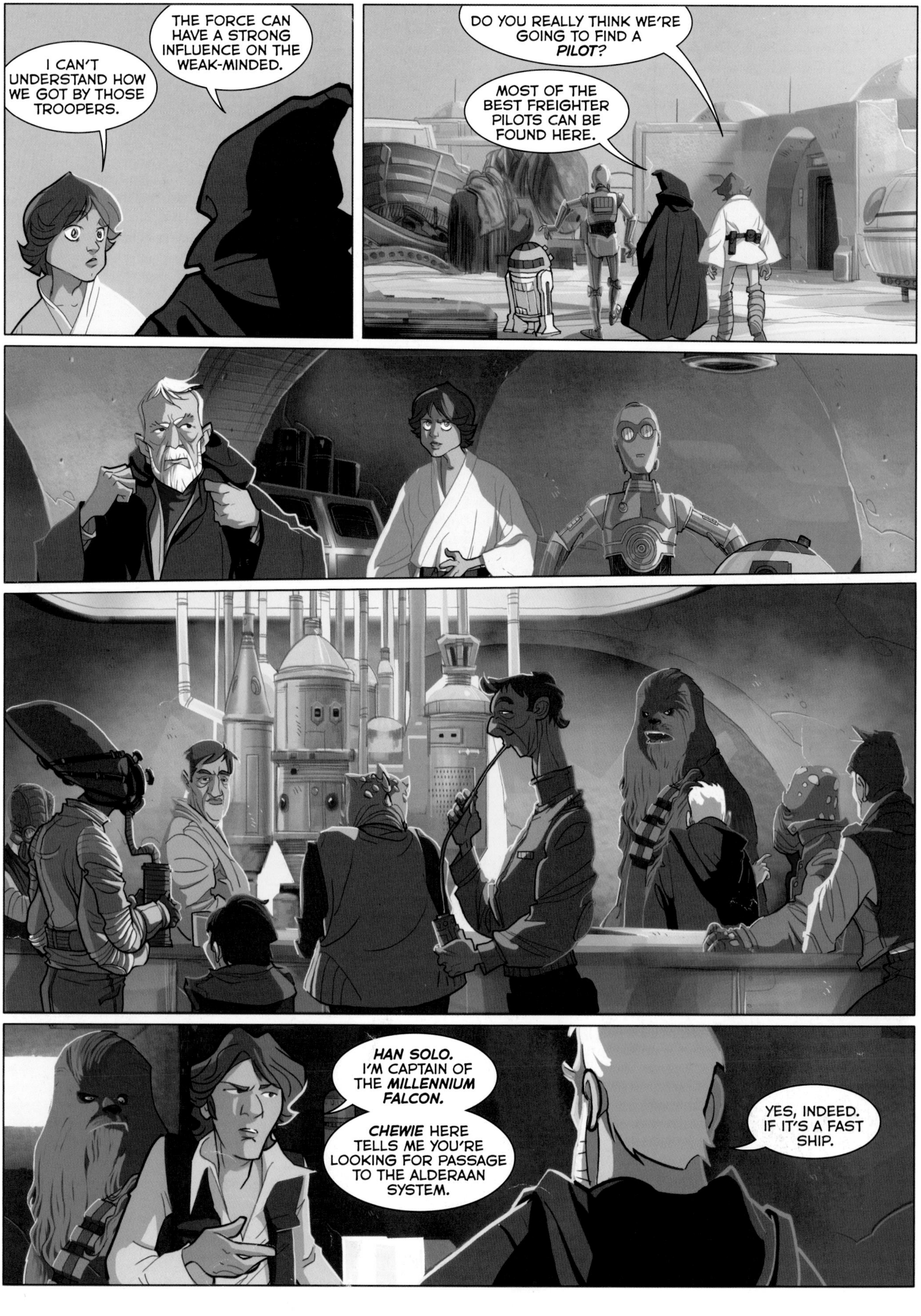
I CAN'T UNDERSTAND HOW WE GOT BY THOSE TROOPERS.
THE FORCE CAN HAVE A STRONG INFLUENCE ON THE WEAK-MINDED.
DO YOU REALLY THINK WE'RE GOING TO FIND A PILOT?
MOST OF THE BEST FREIGHTER PILOTS CAN BE FOUND HERE.
HAN SOLO. I'M CAPTAIN OF THE MILLENNIUM FALCON.
CHEWIE HERE TELLS ME YOU'RE LOOKING FOR PASSAGE TO THE ALDERAAN SYSTEM.
YES, INDEED. IF IT'S A FAST SHIP.

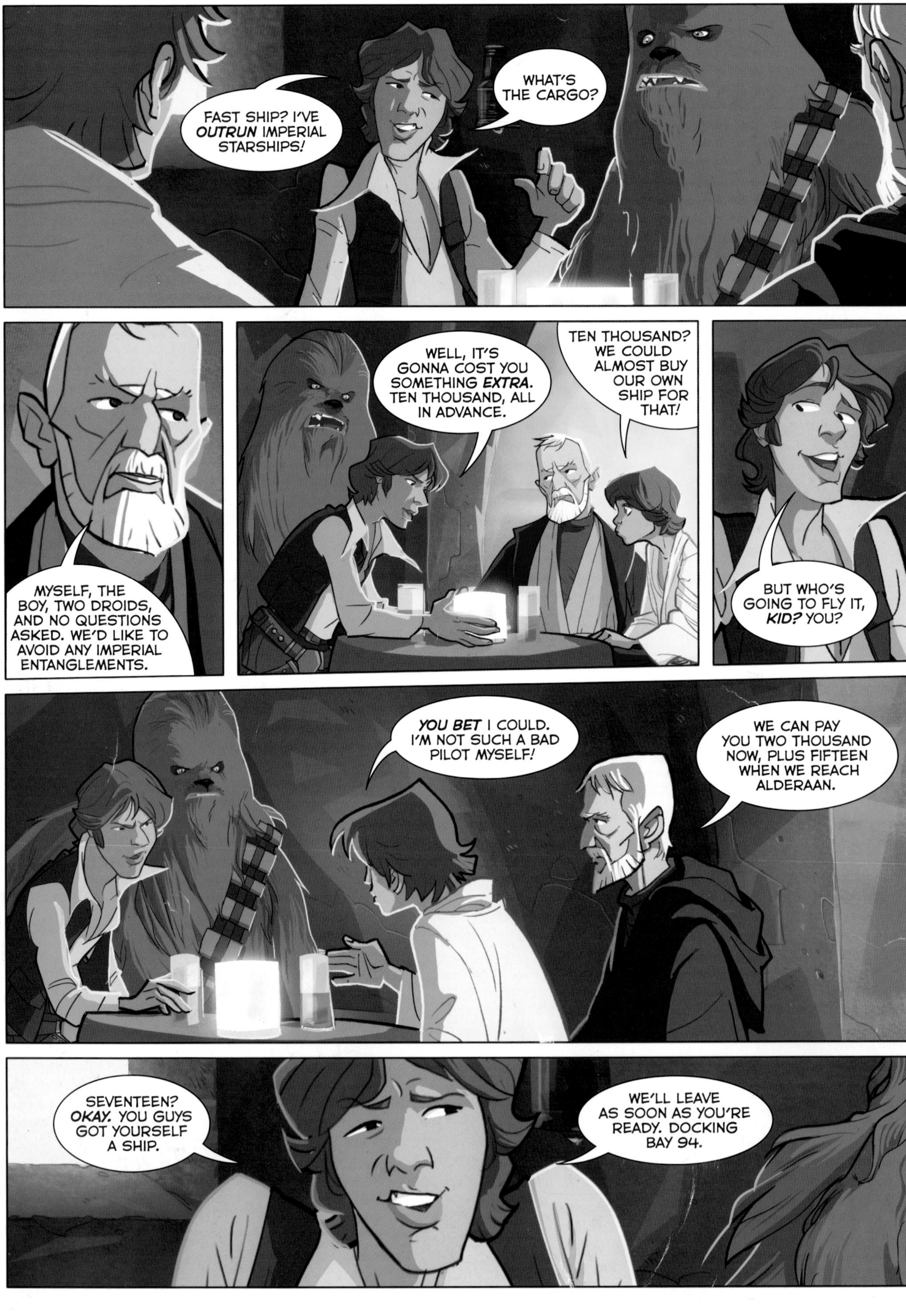
FAST SHIP? I'VE *OUTRUN* IMPERIAL STARSHIPS!
WHAT'S THE CARGO?
MYSELF, THE BOY, TWO DROIDS, AND NO QUESTIONS ASKED. WE'D LIKE TO AVOID ANY IMPERIAL ENTANGLEMENTS.
WELL, IT'S GONNA COST YOU SOMETHING *EXTRA.* TEN THOUSAND, ALL IN ADVANCE.
TEN THOUSAND? WE COULD ALMOST BUY OUR OWN SHIP FOR THAT!
BUT WHO'S GOING TO FLY IT, *KID?* YOU?
YOU BET I COULD. I'M NOT SUCH A BAD PILOT MYSELF!
WE CAN PAY YOU TWO THOUSAND NOW, PLUS FIFTEEN WHEN WE REACH ALDERAAN.
SEVENTEEN? *OKAY.* YOU GUYS GOT YOURSELF A SHIP.
WE'LL LEAVE AS SOON AS YOU'RE READY. DOCKING BAY 94.

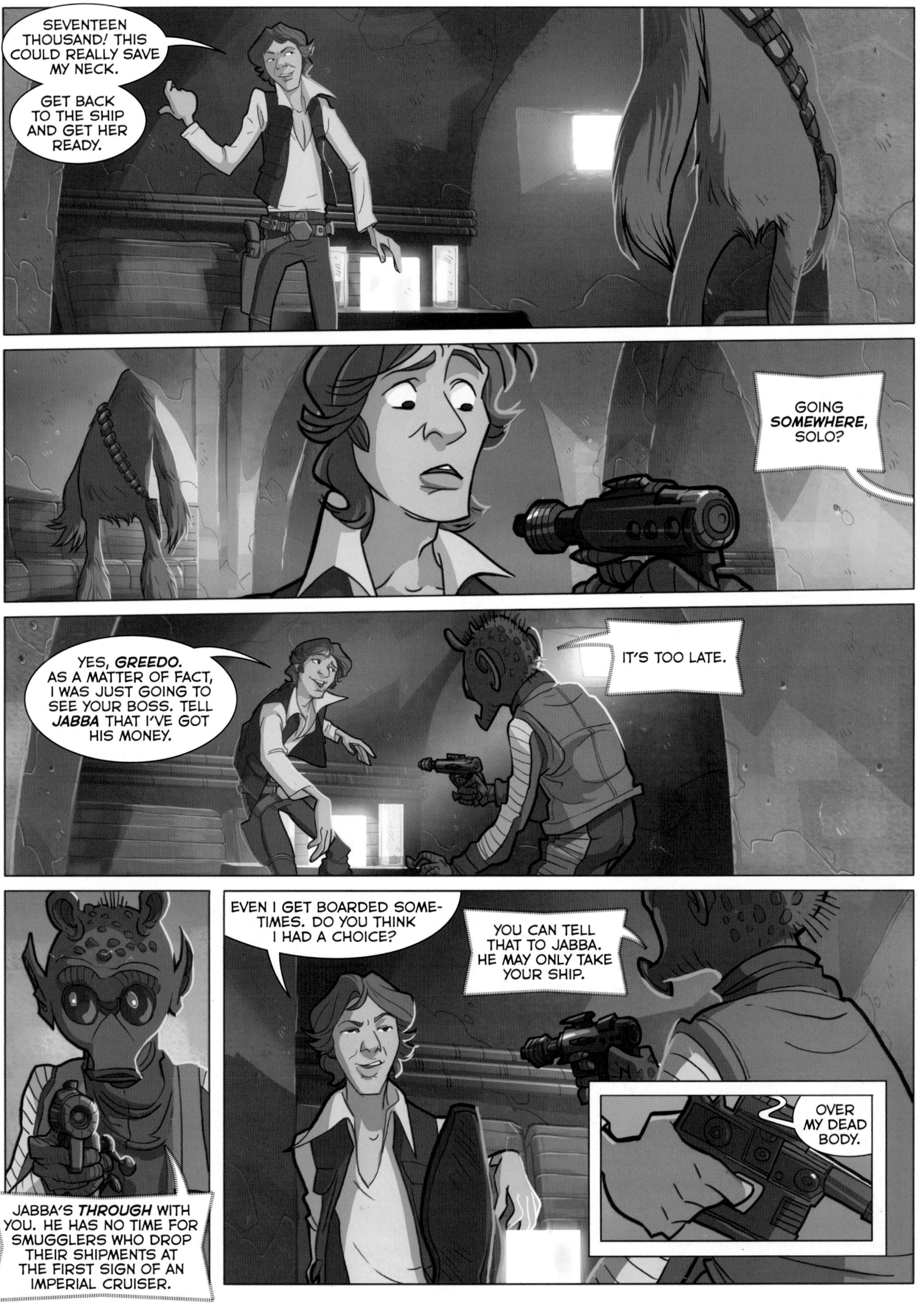
SEVENTEEN THOUSAND! THIS COULD REALLY SAVE MY NECK.
GET BACK TO THE SHIP AND GET HER READY.
GOING *SOMEWHERE*, SOLO?
YES, *GREEDO*. AS A MATTER OF FACT, I WAS JUST GOING TO SEE YOUR BOSS. TELL *JABBA* THAT I'VE GOT HIS MONEY.
IT'S TOO LATE.
JABBA'S *THROUGH* WITH YOU. HE HAS NO TIME FOR SMUGGLERS WHO DROP THEIR SHIPMENTS AT THE FIRST SIGN OF AN IMPERIAL CRUISER.
EVEN I GET BOARDED SOMETIMES. DO YOU THINK I HAD A CHOICE?
YOU CAN TELL THAT TO JABBA. HE MAY ONLY TAKE YOUR SHIP.
OVER MY DEAD BODY.

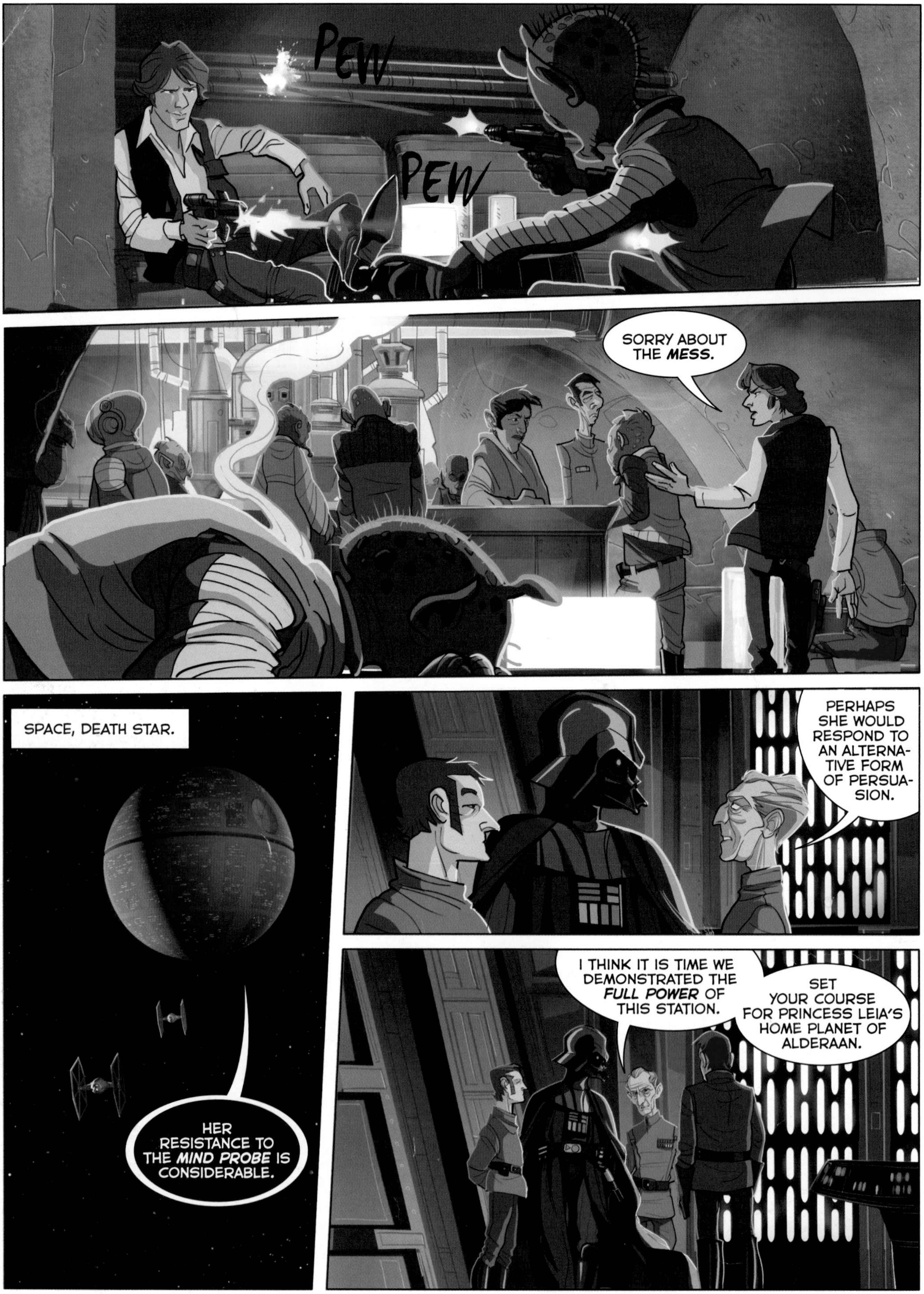
PEW
PEW
SORRY ABOUT THE MESS.
SPACE, DEATH STAR.
HER RESISTANCE TO THE MIND PROBE IS CONSIDERABLE.
PERHAPS SHE WOULD RESPOND TO AN ALTERNATIVE FORM OF PERSUASION.
I THINK IT IS TIME WE DEMONSTRATED THE FULL POWER OF THIS STATION.
SET YOUR COURSE FOR PRINCESS LEIA'S HOME PLANET OF ALDERAAN.

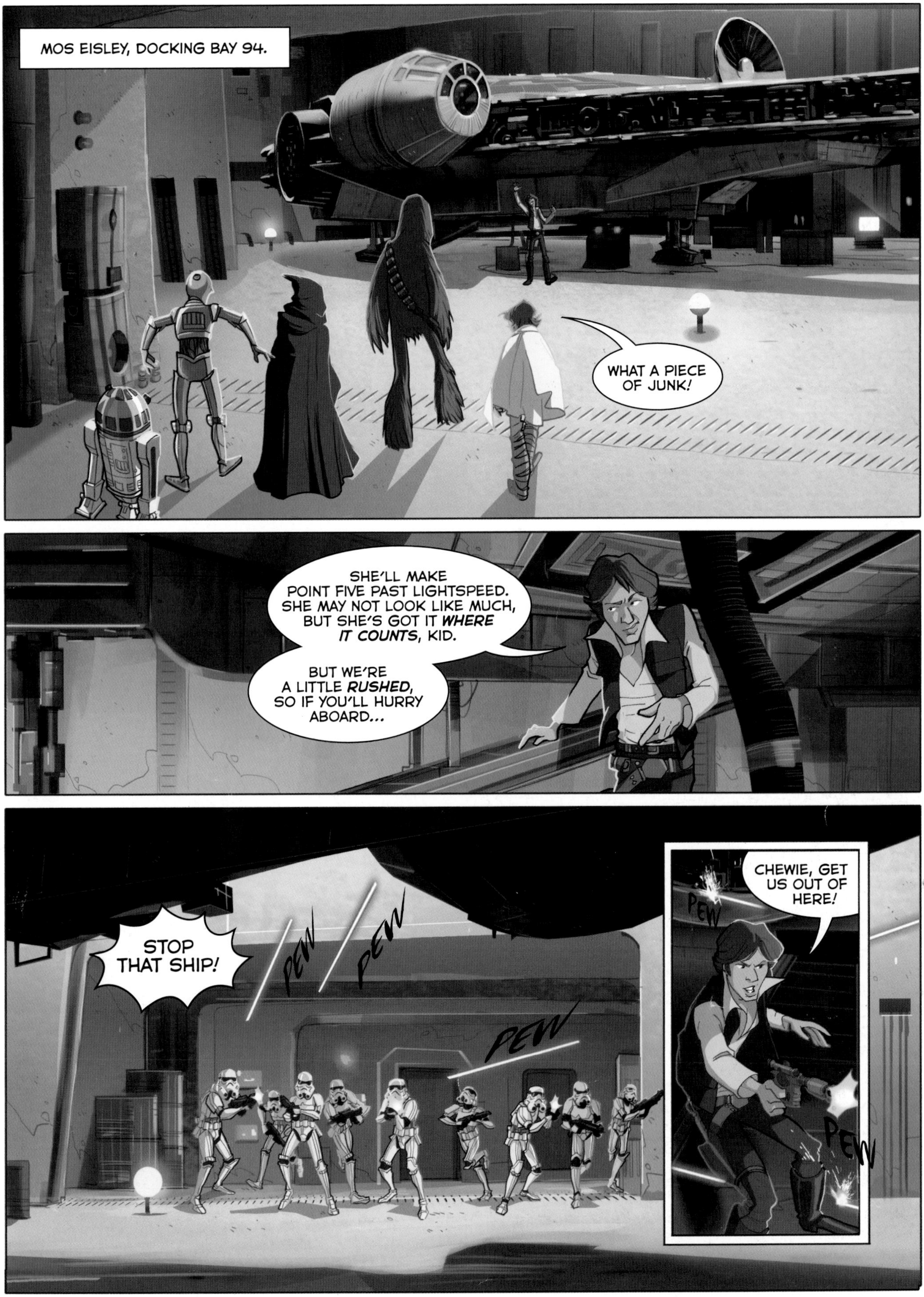
MOS EISLEY, DOCKING BAY 94.
WHAT A PIECE OF JUNK!
SHE'LL MAKE POINT FIVE PAST LIGHTSPEED. SHE MAY NOT LOOK LIKE MUCH, BUT SHE'S GOT IT *WHERE IT COUNTS*, KID.
BUT WE'RE A LITTLE *RUSHED*, SO IF YOU'LL HURRY ABOARD...
STOP THAT SHIP!
PEW
PEW
PEW
CHEWIE, GET US OUT OF HERE!
PEW
PEW

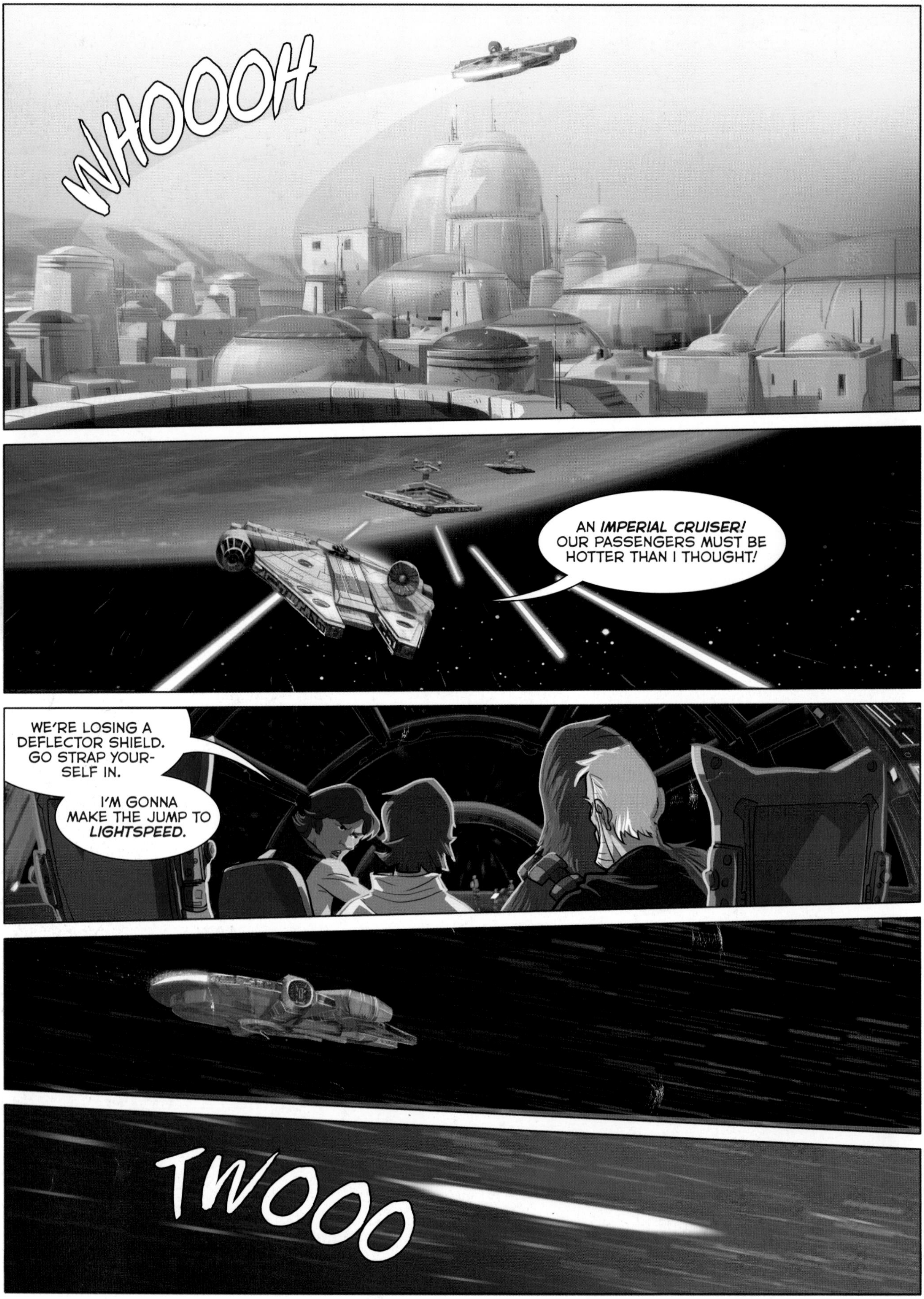
WHOOOH
AN IMPERIAL CRUISER! OUR PASSENGERS MUST BE HOTTER THAN I THOUGHT!
WE'RE LOSING A DEFLECTOR SHIELD. GO STRAP YOURSELF IN.
I'M GONNA MAKE THE JUMP TO LIGHTSPEED.
TWOOO

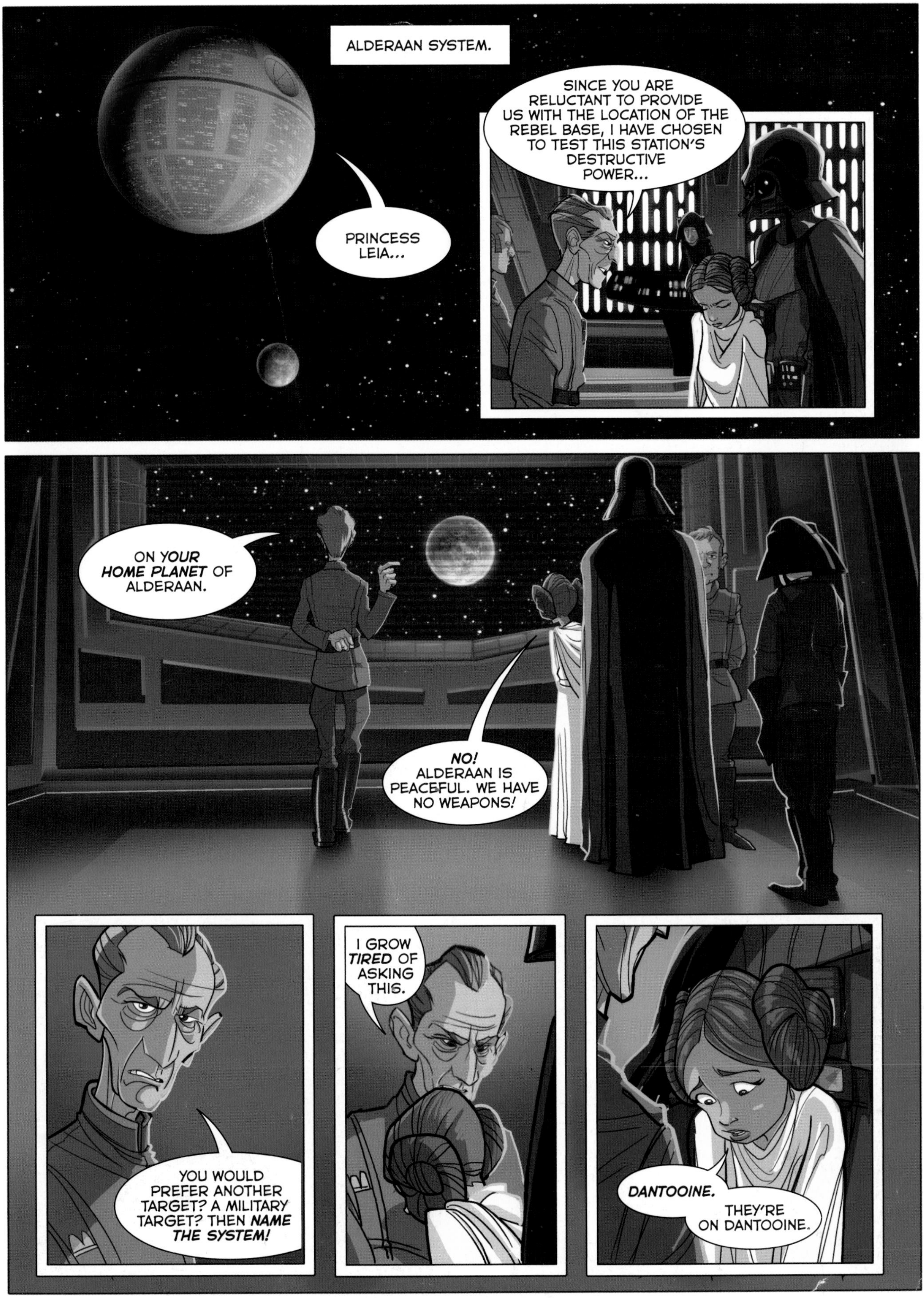
ALDERAAN SYSTEM.
PRINCESS LEIA...
SINCE YOU ARE RELUCTANT TO PROVIDE US WITH THE LOCATION OF THE REBEL BASE, I HAVE CHOSEN TO TEST THIS STATION'S DESTRUCTIVE POWER...
ON *YOUR HOME PLANET* OF ALDERAAN.
NO! ALDERAAN IS PEACEFUL. WE HAVE NO WEAPONS!
YOU WOULD PREFER ANOTHER TARGET? A MILITARY TARGET? THEN *NAME THE SYSTEM!*
I GROW *TIRED* OF ASKING THIS.
DANTOOINE.
THEY'RE ON DANTOOINE.

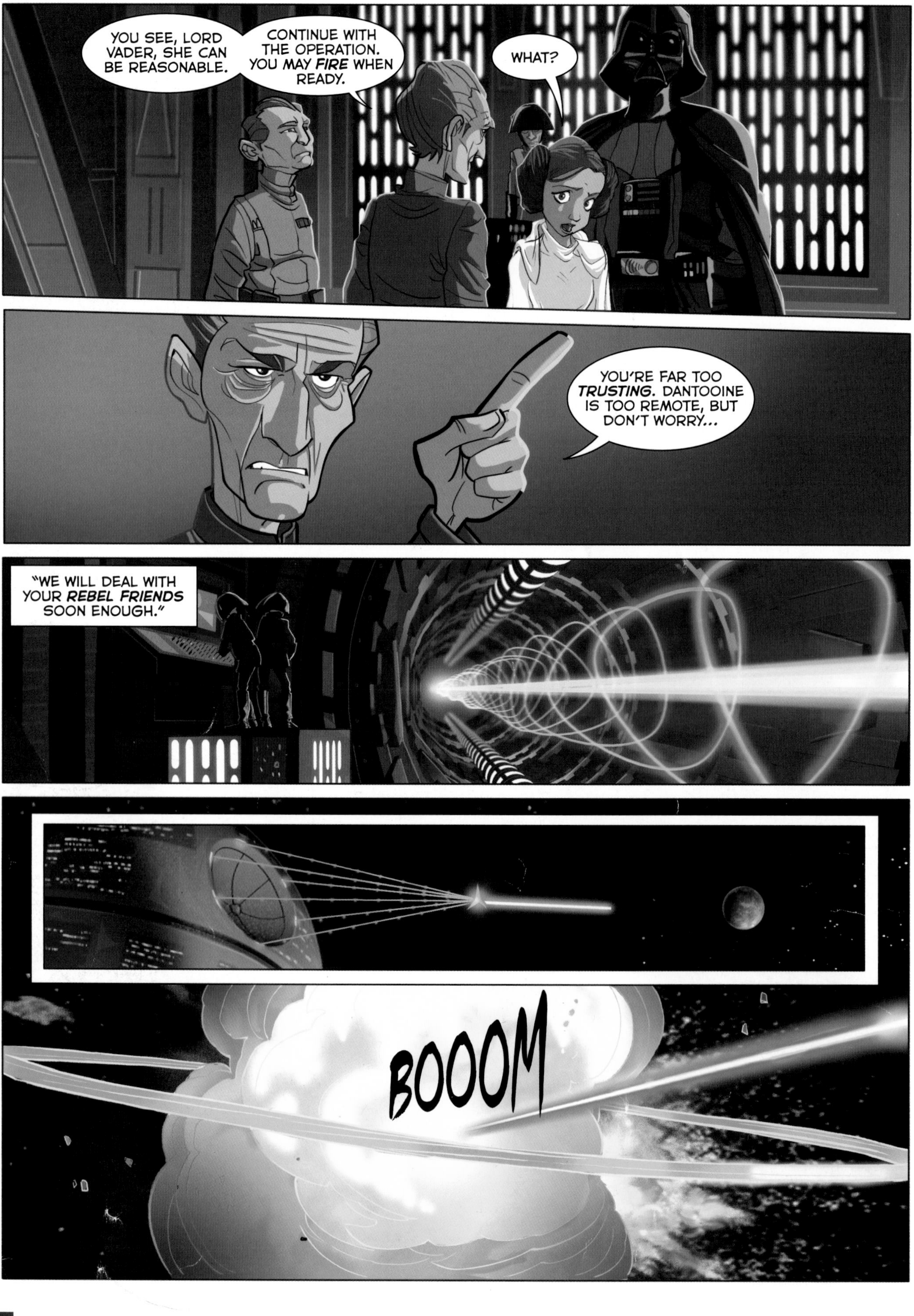
YOU SEE, LORD VADER, SHE CAN BE REASONABLE.
CONTINUE WITH THE OPERATION. YOU MAY FIRE WHEN READY.
WHAT?
YOU'RE FAR TOO TRUSTING. DANTOOINE IS TOO REMOTE, BUT DON'T WORRY...
"WE WILL DEAL WITH YOUR REBEL FRIENDS SOON ENOUGH."
BOOOM

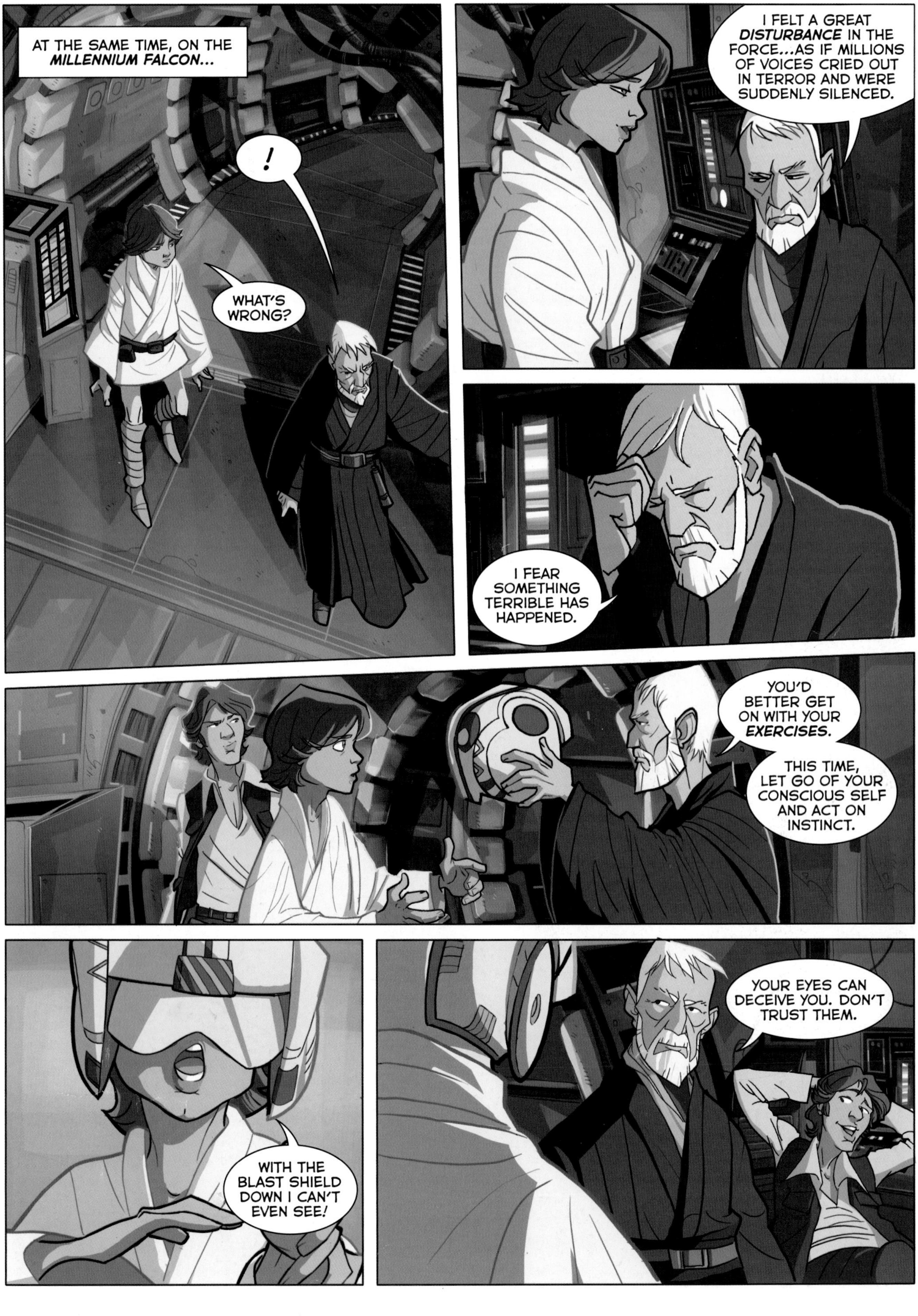
AT THE SAME TIME, ON THE MILLENNIUM FALCON...
!
WHAT'S WRONG?
I FELT A GREAT DISTURBANCE IN THE FORCE...AS IF MILLIONS OF VOICES CRIED OUT IN TERROR AND WERE SUDDENLY SILENCED.
I FEAR SOMETHING TERRIBLE HAS HAPPENED.
YOU'D BETTER GET ON WITH YOUR EXERCISES.
THIS TIME, LET GO OF YOUR CONSCIOUS SELF AND ACT ON INSTINCT.
WITH THE BLAST SHIELD DOWN I CAN'T EVEN SEE!
YOUR EYES CAN DECEIVE YOU. DON'T TRUST THEM.

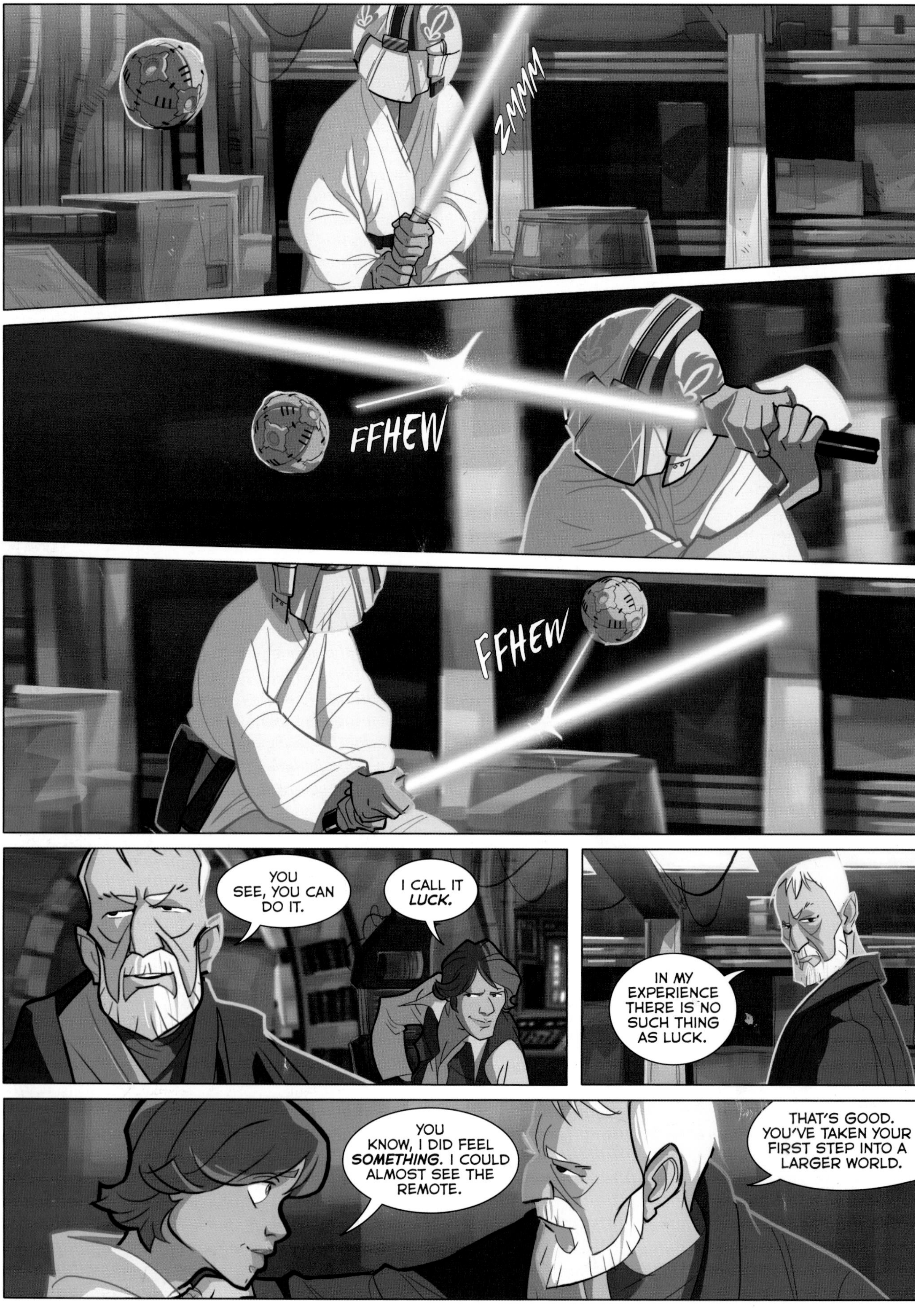
ZMMM
FFHEW
FFHEW
YOU SEE, YOU CAN DO IT.
I CALL IT LUCK.
IN MY EXPERIENCE THERE IS NO SUCH THING AS LUCK.
YOU KNOW, I DID FEEL SOMETHING. I COULD ALMOST SEE THE REMOTE.
THAT'S GOOD. YOU'VE TAKEN YOUR FIRST STEP INTO A LARGER WORLD.

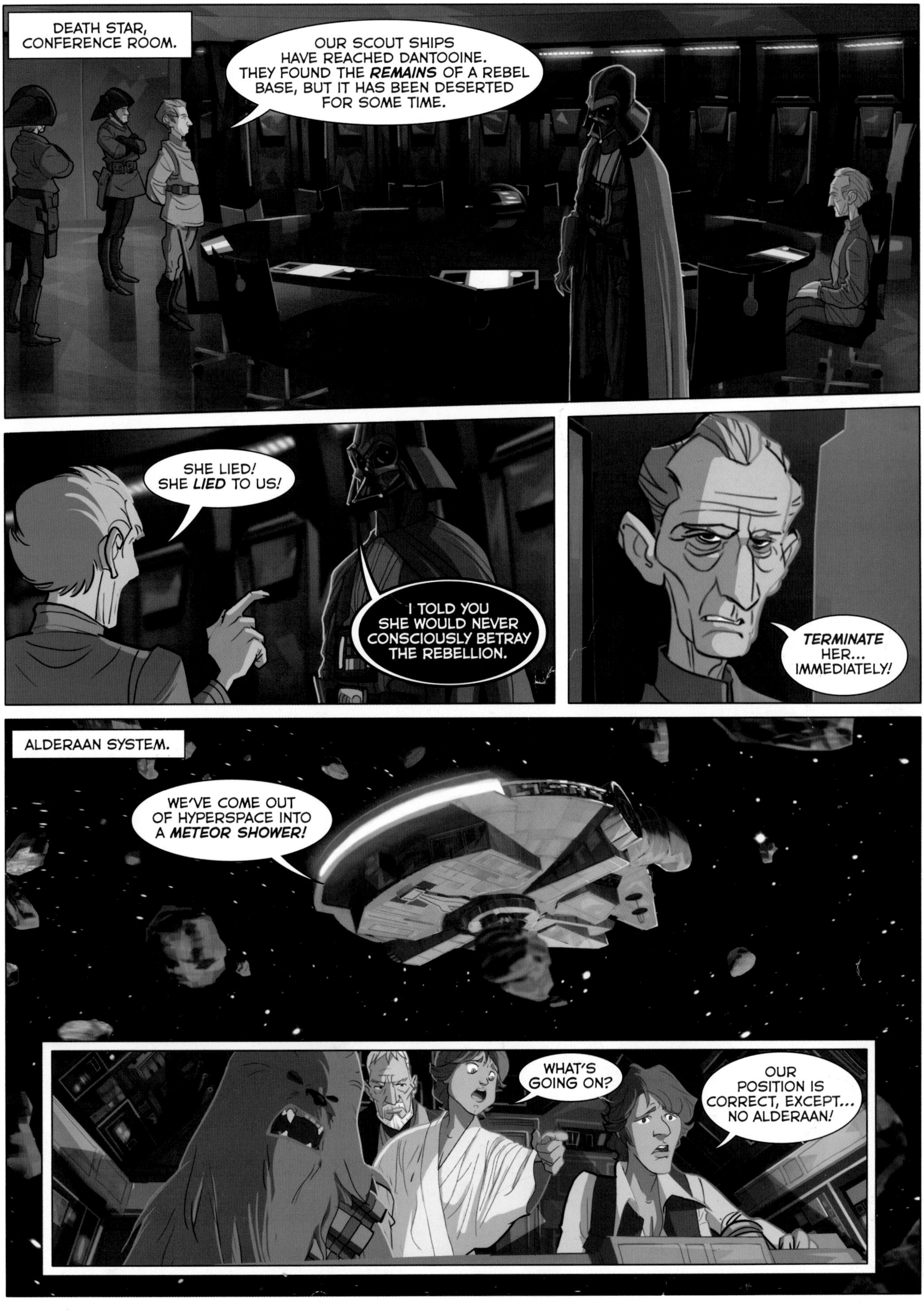
DEATH STAR, CONFERENCE ROOM.
OUR SCOUT SHIPS HAVE REACHED DANTOOINE. THEY FOUND THE *REMAINS* OF A REBEL BASE, BUT IT HAS BEEN DESERTED FOR SOME TIME.
SHE LIED! SHE *LIED* TO US!
I TOLD YOU SHE WOULD NEVER CONSCIOUSLY BETRAY THE REBELLION.
TERMINATE HER... IMMEDIATELY!
ALDERAAN SYSTEM.
WE'VE COME OUT OF HYPERSPACE INTO A *METEOR SHOWER!*
WHAT'S GOING ON?
OUR POSITION IS CORRECT, EXCEPT... NO ALDERAAN!

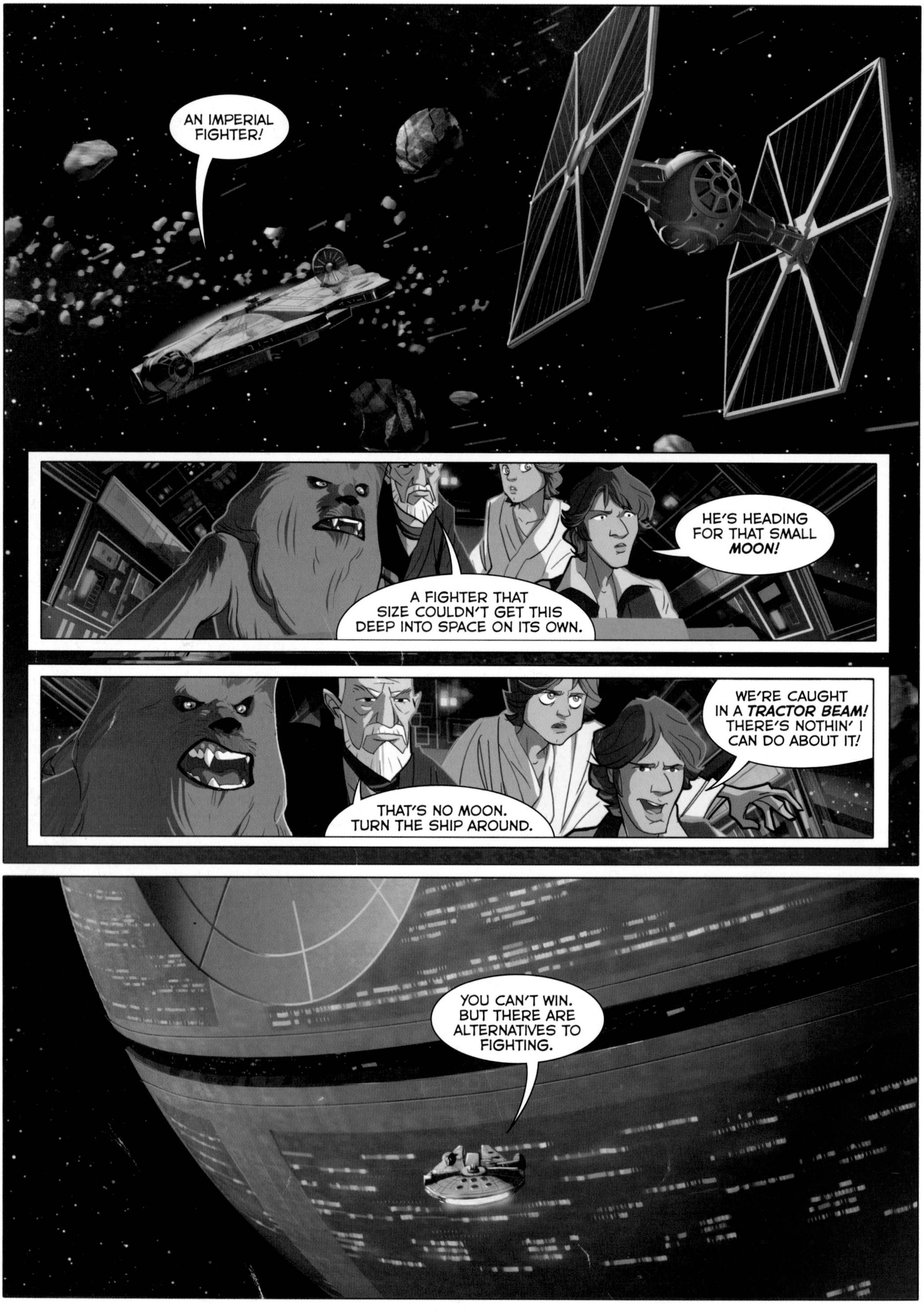
AN IMPERIAL FIGHTER!
HE'S HEADING FOR THAT SMALL MOON!
A FIGHTER THAT SIZE COULDN'T GET THIS DEEP INTO SPACE ON ITS OWN.
WE'RE CAUGHT IN A TRACTOR BEAM! THERE'S NOTHIN' I CAN DO ABOUT IT!
THAT'S NO MOON. TURN THE SHIP AROUND.
YOU CAN'T WIN. BUT THERE ARE ALTERNATIVES TO FIGHTING.

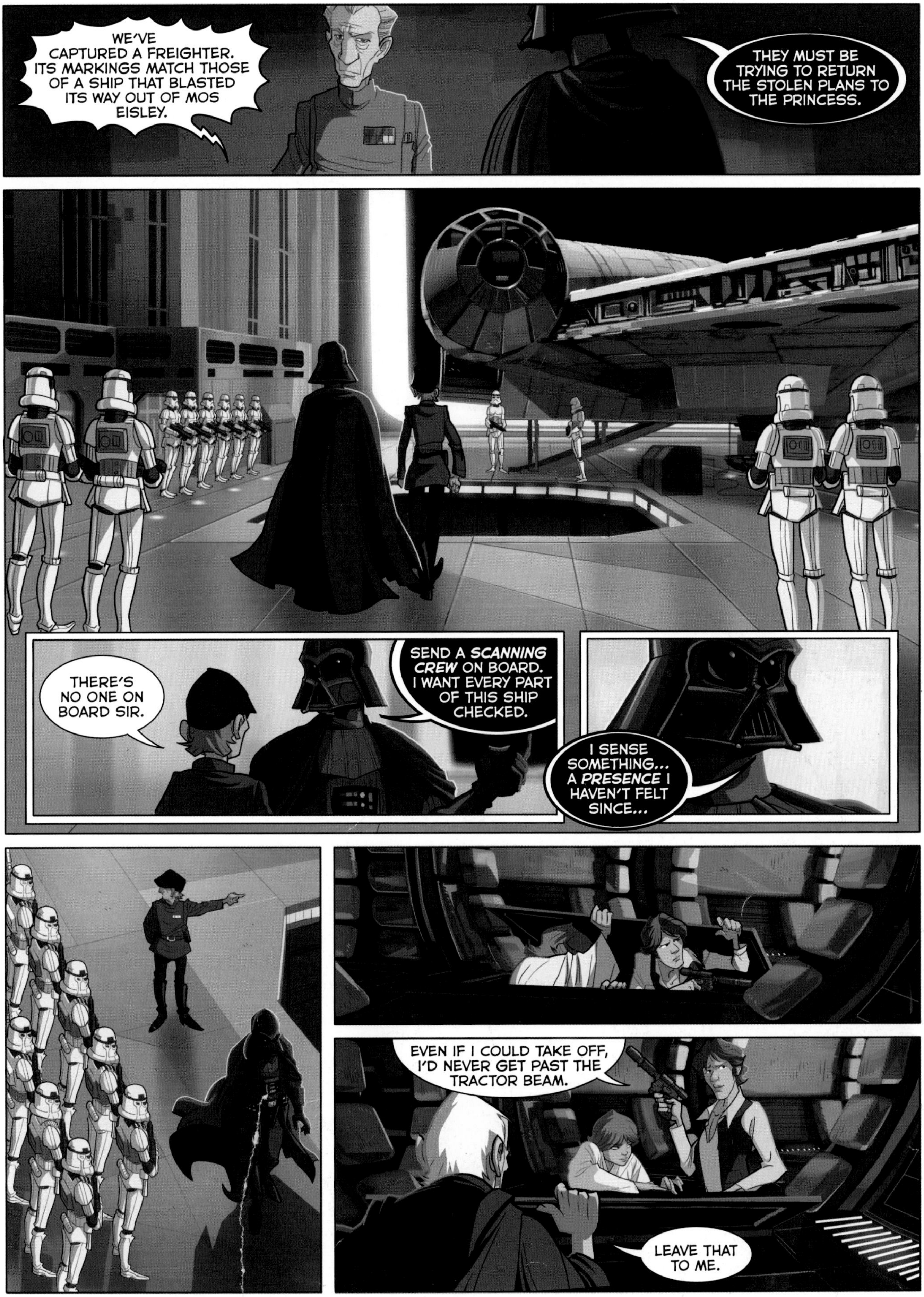
WE'VE CAPTURED A FREIGHTER. ITS MARKINGS MATCH THOSE OF A SHIP THAT BLASTED ITS WAY OUT OF MOS EISLEY.
THEY MUST BE TRYING TO RETURN THE STOLEN PLANS TO THE PRINCESS.
THERE'S NO ONE ON BOARD SIR.
SEND A *SCANNING CREW* ON BOARD. I WANT EVERY PART OF THIS SHIP CHECKED.
I SENSE SOMETHING... A *PRESENCE* I HAVEN'T FELT SINCE...
EVEN IF I COULD TAKE OFF, I'D NEVER GET PAST THE TRACTOR BEAM.
LEAVE THAT TO ME.

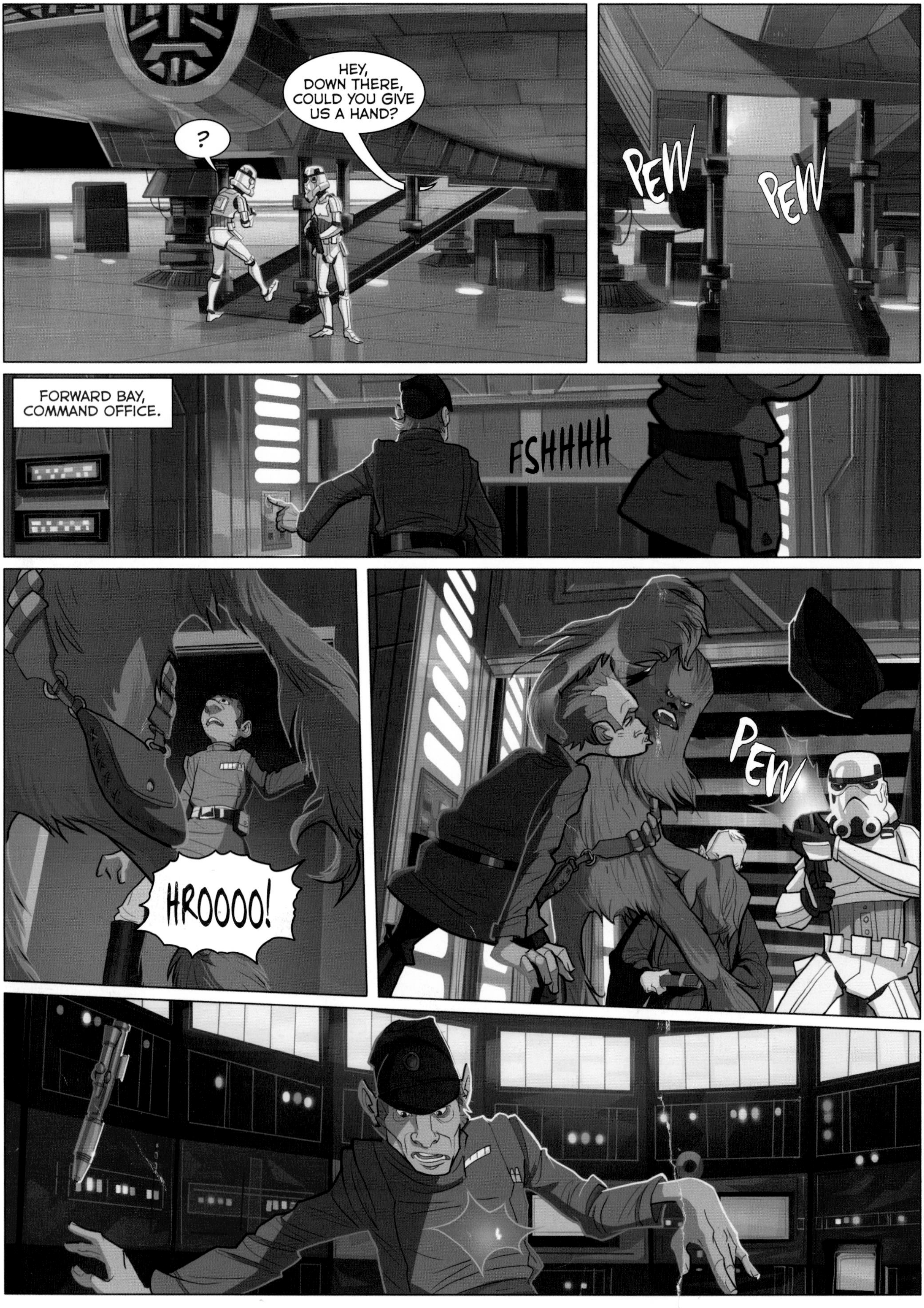
?
HEY, DOWN THERE, COULD YOU GIVE US A HAND?
PEW
PEW
FORWARD BAY, COMMAND OFFICE.
FSHHHH
HROOOO!
PEW

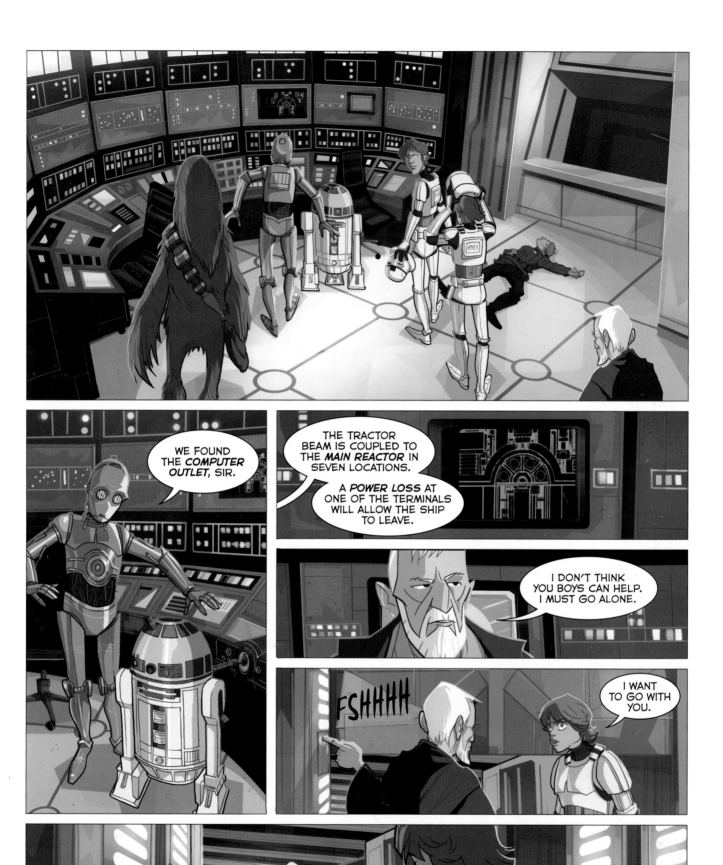

WE FOUND THE *COMPUTER OUTLET*, SIR.

THE TRACTOR BEAM IS COUPLED TO THE *MAIN REACTOR* IN SEVEN LOCATIONS.

A *POWER LOSS* AT ONE OF THE TERMINALS WILL ALLOW THE SHIP TO LEAVE.

I DON'T THINK YOU BOYS CAN HELP. I MUST GO ALONE.

FSHHHH

I WANT TO GO WITH YOU.

YOUR DESTINY LIES ALONG A *DIFFERENT PATH* FROM MINE. THE FORCE WILL BE WITH YOU...ALWAYS!

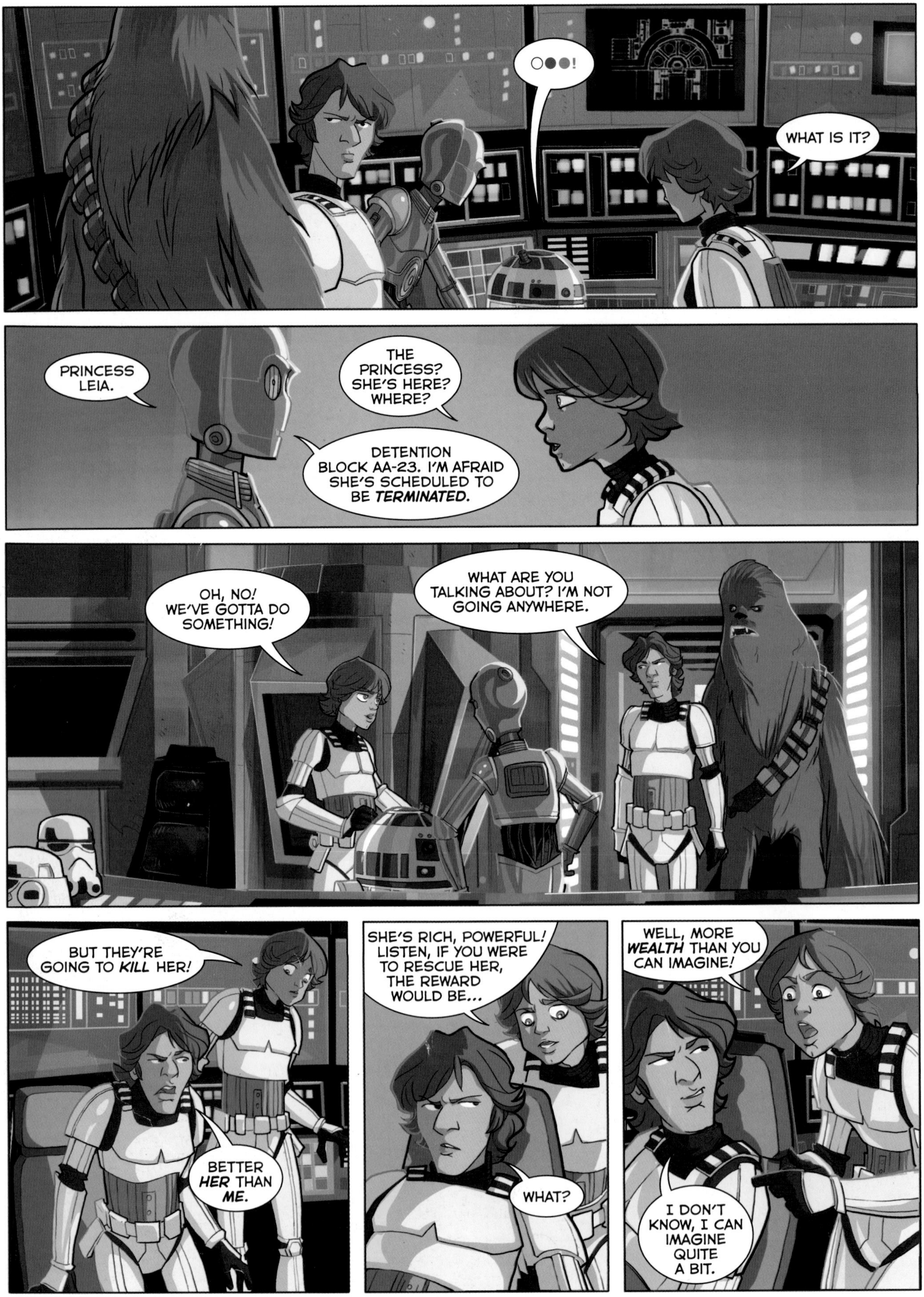
○●●!
WHAT IS IT?
PRINCESS LEIA.
THE PRINCESS? SHE'S HERE? WHERE?
DETENTION BLOCK AA-23. I'M AFRAID SHE'S SCHEDULED TO BE *TERMINATED.*
OH, NO! WE'VE GOTTA DO SOMETHING!
WHAT ARE YOU TALKING ABOUT? I'M NOT GOING ANYWHERE.
BUT THEY'RE GOING TO *KILL* HER!
BETTER *HER* THAN *ME.*
SHE'S RICH, POWERFUL! LISTEN, IF YOU WERE TO RESCUE HER, THE REWARD WOULD BE...
WHAT?
WELL, MORE *WEALTH* THAN YOU CAN IMAGINE!
I DON'T KNOW, I CAN IMAGINE QUITE A BIT.

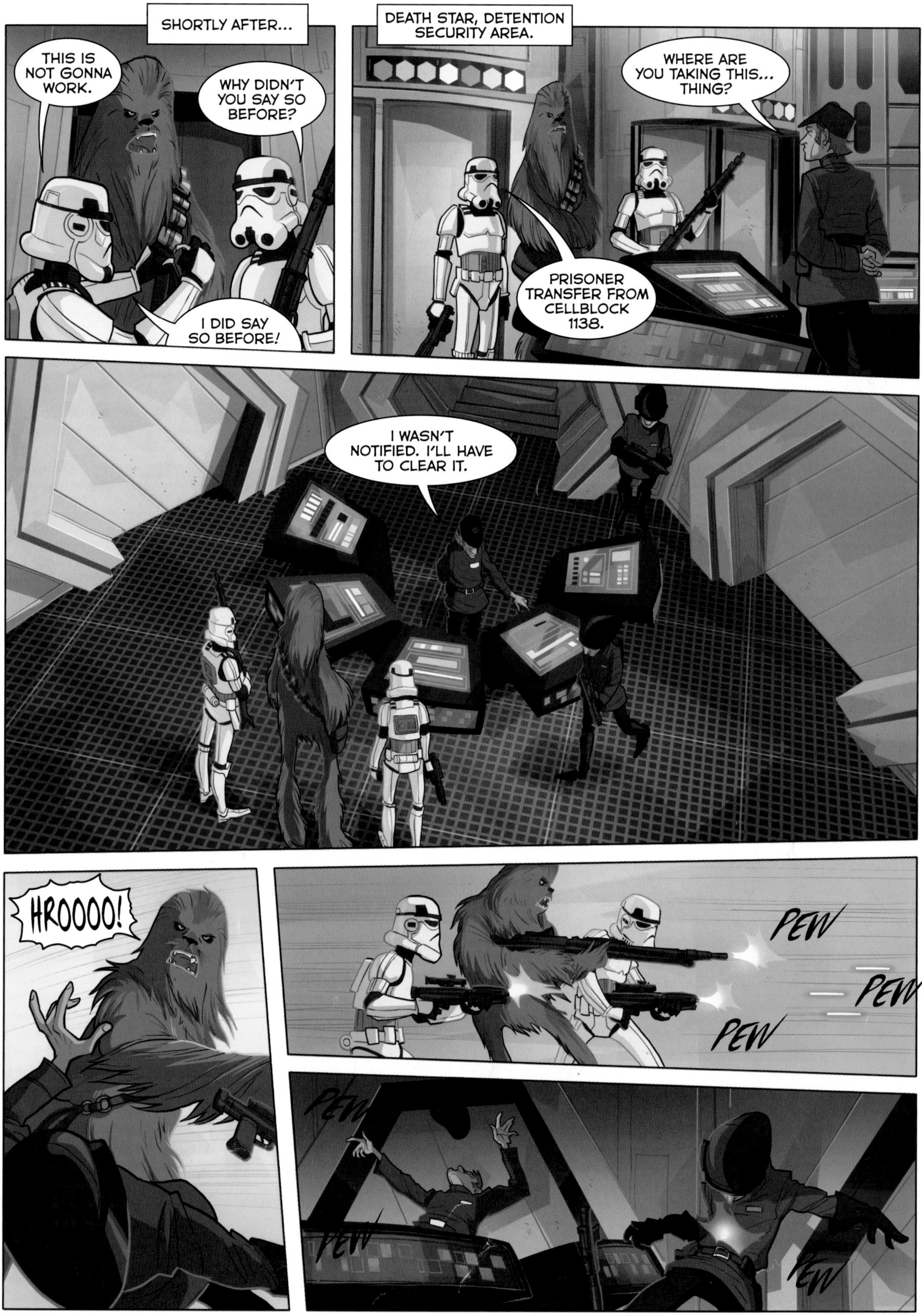
SHORTLY AFTER...
THIS IS NOT GONNA WORK.
WHY DIDN'T YOU SAY SO BEFORE?
I DID SAY SO BEFORE!
DEATH STAR, DETENTION SECURITY AREA.
WHERE ARE YOU TAKING THIS... THING?
PRISONER TRANSFER FROM CELLBLOCK 1138.
I WASN'T NOTIFIED. I'LL HAVE TO CLEAR IT.
HROOOO!
PEW
PEW
PEW
PEW
PEW
PEW

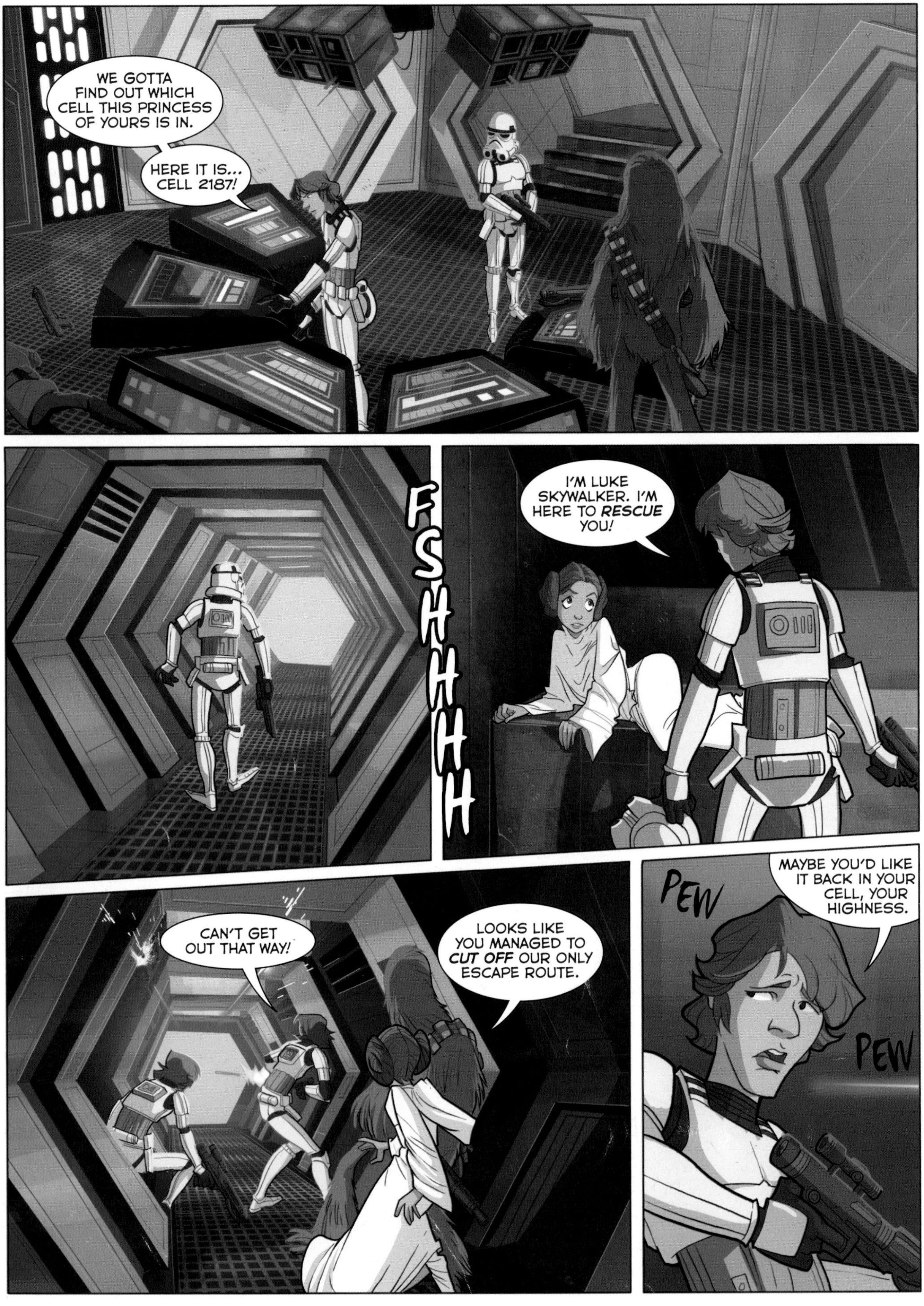
WE GOTTA FIND OUT WHICH CELL THIS PRINCESS OF YOURS IS IN.
HERE IT IS... CELL 2187!
FSHHHH
I'M LUKE SKYWALKER. I'M HERE TO RESCUE YOU!
CAN'T GET OUT THAT WAY!
LOOKS LIKE YOU MANAGED TO CUT OFF OUR ONLY ESCAPE ROUTE.
PEW
MAYBE YOU'D LIKE IT BACK IN YOUR CELL, YOUR HIGHNESS.
PEW

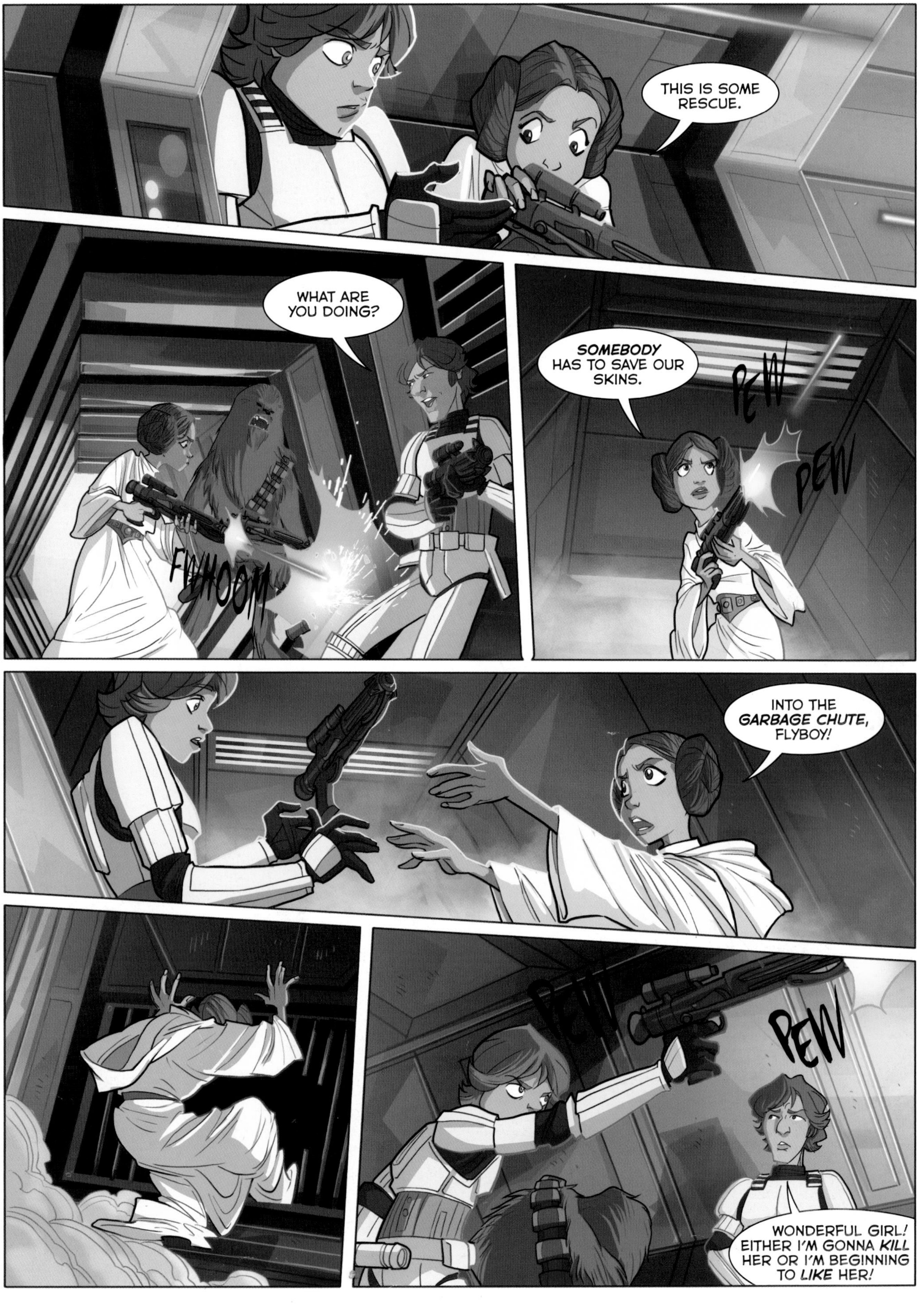
THIS IS SOME RESCUE.
WHAT ARE YOU DOING?
FWHOOM
SOMEBODY HAS TO SAVE OUR SKINS.
PEW
PEW
INTO THE GARBAGE CHUTE, FLYBOY!
PEW
PEW
WONDERFUL GIRL! EITHER I'M GONNA KILL HER OR I'M BEGINNING TO LIKE HER!

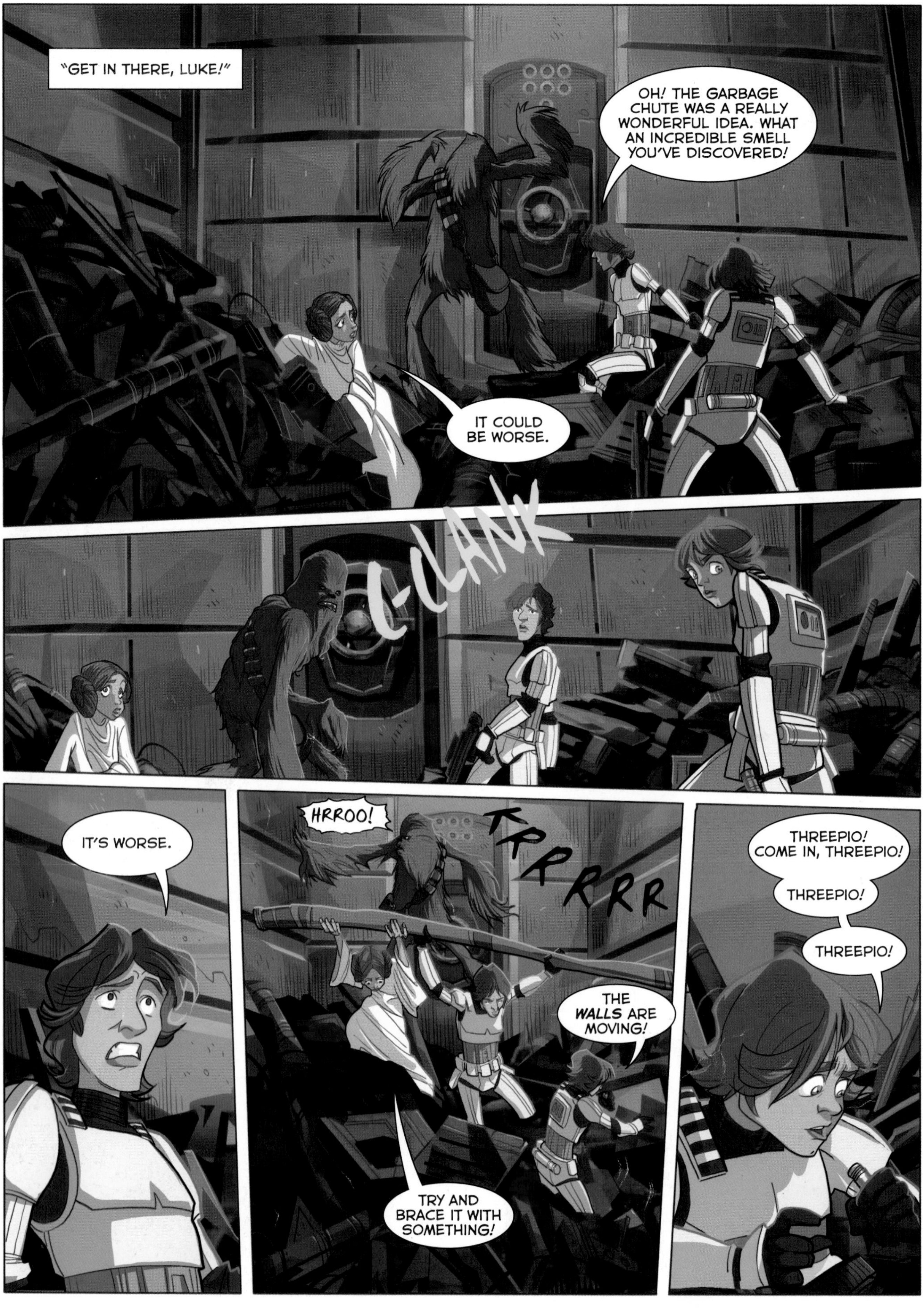
"GET IN THERE, LUKE!"
OH! THE GARBAGE CHUTE WAS A REALLY WONDERFUL IDEA. WHAT AN INCREDIBLE SMELL YOU'VE DISCOVERED!
IT COULD BE WORSE.
C-CLANK
IT'S WORSE.
HRROO!
KRRRRRR
THE WALLS ARE MOVING!
TRY AND BRACE IT WITH SOMETHING!
THREEPIO! COME IN, THREEPIO!
THREEPIO!
THREEPIO!

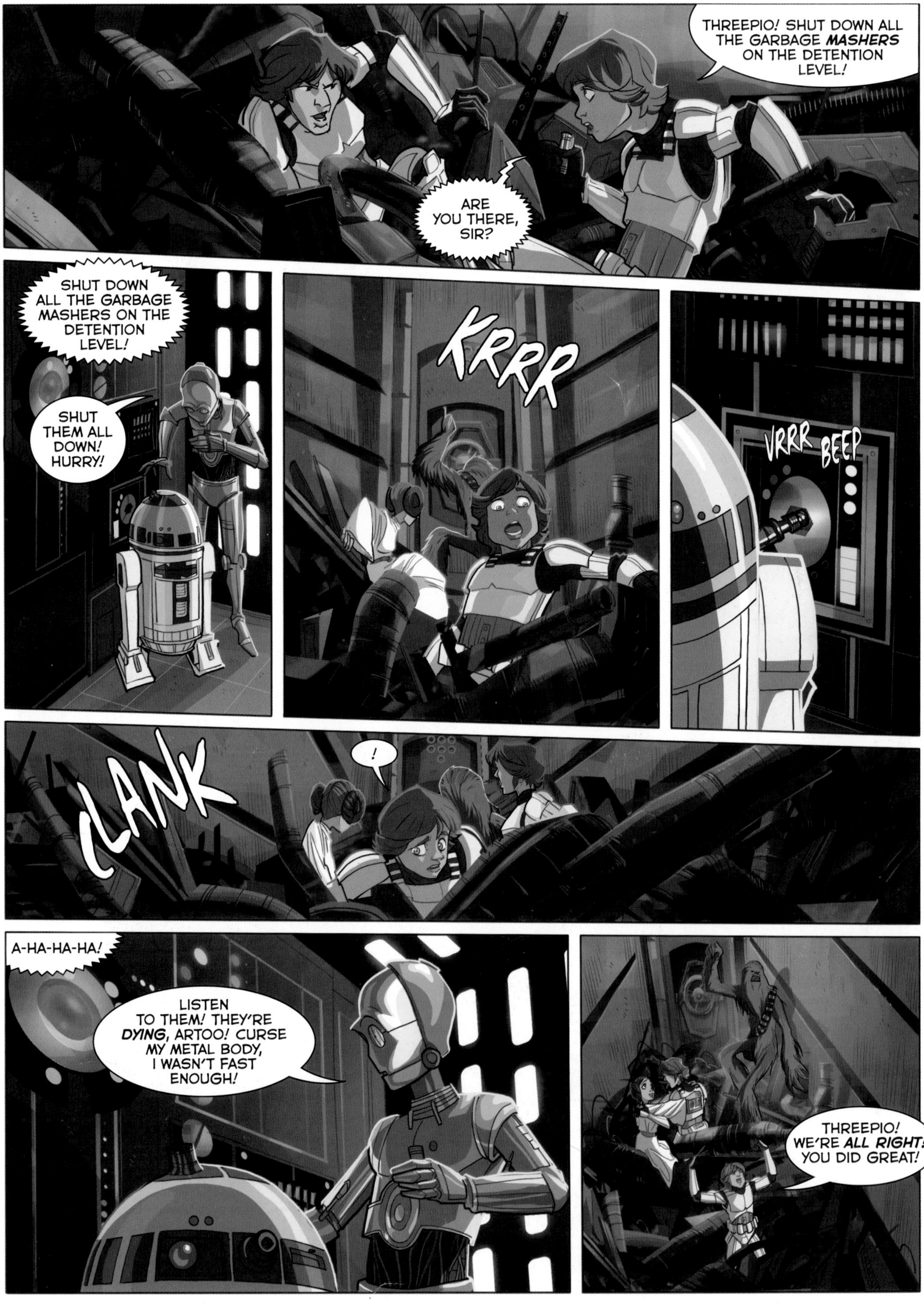
THREEPIO! SHUT DOWN ALL THE GARBAGE MASHERS ON THE DETENTION LEVEL!
ARE YOU THERE, SIR?
SHUT DOWN ALL THE GARBAGE MASHERS ON THE DETENTION LEVEL!
SHUT THEM ALL DOWN! HURRY!
KRRR
VRRR BEEP
CLANK
!
A-HA-HA-HA!
LISTEN TO THEM! THEY'RE DYING, ARTOO! CURSE MY METAL BODY, I WASN'T FAST ENOUGH!
THREEPIO! WE'RE ALL RIGHT! YOU DID GREAT!

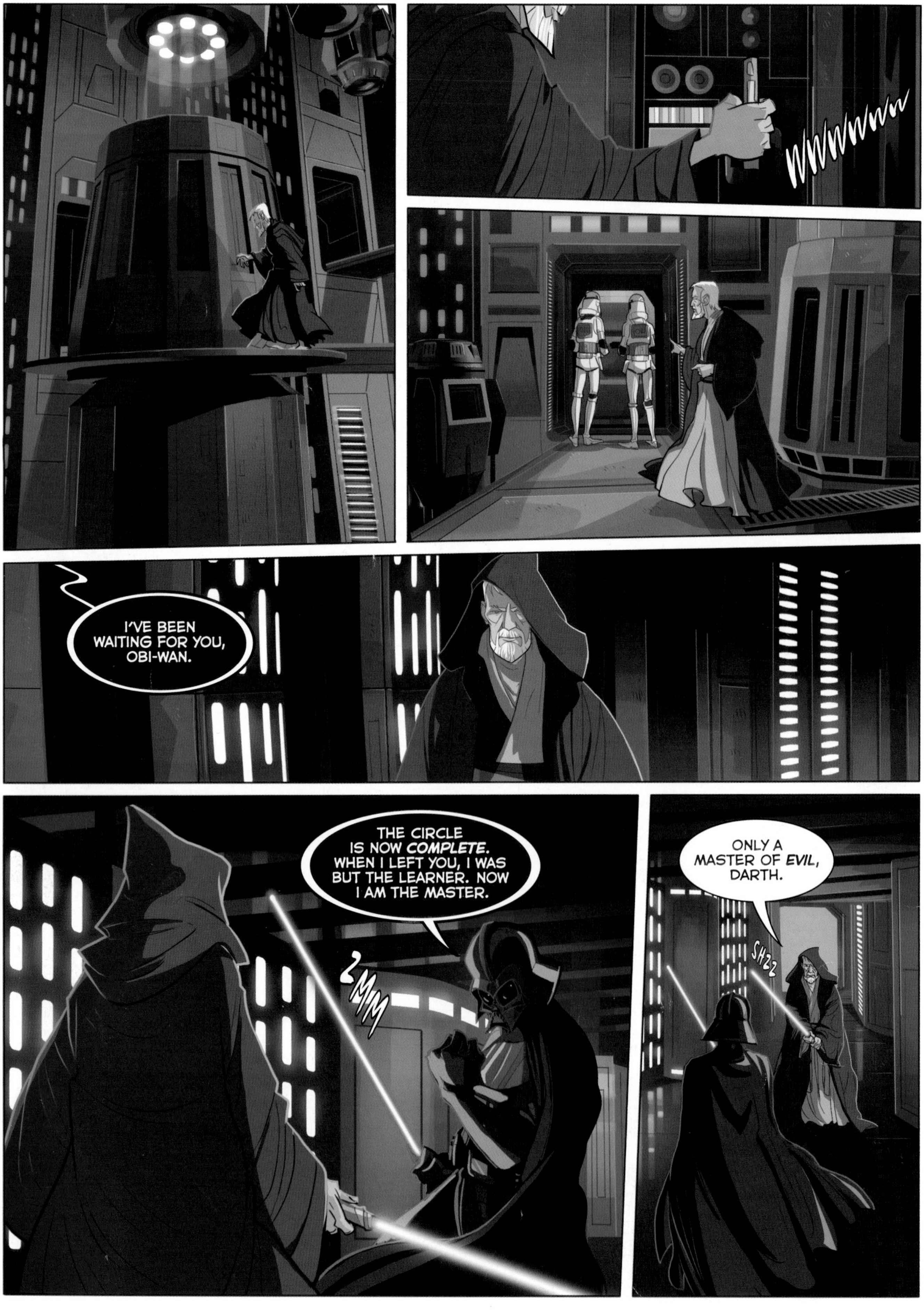
WWWWWW
I'VE BEEN WAITING FOR YOU, OBI-WAN.
THE CIRCLE IS NOW COMPLETE. WHEN I LEFT YOU, I WAS BUT THE LEARNER. NOW I AM THE MASTER.
ZMM
ONLY A MASTER OF EVIL, DARTH.
SHZZ

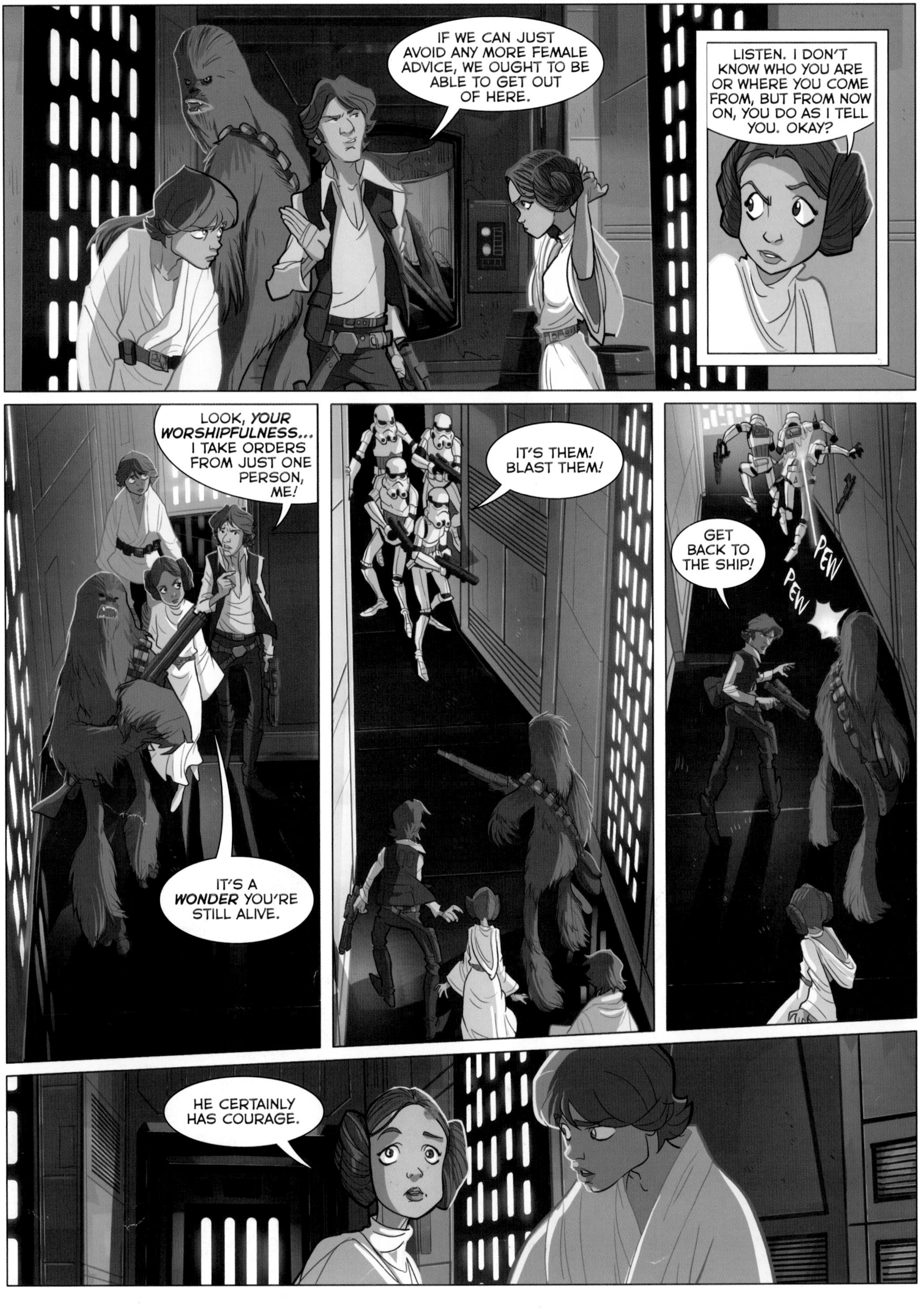

IF WE CAN JUST AVOID ANY MORE FEMALE ADVICE, WE OUGHT TO BE ABLE TO GET OUT OF HERE.
LISTEN. I DON'T KNOW WHO YOU ARE OR WHERE YOU COME FROM, BUT FROM NOW ON, YOU DO AS I TELL YOU. OKAY?
LOOK, *YOUR WORSHIPFULNESS...* I TAKE ORDERS FROM JUST ONE PERSON, ME!
IT'S A *WONDER* YOU'RE STILL ALIVE.
IT'S THEM! BLAST THEM!
GET BACK TO THE SHIP!
PEW
PEW
HE CERTAINLY HAS COURAGE.

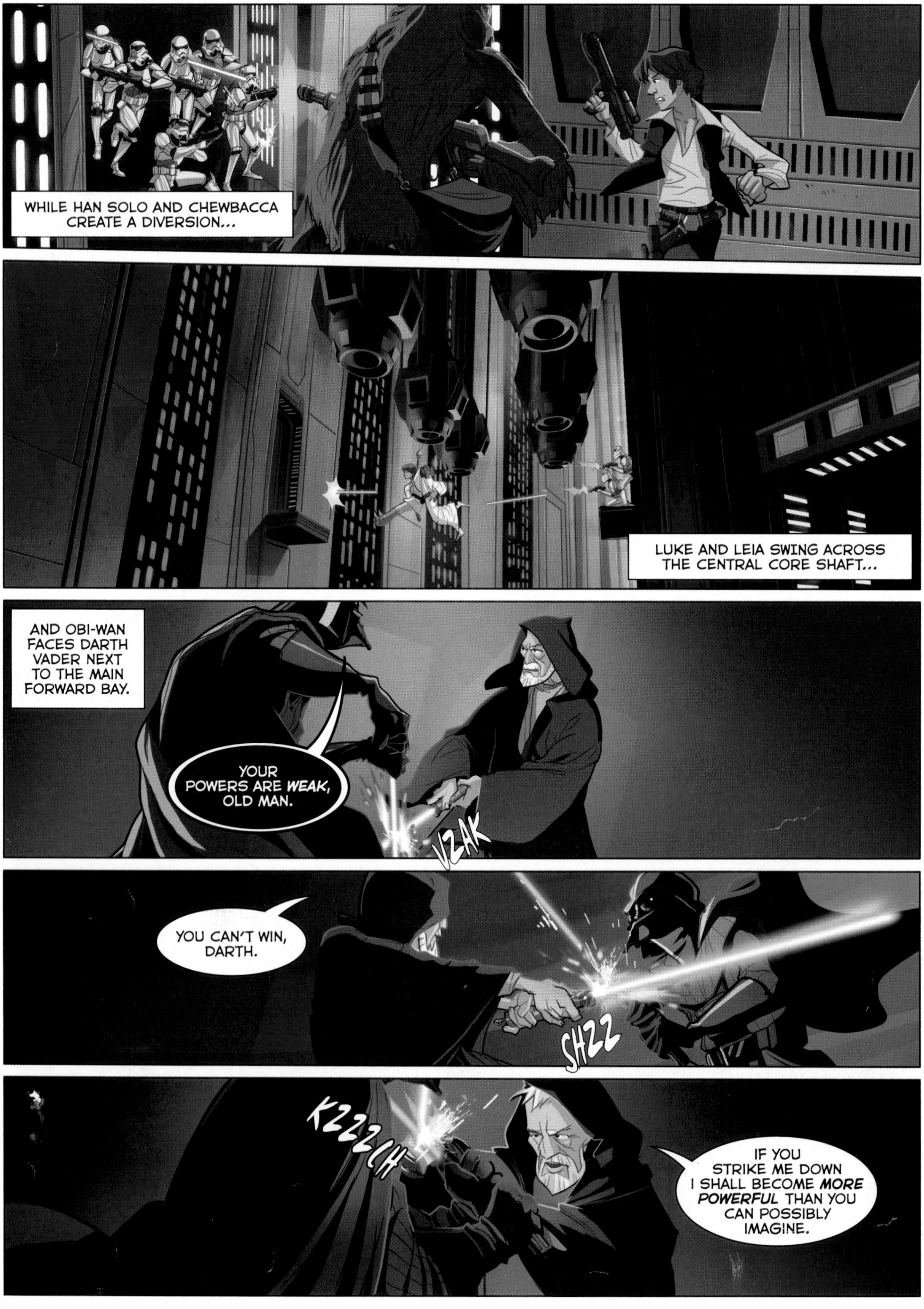
WHILE HAN SOLO AND CHEWBACCA CREATE A DIVERSION...
LUKE AND LEIA SWING ACROSS THE CENTRAL CORE SHAFT...
AND OBI-WAN FACES DARTH VADER NEXT TO THE MAIN FORWARD BAY.
YOUR POWERS ARE *WEAK*, OLD MAN.
VZAK
YOU CAN'T WIN, DARTH.
SHZZ
KZZZCH
IF YOU STRIKE ME DOWN I SHALL BECOME ***MORE POWERFUL*** THAN YOU CAN POSSIBLY IMAGINE.

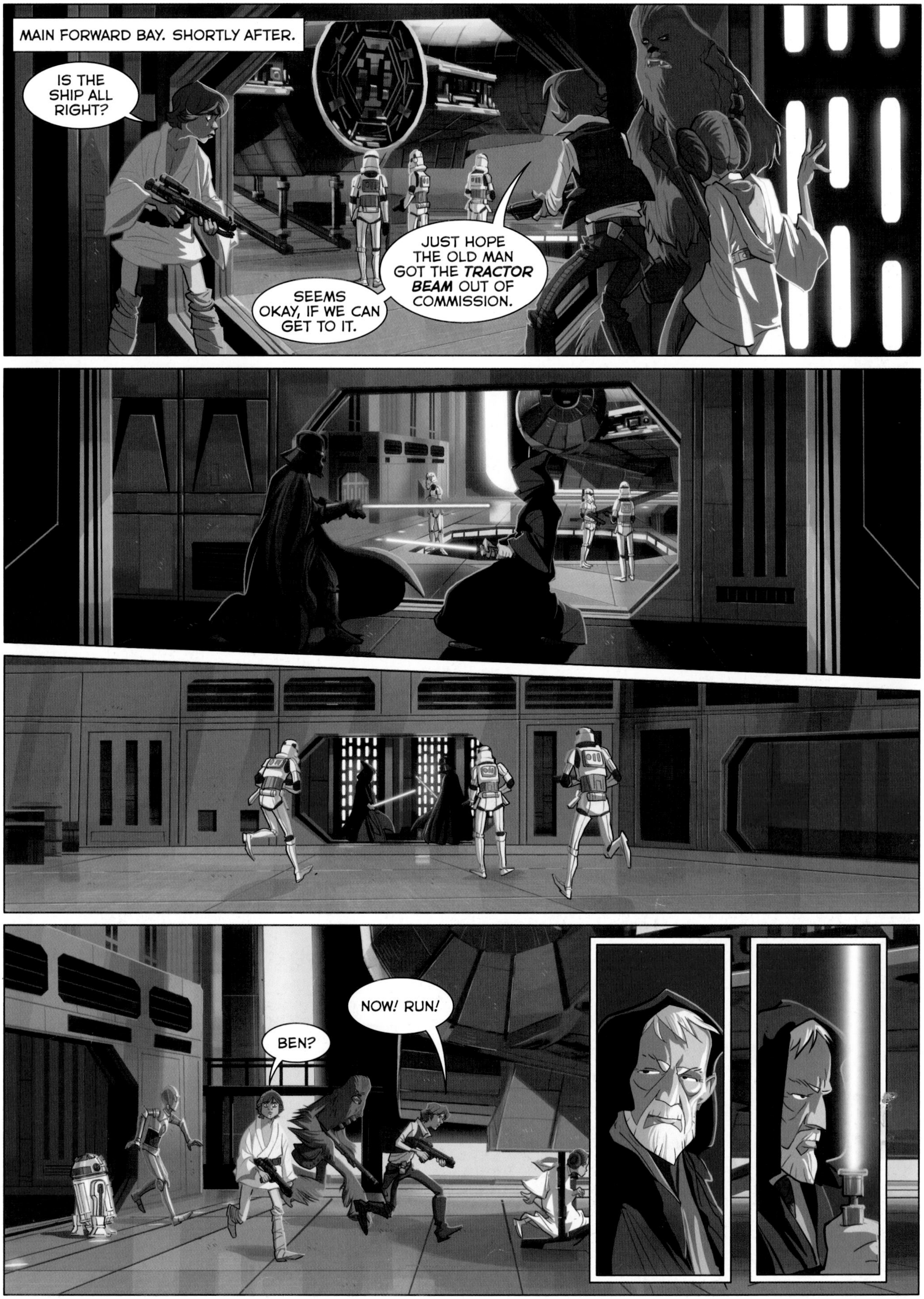
MAIN FORWARD BAY. SHORTLY AFTER.
IS THE SHIP ALL RIGHT?
SEEMS OKAY, IF WE CAN GET TO IT.
JUST HOPE THE OLD MAN GOT THE TRACTOR BEAM OUT OF COMMISSION.
BEN?
NOW! RUN!

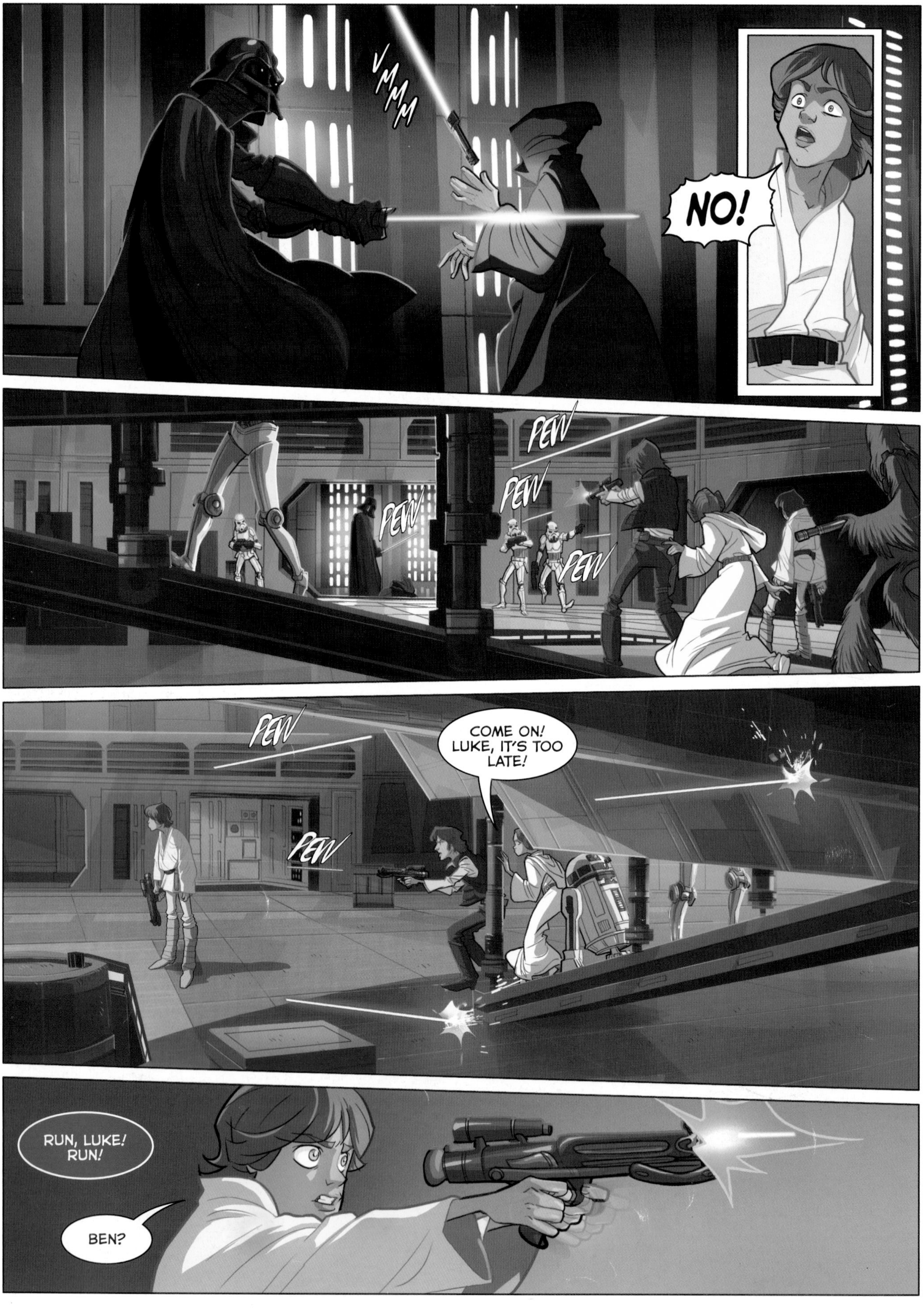
VMMM
NO!
PEW
PEW
PEW
PEW
PEW
COME ON! LUKE, IT'S TOO LATE!
PEW
RUN, LUKE! RUN!
BEN?

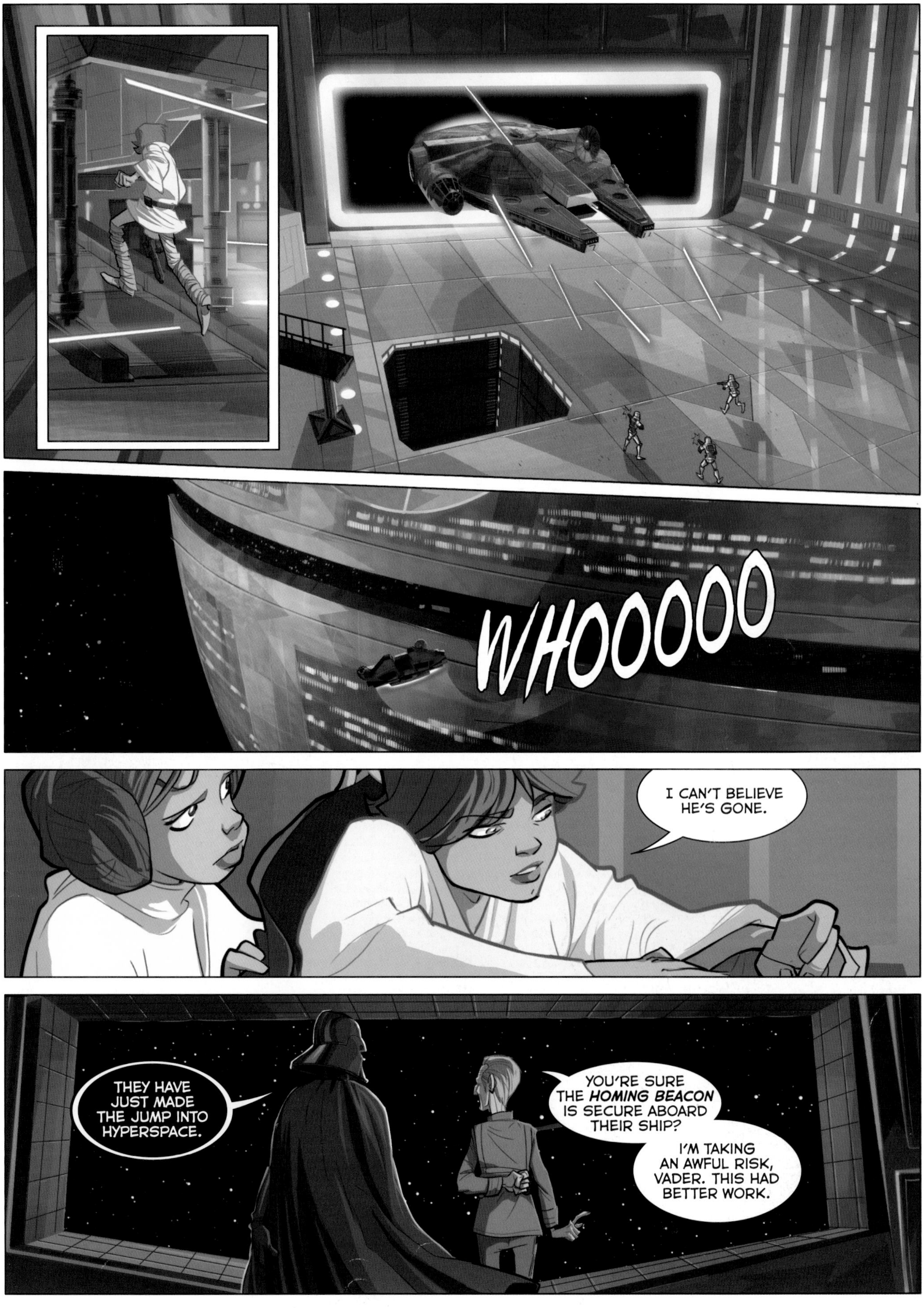
WHOOOOO
I CAN'T BELIEVE HE'S GONE.
THEY HAVE JUST MADE THE JUMP INTO HYPERSPACE.
YOU'RE SURE THE HOMING BEACON IS SECURE ABOARD THEIR SHIP?
I'M TAKING AN AWFUL RISK, VADER. THIS HAD BETTER WORK.

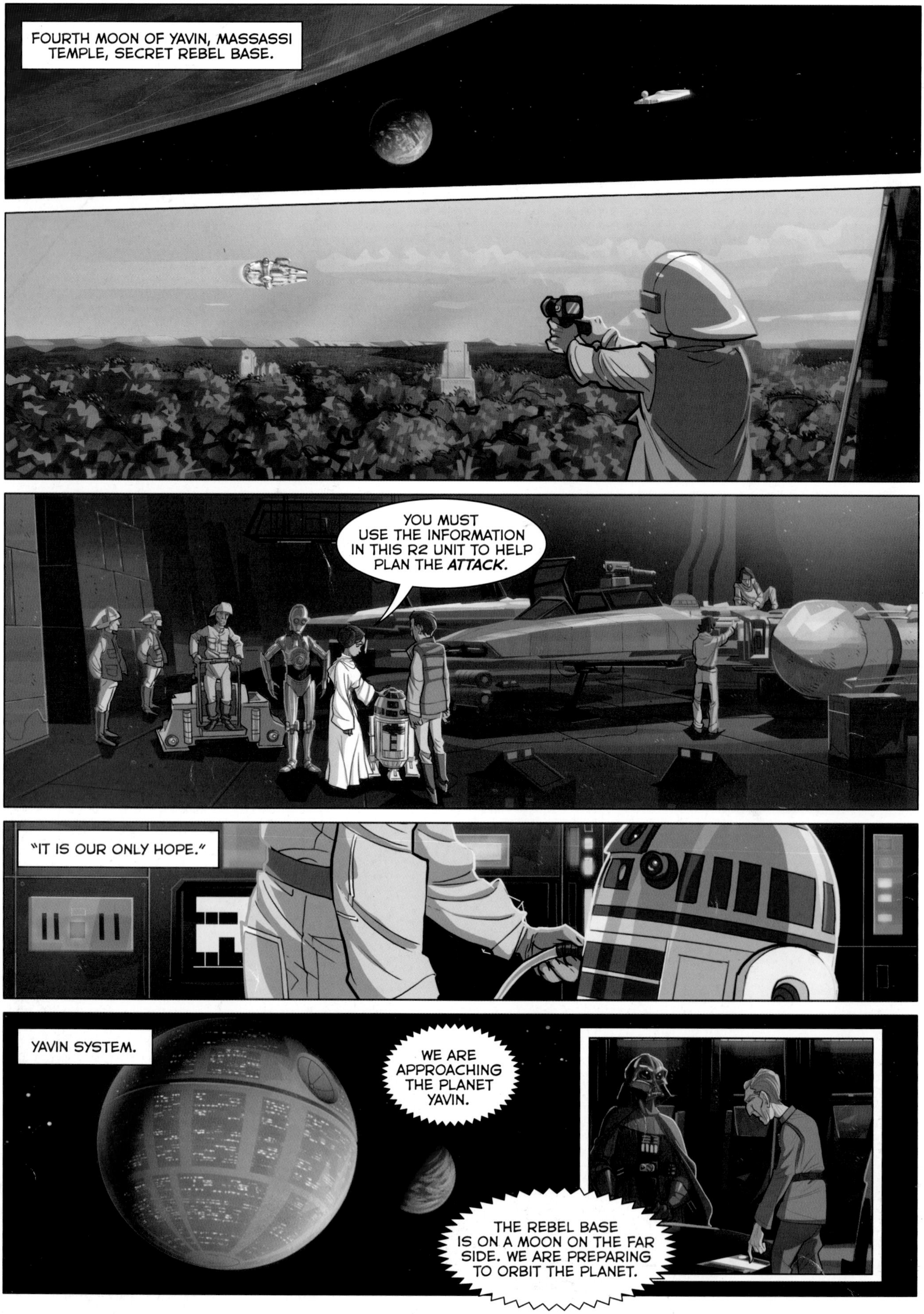
FOURTH MOON OF YAVIN, MASSASSI TEMPLE, SECRET REBEL BASE.
YOU MUST USE THE INFORMATION IN THIS R2 UNIT TO HELP PLAN THE *ATTACK.*
"IT IS OUR ONLY HOPE."
YAVIN SYSTEM.
WE ARE APPROACHING THE PLANET YAVIN.
THE REBEL BASE IS ON A MOON ON THE FAR SIDE. WE ARE PREPARING TO ORBIT THE PLANET.

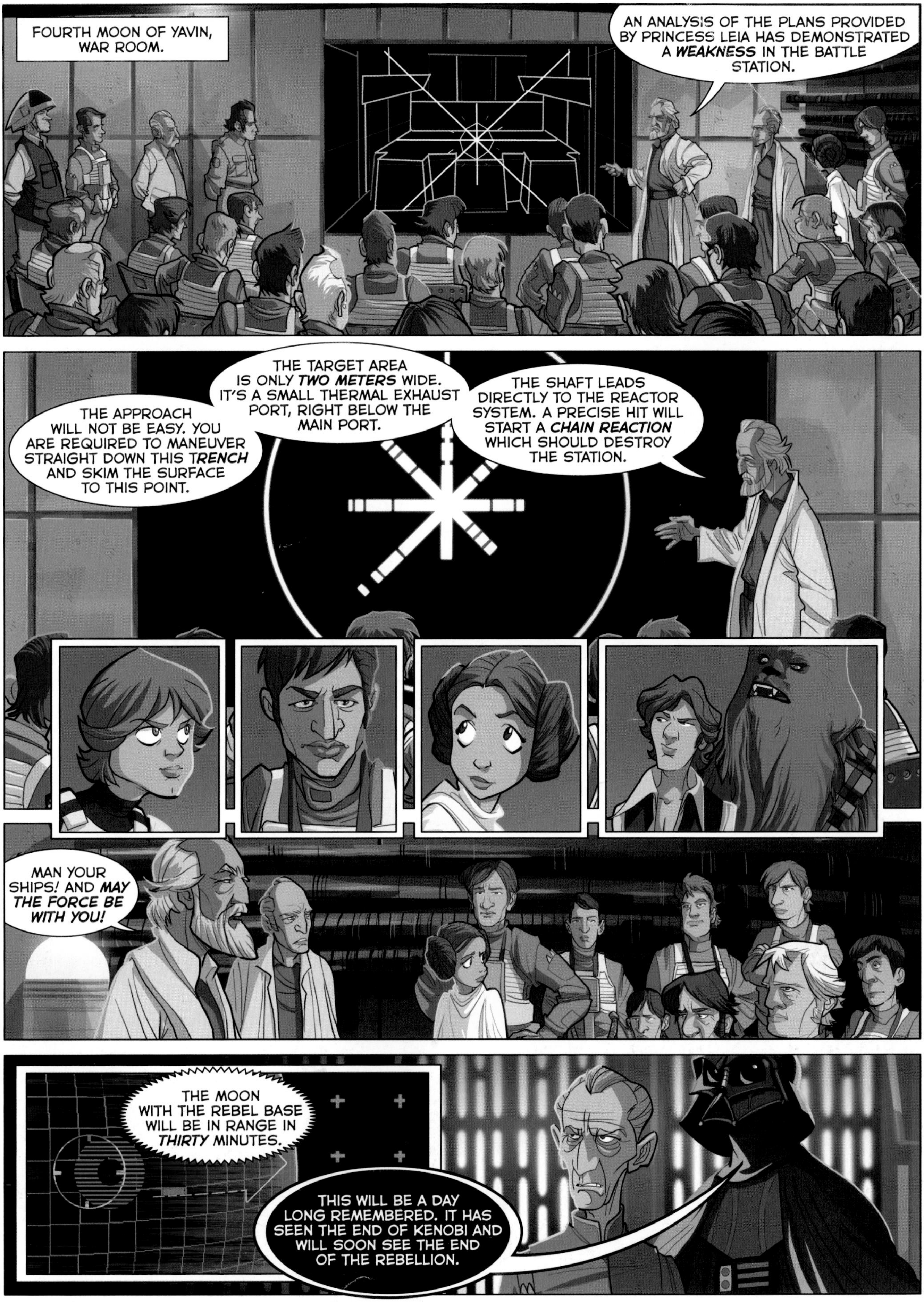
FOURTH MOON OF YAVIN, WAR ROOM.
AN ANALYSIS OF THE PLANS PROVIDED BY PRINCESS LEIA HAS DEMONSTRATED A WEAKNESS IN THE BATTLE STATION.
THE APPROACH WILL NOT BE EASY. YOU ARE REQUIRED TO MANEUVER STRAIGHT DOWN THIS TRENCH AND SKIM THE SURFACE TO THIS POINT.
THE TARGET AREA IS ONLY TWO METERS WIDE. IT'S A SMALL THERMAL EXHAUST PORT, RIGHT BELOW THE MAIN PORT.
THE SHAFT LEADS DIRECTLY TO THE REACTOR SYSTEM. A PRECISE HIT WILL START A CHAIN REACTION WHICH SHOULD DESTROY THE STATION.
MAN YOUR SHIPS! AND MAY THE FORCE BE WITH YOU!
THE MOON WITH THE REBEL BASE WILL BE IN RANGE IN THIRTY MINUTES.
THIS WILL BE A DAY LONG REMEMBERED. IT HAS SEEN THE END OF KENOBI AND WILL SOON SEE THE END OF THE REBELLION.

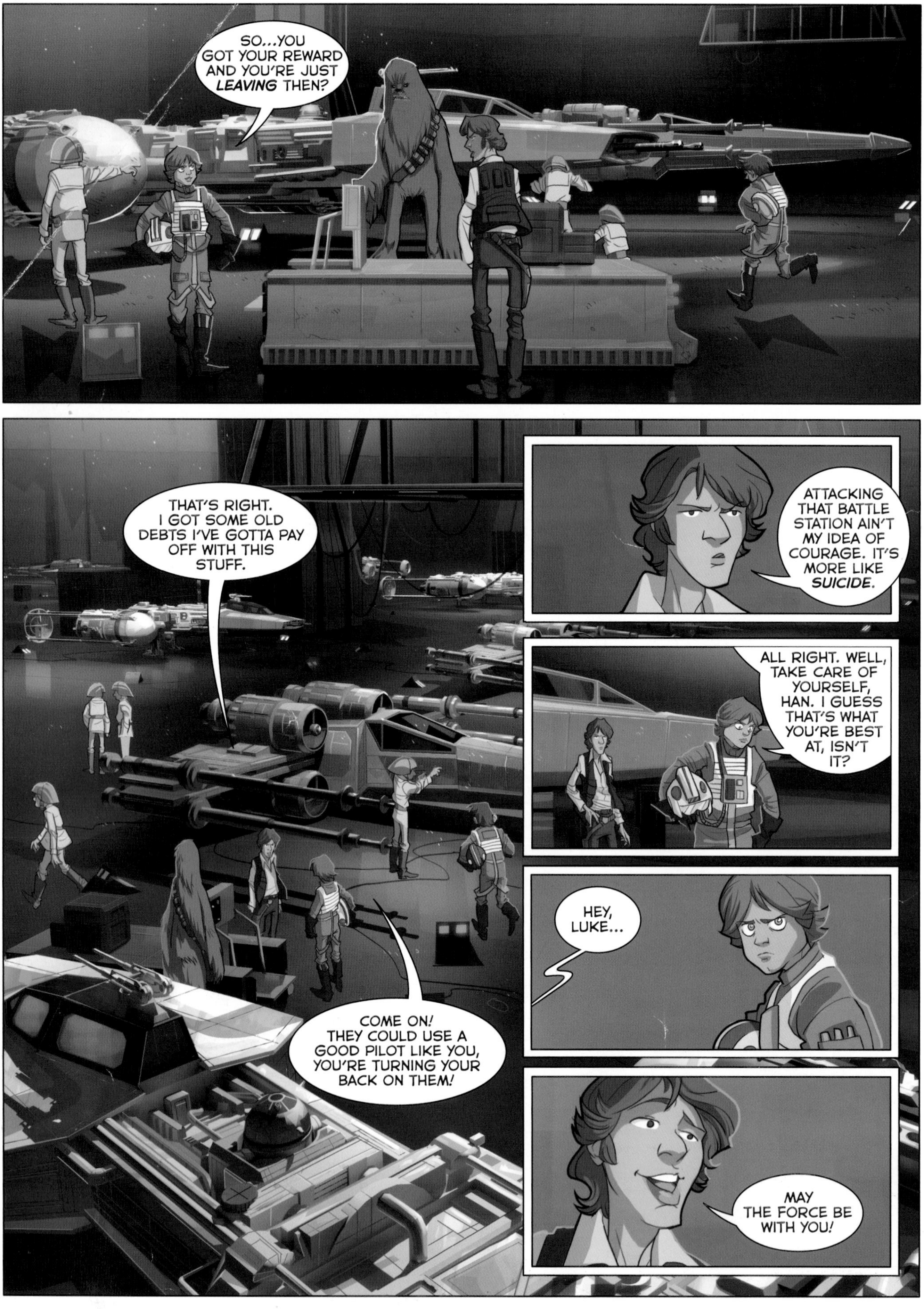

SO...YOU GOT YOUR REWARD AND YOU'RE JUST *LEAVING* THEN?
THAT'S RIGHT. I GOT SOME OLD DEBTS I'VE GOTTA PAY OFF WITH THIS STUFF.
ATTACKING THAT BATTLE STATION AIN'T MY IDEA OF COURAGE. IT'S MORE LIKE *SUICIDE*.
COME ON! THEY COULD USE A GOOD PILOT LIKE YOU, YOU'RE TURNING YOUR BACK ON THEM!
ALL RIGHT. WELL, TAKE CARE OF YOURSELF, HAN. I GUESS THAT'S WHAT YOU'RE BEST AT, ISN'T IT?
HEY, LUKE...
MAY THE FORCE BE WITH YOU!

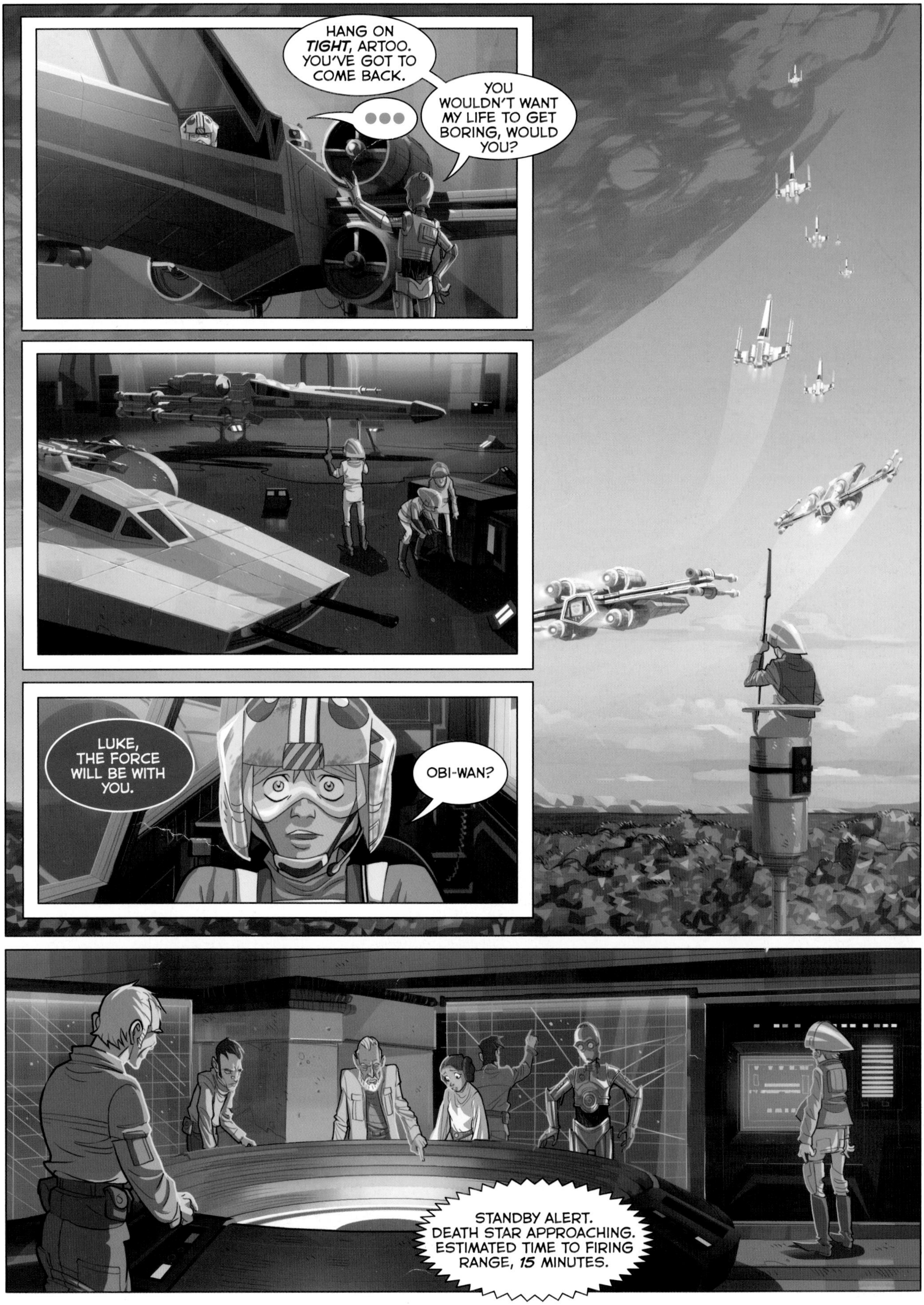
HANG ON *TIGHT*, ARTOO. YOU'VE GOT TO COME BACK.
YOU WOULDN'T WANT MY LIFE TO GET BORING, WOULD YOU?
●●●
LUKE, THE FORCE WILL BE WITH YOU.
OBI-WAN?
STANDBY ALERT. DEATH STAR APPROACHING. ESTIMATED TIME TO FIRING RANGE, *15* MINUTES.

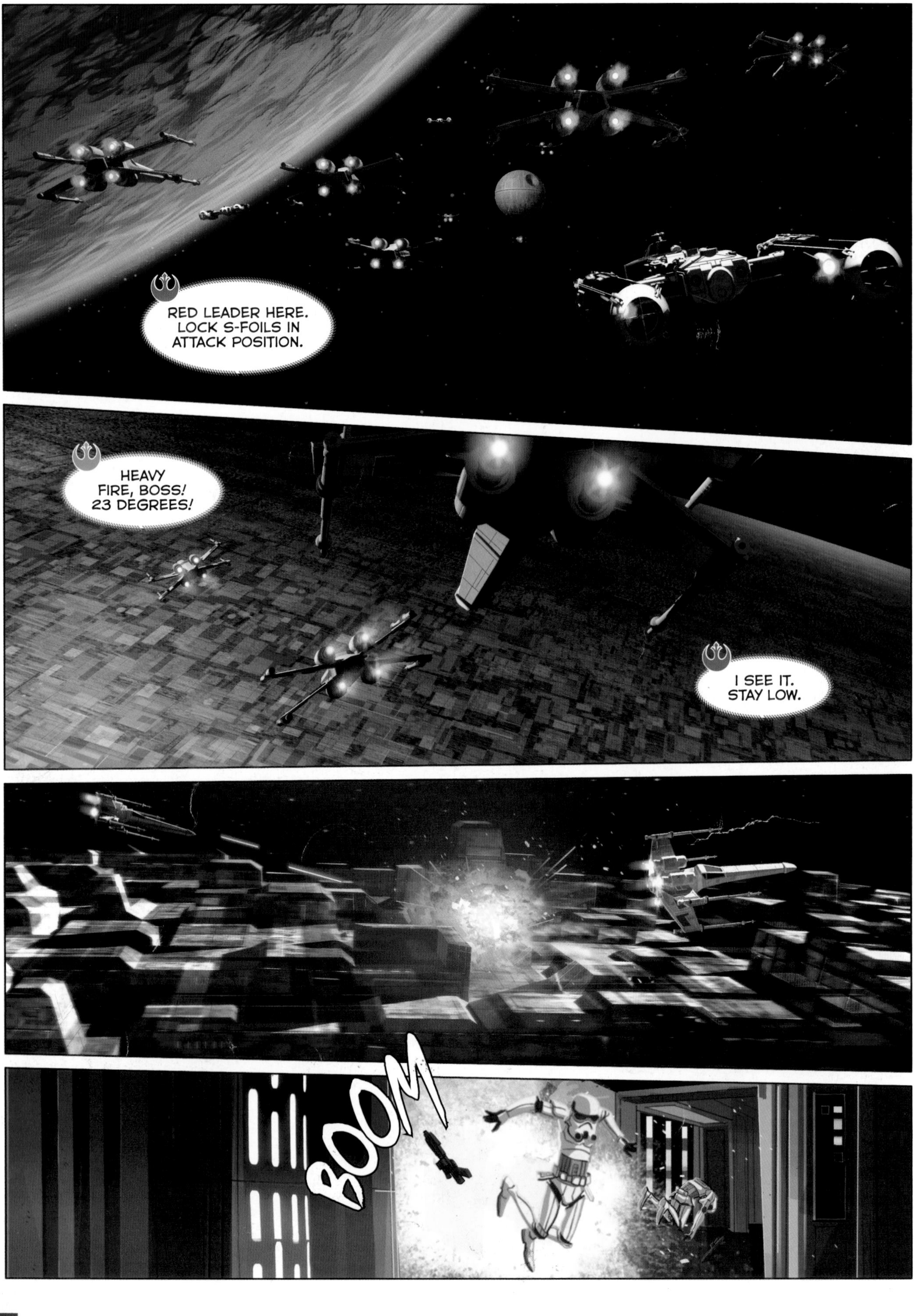
RED LEADER HERE. LOCK S-FOILS IN ATTACK POSITION.
HEAVY FIRE, BOSS! 23 DEGREES!
I SEE IT. STAY LOW.
BOOM

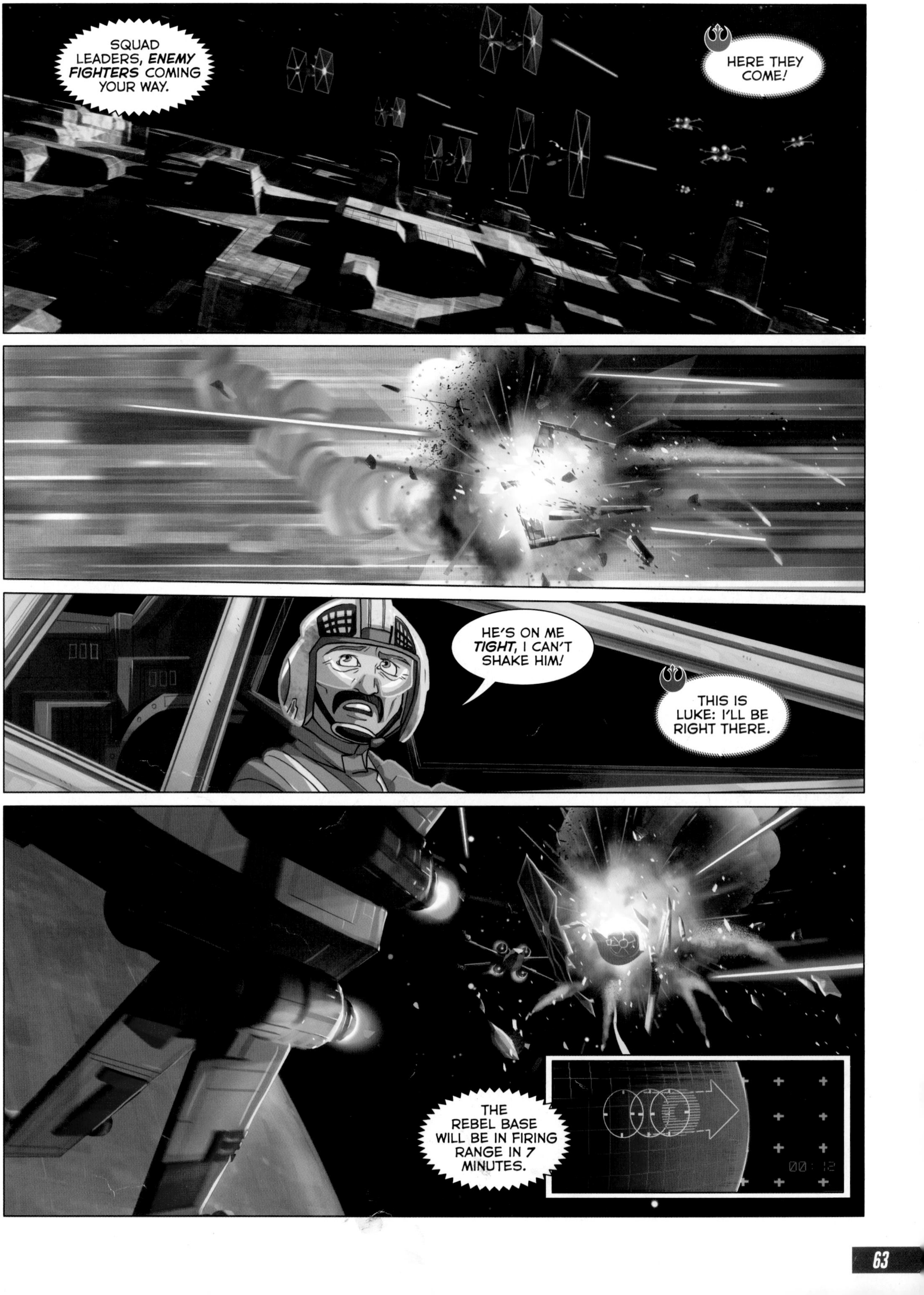
SQUAD LEADERS, ENEMY FIGHTERS COMING YOUR WAY.
HERE THEY COME!
HE'S ON ME TIGHT, I CAN'T SHAKE HIM!
THIS IS LUKE: I'LL BE RIGHT THERE.
THE REBEL BASE WILL BE IN FIRING RANGE IN 7 MINUTES.

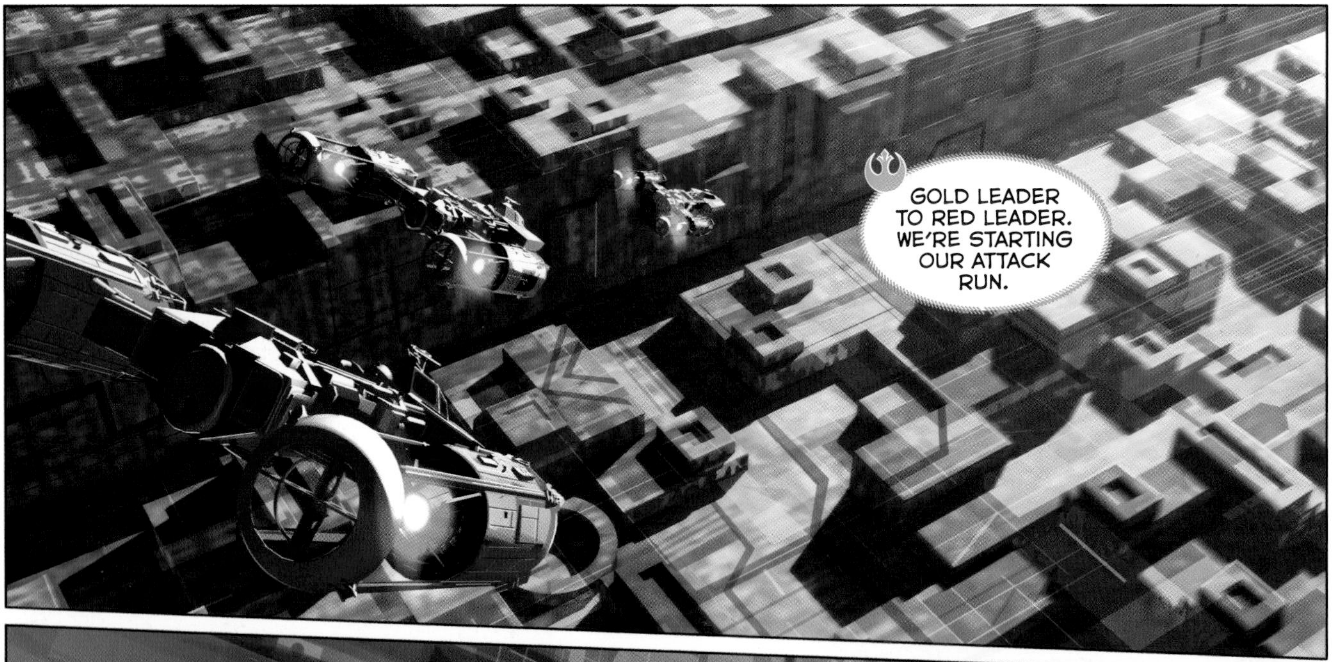
GOLD LEADER TO RED LEADER. WE'RE STARTING OUR ATTACK RUN.
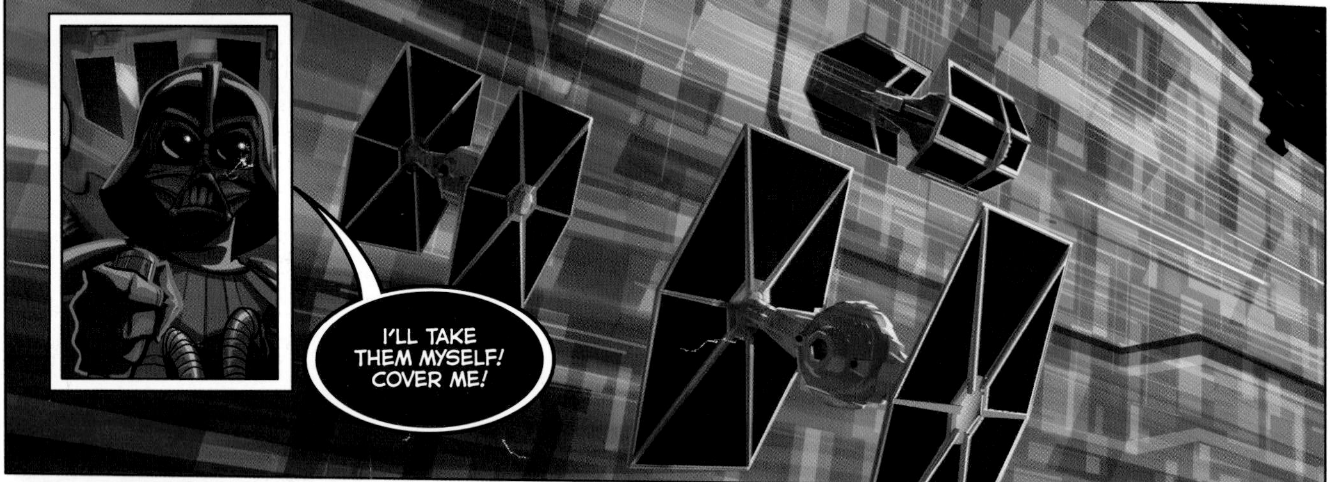
I'LL TAKE THEM MYSELF! COVER ME!
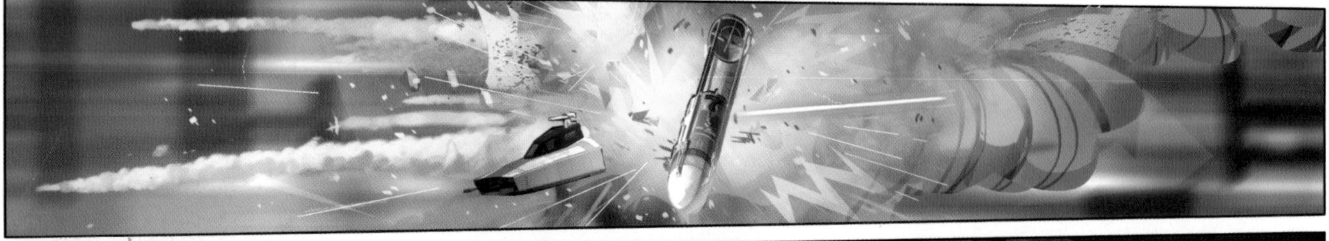
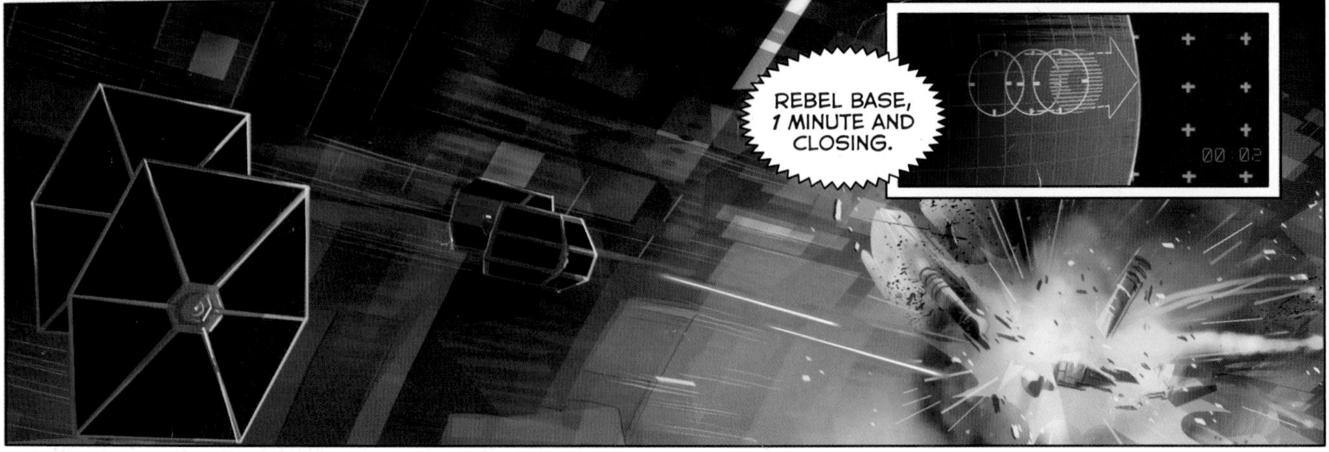
REBEL BASE, 1 MINUTE AND CLOSING.

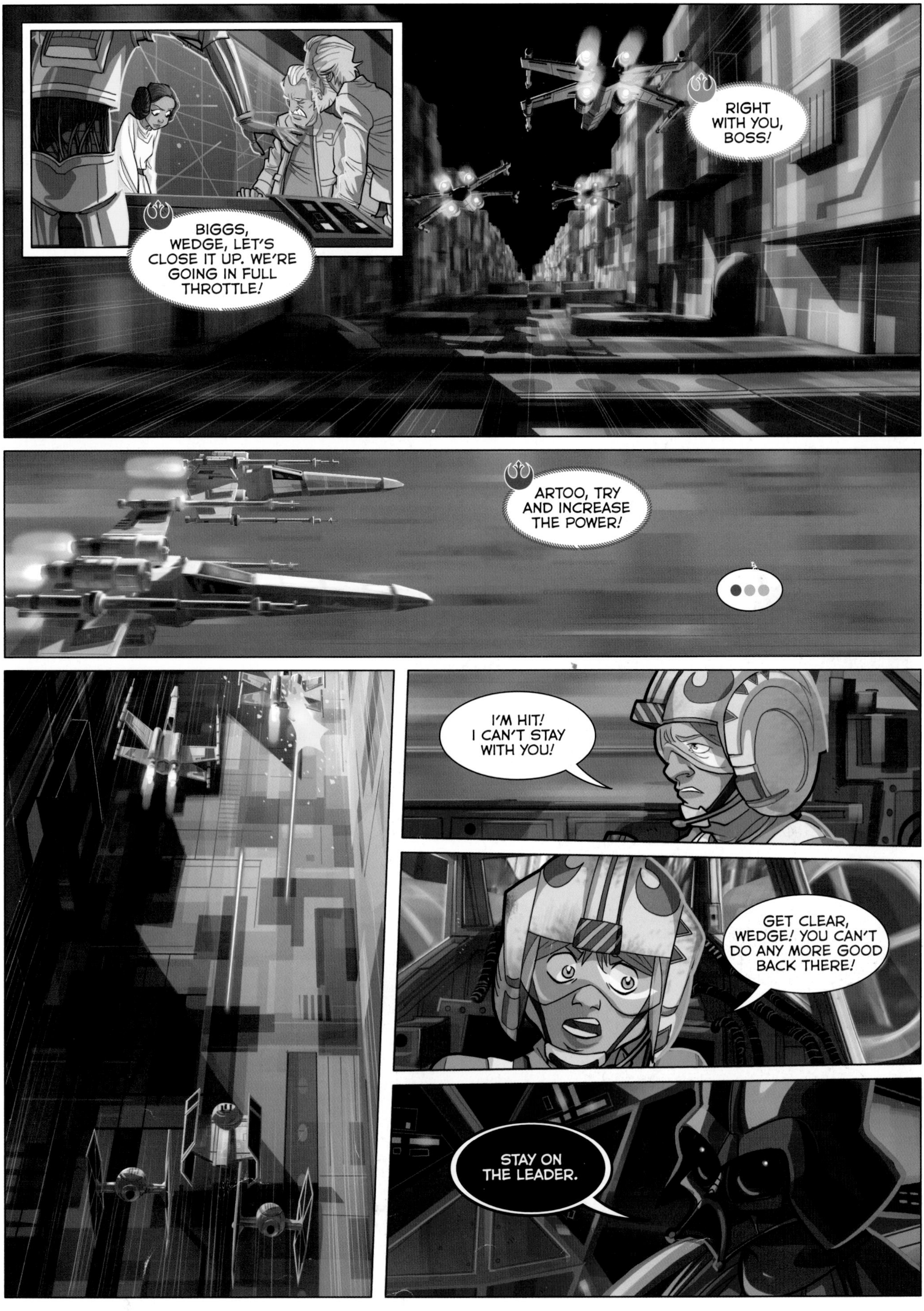
BIGGS, WEDGE, LET'S CLOSE IT UP. WE'RE GOING IN FULL THROTTLE!
RIGHT WITH YOU, BOSS!
ARTOO, TRY AND INCREASE THE POWER!
I'M HIT! I CAN'T STAY WITH YOU!
GET CLEAR, WEDGE! YOU CAN'T DO ANY MORE GOOD BACK THERE!
STAY ON THE LEADER.

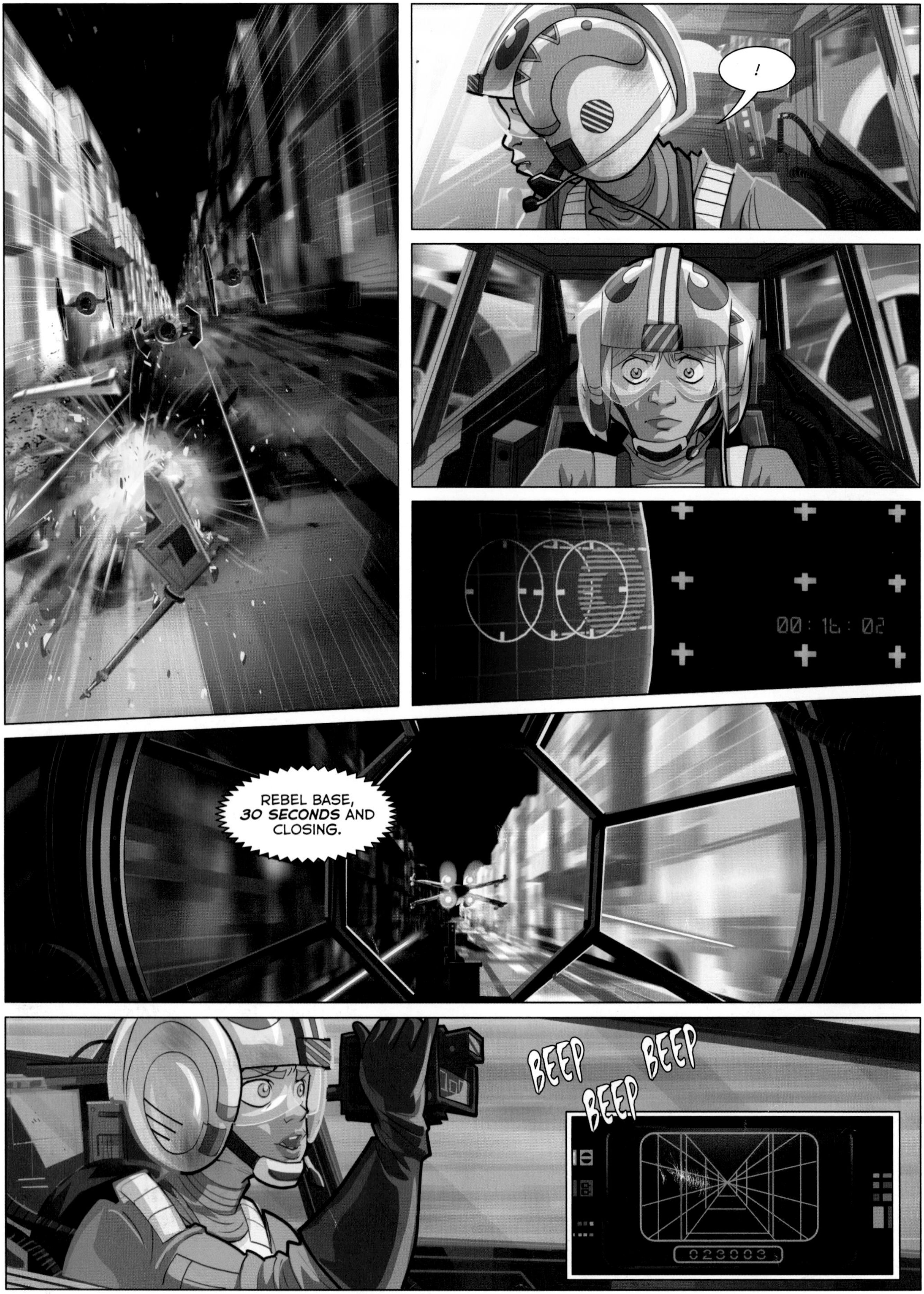
!
00 : 16 : 02
REBEL BASE, 30 SECONDS AND CLOSING.
BEEP BEEP BEEP
023003

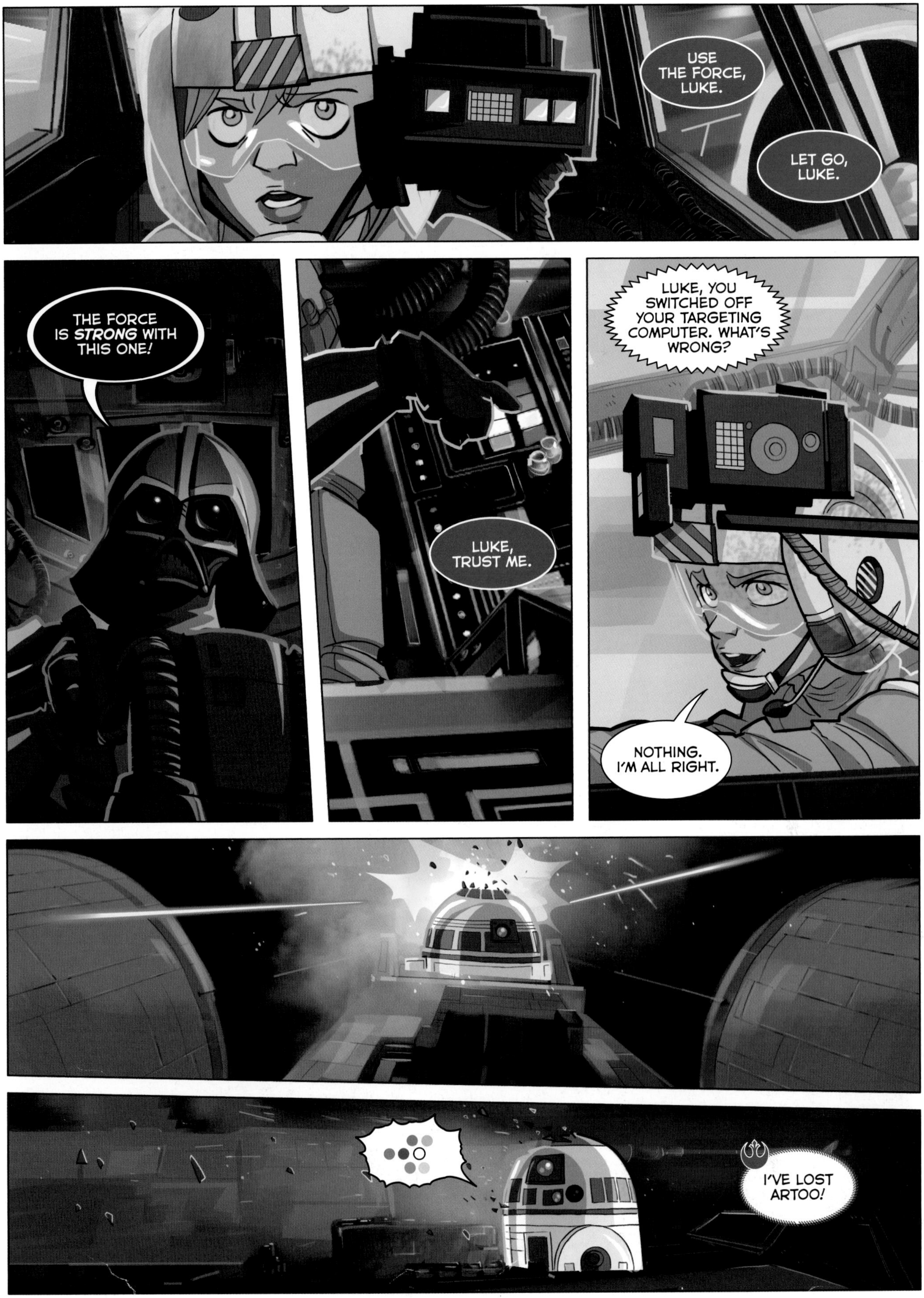
USE THE FORCE, LUKE.
LET GO, LUKE.
THE FORCE IS *STRONG* WITH THIS ONE!
LUKE, TRUST ME.
LUKE, YOU SWITCHED OFF YOUR TARGETING COMPUTER. WHAT'S WRONG?
NOTHING. I'M ALL RIGHT.
I'VE LOST ARTOO!

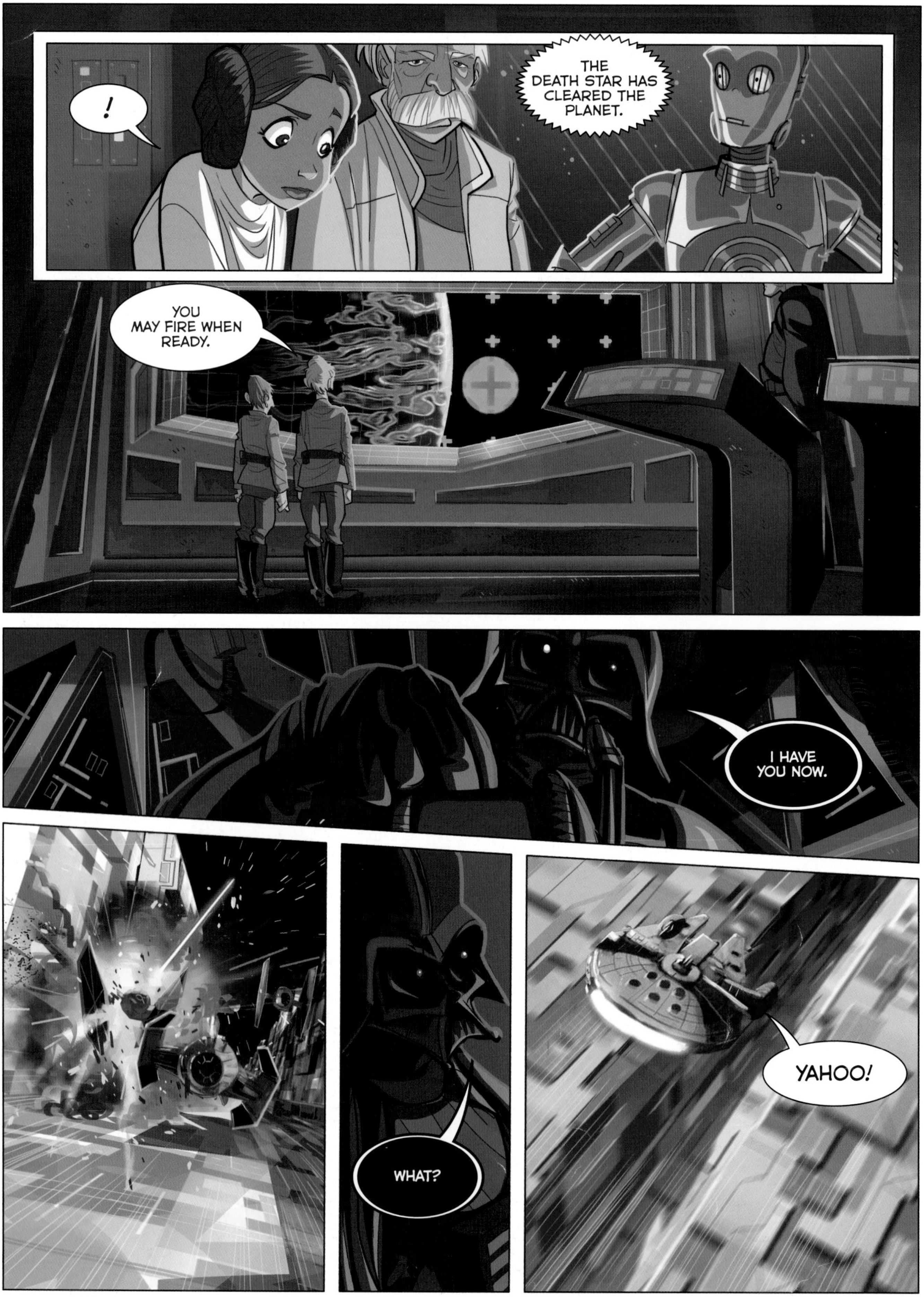
!
THE DEATH STAR HAS CLEARED THE PLANET.
YOU MAY FIRE WHEN READY.
I HAVE YOU NOW.
WHAT?
YAHOO!

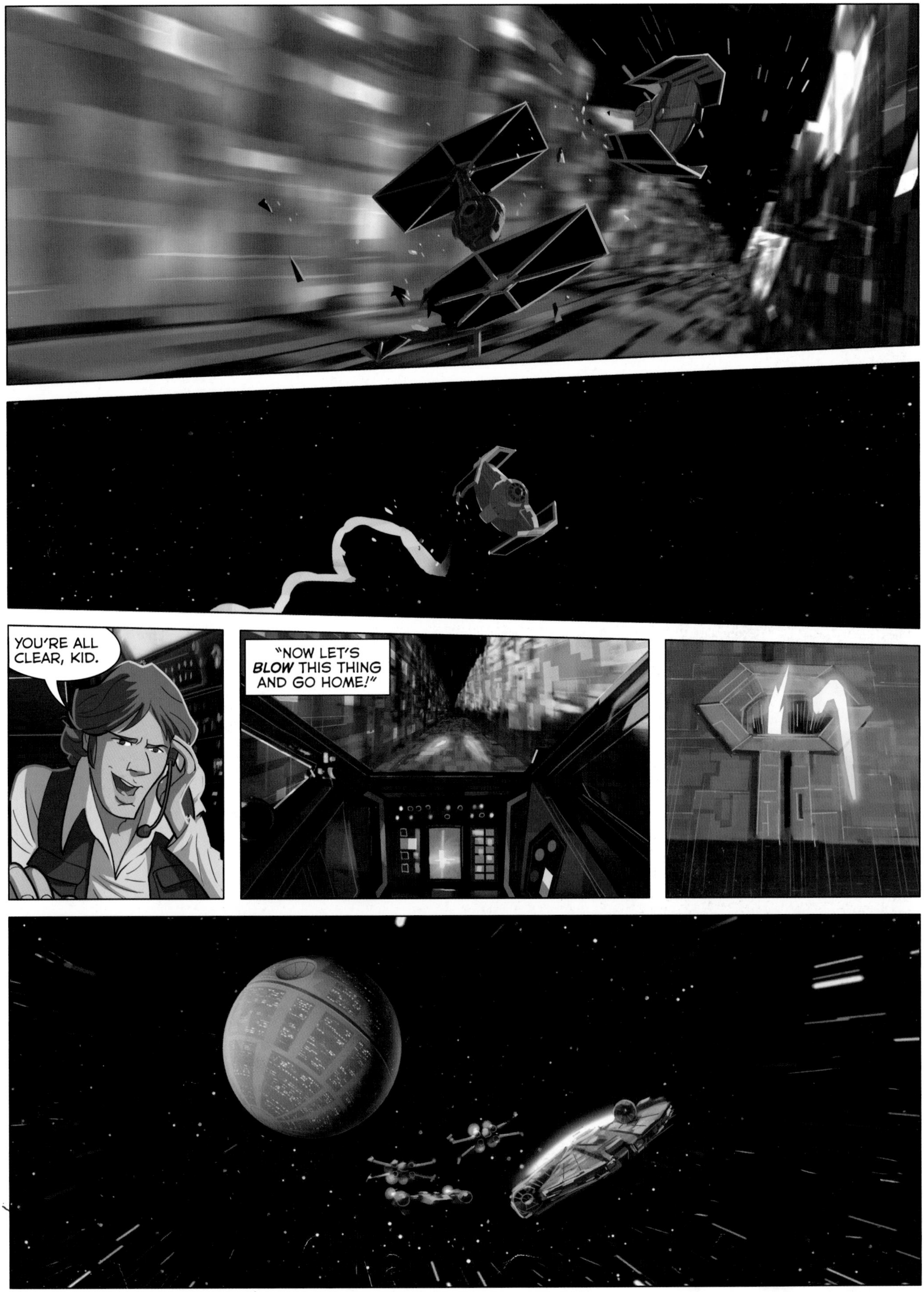
YOU'RE ALL CLEAR, KID.
"NOW LET'S *BLOW* THIS THING AND GO HOME!"

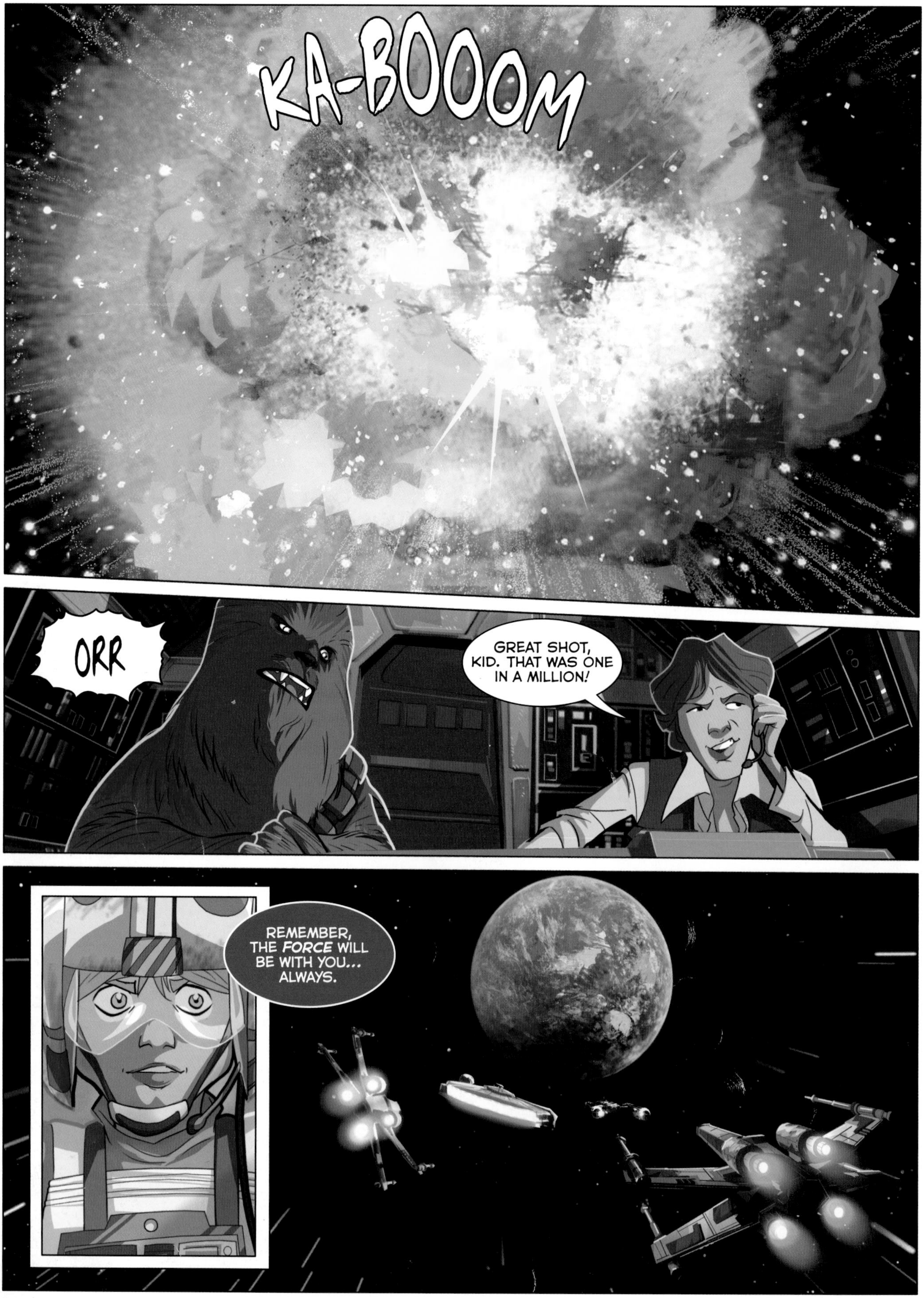
KA-BOOOM
ORR
GREAT SHOT, KID. THAT WAS ONE IN A MILLION!
REMEMBER, THE FORCE WILL BE WITH YOU... ALWAYS.

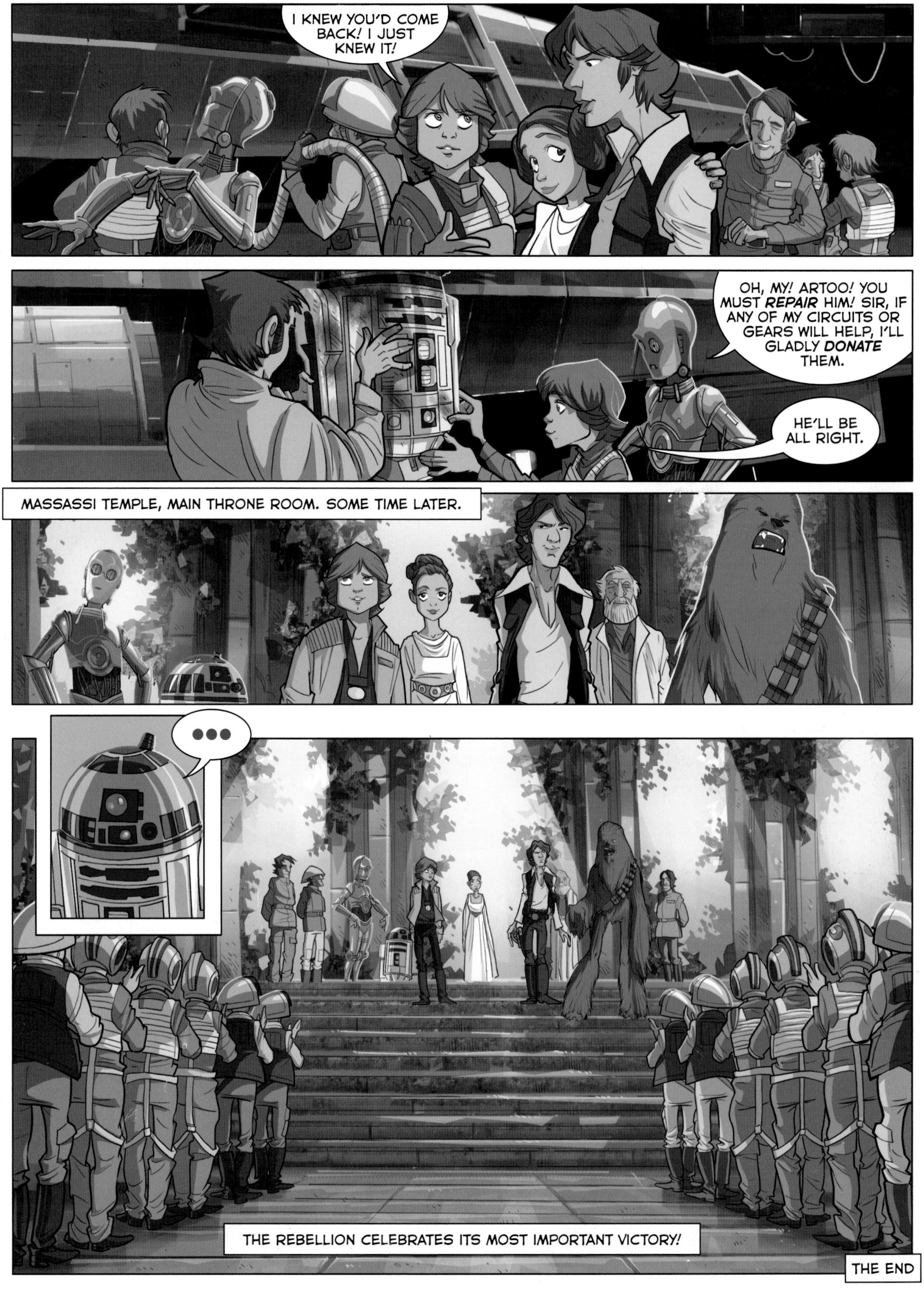
I KNEW YOU'D COME BACK! I JUST KNEW IT!
OH, MY! ARTOO! YOU MUST **REPAIR** HIM! SIR, IF ANY OF MY CIRCUITS OR GEARS WILL HELP, I'LL GLADLY **DONATE** THEM.
HE'LL BE ALL RIGHT.
MASSASSI TEMPLE, MAIN THRONE ROOM. SOME TIME LATER.
•••
THE REBELLION CELEBRATES ITS MOST IMPORTANT VICTORY!
THE END

STAR WARS®

THE EMPIRE STRIKES BACK

*A LONG TIME AGO
IN A GALAXY FAR, FAR AWAY....*

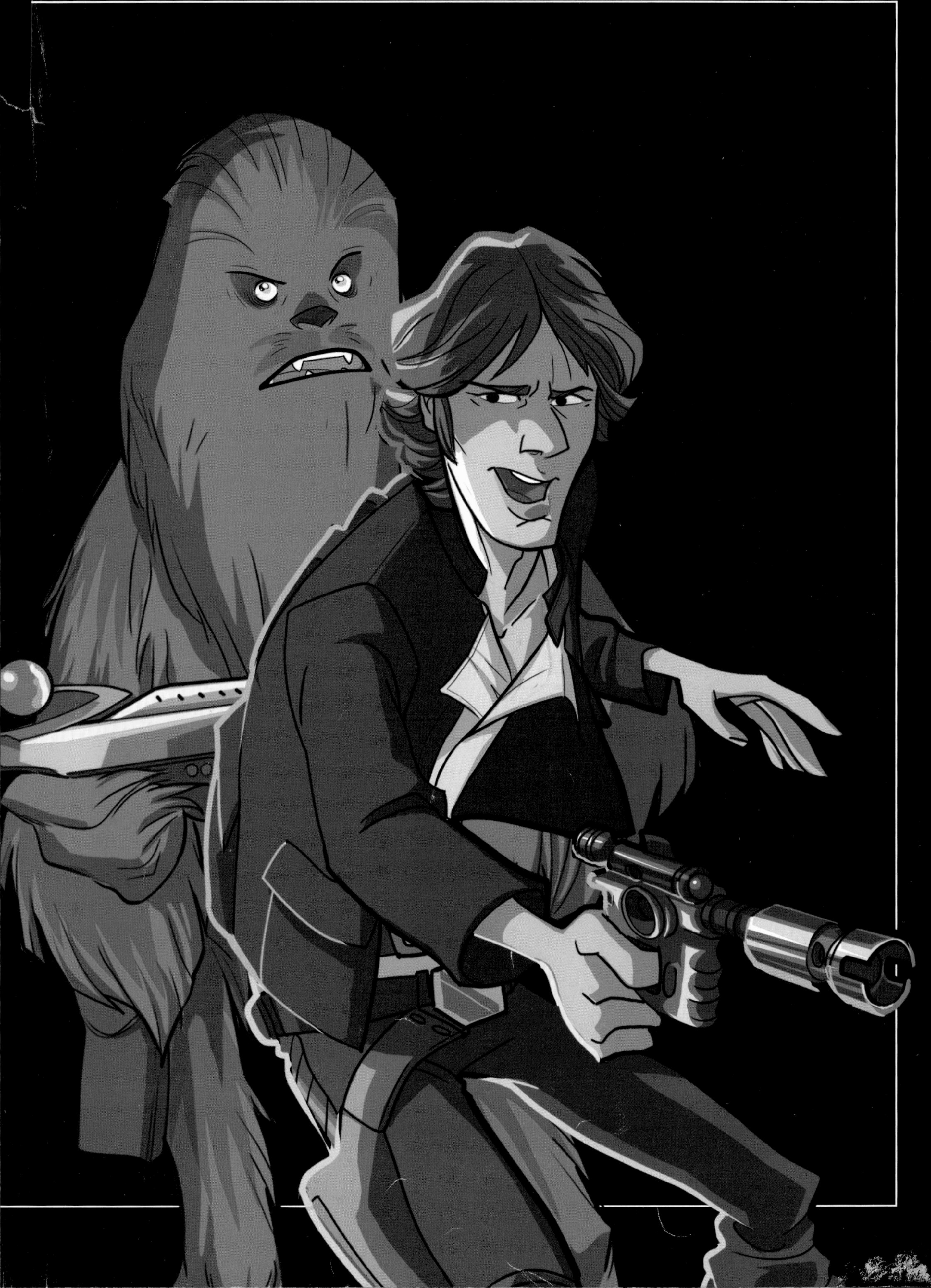

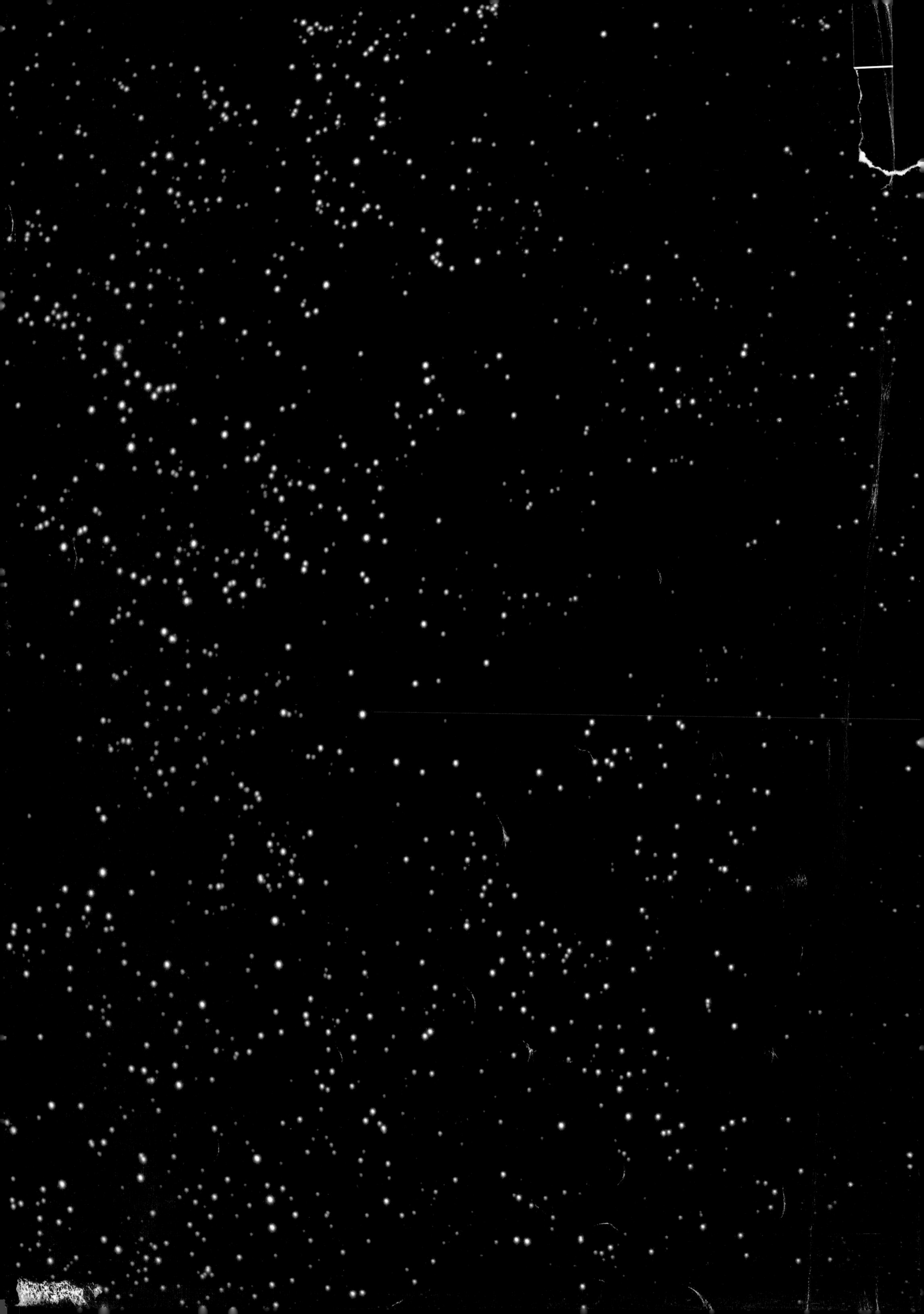

Episode V
THE EMPIRE STRIKES BACK

It is a dark time for the Rebellion. Although the Death Star has been destroyed, Imperial troops have driven the Rebel forces from their hidden base and pursued them across the galaxy.

Evading the dreaded Imperial Starfleet, a group of freedom fighters led by Luke Skywalker has established a new secret base on the remote ice world of Hoth.

The evil lord Darth Vader, obsessed with finding young Skywalker, has dispatched thousands of remote probes into the far reaches of space. . . .

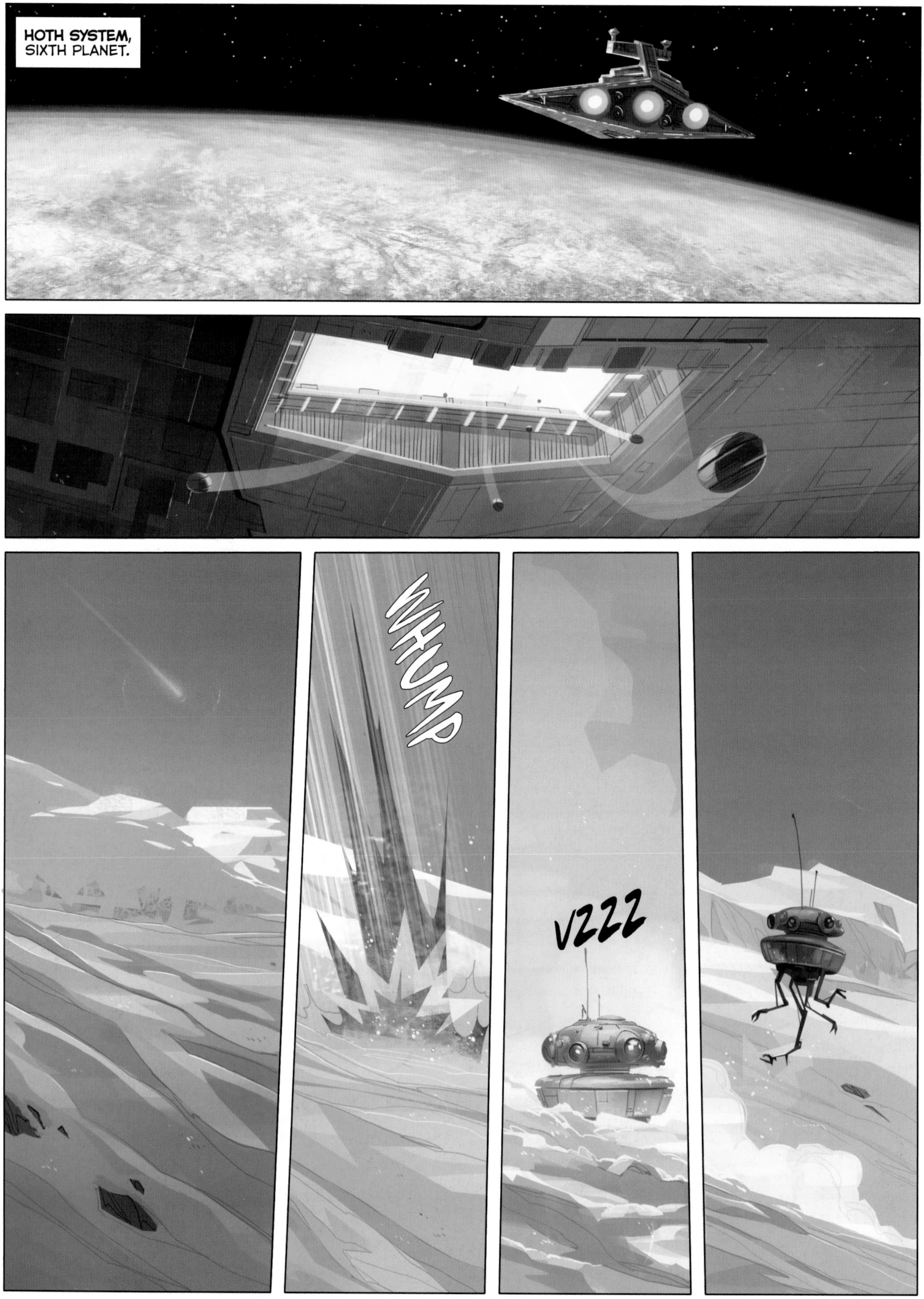
HOTH SYSTEM,
SIXTH PLANET.
WHUMP
VZZZ

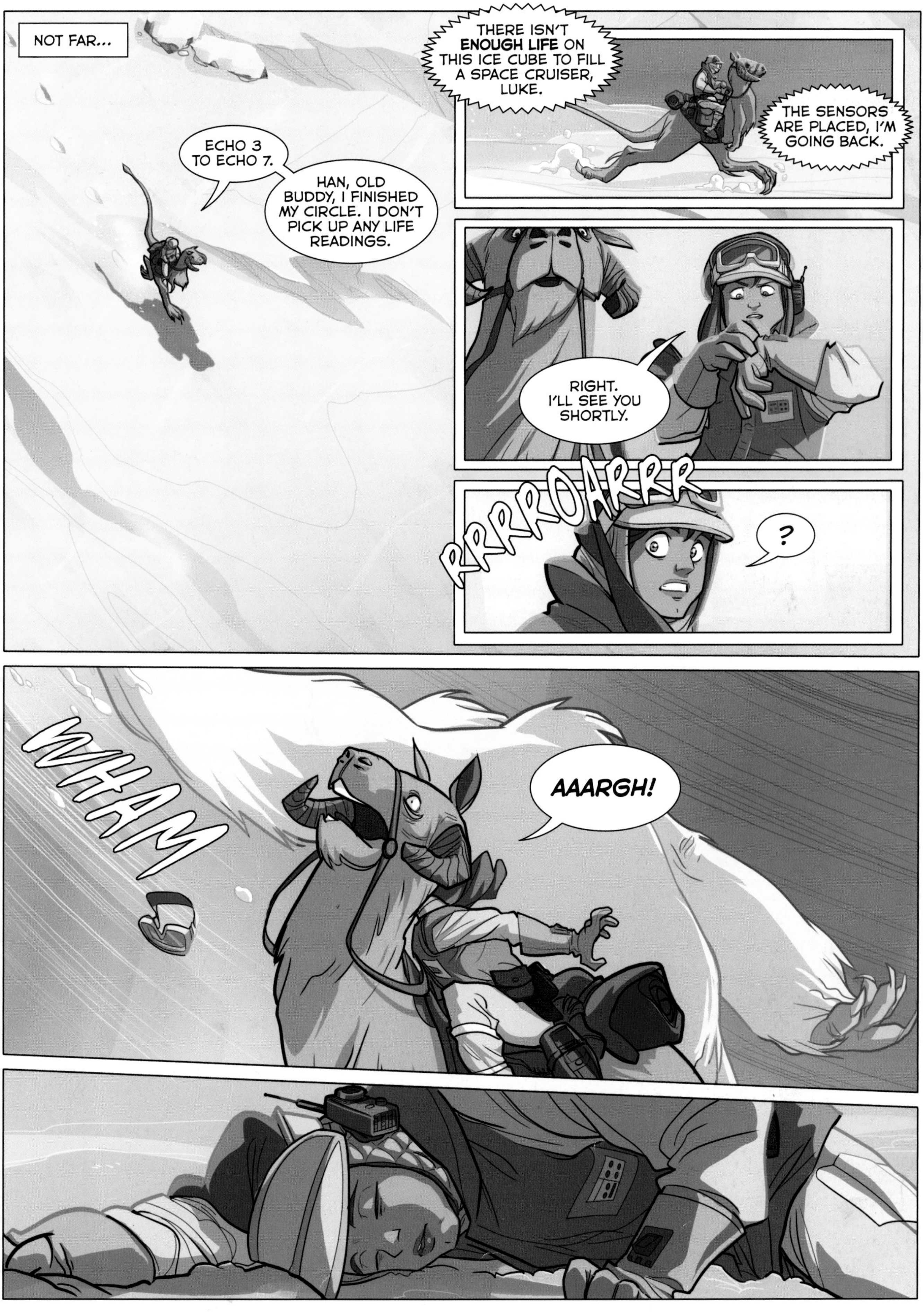
NOT FAR...
ECHO 3 TO ECHO 7.
HAN, OLD BUDDY, I FINISHED MY CIRCLE. I DON'T PICK UP ANY LIFE READINGS.
THERE ISN'T **ENOUGH LIFE** ON THIS ICE CUBE TO FILL A SPACE CRUISER, LUKE.
THE SENSORS ARE PLACED, I'M GOING BACK.
RIGHT. I'LL SEE YOU SHORTLY.
RRRROARRR
?
WHAM
AAARGH!

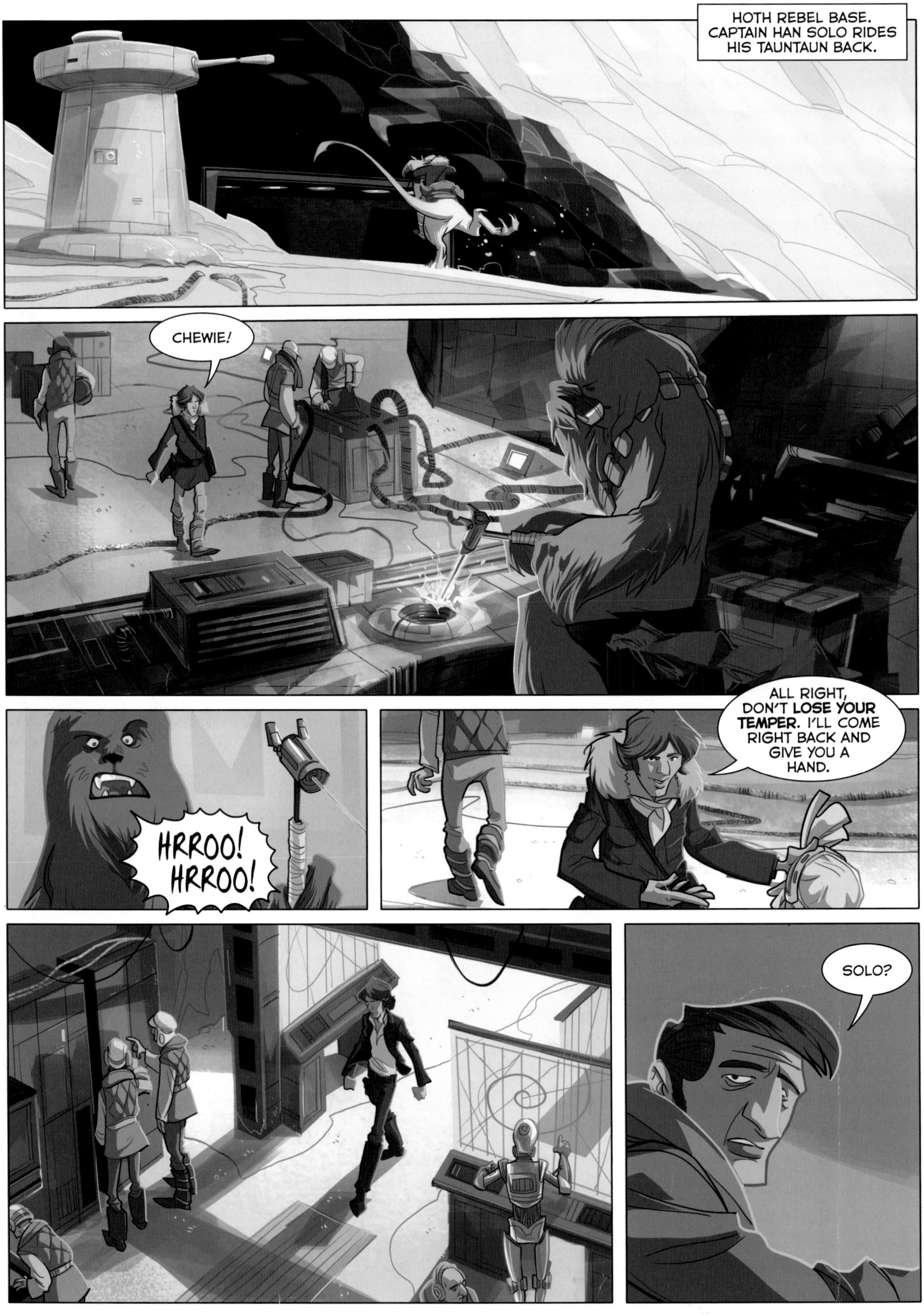
HOTH REBEL BASE. CAPTAIN HAN SOLO RIDES HIS TAUNTAUN BACK.
CHEWIE!
HRROO! HRROO!
ALL RIGHT, DON'T **LOSE YOUR TEMPER.** I'LL COME RIGHT BACK AND GIVE YOU A HAND.
SOLO?

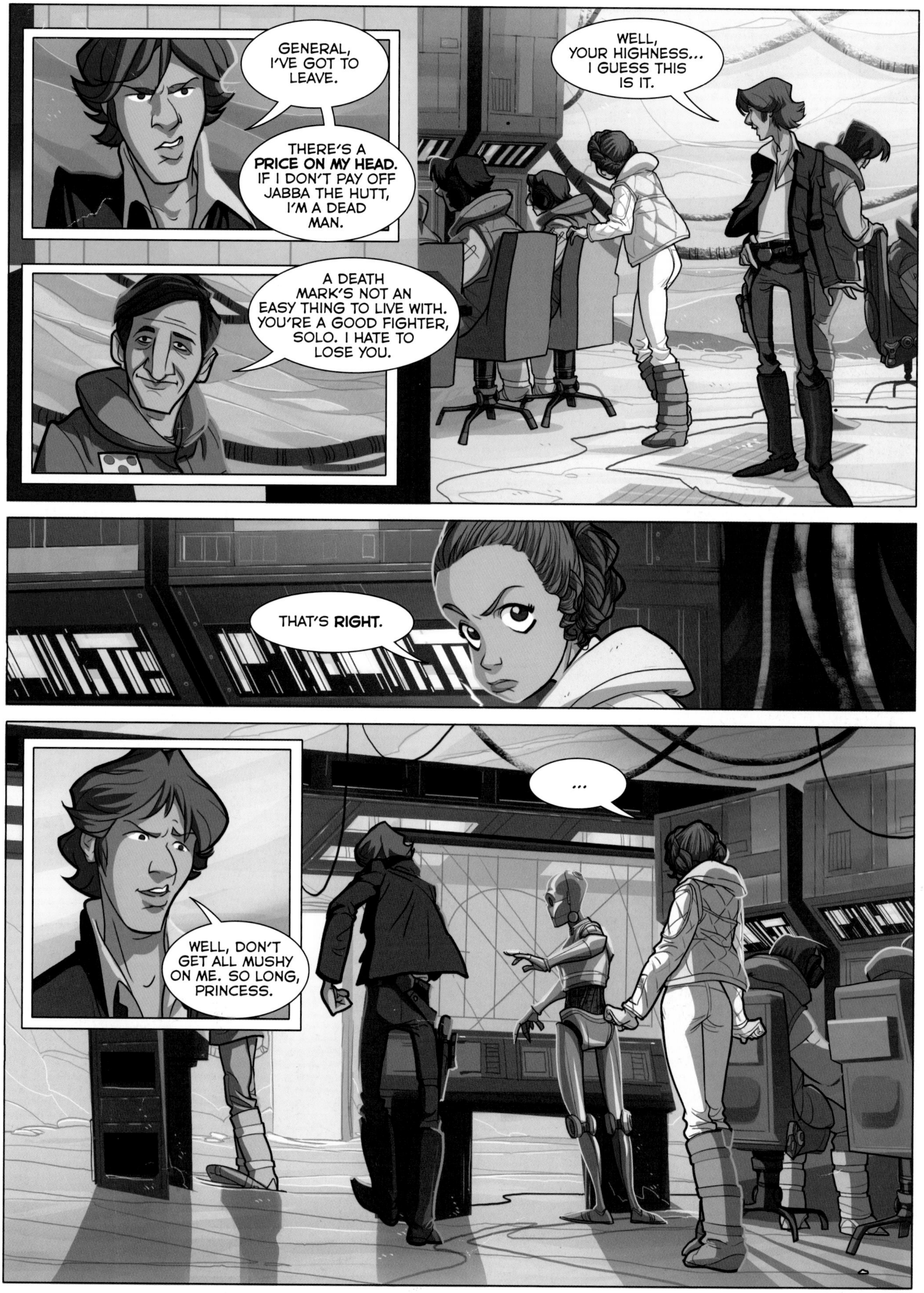
GENERAL, I'VE GOT TO LEAVE.
THERE'S A **PRICE ON MY HEAD.** IF I DON'T PAY OFF JABBA THE HUTT, I'M A DEAD MAN.
A DEATH MARK'S NOT AN EASY THING TO LIVE WITH. YOU'RE A GOOD FIGHTER, SOLO. I HATE TO LOSE YOU.
WELL, YOUR HIGHNESS... I GUESS THIS IS IT.
THAT'S **RIGHT.**
WELL, DON'T GET ALL MUSHY ON ME. SO LONG, PRINCESS.
...

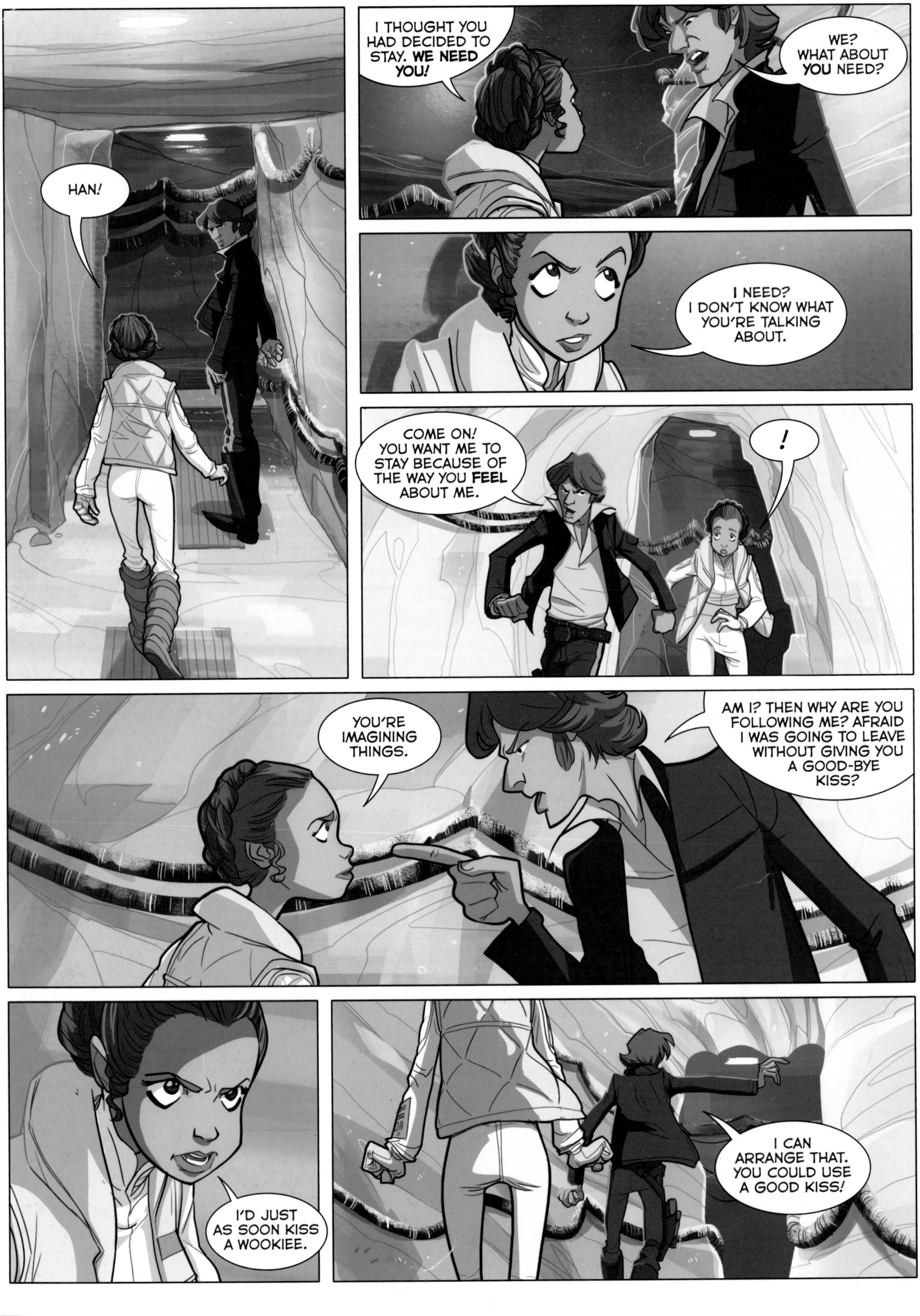
HAN!
I THOUGHT YOU HAD DECIDED TO STAY. WE NEED YOU!
WE? WHAT ABOUT YOU NEED?
I NEED? I DON'T KNOW WHAT YOU'RE TALKING ABOUT.
COME ON! YOU WANT ME TO STAY BECAUSE OF THE WAY YOU FEEL ABOUT ME.
!
YOU'RE IMAGINING THINGS.
AM I? THEN WHY ARE YOU FOLLOWING ME? AFRAID I WAS GOING TO LEAVE WITHOUT GIVING YOU A GOOD-BYE KISS?
I'D JUST AS SOON KISS A WOOKIEE.
I CAN ARRANGE THAT. YOU COULD USE A GOOD KISS!

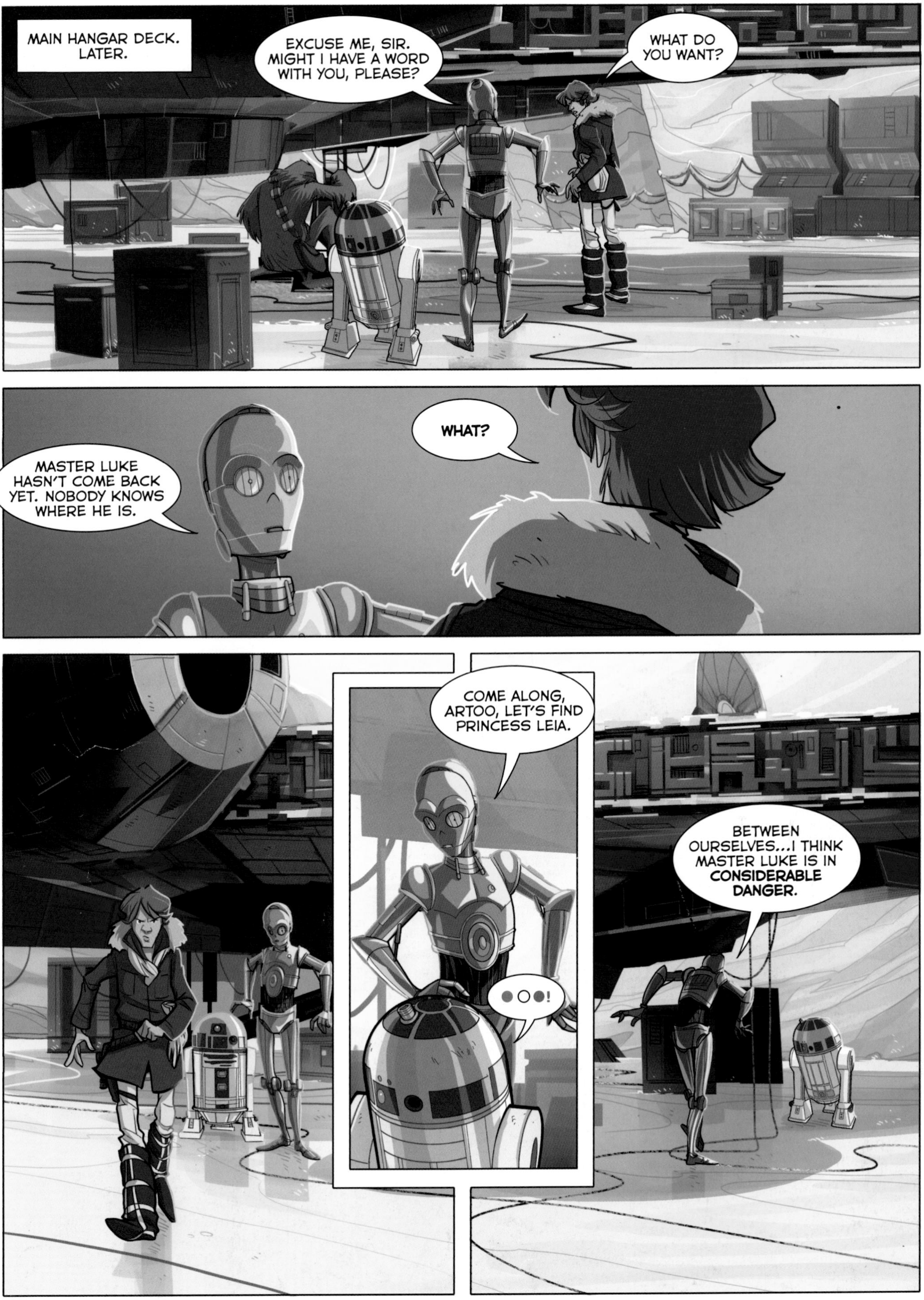
MAIN HANGAR DECK. LATER.
EXCUSE ME, SIR. MIGHT I HAVE A WORD WITH YOU, PLEASE?
WHAT DO YOU WANT?
MASTER LUKE HASN'T COME BACK YET. NOBODY KNOWS WHERE HE IS.
WHAT?
COME ALONG, ARTOO, LET'S FIND PRINCESS LEIA.
●○●!
BETWEEN OURSELVES...I THINK MASTER LUKE IS IN **CONSIDERABLE DANGER.**

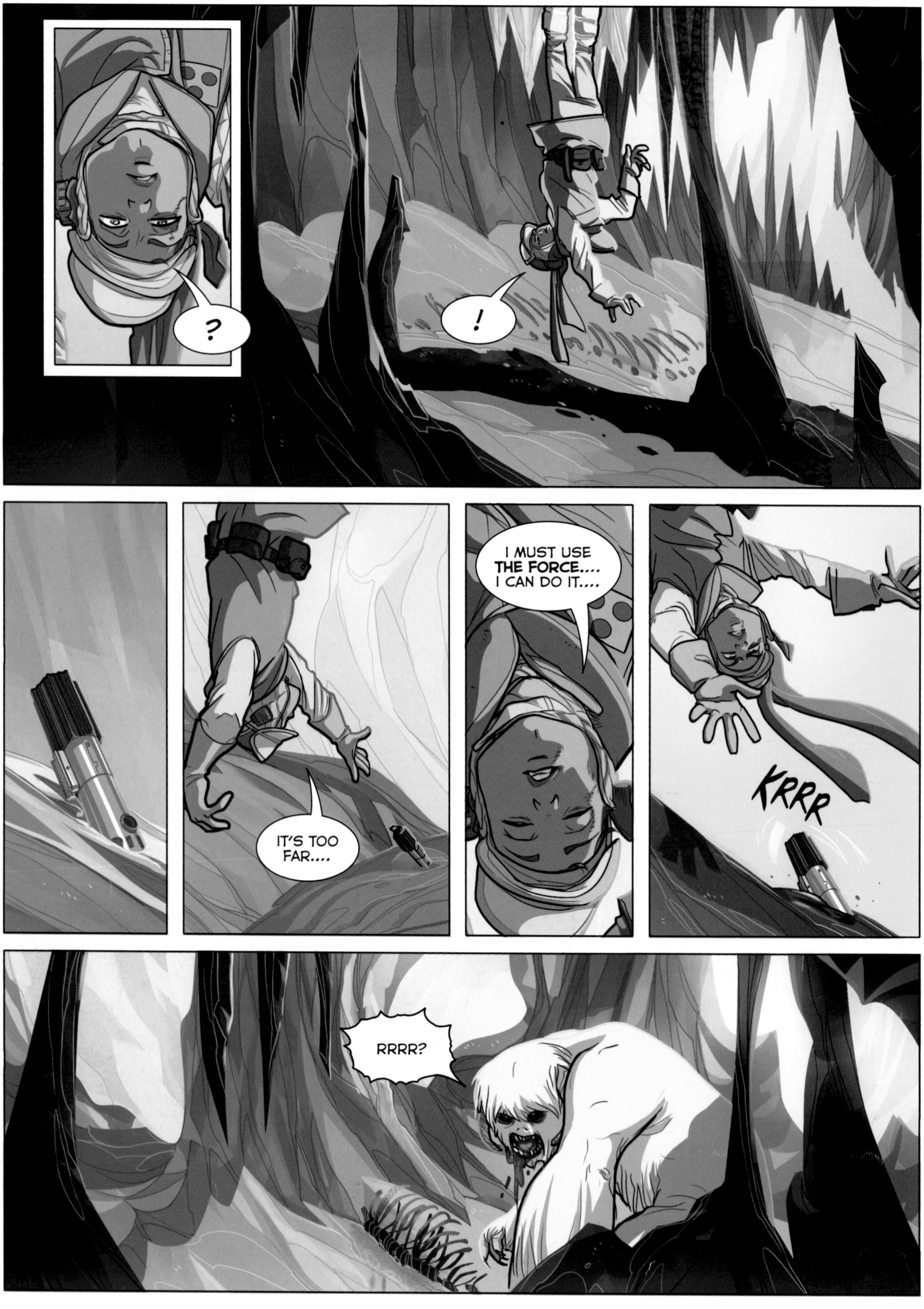
?
!
IT'S TOO FAR....
I MUST USE THE FORCE.... I CAN DO IT....
KRRR
RRRR?

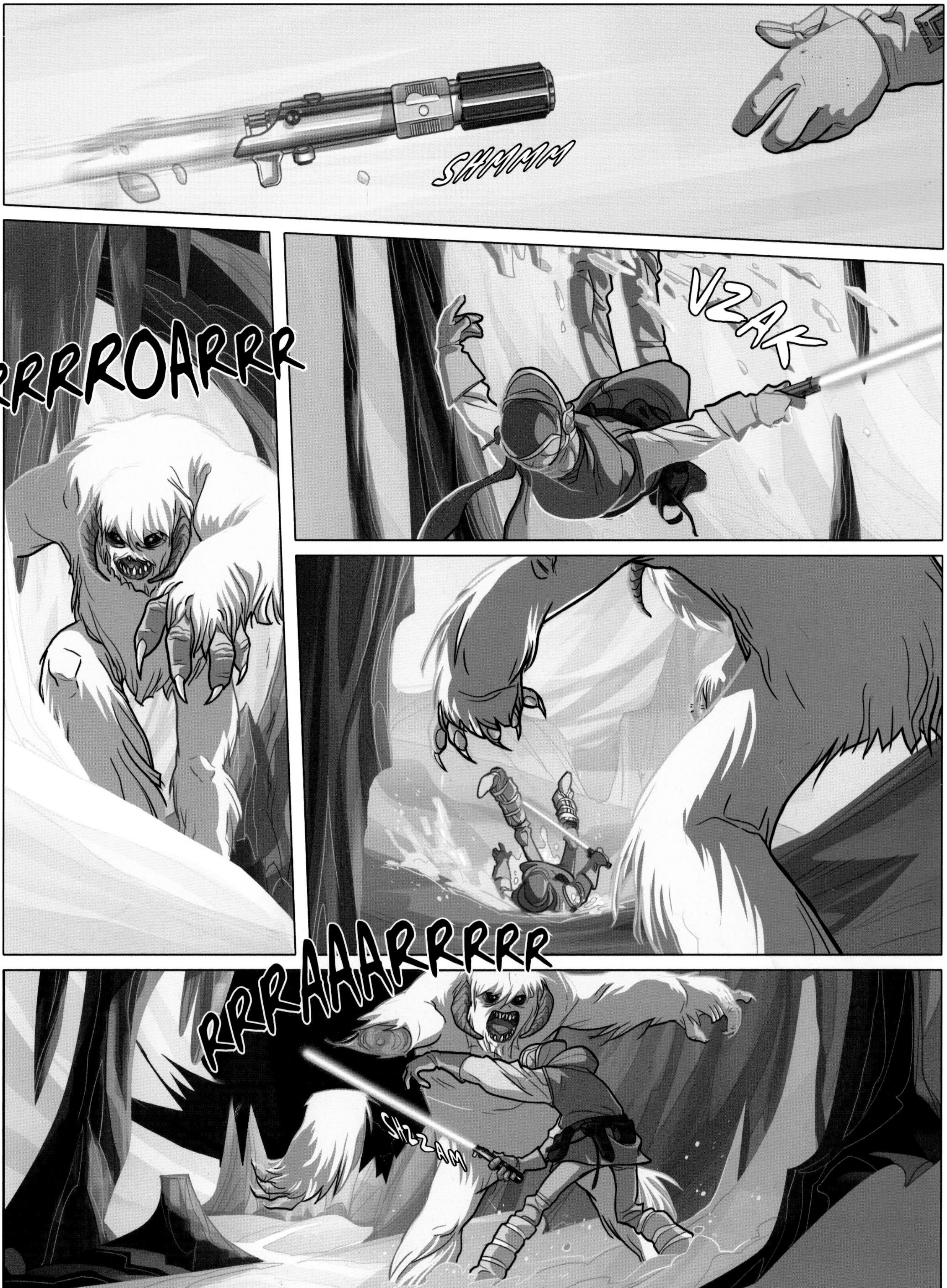
SHHMMM
RRRROARRR
VZAK
RRRAAARRRRR
SHZZAM

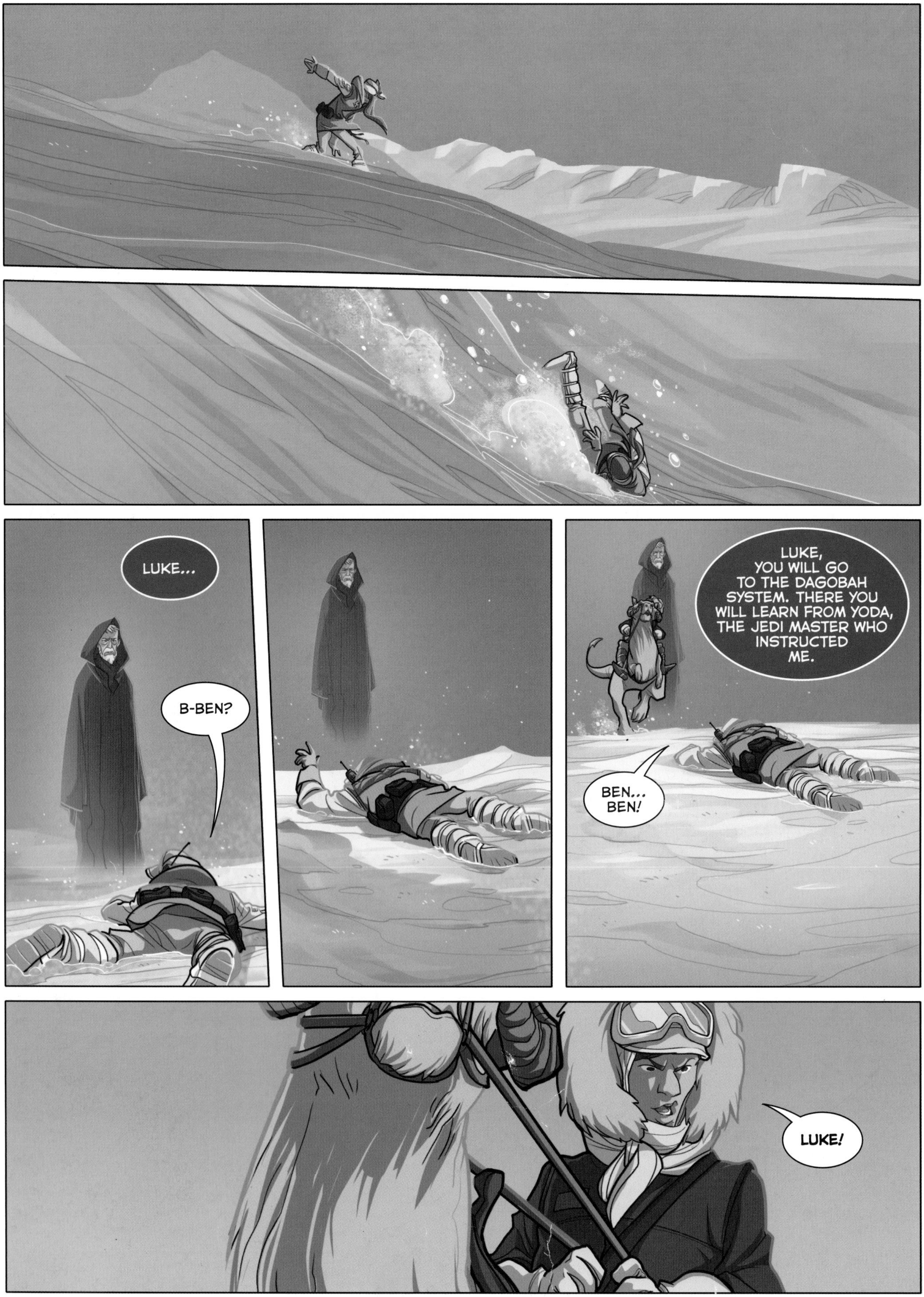

LUKE...
B-BEN?
LUKE, YOU WILL GO TO THE DAGOBAH SYSTEM. THERE YOU WILL LEARN FROM YODA, THE JEDI MASTER WHO INSTRUCTED ME.
BEN... BEN!
LUKE!

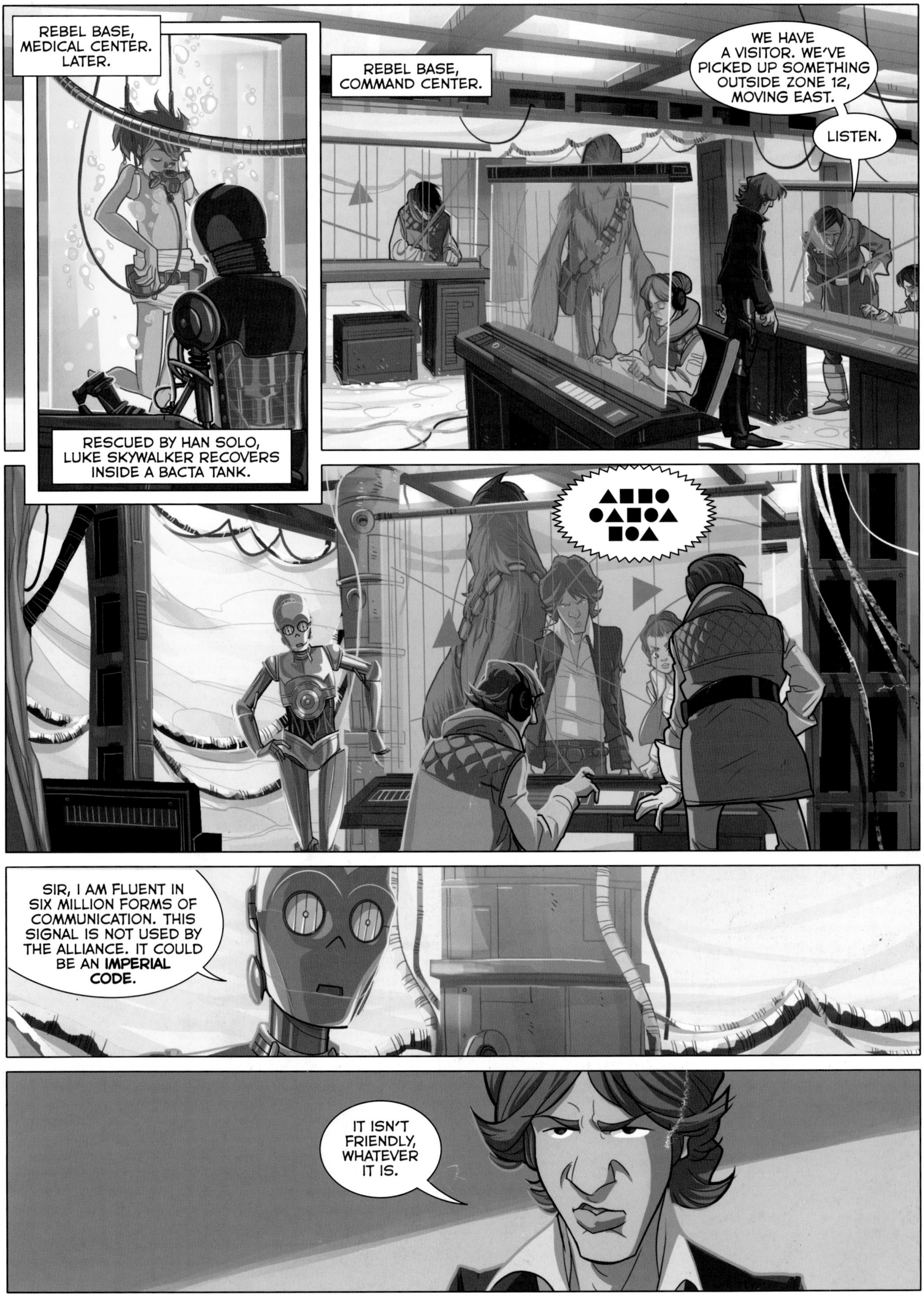
REBEL BASE, MEDICAL CENTER. LATER.
RESCUED BY HAN SOLO, LUKE SKYWALKER RECOVERS INSIDE A BACTA TANK.
REBEL BASE, COMMAND CENTER.
WE HAVE A VISITOR. WE'VE PICKED UP SOMETHING OUTSIDE ZONE 12, MOVING EAST.
LISTEN.
SIR, I AM FLUENT IN SIX MILLION FORMS OF COMMUNICATION. THIS SIGNAL IS NOT USED BY THE ALLIANCE. IT COULD BE AN **IMPERIAL CODE**.
IT ISN'T FRIENDLY, WHATEVER IT IS.

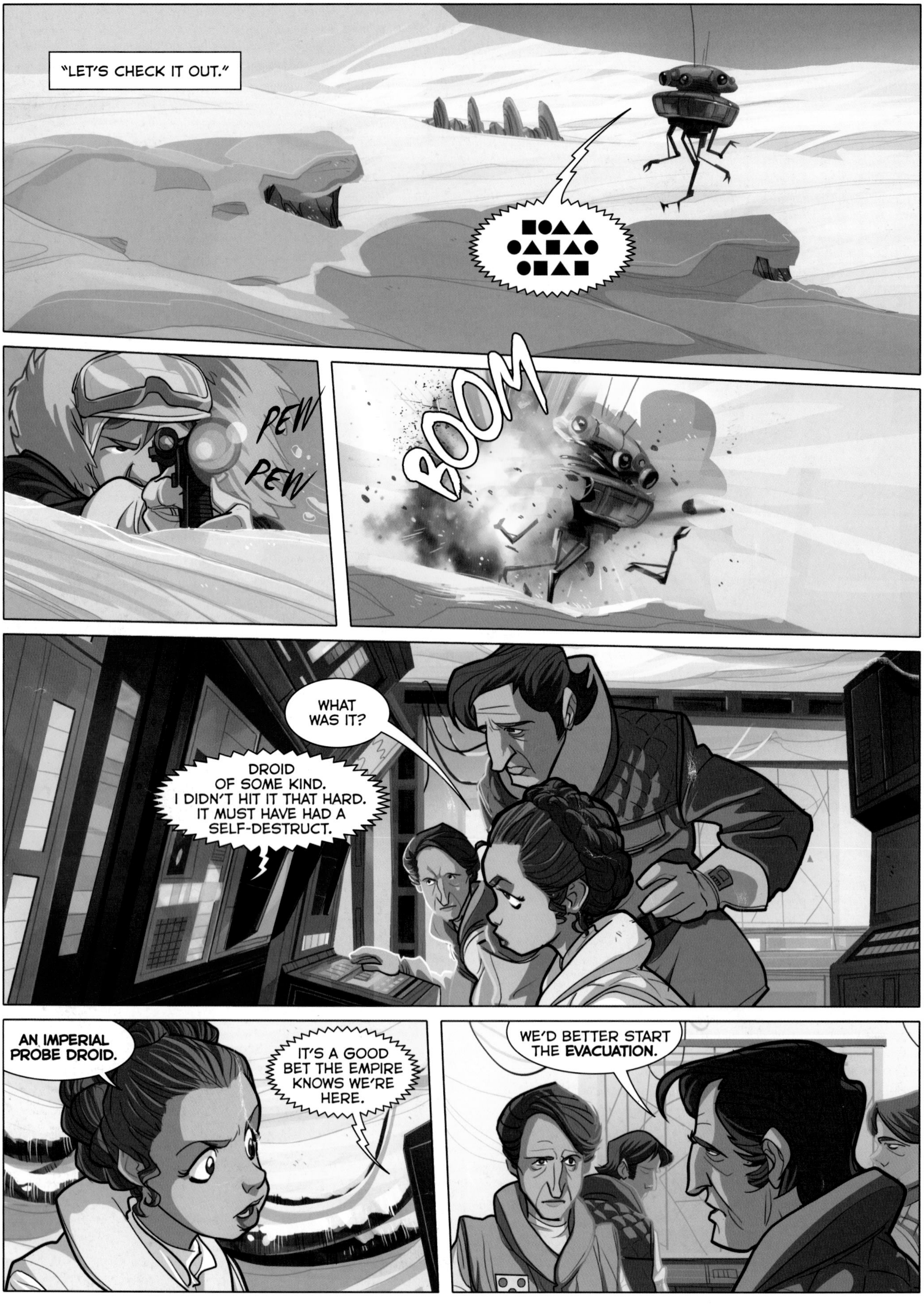

"LET'S CHECK IT OUT."
BOOM
PEW
PEW
WHAT WAS IT?
DROID OF SOME KIND. I DIDN'T HIT IT THAT HARD. IT MUST HAVE HAD A SELF-DESTRUCT.
AN IMPERIAL PROBE DROID.
IT'S A GOOD BET THE EMPIRE KNOWS WE'RE HERE.
WE'D BETTER START THE EVACUATION.

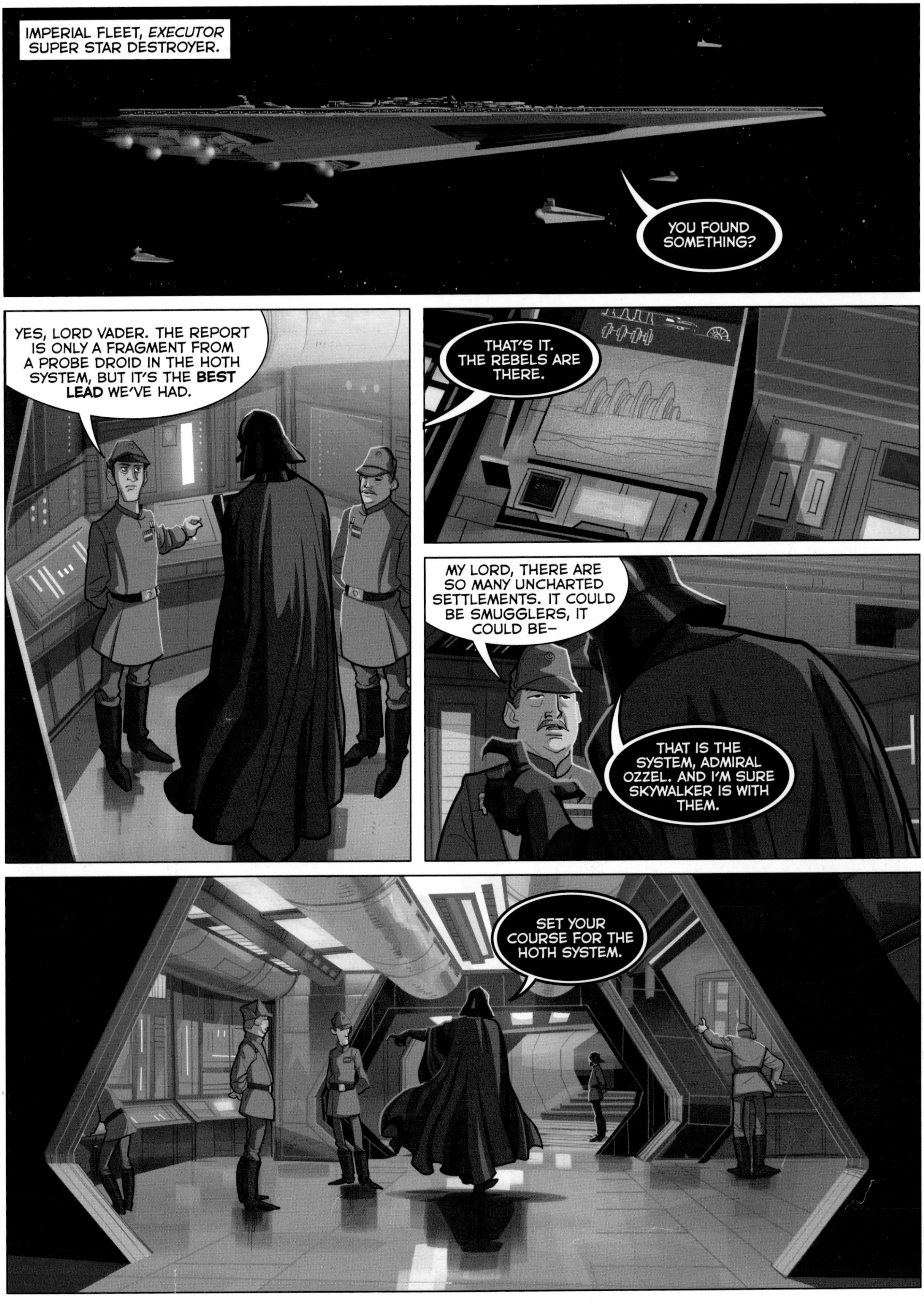
IMPERIAL FLEET, *EXECUTOR* SUPER STAR DESTROYER.
YOU FOUND SOMETHING?
YES, LORD VADER. THE REPORT IS ONLY A FRAGMENT FROM A PROBE DROID IN THE HOTH SYSTEM, BUT IT'S THE **BEST LEAD** WE'VE HAD.
THAT'S IT. THE REBELS ARE THERE.
MY LORD, THERE ARE SO MANY UNCHARTED SETTLEMENTS. IT COULD BE SMUGGLERS, IT COULD BE–
THAT IS THE SYSTEM, ADMIRAL OZZEL. AND I'M SURE SKYWALKER IS WITH THEM.
SET YOUR COURSE FOR THE HOTH SYSTEM.

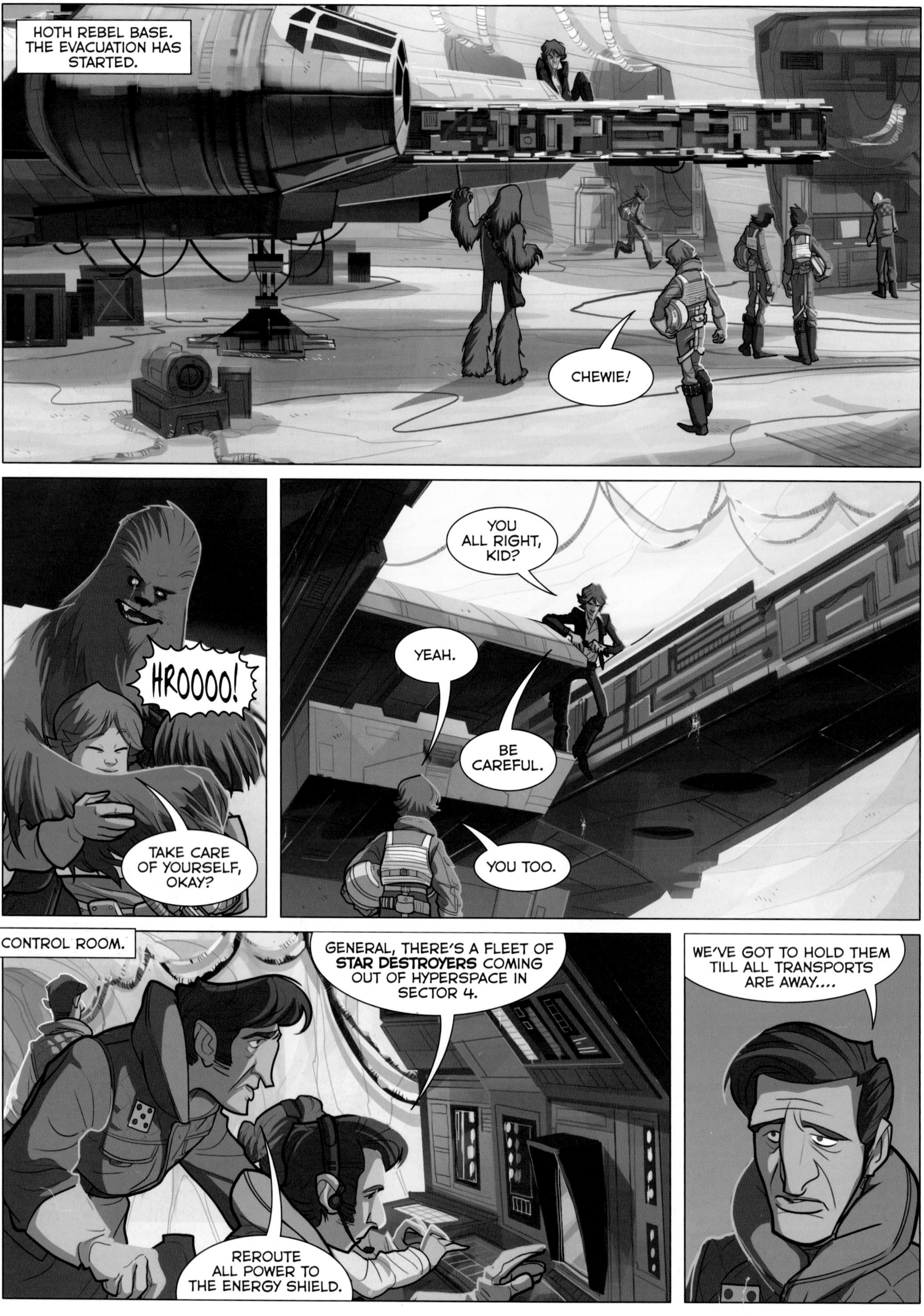
HOTH REBEL BASE. THE EVACUATION HAS STARTED.
CHEWIE!
HROOOO!
TAKE CARE OF YOURSELF, OKAY?
YOU ALL RIGHT, KID?
YEAH.
BE CAREFUL.
YOU TOO.
CONTROL ROOM.
GENERAL, THERE'S A FLEET OF **STAR DESTROYERS** COMING OUT OF HYPERSPACE IN SECTOR 4.
REROUTE ALL POWER TO THE ENERGY SHIELD.
WE'VE GOT TO HOLD THEM TILL ALL TRANSPORTS ARE AWAY....

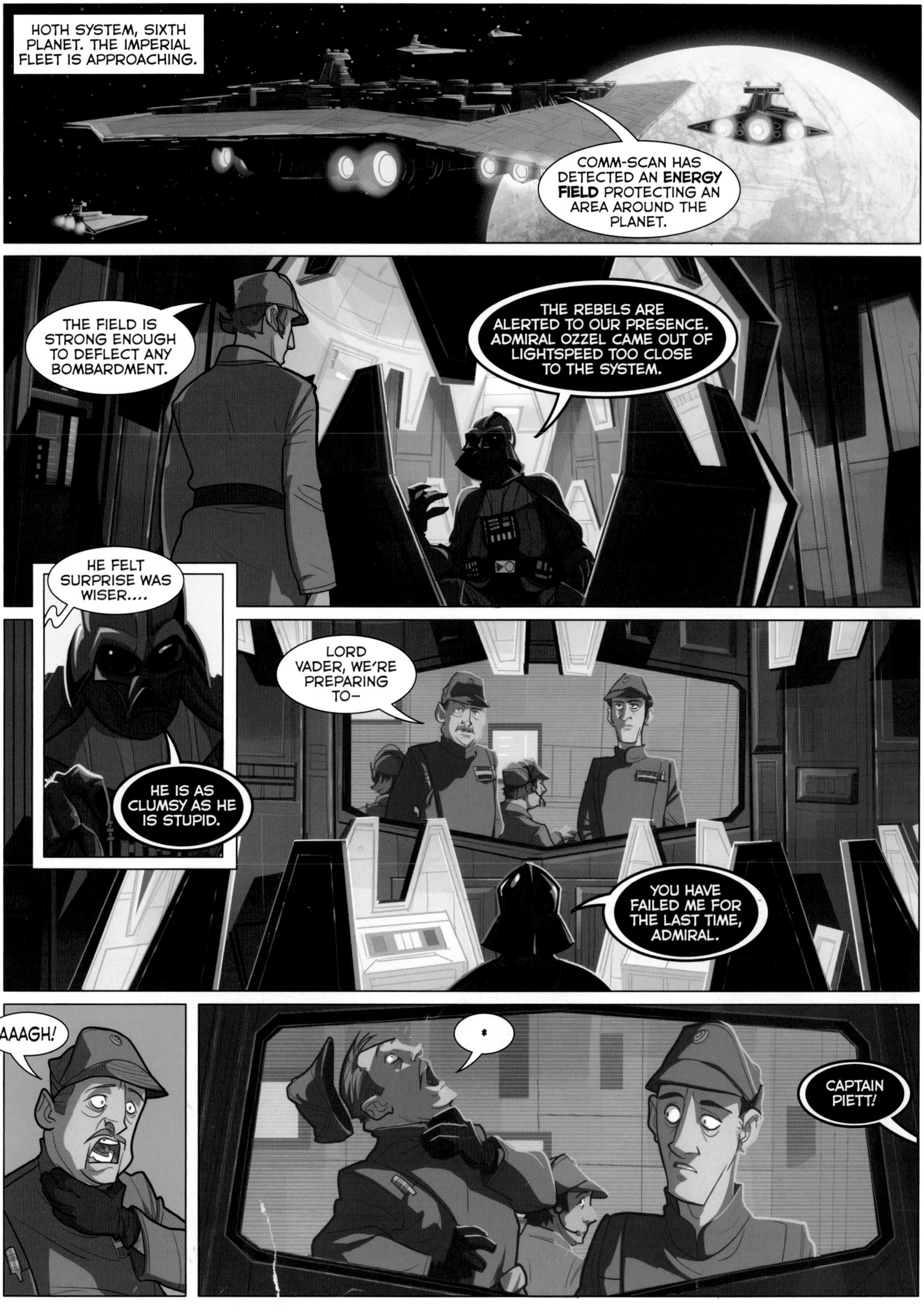
HOTH SYSTEM, SIXTH PLANET. THE IMPERIAL FLEET IS APPROACHING.
COMM-SCAN HAS DETECTED AN **ENERGY FIELD** PROTECTING AN AREA AROUND THE PLANET.
THE FIELD IS STRONG ENOUGH TO DEFLECT ANY BOMBARDMENT.
THE REBELS ARE ALERTED TO OUR PRESENCE. ADMIRAL OZZEL CAME OUT OF LIGHTSPEED TOO CLOSE TO THE SYSTEM.
HE FELT SURPRISE WAS WISER....
HE IS AS CLUMSY AS HE IS STUPID.
LORD VADER, WE'RE PREPARING TO–
YOU HAVE FAILED ME FOR THE LAST TIME, ADMIRAL.
AAAGH!
*
CAPTAIN PIETT!

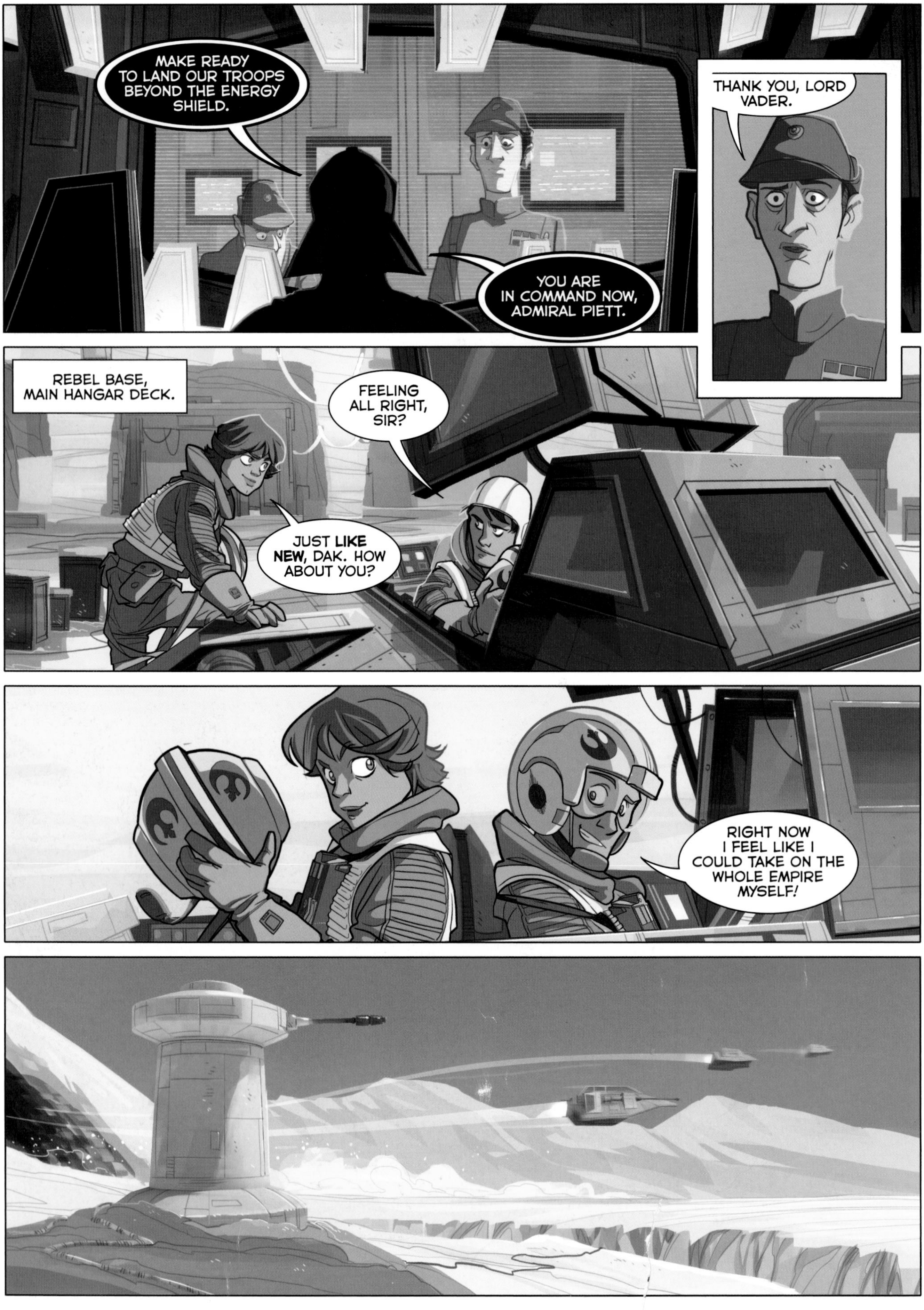
MAKE READY TO LAND OUR TROOPS BEYOND THE ENERGY SHIELD.
YOU ARE IN COMMAND NOW, ADMIRAL PIETT.
THANK YOU, LORD VADER.
REBEL BASE, MAIN HANGAR DECK.
FEELING ALL RIGHT, SIR?
JUST LIKE NEW, DAK. HOW ABOUT YOU?
RIGHT NOW I FEEL LIKE I COULD TAKE ON THE WHOLE EMPIRE MYSELF!

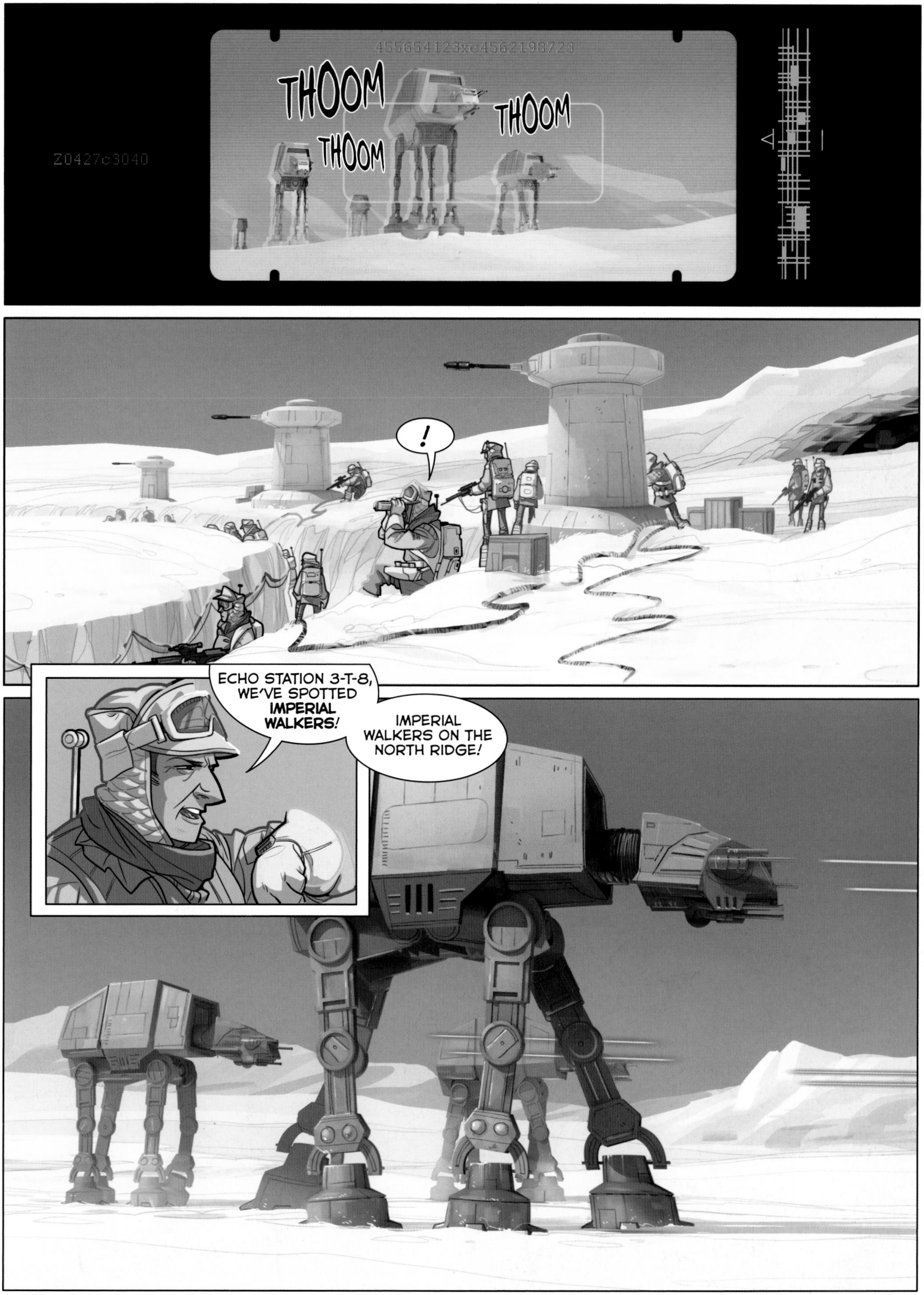
455654123xc4562198723
THOOM
THOOM
THOOM
Z0427c3040
!
ECHO STATION 3-T-8, WE'VE SPOTTED IMPERIAL WALKERS!
IMPERIAL WALKERS ON THE NORTH RIDGE!

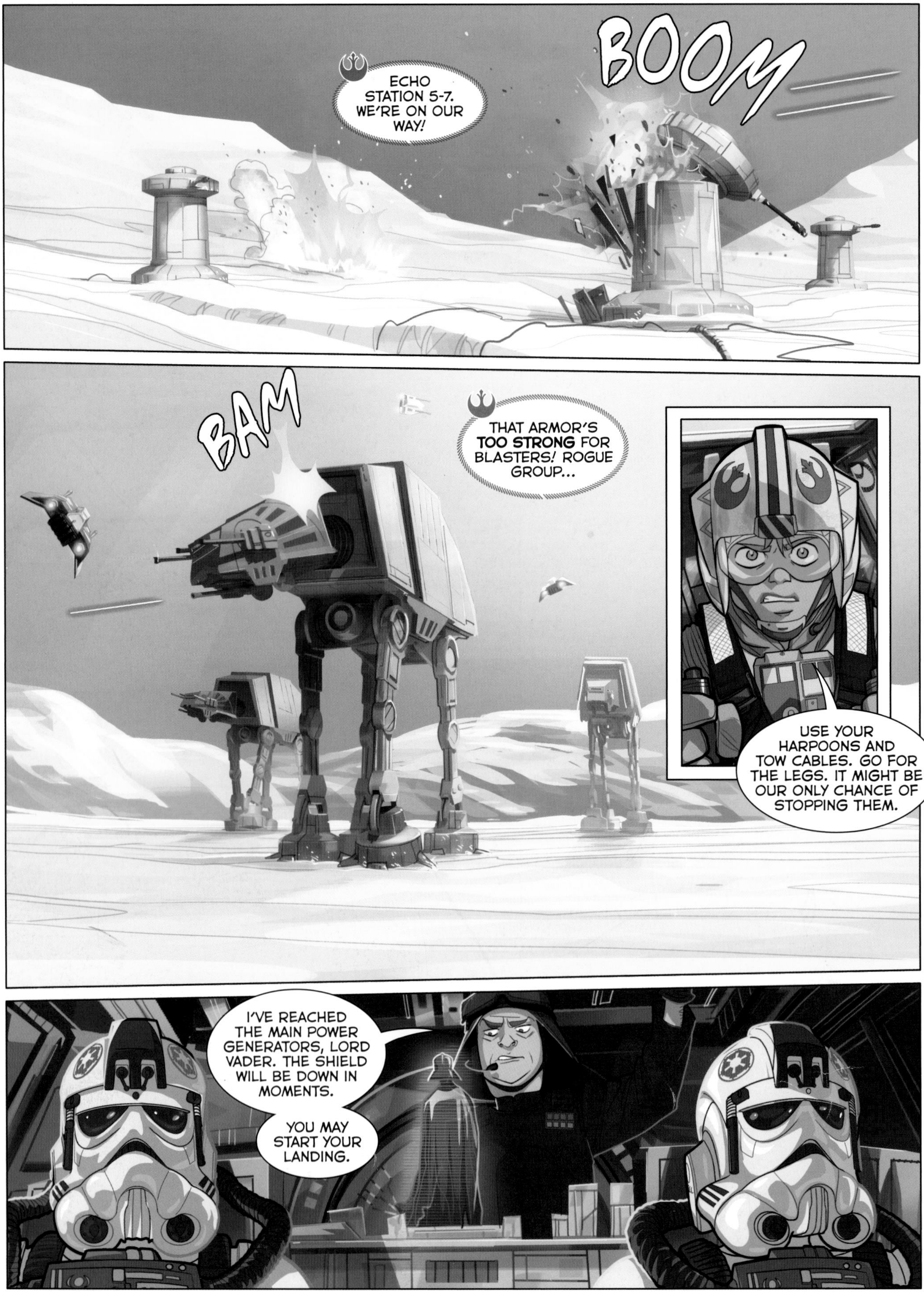
ECHO STATION 5-7. WE'RE ON OUR WAY!
BOOM
BAM
THAT ARMOR'S **TOO STRONG** FOR BLASTERS! ROGUE GROUP...
USE YOUR HARPOONS AND TOW CABLES. GO FOR THE LEGS. IT MIGHT BE OUR ONLY CHANCE OF STOPPING THEM.
I'VE REACHED THE MAIN POWER GENERATORS, LORD VADER. THE SHIELD WILL BE DOWN IN MOMENTS.
YOU MAY START YOUR LANDING.

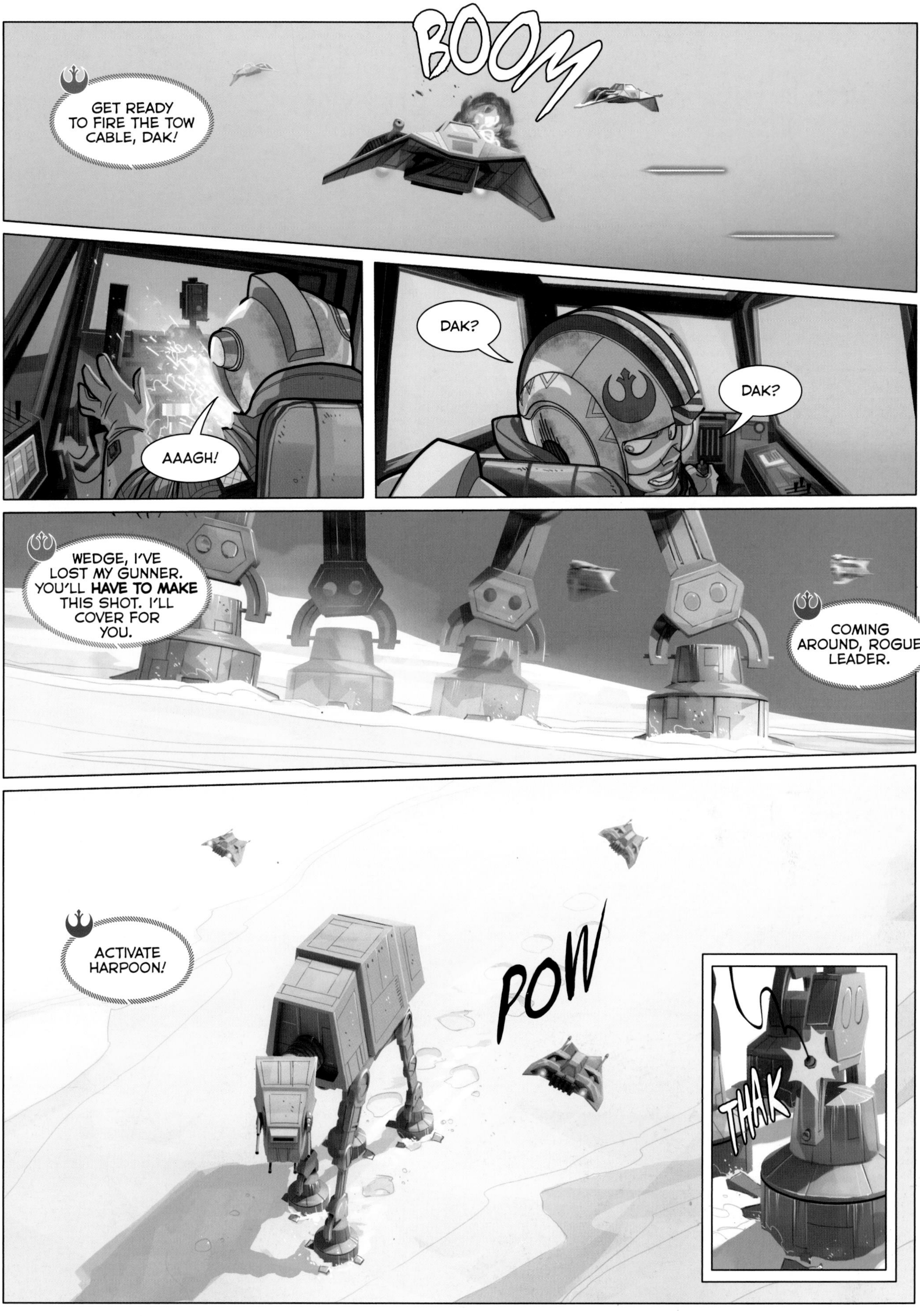
BOOM
GET READY TO FIRE THE TOW CABLE, DAK!
AAAGH!
DAK?
DAK?
WEDGE, I'VE LOST MY GUNNER. YOU'LL **HAVE TO MAKE** THIS SHOT. I'LL COVER FOR YOU.
COMING AROUND, ROGUE LEADER.
ACTIVATE HARPOON!
POW
THAK

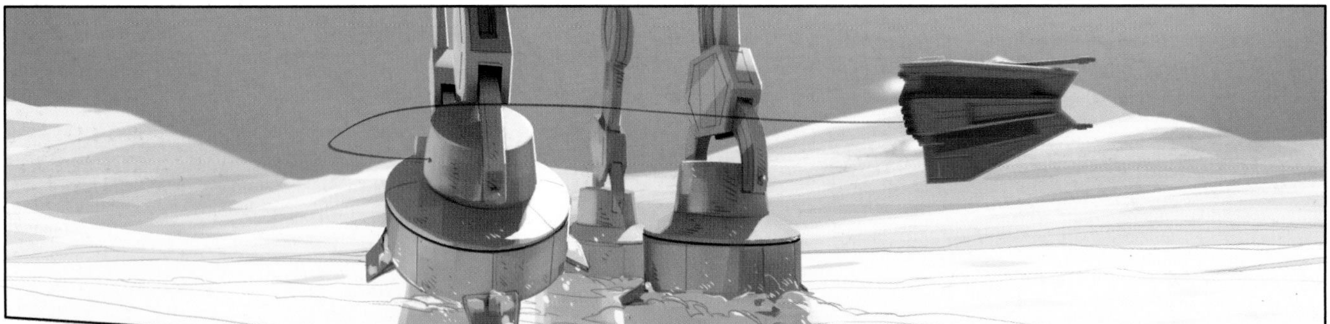

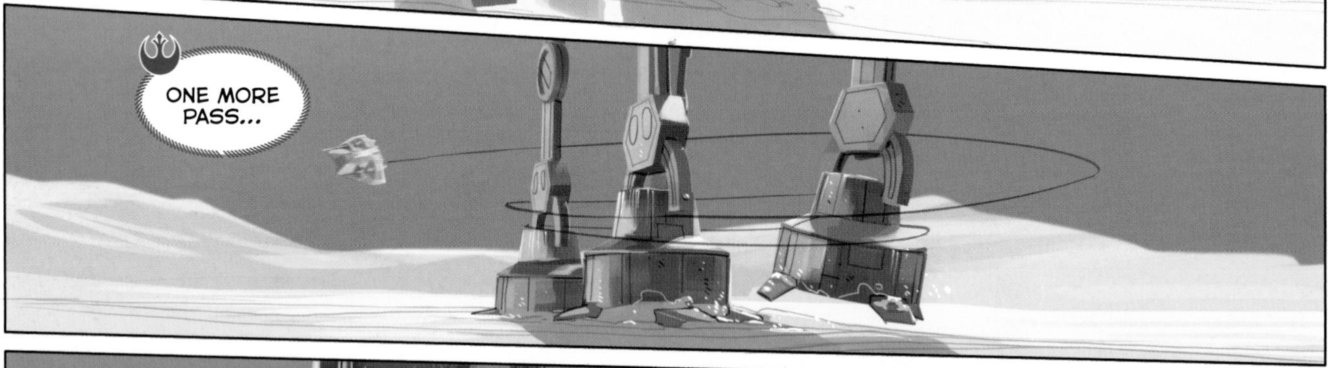

ONE MORE PASS...

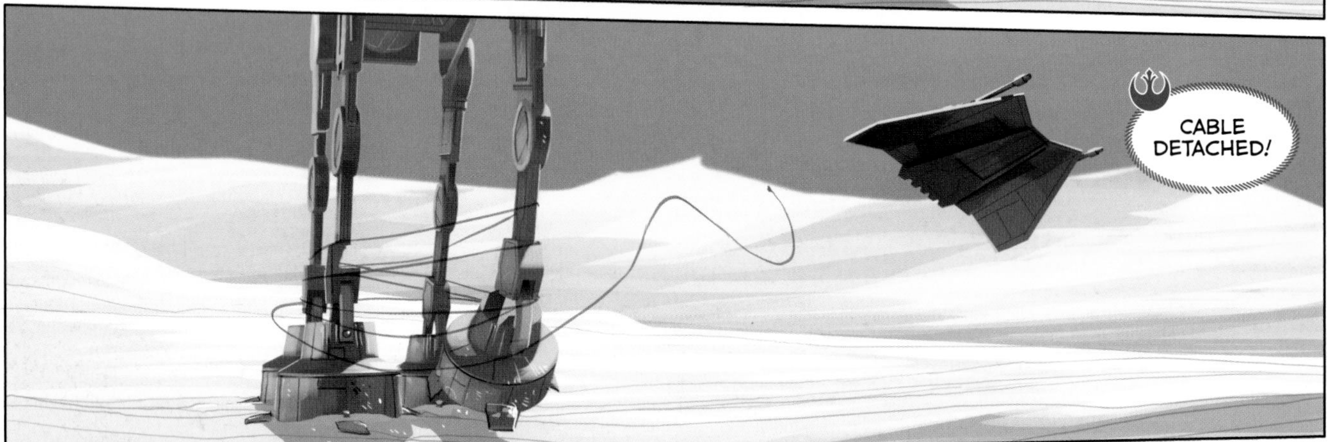

CABLE DETACHED!

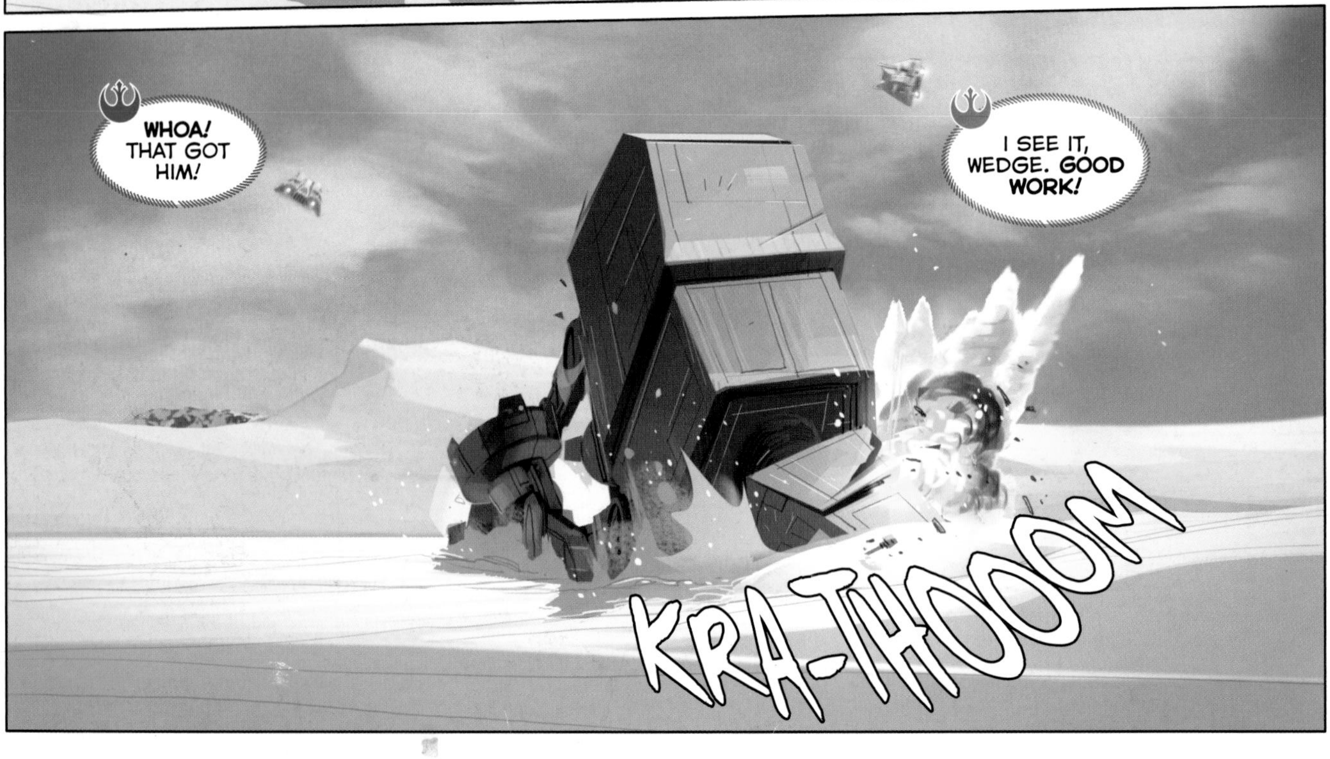

WHOA! THAT GOT HIM!
I SEE IT, WEDGE. GOOD WORK!
KRA-THOOOM

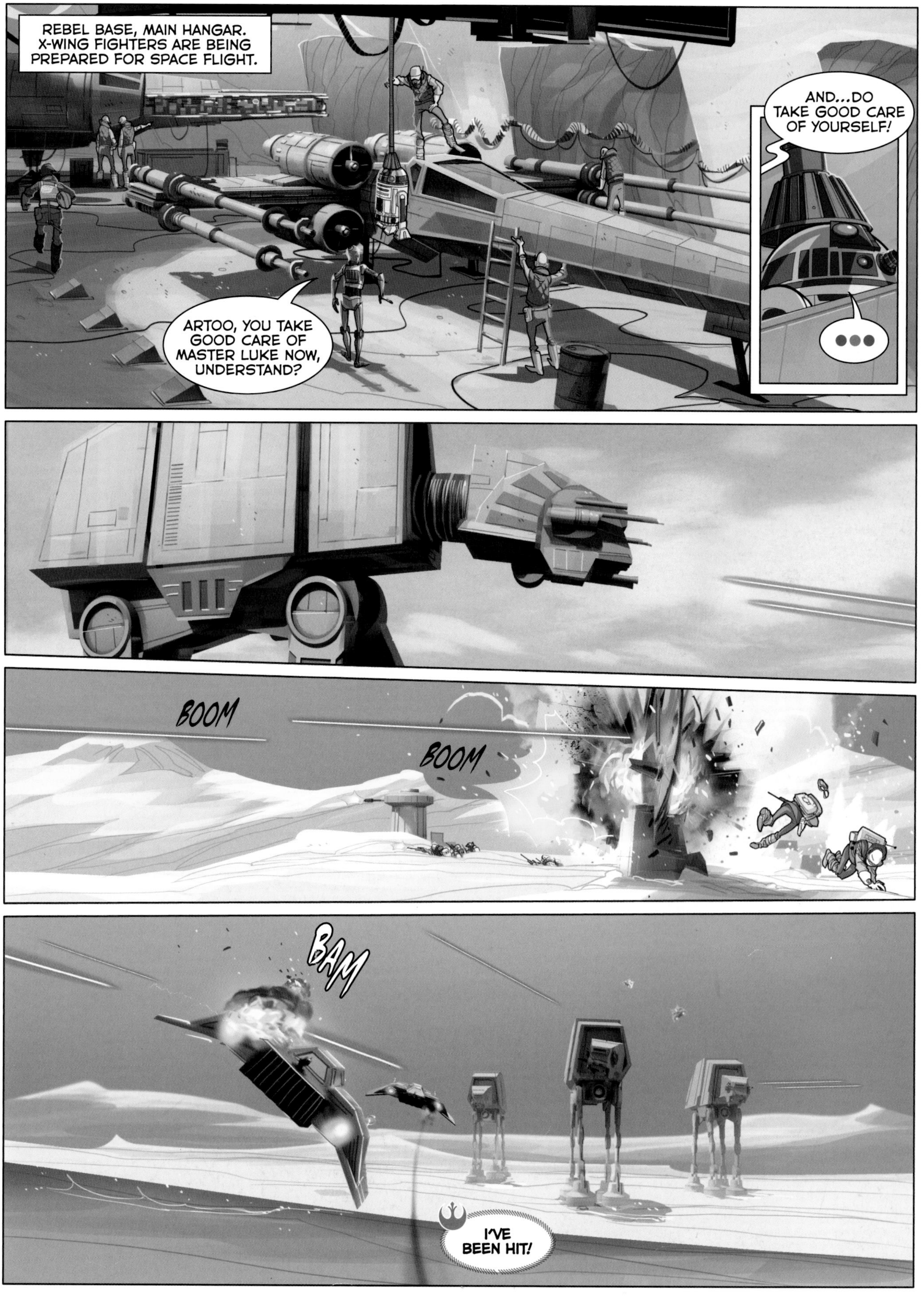
REBEL BASE, MAIN HANGAR. X-WING FIGHTERS ARE BEING PREPARED FOR SPACE FLIGHT.
ARTOO, YOU TAKE GOOD CARE OF MASTER LUKE NOW, UNDERSTAND?
AND...DO TAKE GOOD CARE OF YOURSELF!
•••
BOOM
BOOM
BAM
I'VE BEEN HIT!

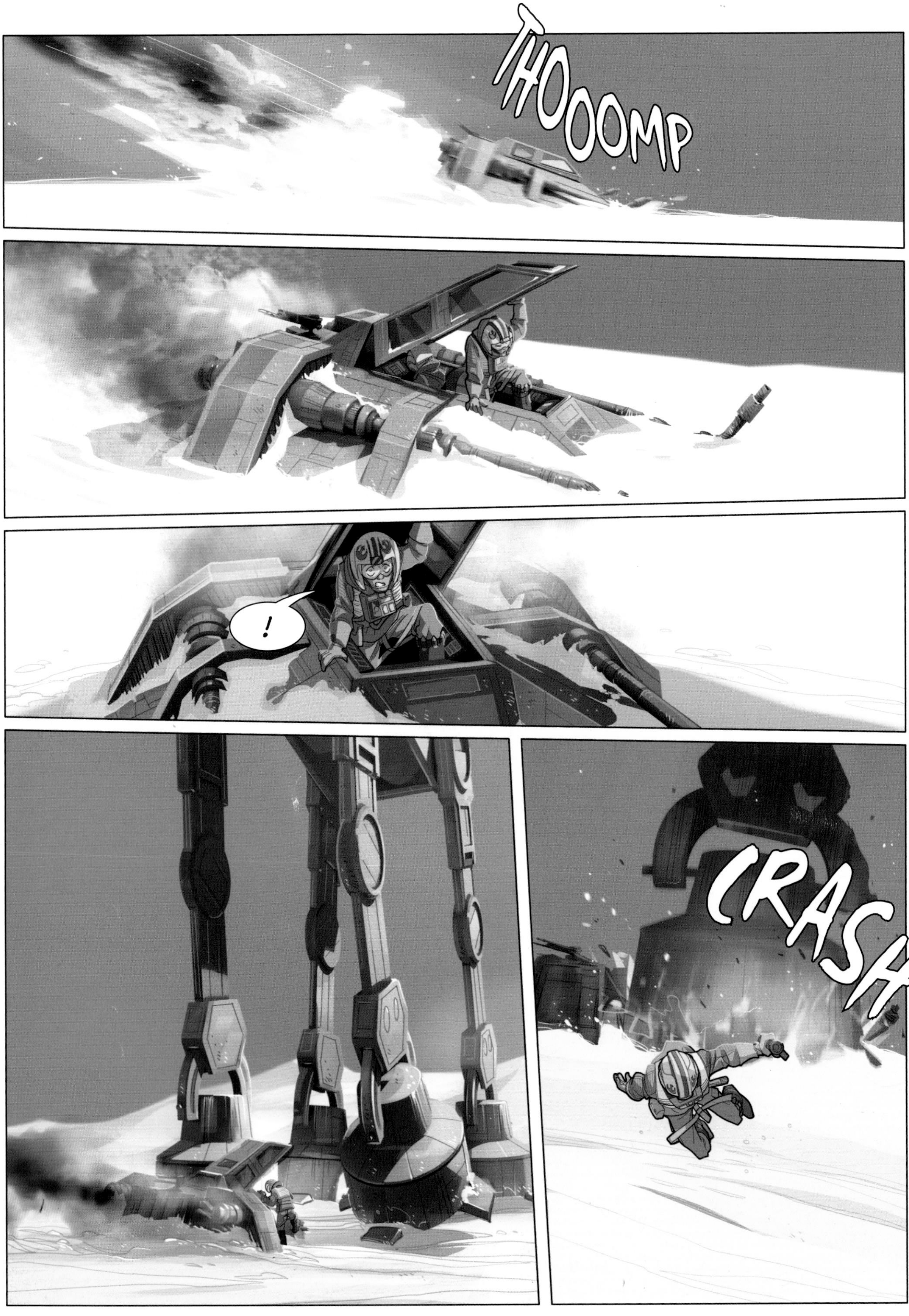
THOOOMP
!
CRASH

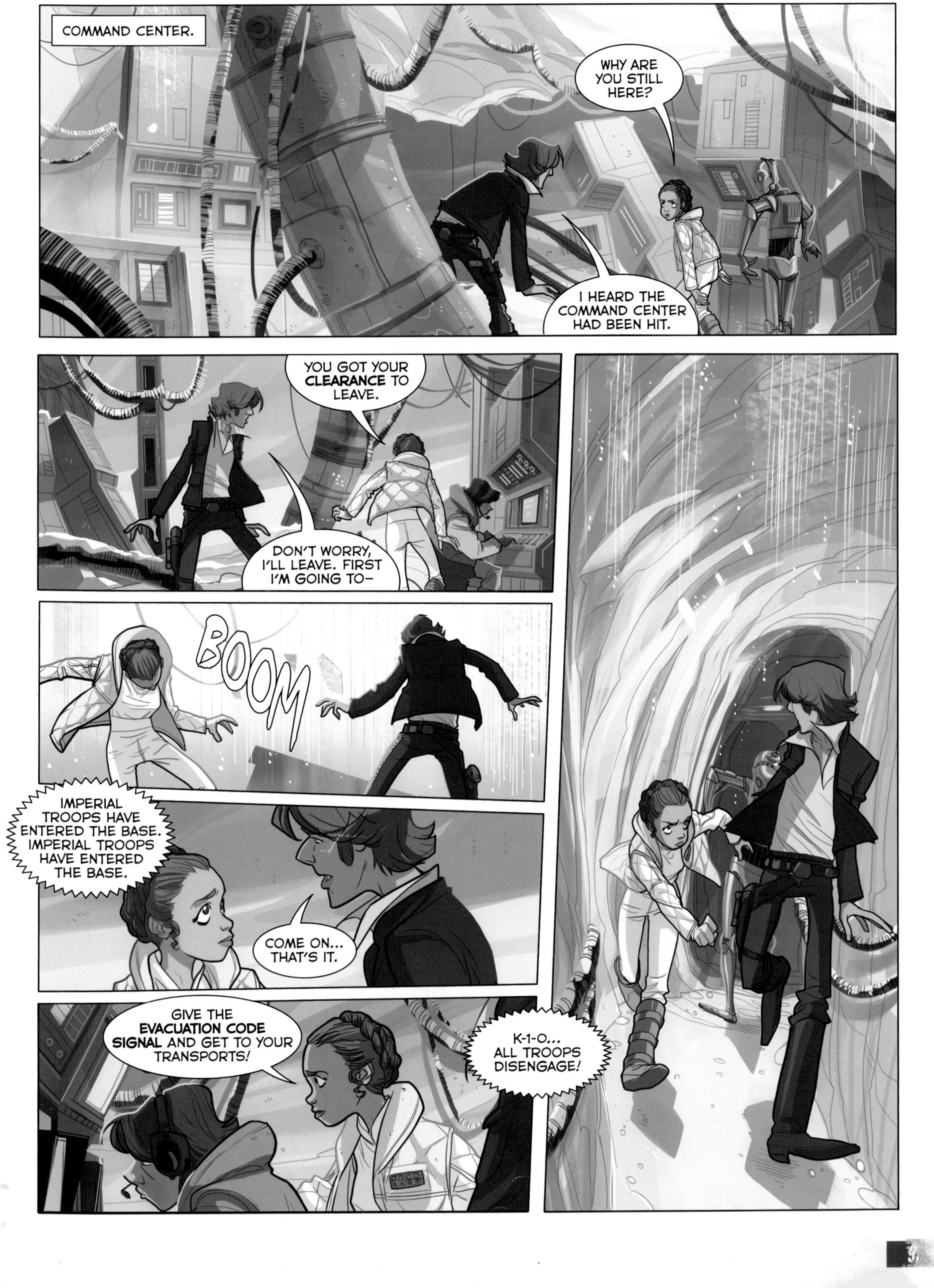
COMMAND CENTER.
WHY ARE YOU STILL HERE?
I HEARD THE COMMAND CENTER HAD BEEN HIT.
YOU GOT YOUR **CLEARANCE** TO LEAVE.
DON'T WORRY, I'LL LEAVE. FIRST I'M GOING TO–
BOOM
IMPERIAL TROOPS HAVE ENTERED THE BASE. IMPERIAL TROOPS HAVE ENTERED THE BASE.
COME ON... THAT'S IT.
GIVE THE **EVACUATION CODE SIGNAL** AND GET TO YOUR TRANSPORTS!
K-1-0... ALL TROOPS DISENGAGE!

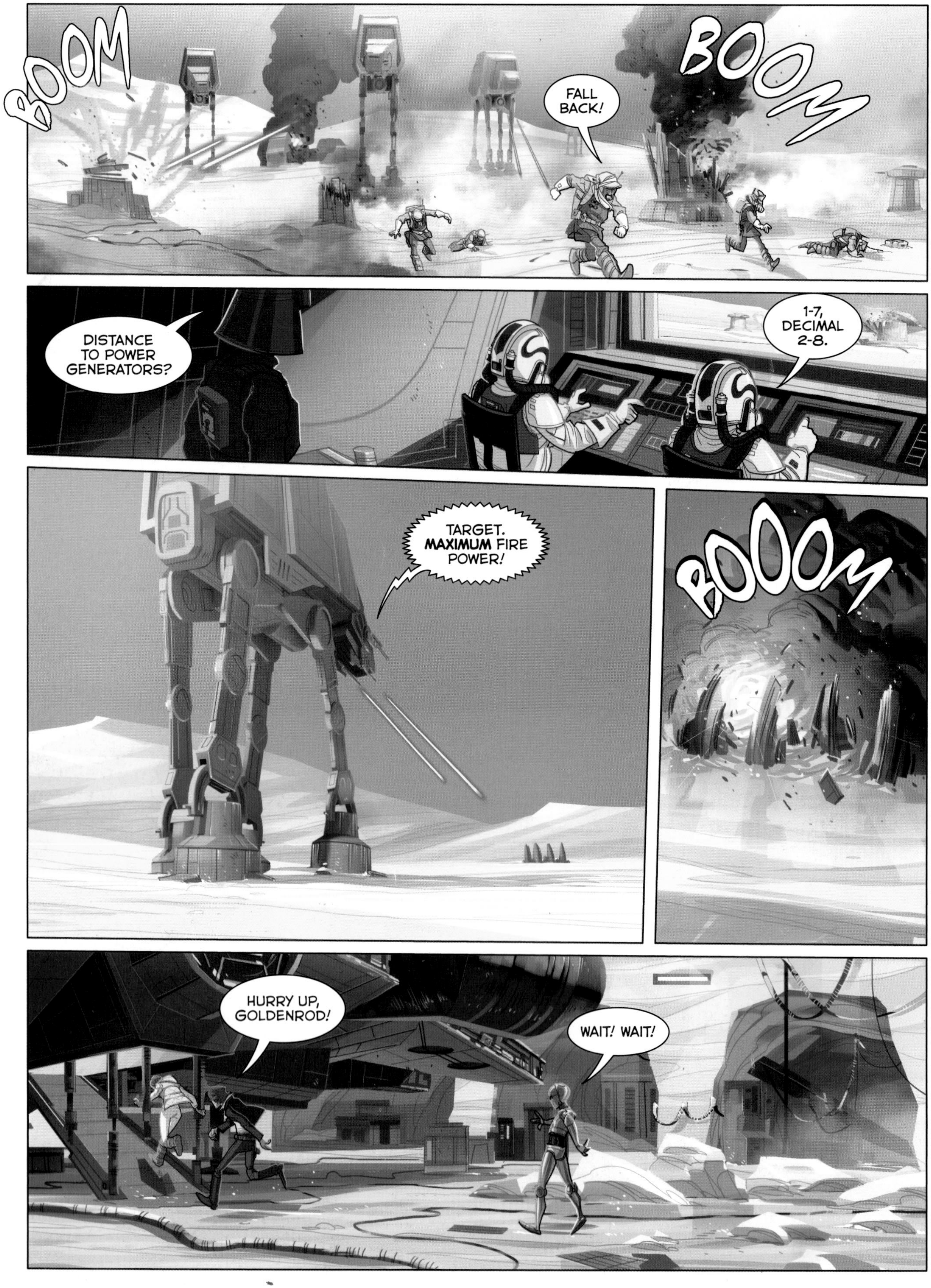
BOOM
FALL BACK!
BOOM
DISTANCE TO POWER GENERATORS?
1-7, DECIMAL 2-8.
TARGET. **MAXIMUM** FIRE POWER!
BOOOM
HURRY UP, GOLDENROD!
WAIT! WAIT!

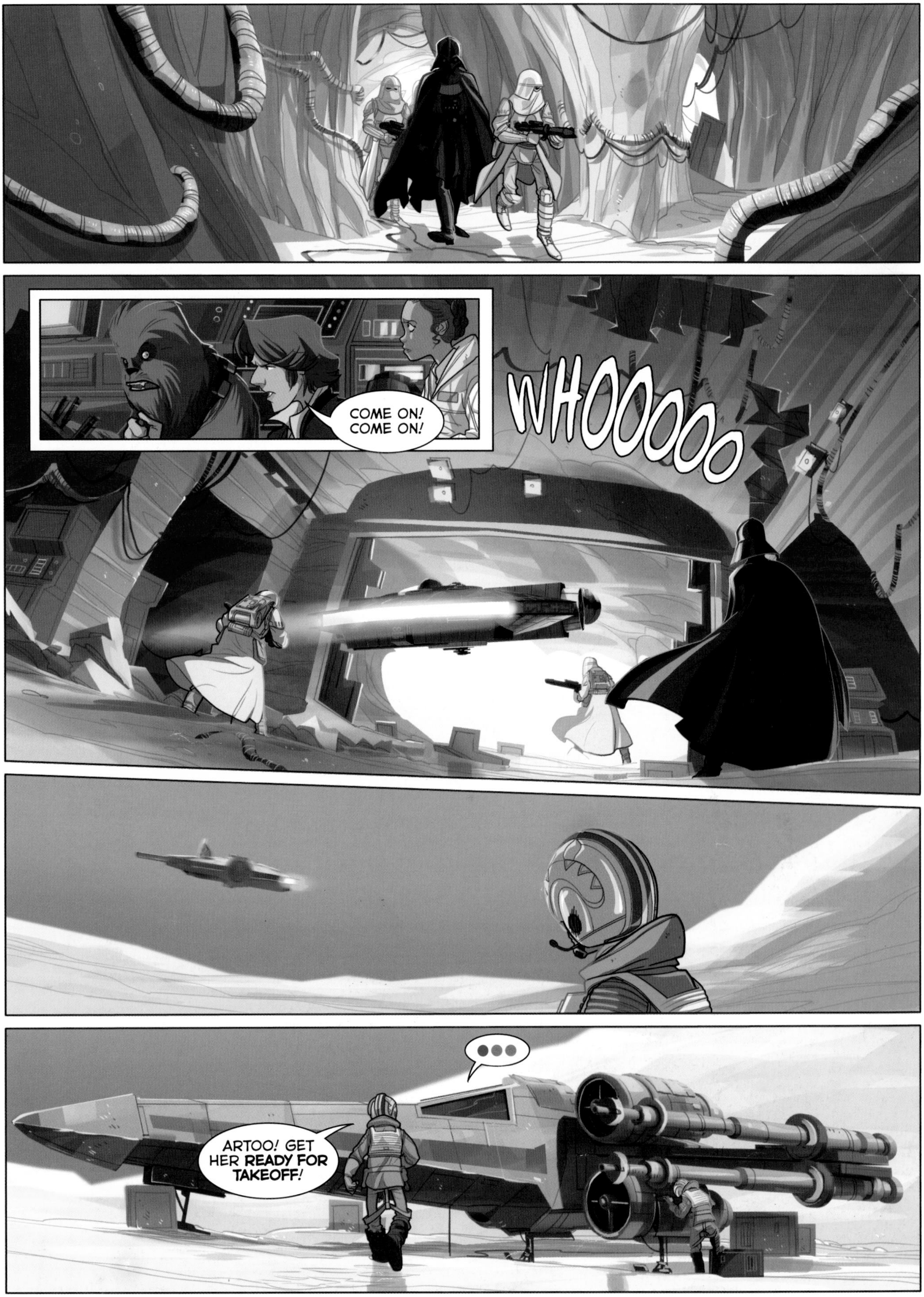
COME ON! COME ON!
WHOOOOO
•••
ARTOO! GET HER READY FOR TAKEOFF!

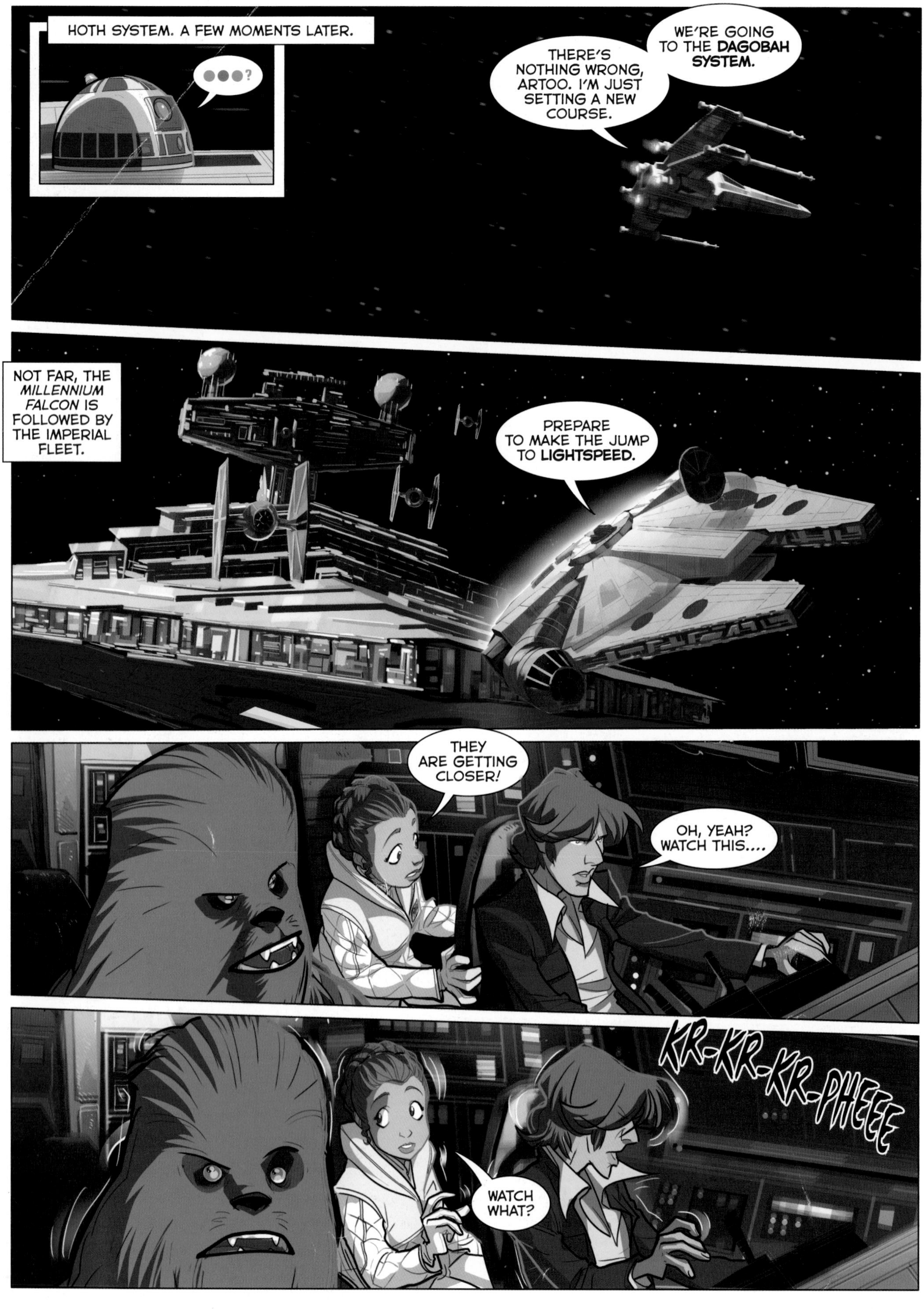
HOTH SYSTEM. A FEW MOMENTS LATER.
●●●?
THERE'S NOTHING WRONG, ARTOO. I'M JUST SETTING A NEW COURSE.
WE'RE GOING TO THE **DAGOBAH SYSTEM.**
NOT FAR, THE *MILLENNIUM FALCON* IS FOLLOWED BY THE IMPERIAL FLEET.
PREPARE TO MAKE THE JUMP TO **LIGHTSPEED.**
THEY ARE GETTING CLOSER!
OH, YEAH? WATCH THIS....
KR-KR-KR-PHEEE
WATCH WHAT?

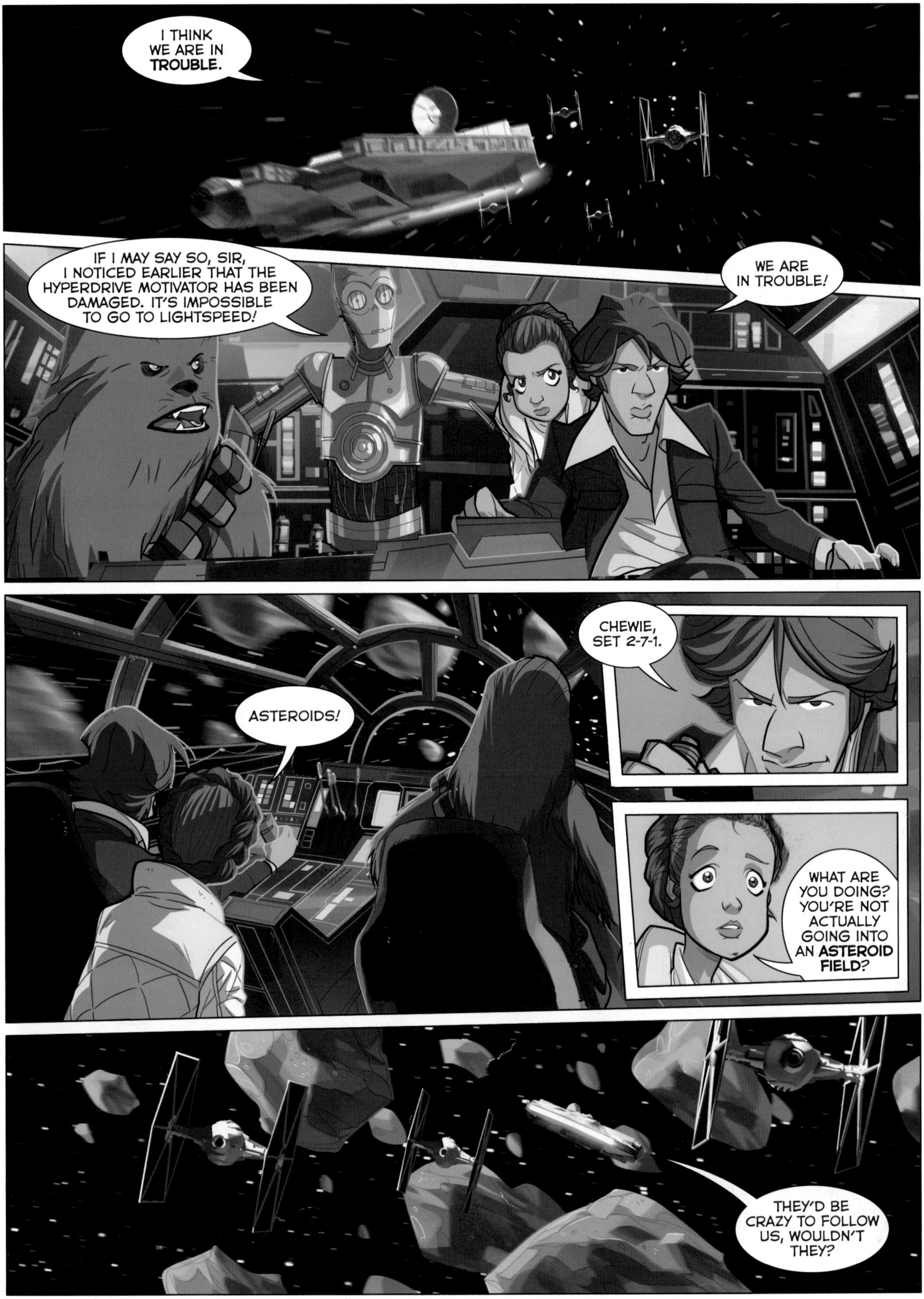

I THINK WE ARE IN TROUBLE.
IF I MAY SAY SO, SIR, I NOTICED EARLIER THAT THE HYPERDRIVE MOTIVATOR HAS BEEN DAMAGED. IT'S IMPOSSIBLE TO GO TO LIGHTSPEED!
WE ARE IN TROUBLE!
ASTEROIDS!
CHEWIE, SET 2-7-1.
WHAT ARE YOU DOING? YOU'RE NOT ACTUALLY GOING INTO AN ASTEROID FIELD?
THEY'D BE CRAZY TO FOLLOW US, WOULDN'T THEY?

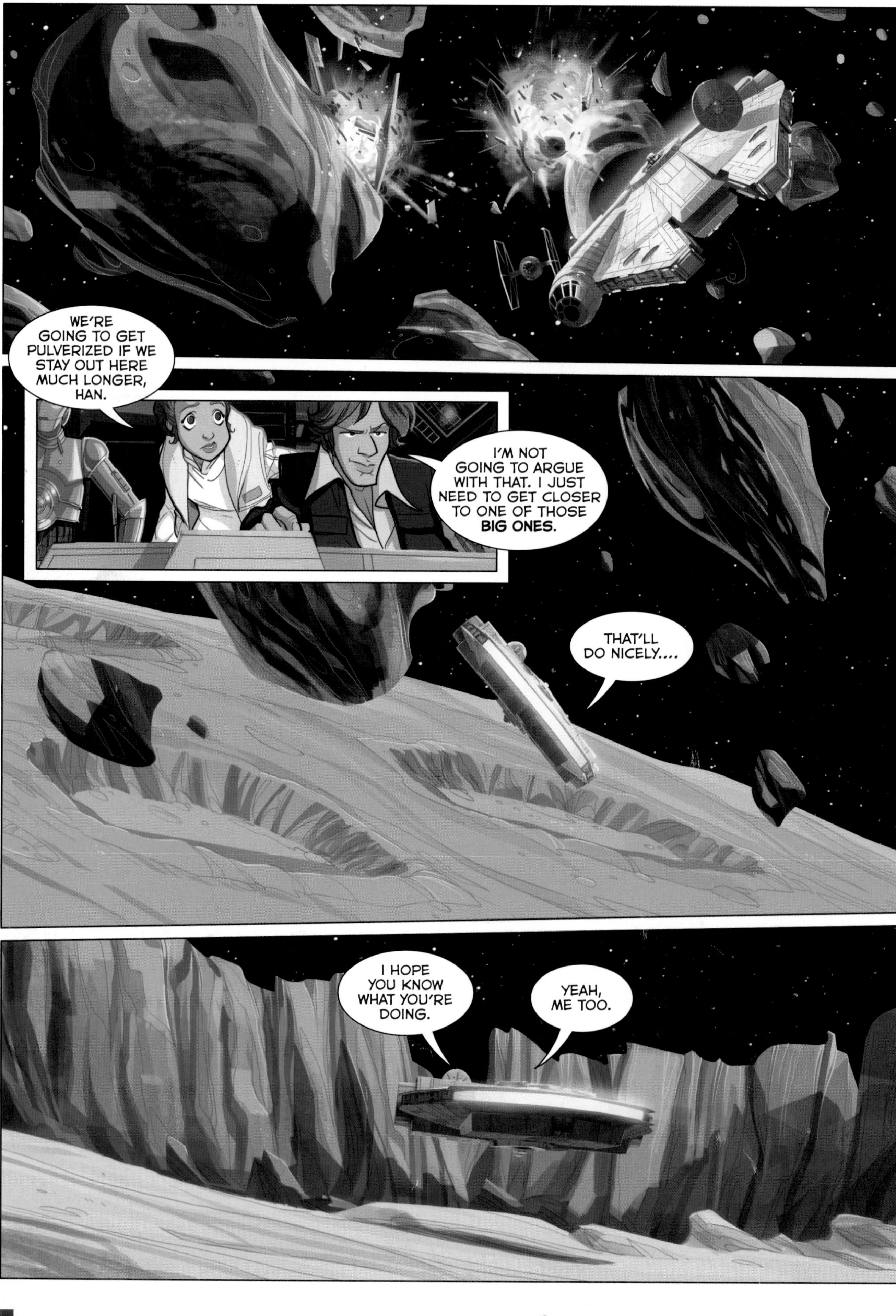
WE'RE GOING TO GET PULVERIZED IF WE STAY OUT HERE MUCH LONGER, HAN.
I'M NOT GOING TO ARGUE WITH THAT. I JUST NEED TO GET CLOSER TO ONE OF THOSE **BIG ONES.**
THAT'LL DO NICELY....
I HOPE YOU KNOW WHAT YOU'RE DOING.
YEAH, ME TOO.

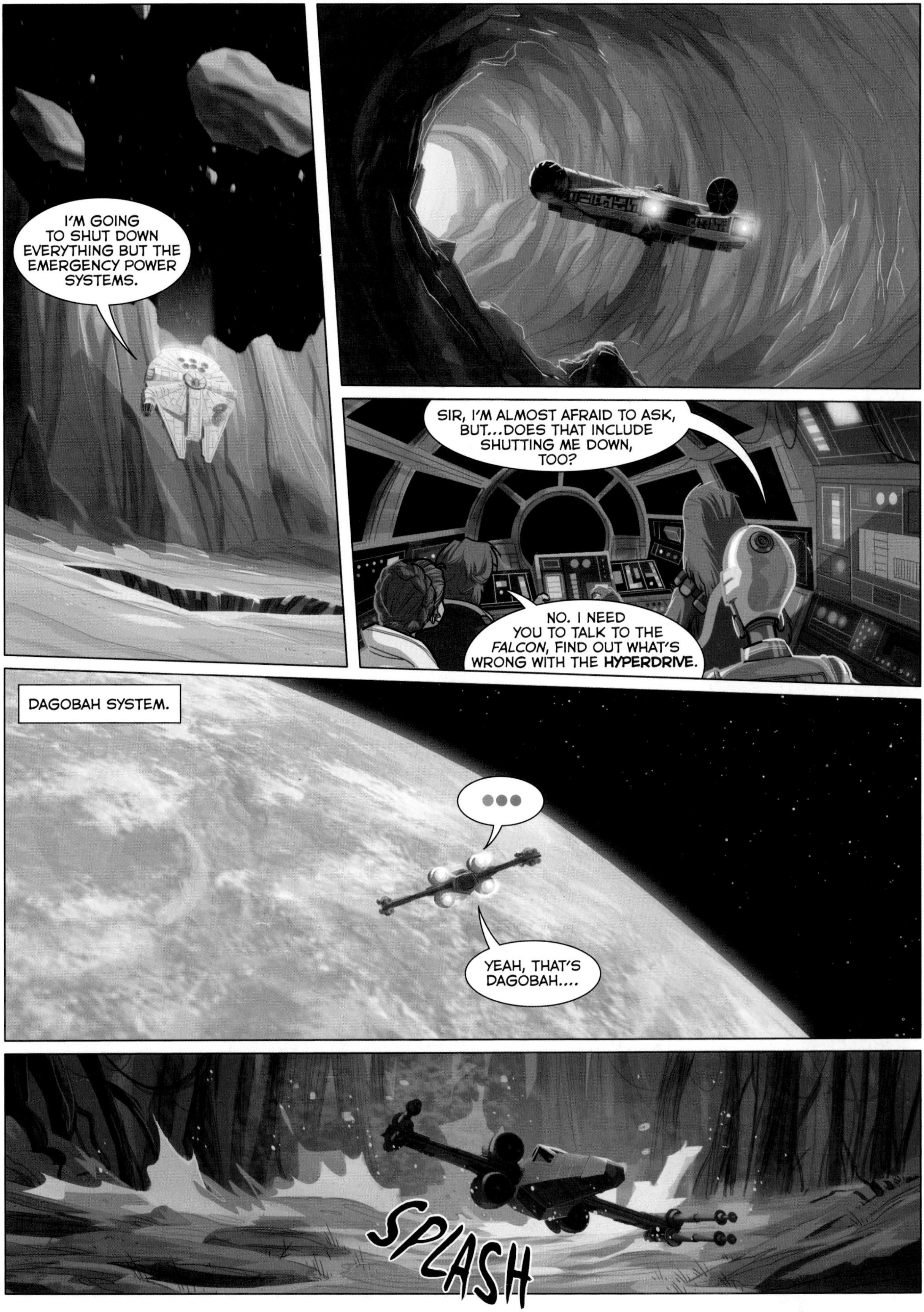

I'M GOING TO SHUT DOWN EVERYTHING BUT THE EMERGENCY POWER SYSTEMS.
SIR, I'M ALMOST AFRAID TO ASK, BUT...DOES THAT INCLUDE SHUTTING ME DOWN, TOO?
NO. I NEED YOU TO TALK TO THE *FALCON*, FIND OUT WHAT'S WRONG WITH THE **HYPERDRIVE**.
DAGOBAH SYSTEM.
YEAH, THAT'S DAGOBAH....
SPLASH

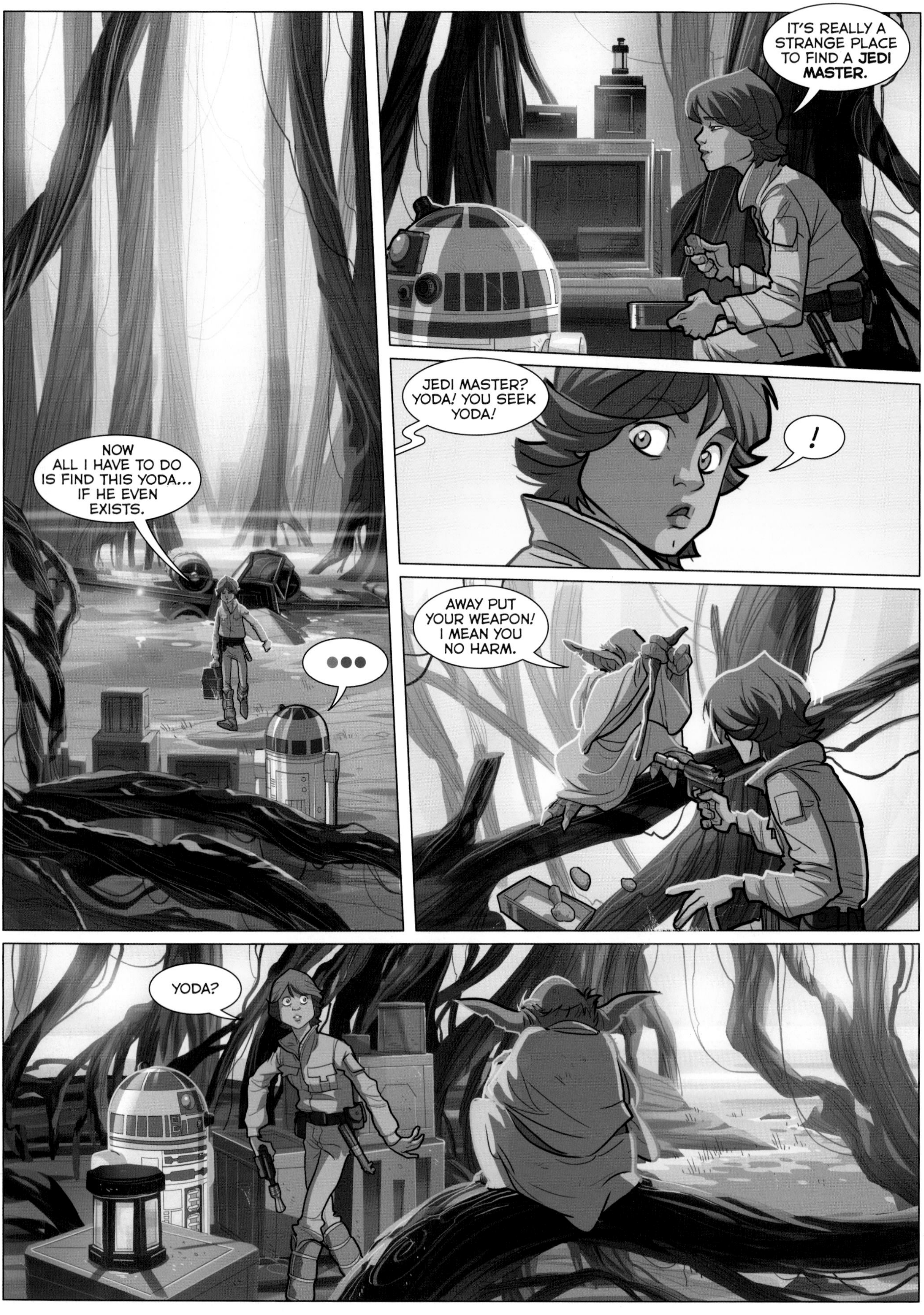

NOW ALL I HAVE TO DO IS FIND THIS YODA... IF HE EVEN EXISTS.
•••
IT'S REALLY A STRANGE PLACE TO FIND A **JEDI MASTER.**
JEDI MASTER? YODA! YOU SEEK YODA!
!
AWAY PUT YOUR WEAPON! I MEAN YOU NO HARM.
YODA?

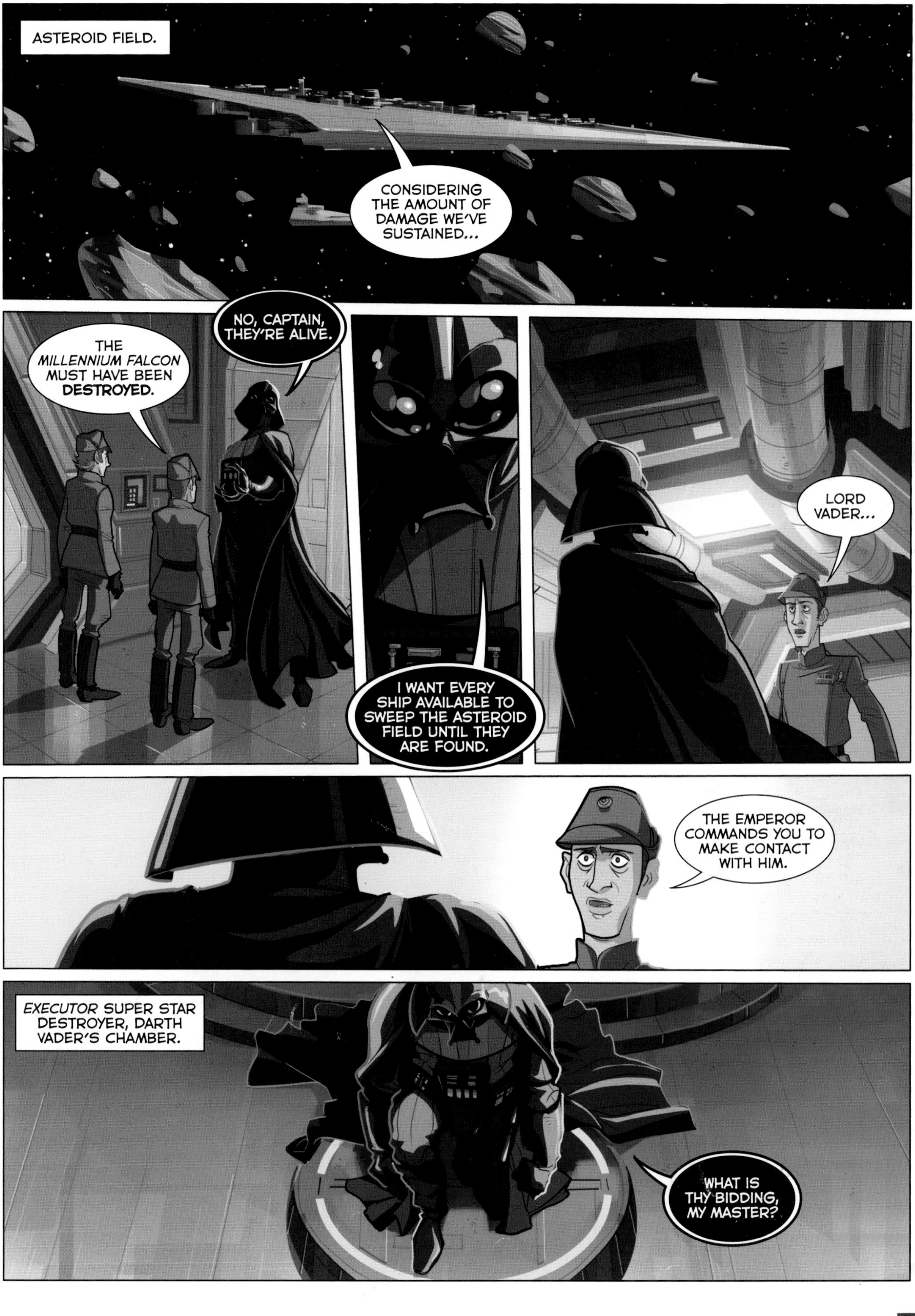
ASTEROID FIELD.
CONSIDERING THE AMOUNT OF DAMAGE WE'VE SUSTAINED...
THE *MILLENNIUM FALCON* MUST HAVE BEEN **DESTROYED.**
NO, CAPTAIN, THEY'RE ALIVE.
I WANT EVERY SHIP AVAILABLE TO SWEEP THE ASTEROID FIELD UNTIL THEY ARE FOUND.
LORD VADER...
THE EMPEROR COMMANDS YOU TO MAKE CONTACT WITH HIM.
EXECUTOR SUPER STAR DESTROYER, DARTH VADER'S CHAMBER.
WHAT IS THY BIDDING, MY MASTER?

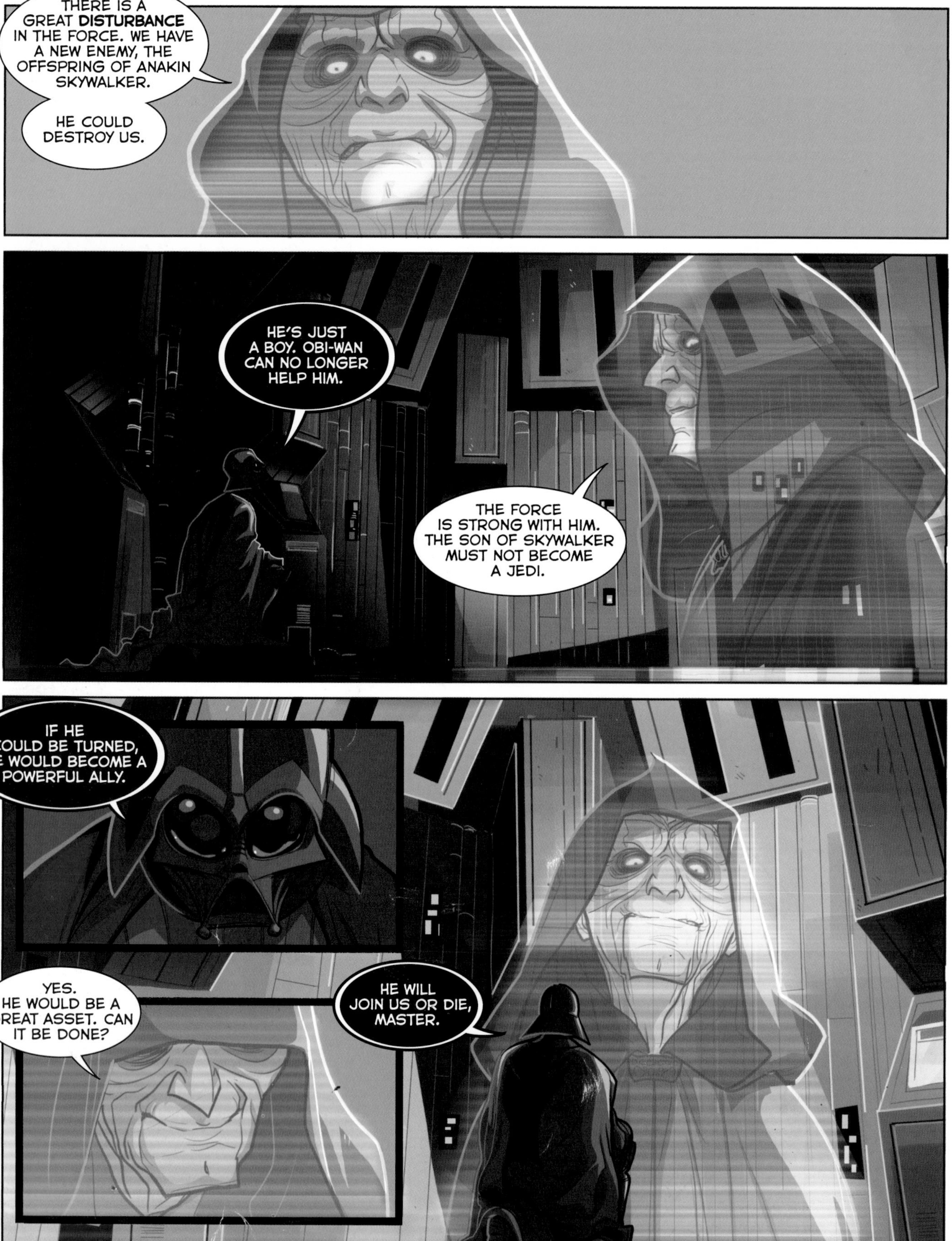

THERE IS A GREAT **DISTURBANCE** IN THE FORCE. WE HAVE A NEW ENEMY, THE OFFSPRING OF ANAKIN SKYWALKER.
HE COULD DESTROY US.
HE'S JUST A BOY. OBI-WAN CAN NO LONGER HELP HIM.
THE FORCE IS STRONG WITH HIM. THE SON OF SKYWALKER MUST NOT BECOME A JEDI.
IF HE COULD BE TURNED, HE WOULD BECOME A POWERFUL ALLY.
YES. HE WOULD BE A GREAT ASSET. CAN IT BE DONE?
HE WILL JOIN US OR DIE, MASTER.

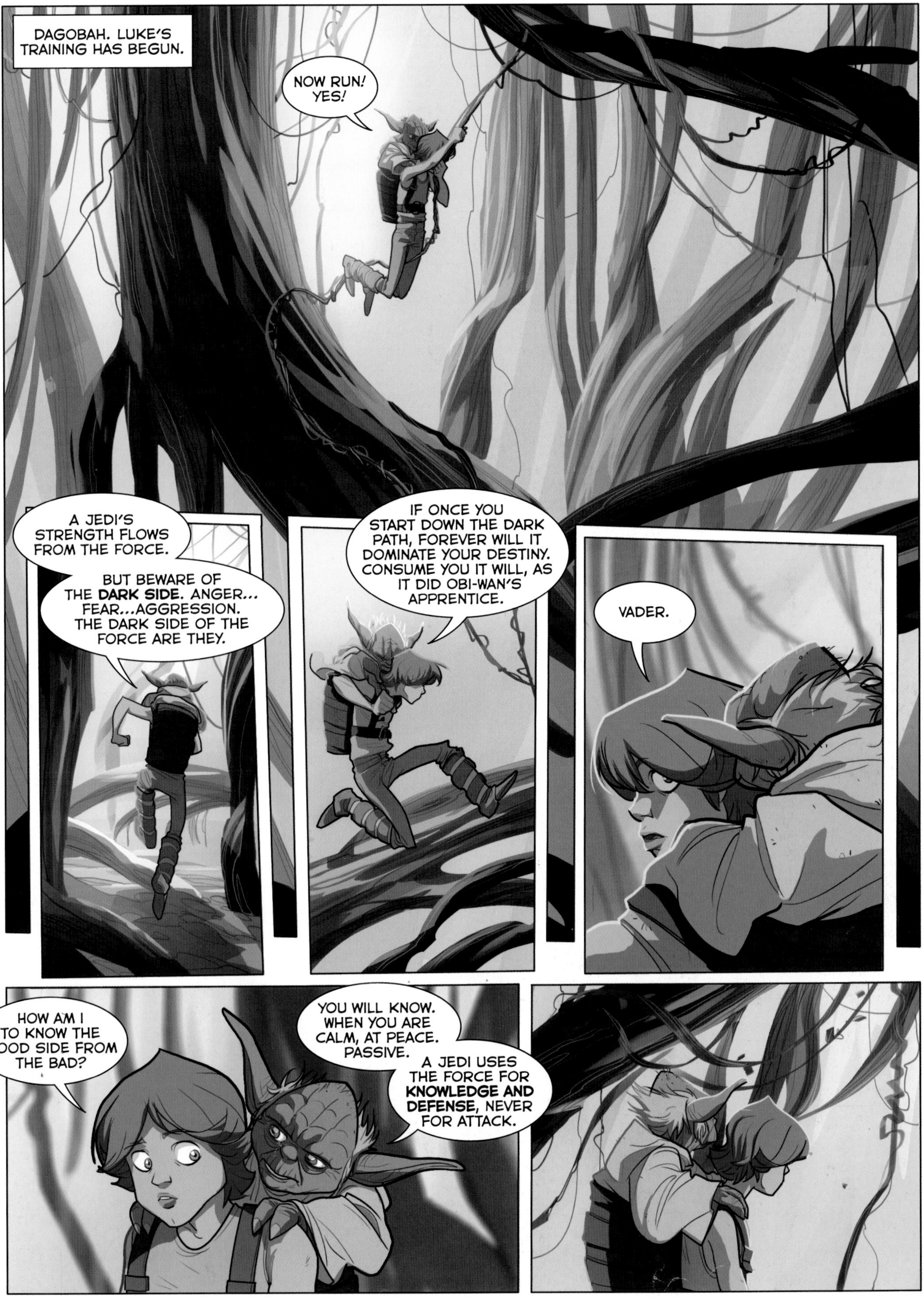
DAGOBAH. LUKE'S TRAINING HAS BEGUN.
NOW RUN! YES!
A JEDI'S STRENGTH FLOWS FROM THE FORCE.
BUT BEWARE OF THE **DARK SIDE**. ANGER... FEAR...AGGRESSION. THE DARK SIDE OF THE FORCE ARE THEY.
IF ONCE YOU START DOWN THE DARK PATH, FOREVER WILL IT DOMINATE YOUR DESTINY. CONSUME YOU IT WILL, AS IT DID OBI-WAN'S APPRENTICE.
VADER.
HOW AM I TO KNOW THE GOOD SIDE FROM THE BAD?
YOU WILL KNOW. WHEN YOU ARE CALM, AT PEACE. PASSIVE.
A JEDI USES THE FORCE FOR **KNOWLEDGE AND DEFENSE**, NEVER FOR ATTACK.

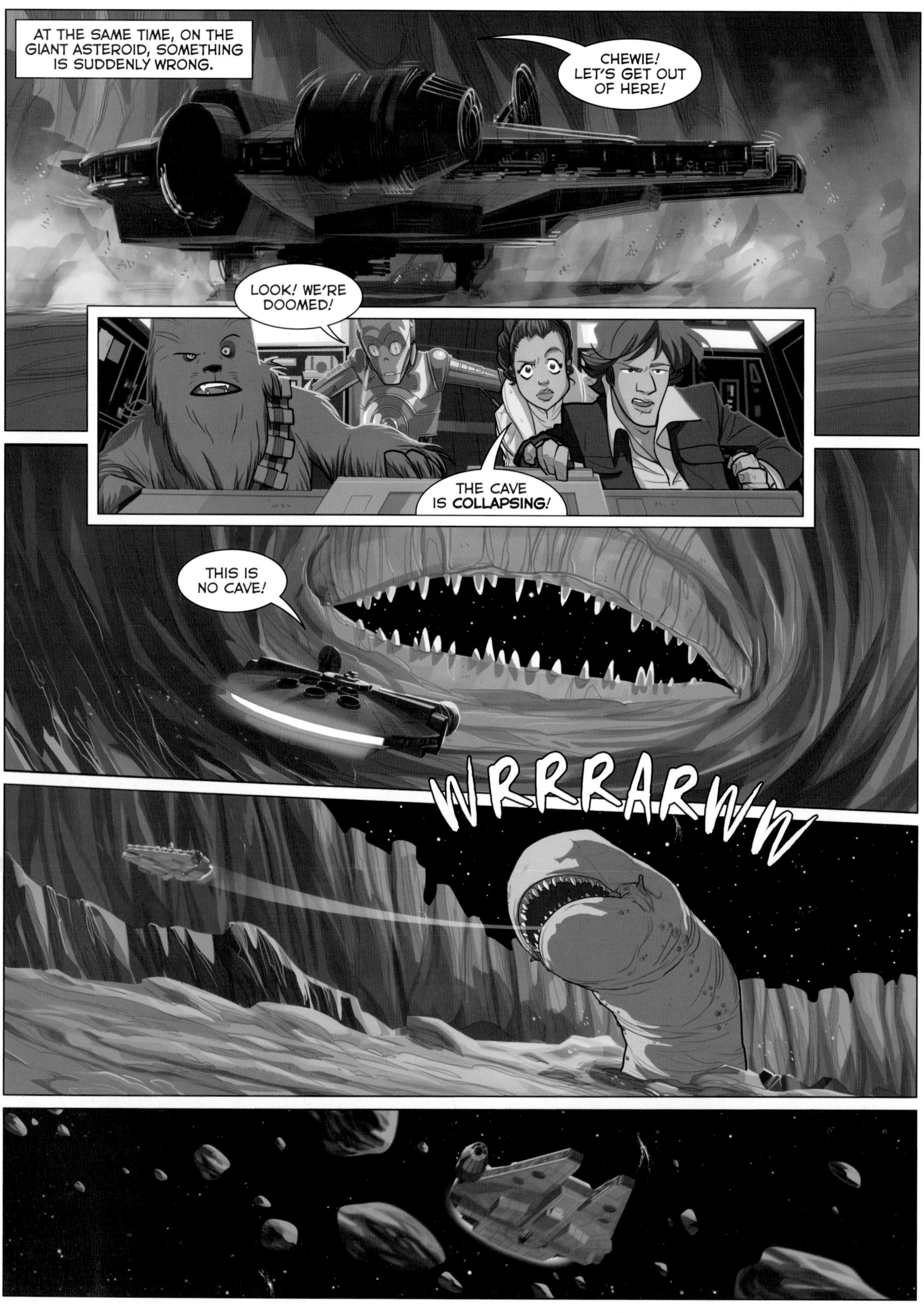
AT THE SAME TIME, ON THE GIANT ASTEROID, SOMETHING IS SUDDENLY WRONG.
CHEWIE! LET'S GET OUT OF HERE!
LOOK! WE'RE DOOMED!
THE CAVE IS **COLLAPSING**!
THIS IS NO CAVE!
WRRRARWW

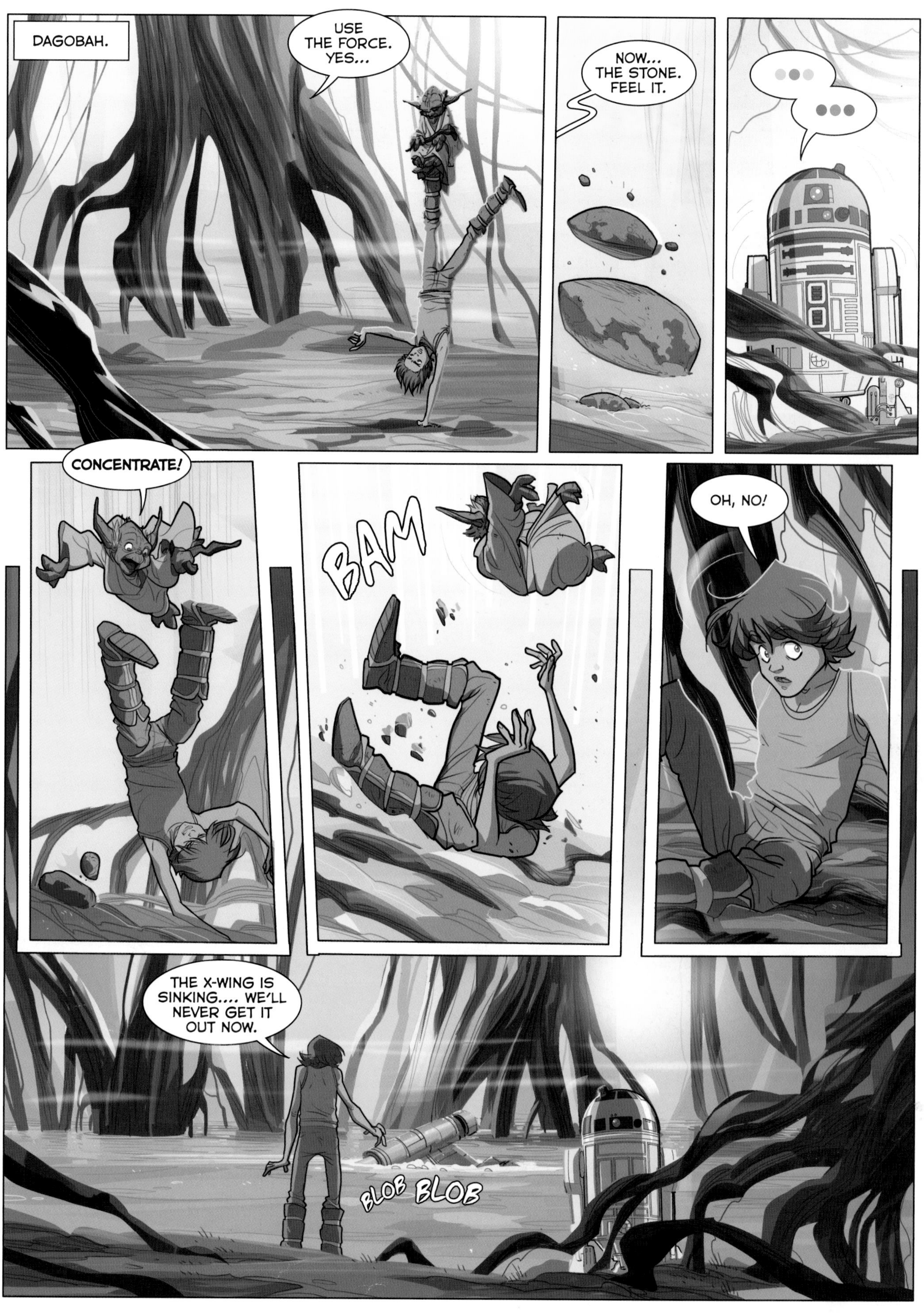
DAGOBAH.
USE THE FORCE. YES...
NOW... THE STONE. FEEL IT.
CONCENTRATE!
BAM
OH, NO!
THE X-WING IS SINKING.... WE'LL NEVER GET IT OUT NOW.
BLOB BLOB

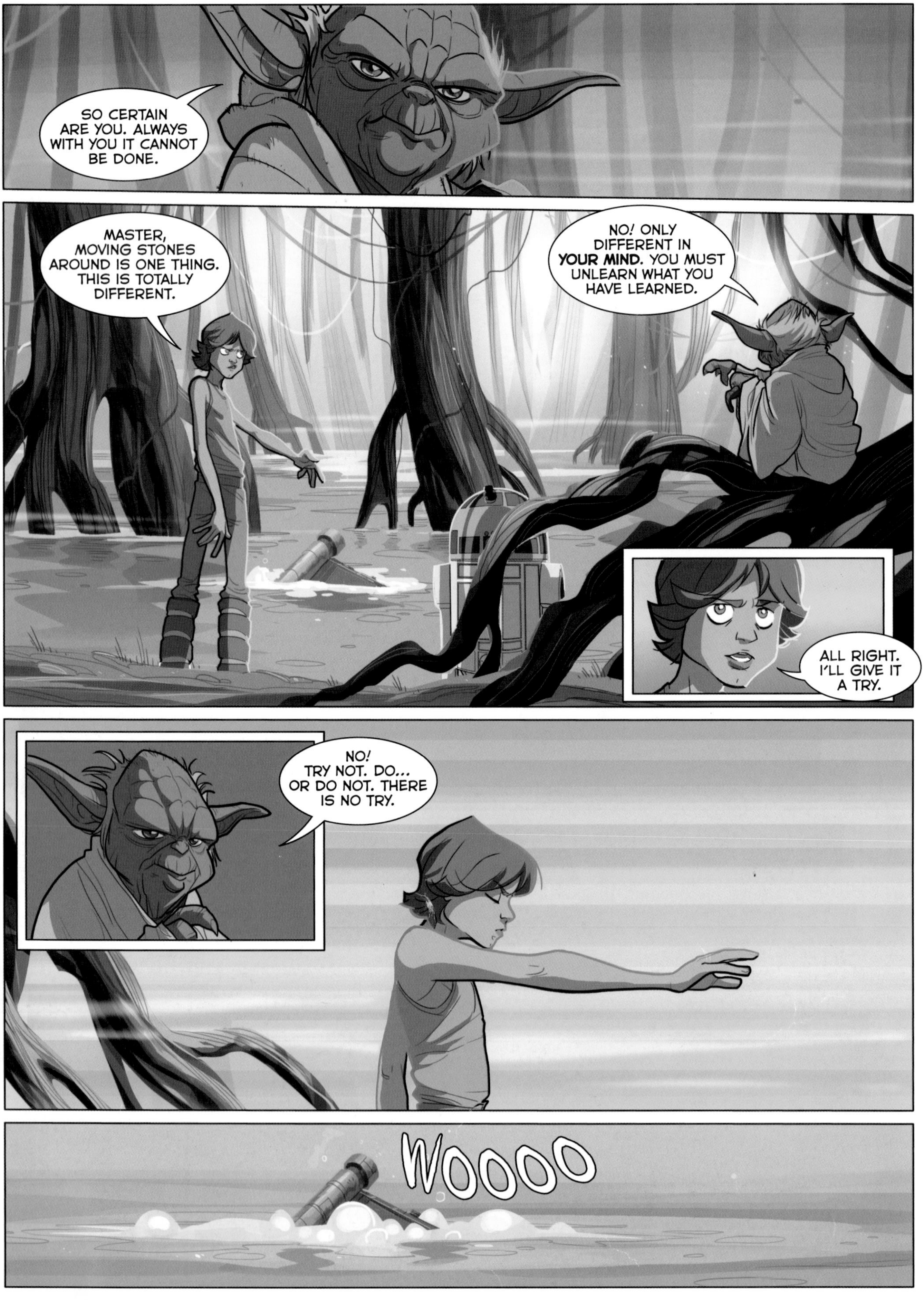
SO CERTAIN ARE YOU. ALWAYS WITH YOU IT CANNOT BE DONE.
MASTER, MOVING STONES AROUND IS ONE THING. THIS IS TOTALLY DIFFERENT.
NO! ONLY DIFFERENT IN **YOUR MIND**. YOU MUST UNLEARN WHAT YOU HAVE LEARNED.
ALL RIGHT. I'LL GIVE IT A TRY.
NO! TRY NOT. DO... OR DO NOT. THERE IS NO TRY.
WOOOO

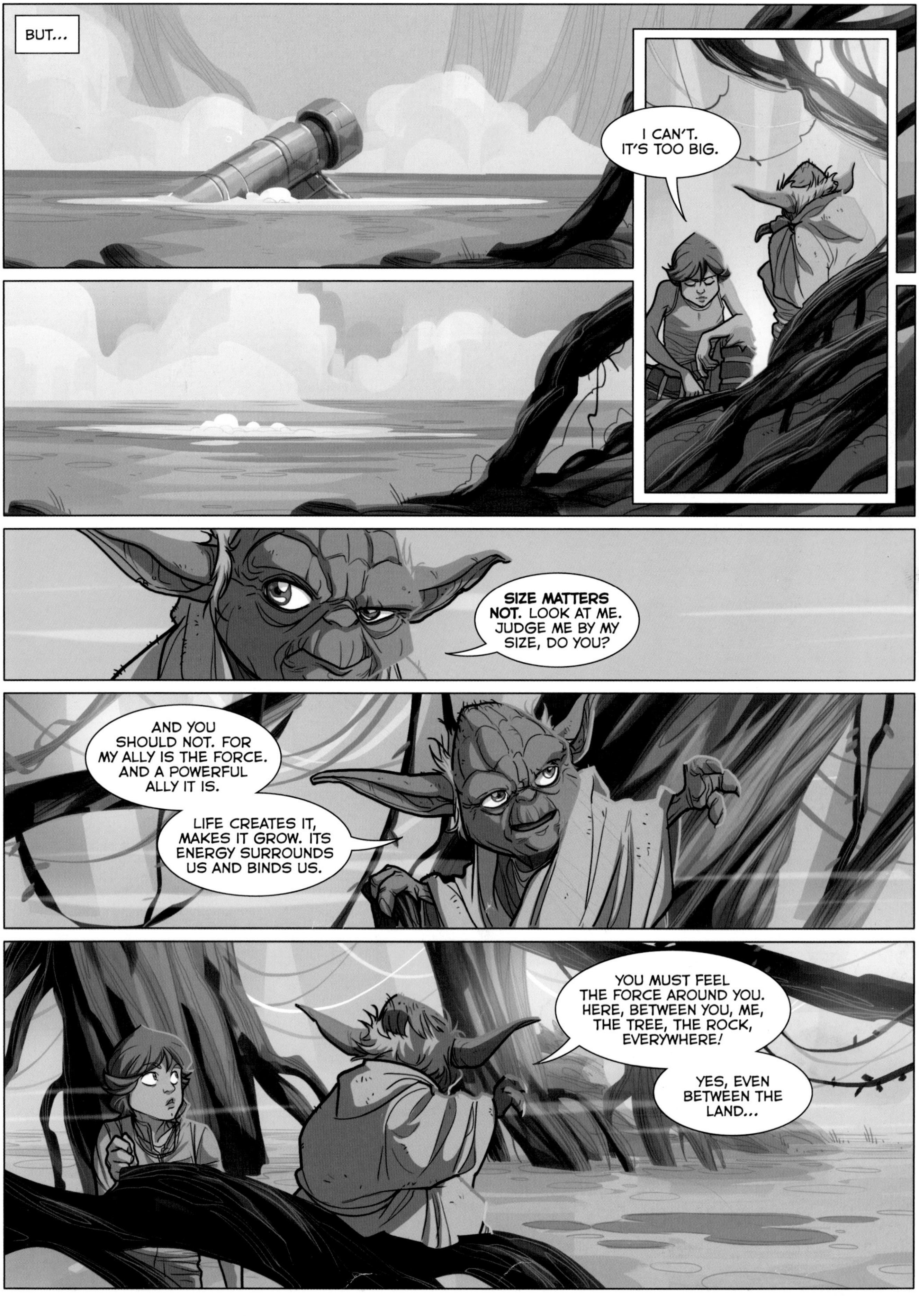
BUT...
I CAN'T. IT'S TOO BIG.
SIZE MATTERS NOT. LOOK AT ME. JUDGE ME BY MY SIZE, DO YOU?
AND YOU SHOULD NOT. FOR MY ALLY IS THE FORCE. AND A POWERFUL ALLY IT IS.
LIFE CREATES IT, MAKES IT GROW. ITS ENERGY SURROUNDS US AND BINDS US.
YOU MUST FEEL THE FORCE AROUND YOU. HERE, BETWEEN YOU, ME, THE TREE, THE ROCK, EVERYWHERE!
YES, EVEN BETWEEN THE LAND...

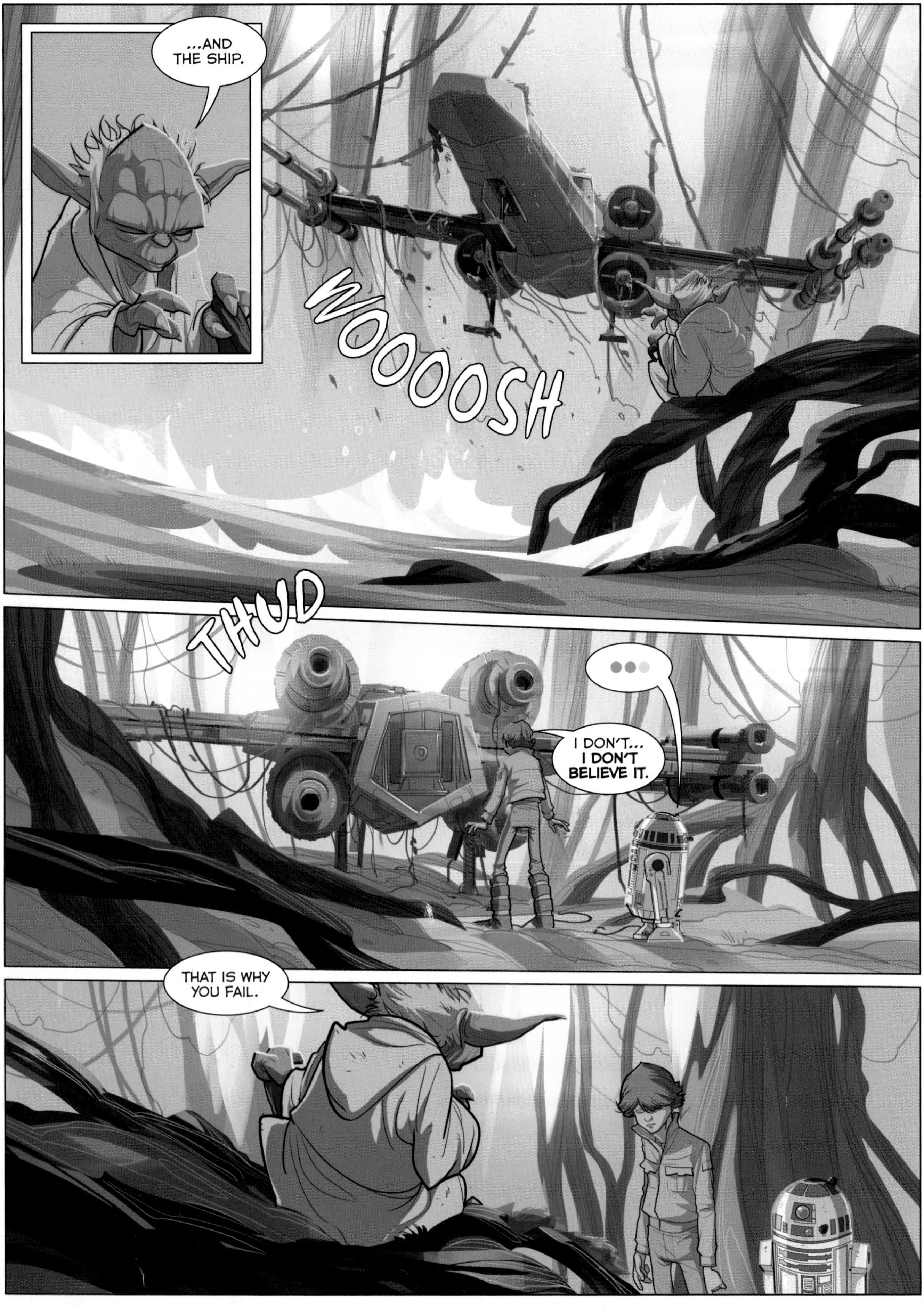
...AND THE SHIP.
WOOOOSH
THUD
...
I DON'T... I DON'T BELIEVE IT.
THAT IS WHY YOU FAIL.

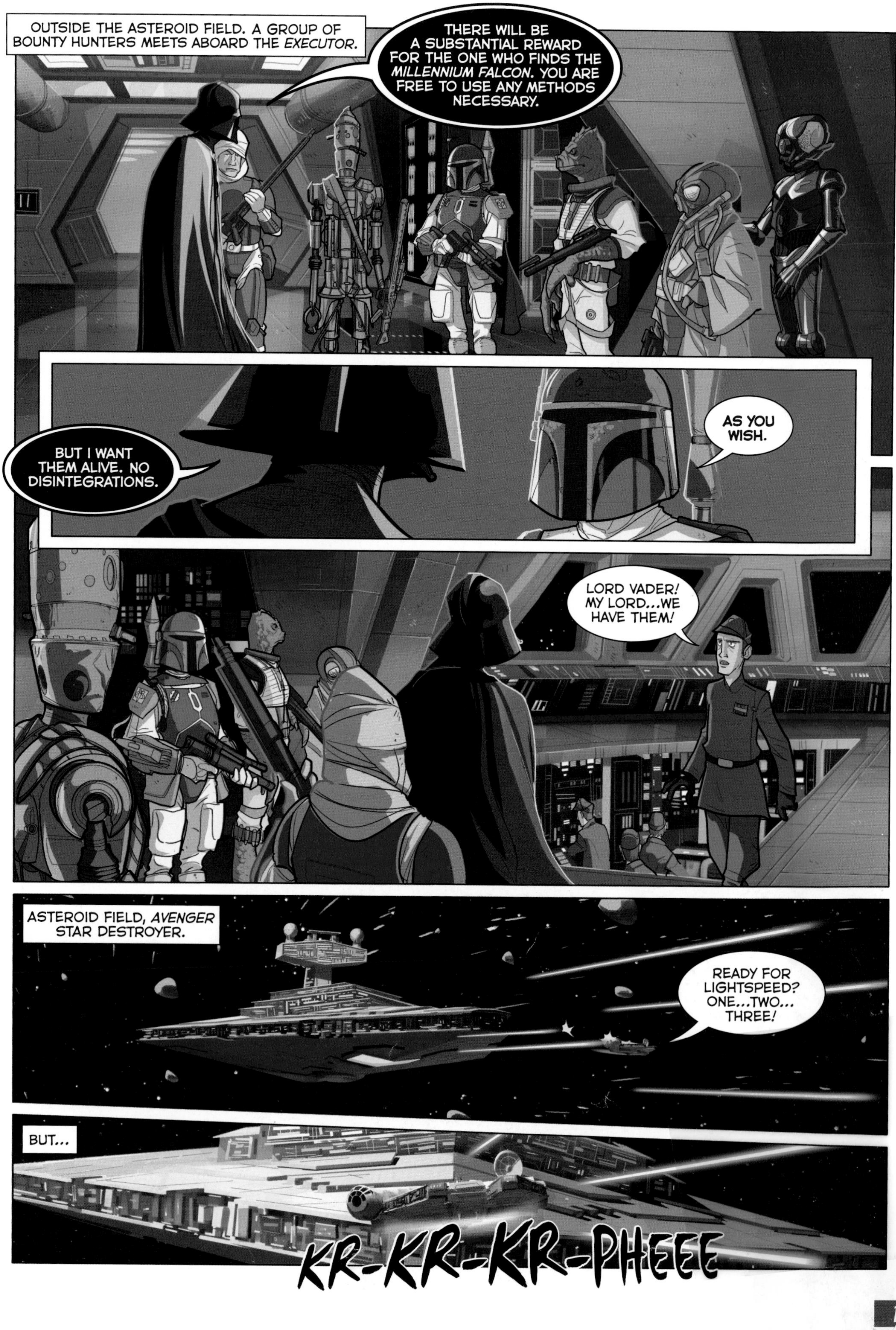
OUTSIDE THE ASTEROID FIELD. A GROUP OF BOUNTY HUNTERS MEETS ABOARD THE *EXECUTOR*.
THERE WILL BE A SUBSTANTIAL REWARD FOR THE ONE WHO FINDS THE *MILLENNIUM FALCON*. YOU ARE FREE TO USE ANY METHODS NECESSARY.
BUT I WANT THEM ALIVE. NO DISINTEGRATIONS.
AS YOU WISH.
LORD VADER! MY LORD...WE HAVE THEM!
ASTEROID FIELD, *AVENGER* STAR DESTROYER.
READY FOR LIGHTSPEED? ONE...TWO... THREE!
BUT...
KR-KR-KR-PHEEE

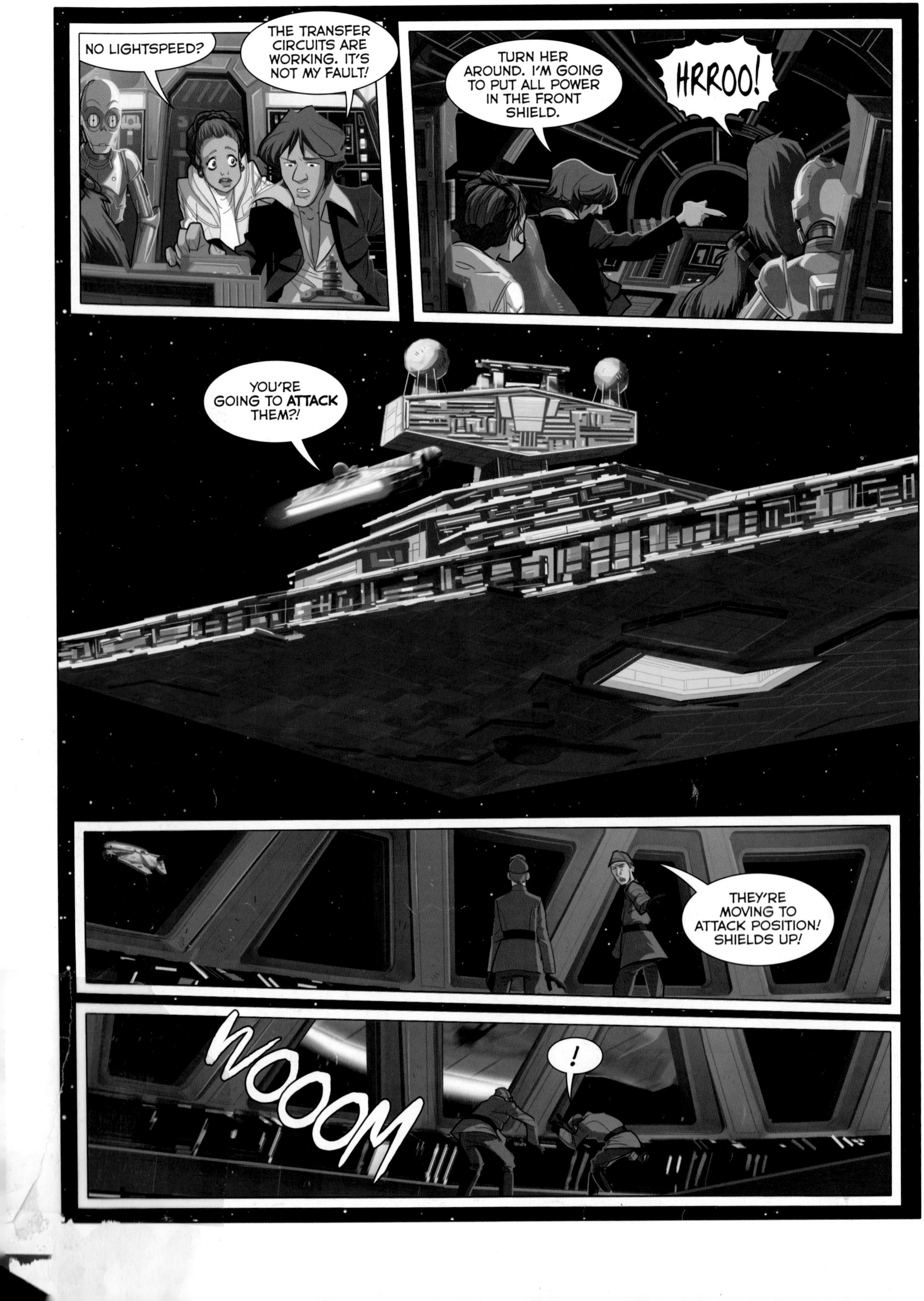
NO LIGHTSPEED?
THE TRANSFER CIRCUITS ARE WORKING. IT'S NOT MY FAULT!
TURN HER AROUND. I'M GOING TO PUT ALL POWER IN THE FRONT SHIELD.
HRROO!
YOU'RE GOING TO ATTACK THEM?!
THEY'RE MOVING TO ATTACK POSITION! SHIELDS UP!
WOOOM
!

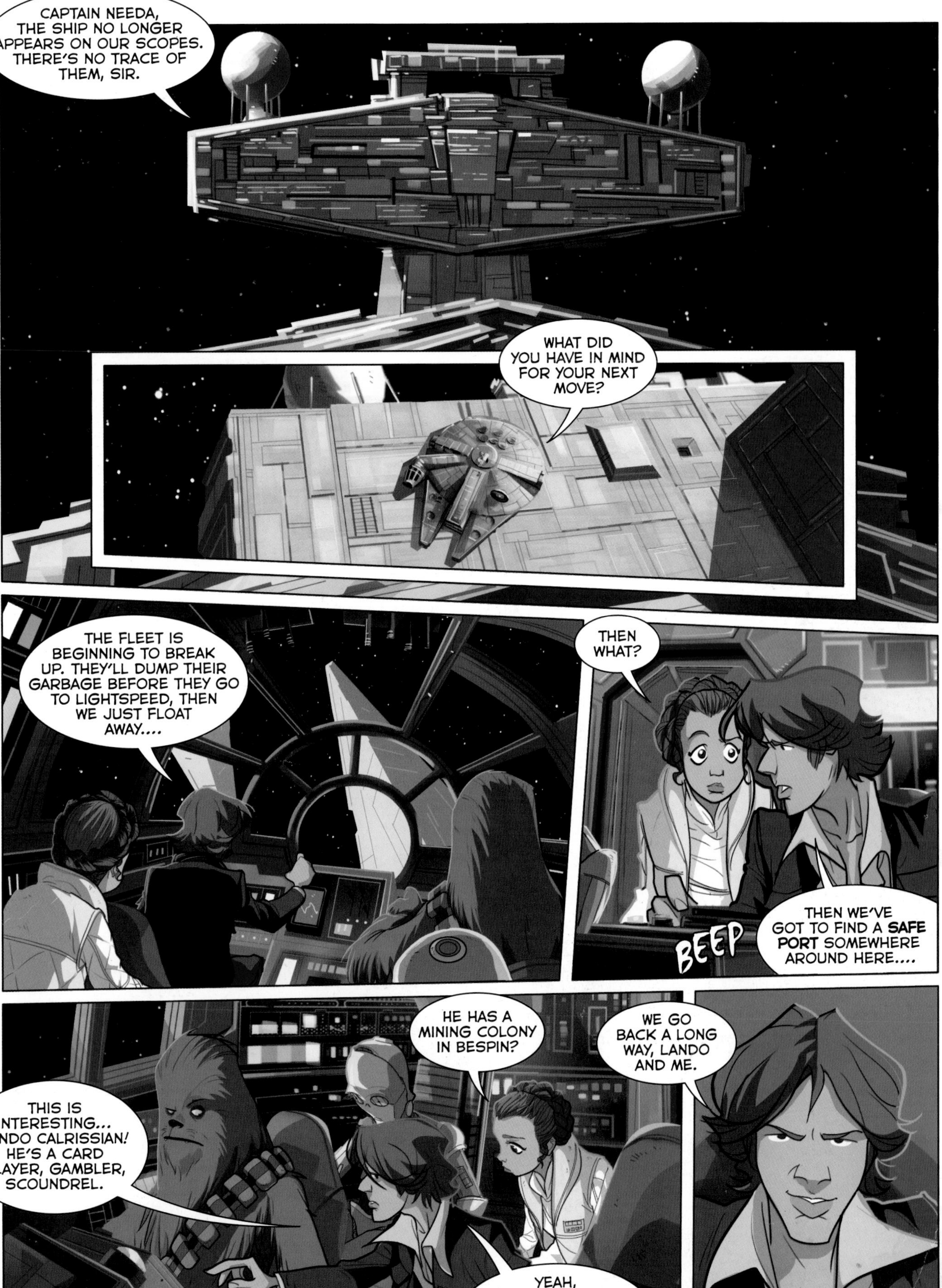
CAPTAIN NEEDA, THE SHIP NO LONGER APPEARS ON OUR SCOPES. THERE'S NO TRACE OF THEM, SIR.
WHAT DID YOU HAVE IN MIND FOR YOUR NEXT MOVE?
THE FLEET IS BEGINNING TO BREAK UP. THEY'LL DUMP THEIR GARBAGE BEFORE THEY GO TO LIGHTSPEED, THEN WE JUST FLOAT AWAY....
THEN WHAT?
THEN WE'VE GOT TO FIND A **SAFE PORT** SOMEWHERE AROUND HERE....
BEEP
THIS IS INTERESTING... LANDO CALRISSIAN! HE'S A CARD PLAYER, GAMBLER, SCOUNDREL.
HE HAS A MINING COLONY IN BESPIN?
YEAH, A TIBANNA GAS MINE. LANDO CONNED SOMEBODY OUT OF IT.
WE GO BACK A LONG WAY, LANDO AND ME.

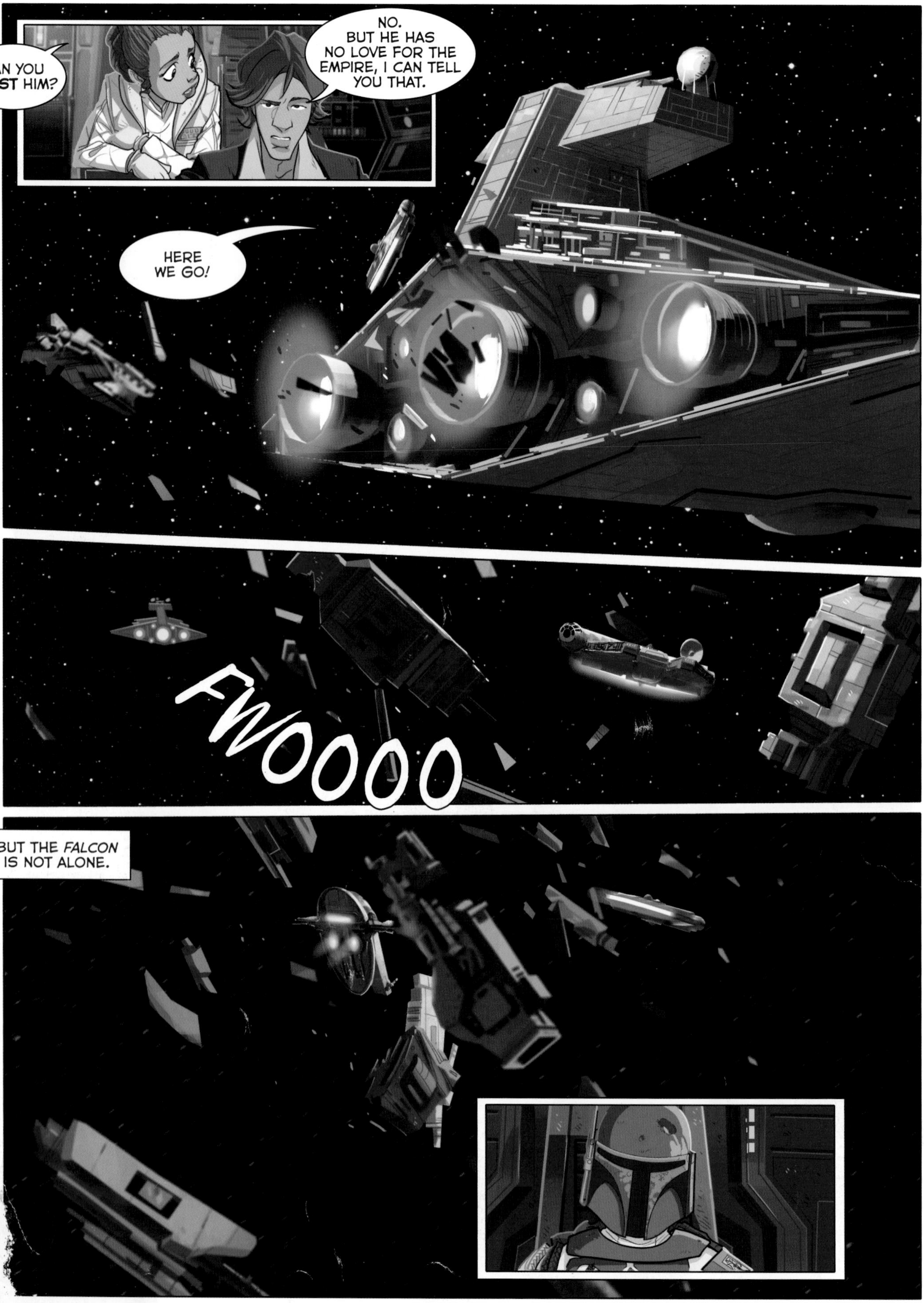
CAN YOU **TRUST** HIM?
NO. BUT HE HAS NO LOVE FOR THE EMPIRE, I CAN TELL YOU THAT.
HERE WE GO!
FWOOOO
BUT THE *FALCON* IS NOT ALONE.

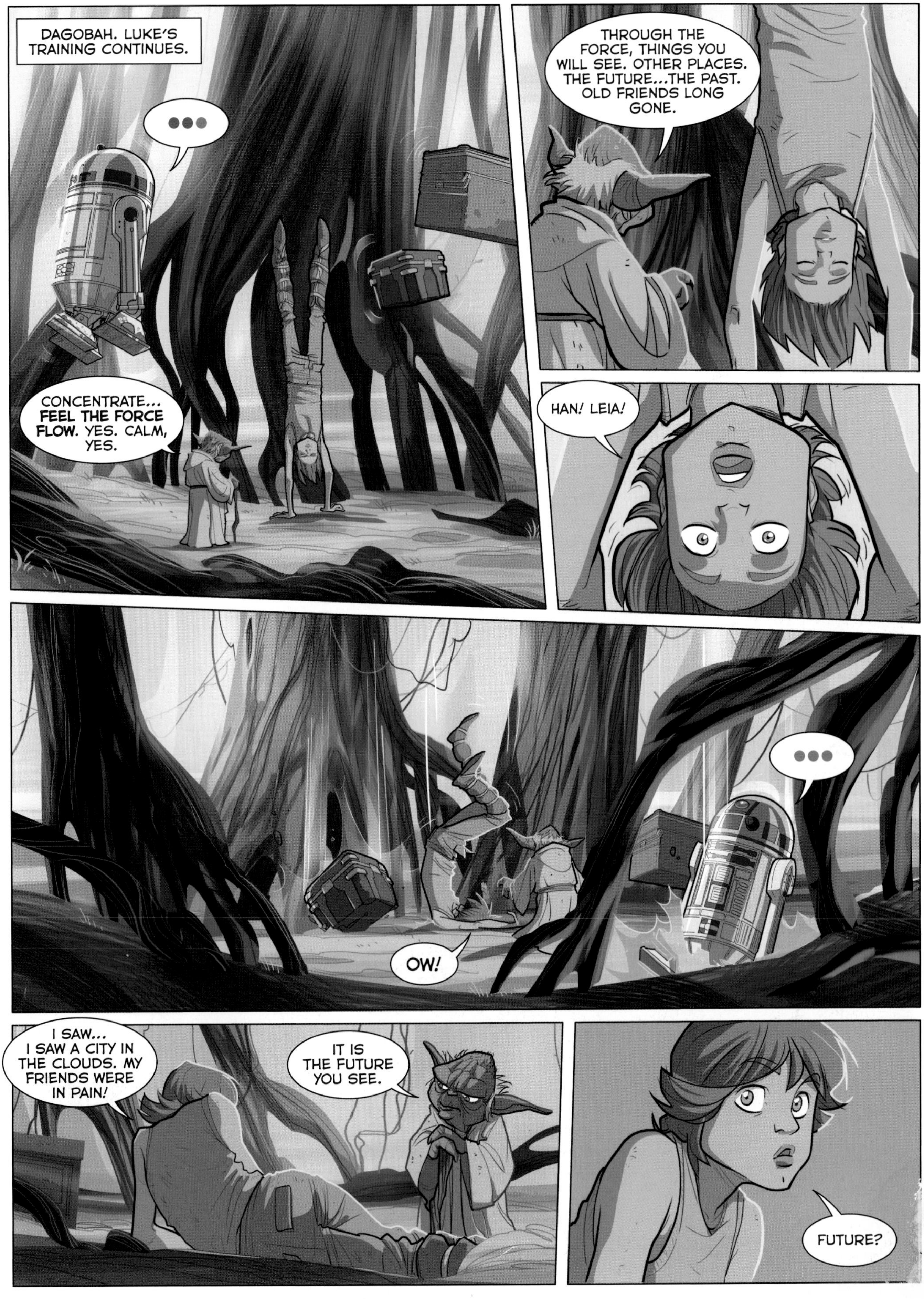

DAGOBAH. LUKE'S TRAINING CONTINUES.
CONCENTRATE... FEEL THE FORCE FLOW. YES. CALM, YES.
THROUGH THE FORCE, THINGS YOU WILL SEE. OTHER PLACES. THE FUTURE...THE PAST. OLD FRIENDS LONG GONE.
HAN! LEIA!
OW!
I SAW... I SAW A CITY IN THE CLOUDS. MY FRIENDS WERE IN PAIN!
IT IS THE FUTURE YOU SEE.
FUTURE?

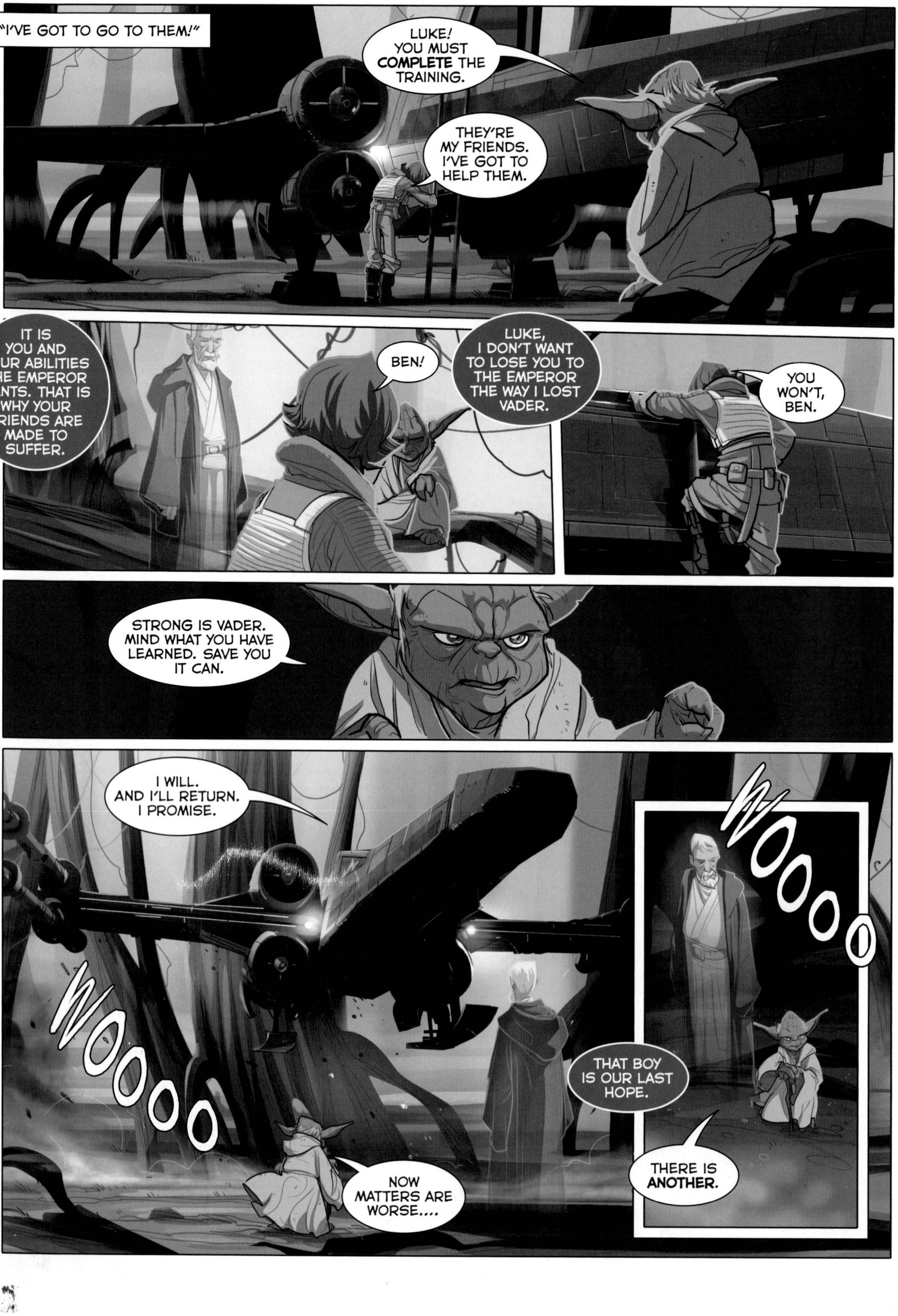

"I'VE GOT TO GO TO THEM!"
LUKE! YOU MUST **COMPLETE** THE TRAINING.
THEY'RE MY FRIENDS. I'VE GOT TO HELP THEM.
IT IS YOU AND YOUR ABILITIES THE EMPEROR WANTS. THAT IS WHY YOUR FRIENDS ARE MADE TO SUFFER.
BEN!
LUKE, I DON'T WANT TO LOSE YOU TO THE EMPEROR THE WAY I LOST VADER.
YOU WON'T, BEN.
STRONG IS VADER. MIND WHAT YOU HAVE LEARNED. SAVE YOU IT CAN.
I WILL. AND I'LL RETURN. I PROMISE.
WOOOO
WOOOO
NOW MATTERS ARE WORSE....
THAT BOY IS OUR LAST HOPE.
THERE IS **ANOTHER**.

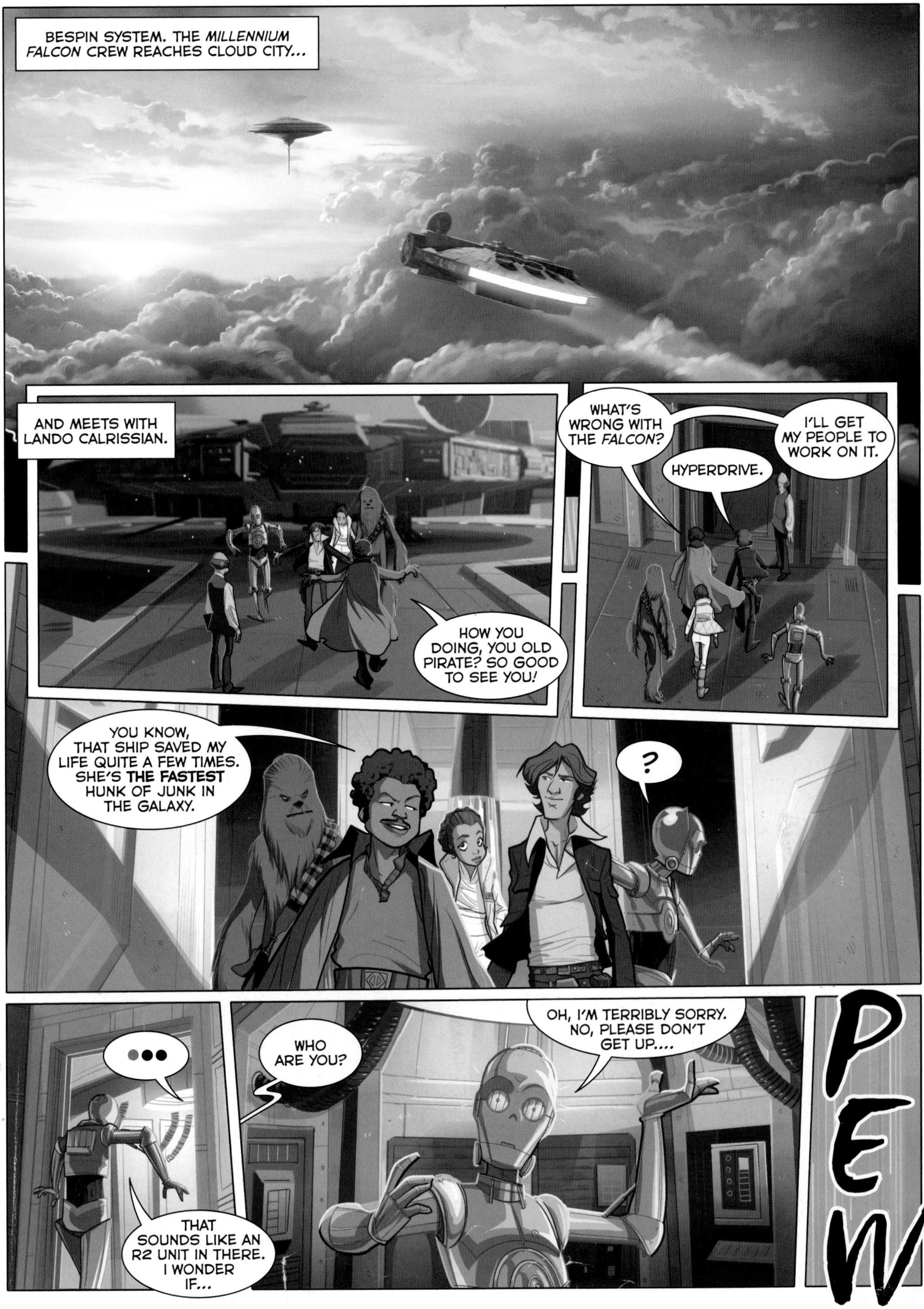
BESPIN SYSTEM. THE MILLENNIUM FALCON CREW REACHES CLOUD CITY...
AND MEETS WITH LANDO CALRISSIAN.
HOW YOU DOING, YOU OLD PIRATE? SO GOOD TO SEE YOU!
WHAT'S WRONG WITH THE FALCON?
HYPERDRIVE.
I'LL GET MY PEOPLE TO WORK ON IT.
YOU KNOW, THAT SHIP SAVED MY LIFE QUITE A FEW TIMES. SHE'S THE FASTEST HUNK OF JUNK IN THE GALAXY.
?
•••
THAT SOUNDS LIKE AN R2 UNIT IN THERE. I WONDER IF...
WHO ARE YOU?
OH, I'M TERRIBLY SORRY. NO, PLEASE DON'T GET UP....
PEW

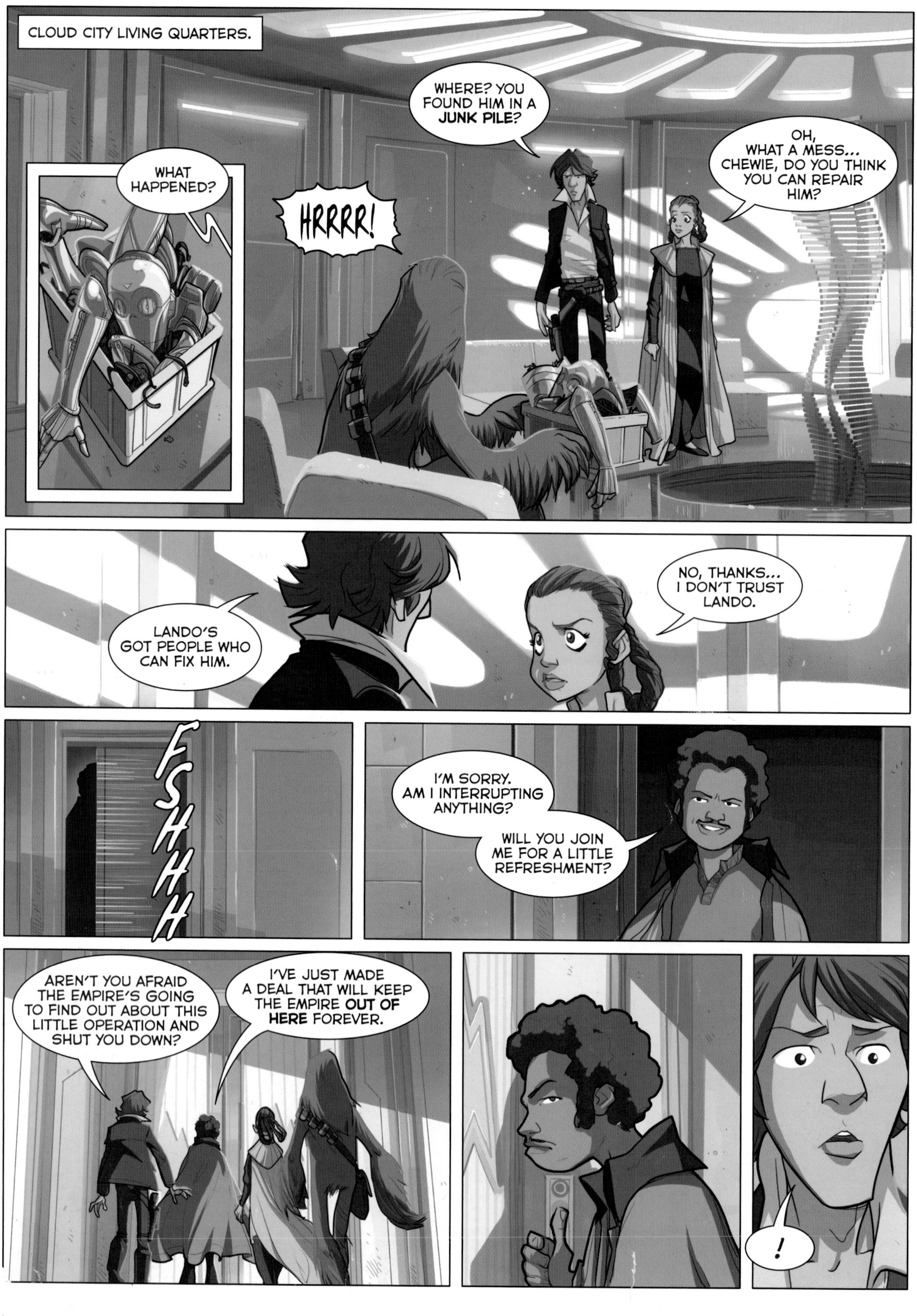

CLOUD CITY LIVING QUARTERS.
WHAT HAPPENED?
HRRRR!
WHERE? YOU FOUND HIM IN A **JUNK PILE**?
OH, WHAT A MESS... CHEWIE, DO YOU THINK YOU CAN REPAIR HIM?
LANDO'S GOT PEOPLE WHO CAN FIX HIM.
NO, THANKS... I DON'T TRUST LANDO.
FSHHHH
I'M SORRY. AM I INTERRUPTING ANYTHING?
WILL YOU JOIN ME FOR A LITTLE REFRESHMENT?
AREN'T YOU AFRAID THE EMPIRE'S GOING TO FIND OUT ABOUT THIS LITTLE OPERATION AND SHUT YOU DOWN?
I'VE JUST MADE A DEAL THAT WILL KEEP THE EMPIRE **OUT OF HERE** FOREVER.
!

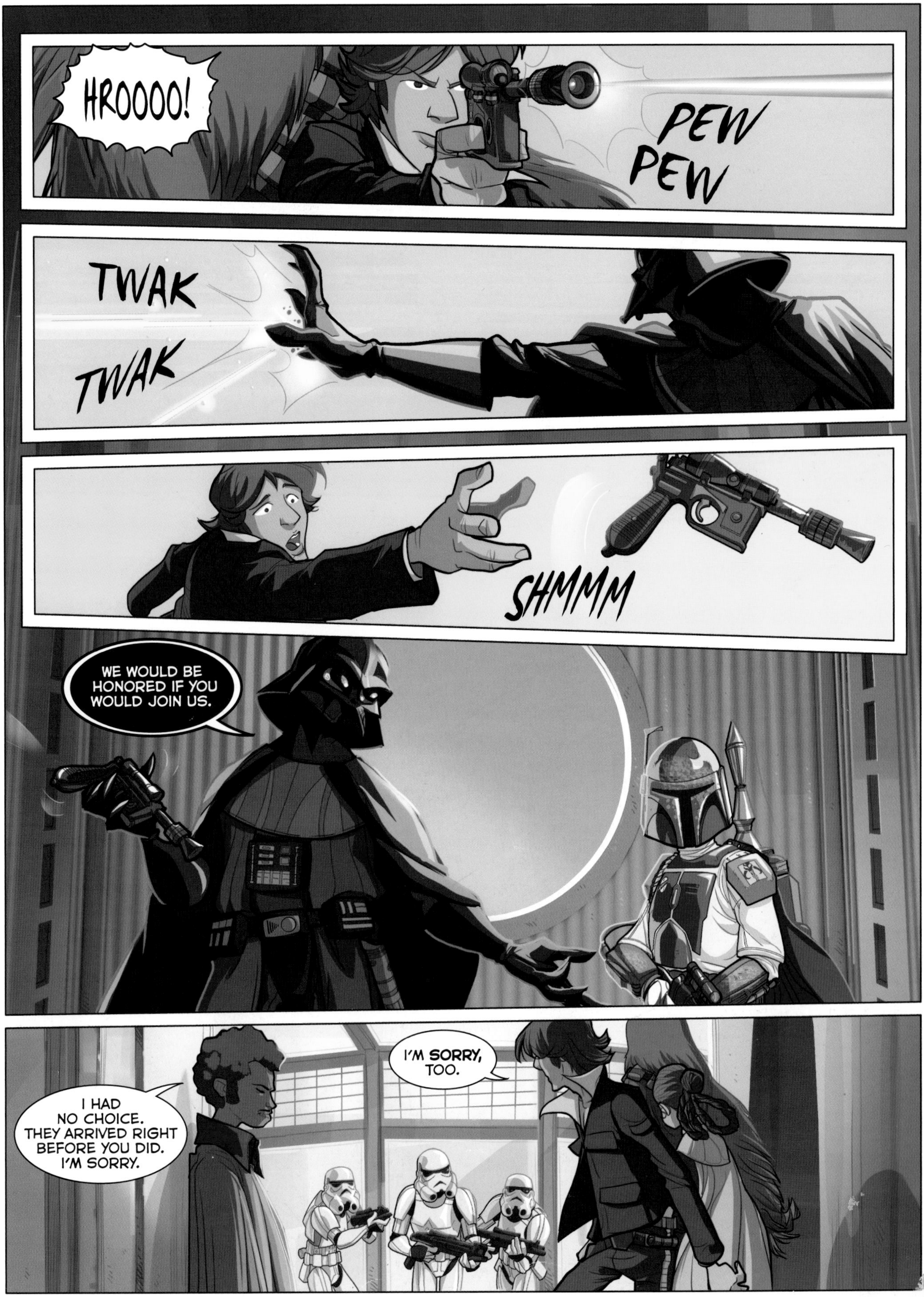
HROOOO!
PEW PEW
TWAK
TWAK
SHMMM
WE WOULD BE HONORED IF YOU WOULD JOIN US.
I HAD NO CHOICE. THEY ARRIVED RIGHT BEFORE YOU DID. I'M SORRY.
I'M SORRY, TOO.

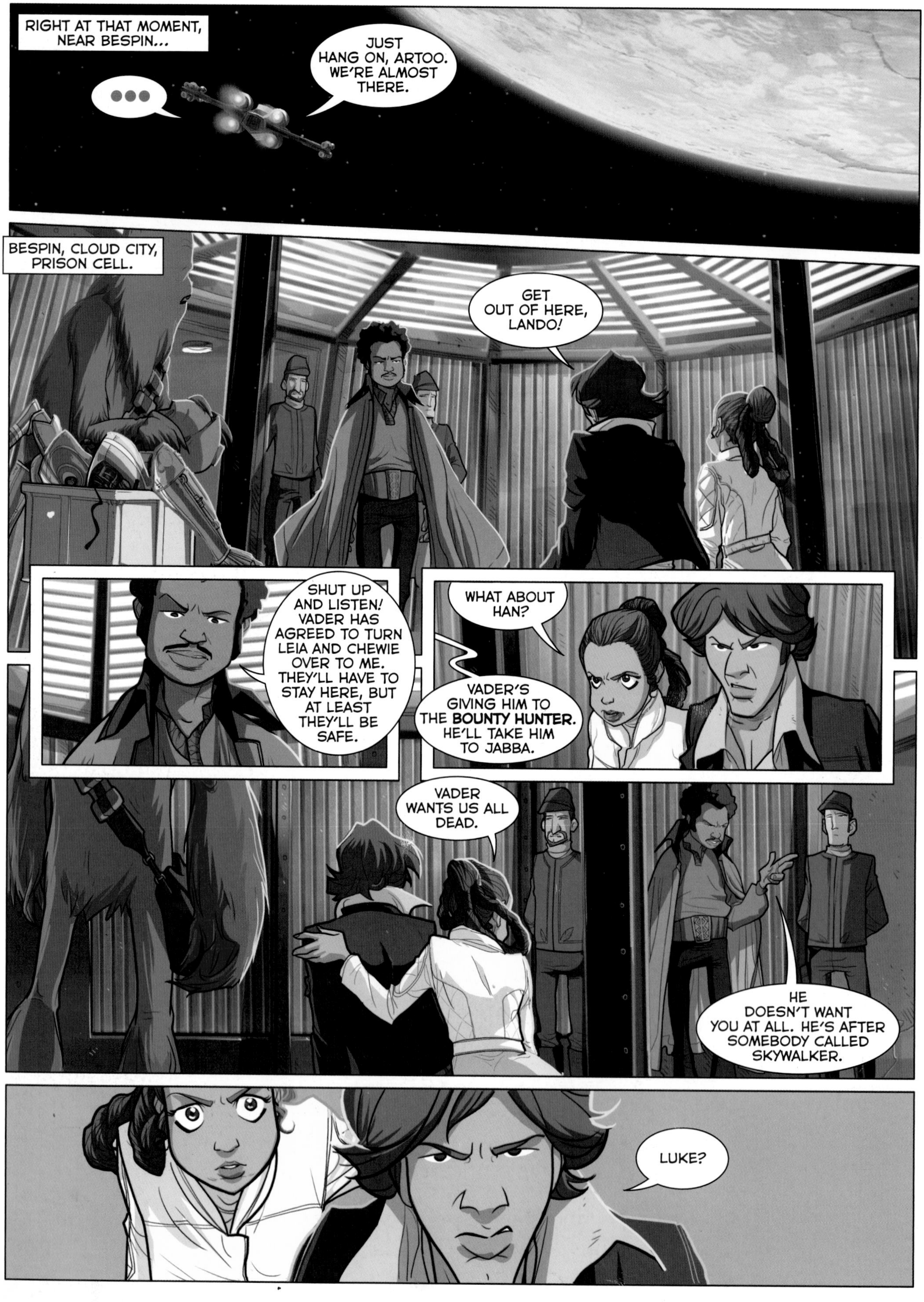
RIGHT AT THAT MOMENT, NEAR BESPIN...
•••
JUST HANG ON, ARTOO. WE'RE ALMOST THERE.
BESPIN, CLOUD CITY, PRISON CELL.
GET OUT OF HERE, LANDO!
SHUT UP AND LISTEN! VADER HAS AGREED TO TURN LEIA AND CHEWIE OVER TO ME. THEY'LL HAVE TO STAY HERE, BUT AT LEAST THEY'LL BE SAFE.
WHAT ABOUT HAN?
VADER'S GIVING HIM TO THE **BOUNTY HUNTER**. HE'LL TAKE HIM TO JABBA.
VADER WANTS US ALL DEAD.
HE DOESN'T WANT YOU AT ALL. HE'S AFTER SOMEBODY CALLED SKYWALKER.
LUKE?

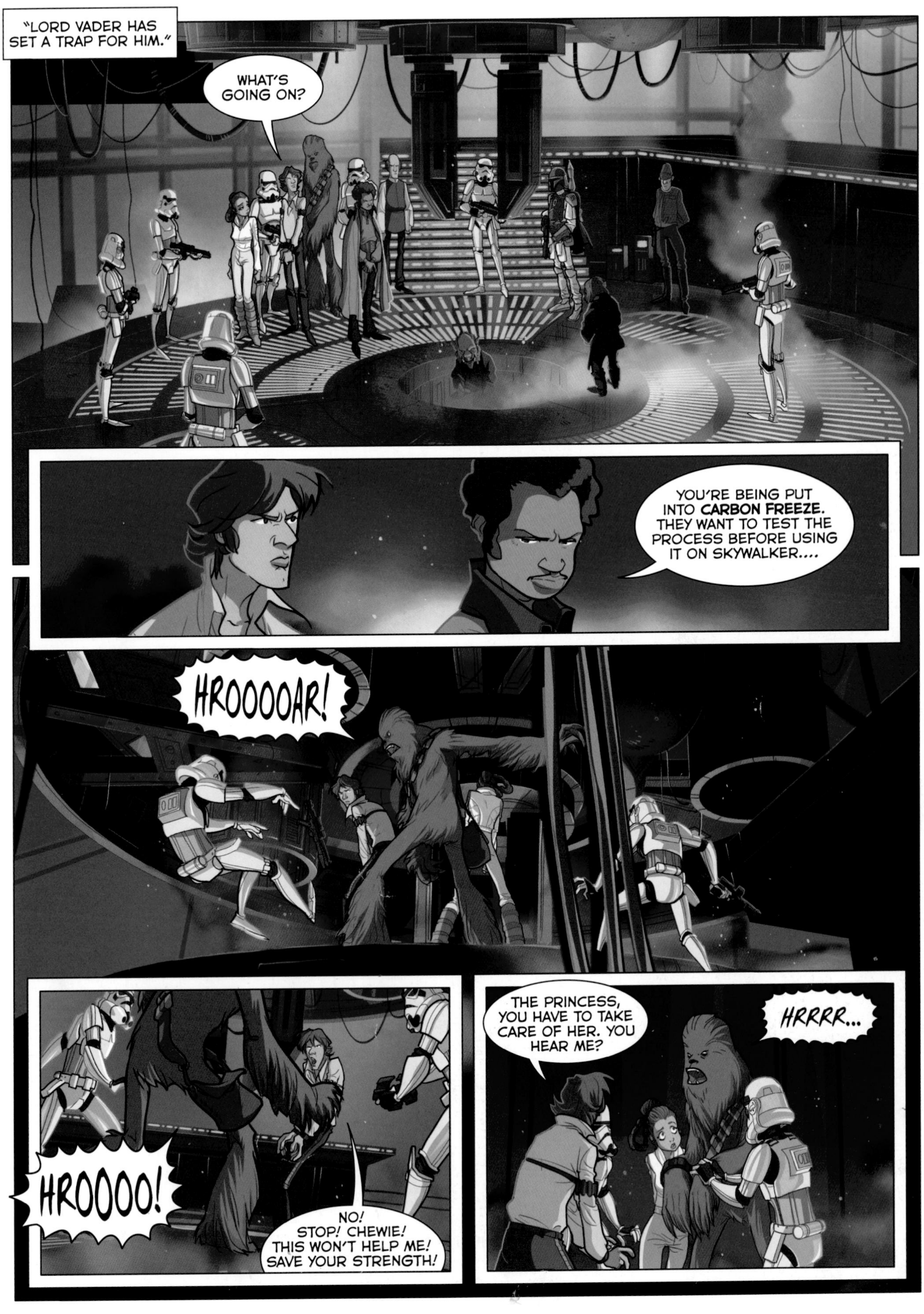

"LORD VADER HAS SET A TRAP FOR HIM."
WHAT'S GOING ON?
YOU'RE BEING PUT INTO **CARBON FREEZE.** THEY WANT TO TEST THE PROCESS BEFORE USING IT ON SKYWALKER....
HROOOOAR!
HROOOO!
NO! STOP! CHEWIE! THIS WON'T HELP ME! SAVE YOUR STRENGTH!
THE PRINCESS, YOU HAVE TO TAKE CARE OF HER. YOU HEAR ME?
HRRRR...

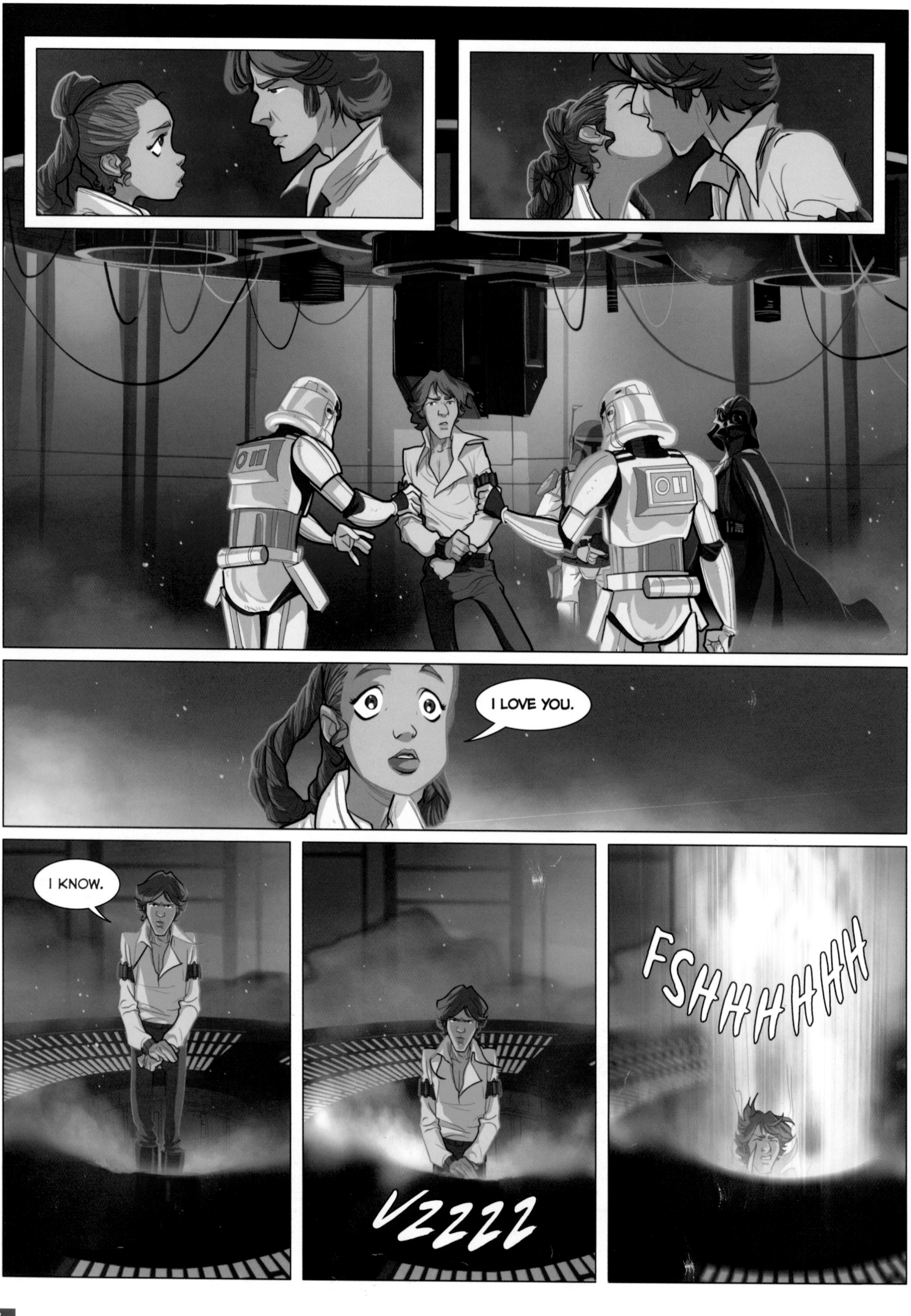
I LOVE YOU.
I KNOW.
VZZZZ
FSHHHHHHH

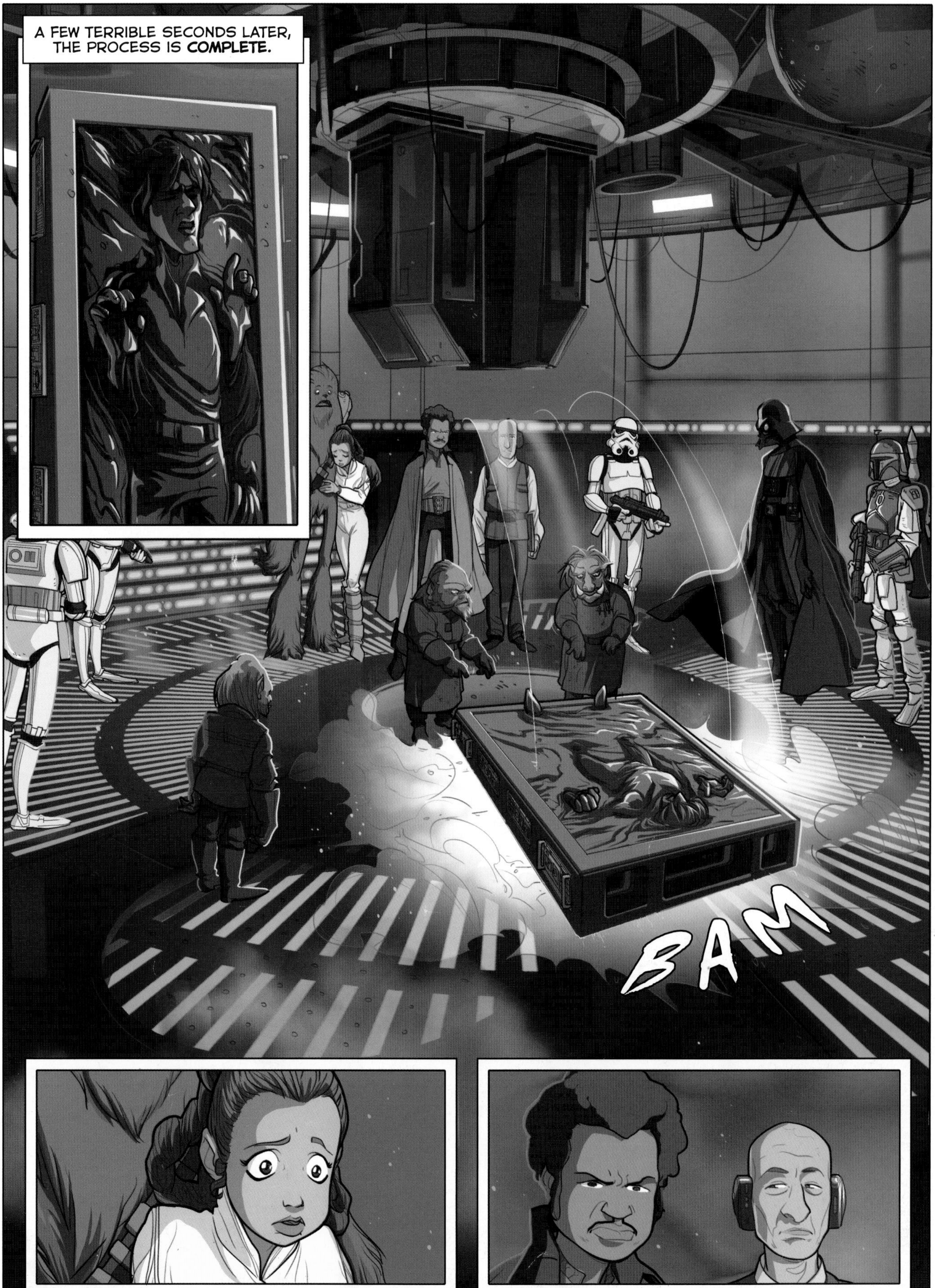
A FEW TERRIBLE SECONDS LATER, THE PROCESS IS COMPLETE.
BAM

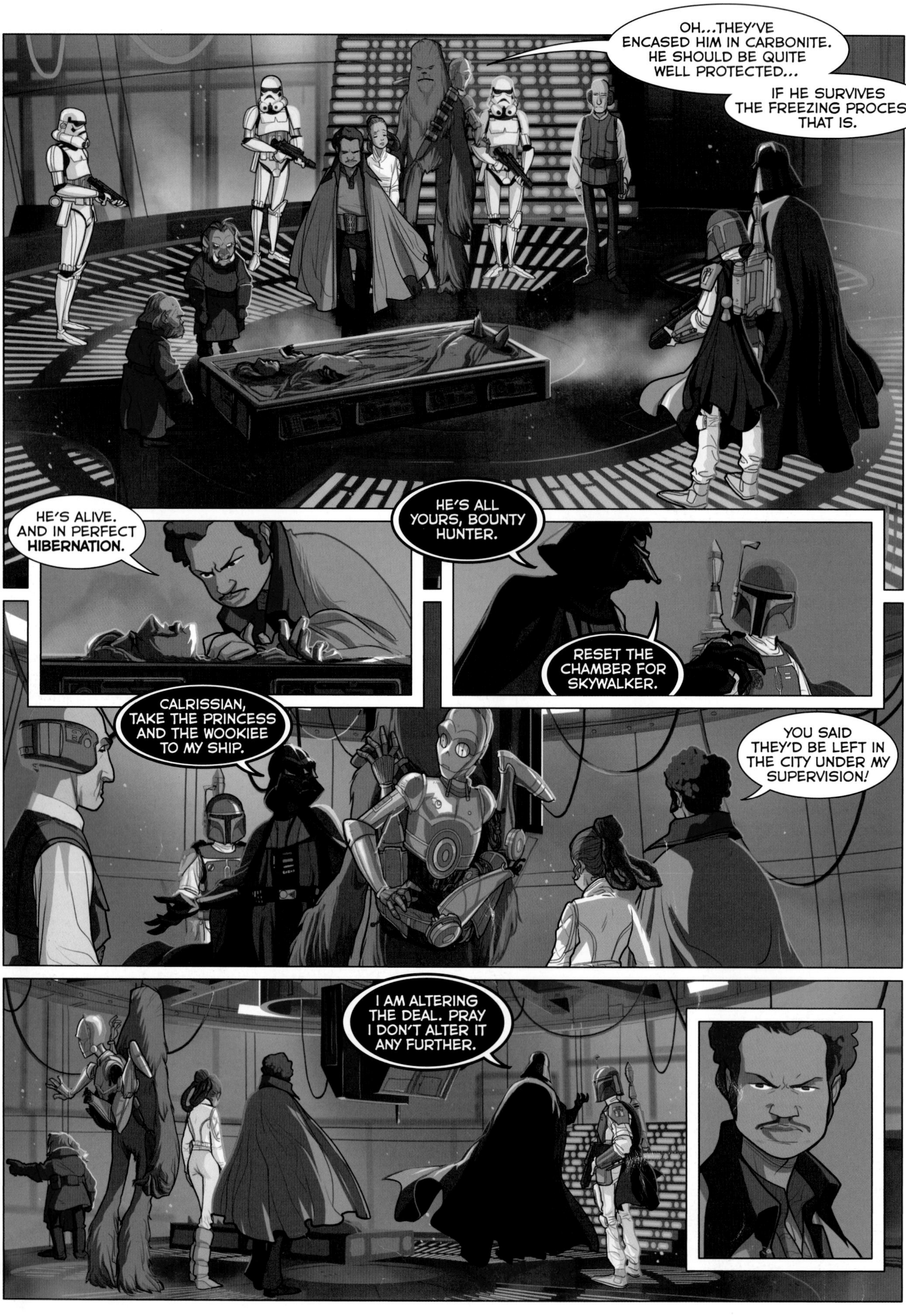

OH...THEY'VE ENCASED HIM IN CARBONITE. HE SHOULD BE QUITE WELL PROTECTED...
IF HE SURVIVES THE FREEZING PROCESS, THAT IS.
HE'S ALIVE. AND IN PERFECT HIBERNATION.
HE'S ALL YOURS, BOUNTY HUNTER.
RESET THE CHAMBER FOR SKYWALKER.
CALRISSIAN, TAKE THE PRINCESS AND THE WOOKIEE TO MY SHIP.
YOU SAID THEY'D BE LEFT IN THE CITY UNDER MY SUPERVISION!
I AM ALTERING THE DEAL. PRAY I DON'T ALTER IT ANY FURTHER.

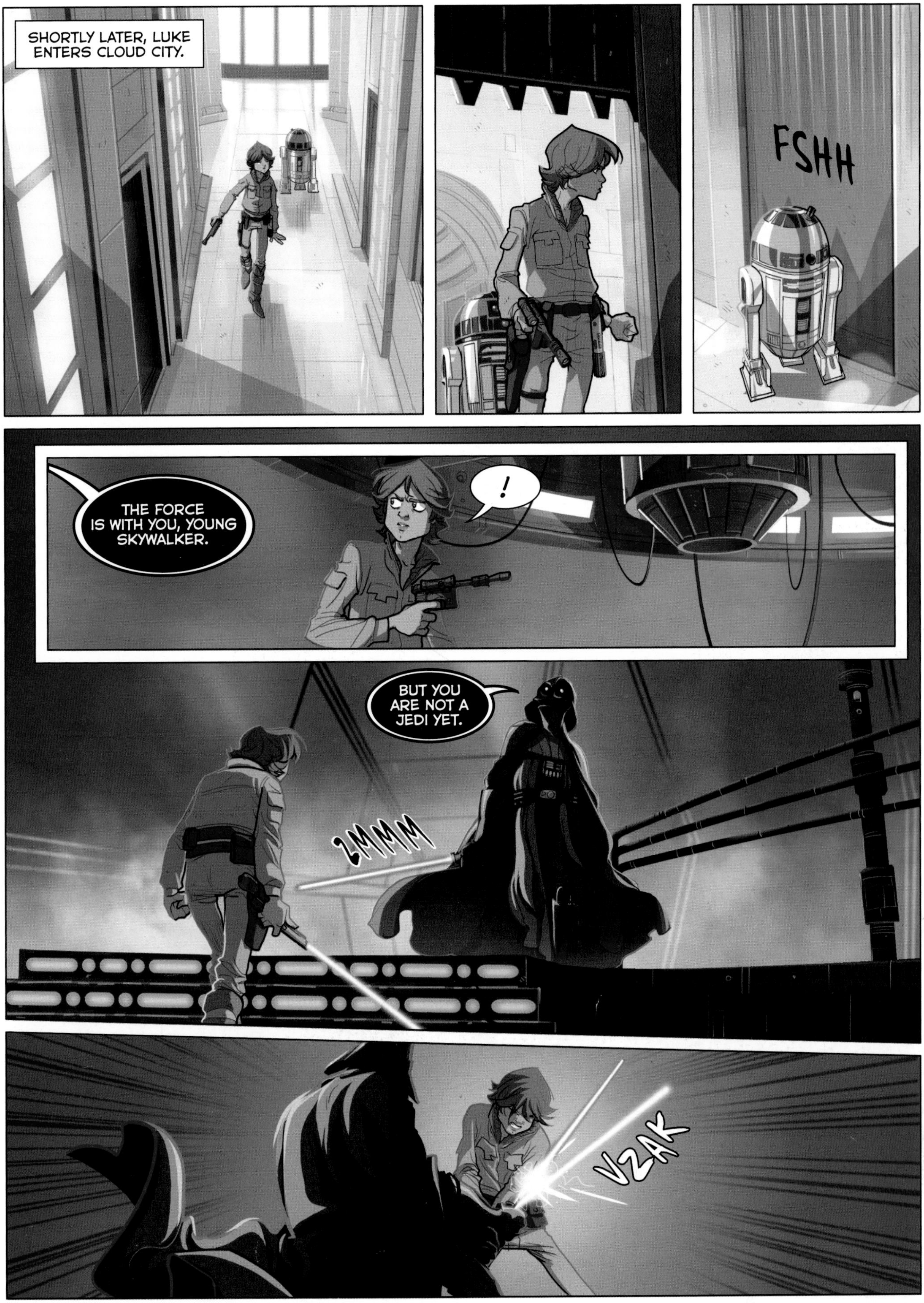

SHORTLY LATER, LUKE ENTERS CLOUD CITY.
FSHH
THE FORCE IS WITH YOU, YOUNG SKYWALKER.
!
BUT YOU ARE NOT A JEDI YET.
ZMMM
VZAK

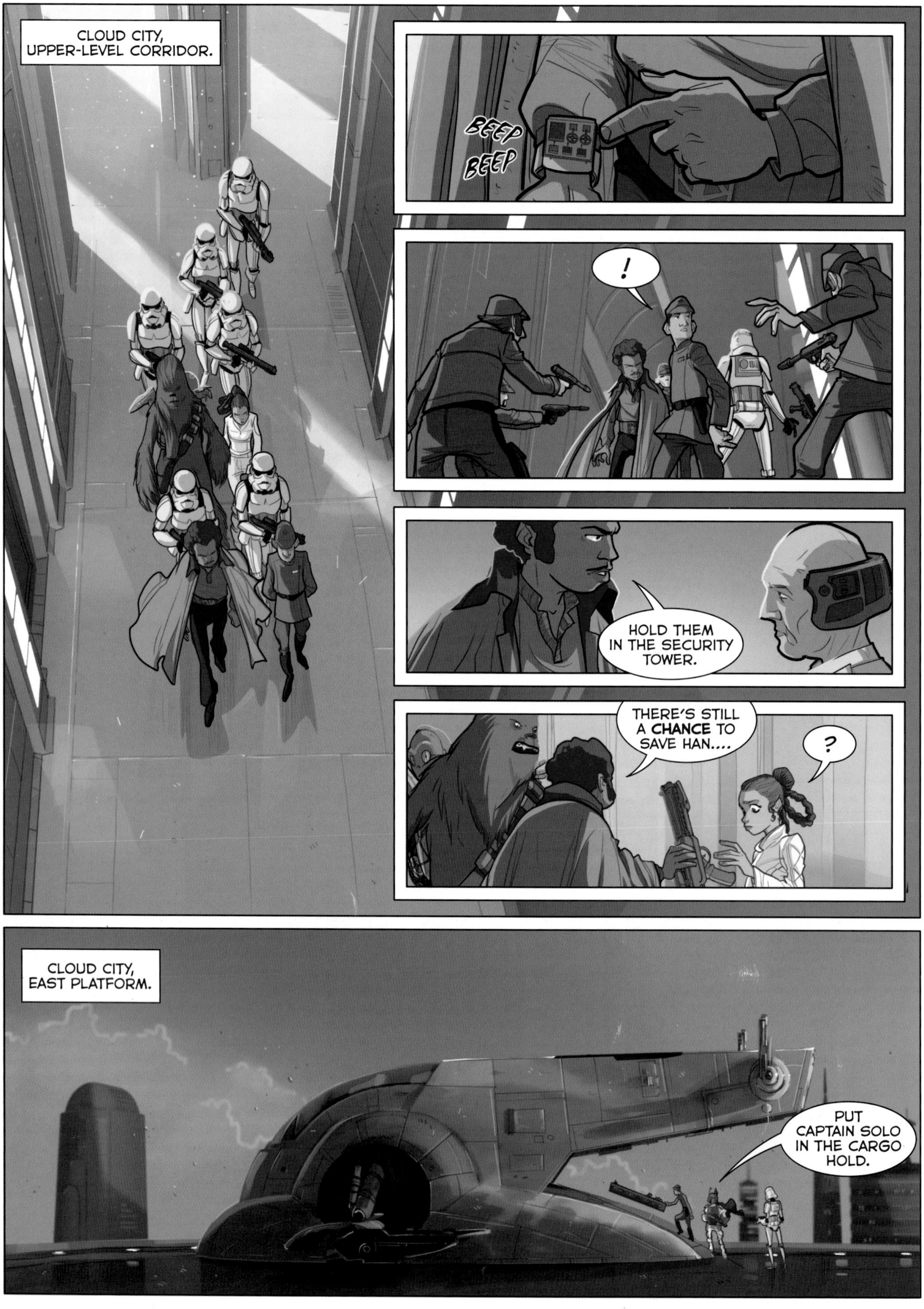
CLOUD CITY, UPPER-LEVEL CORRIDOR.
BEEP BEEP
!
HOLD THEM IN THE SECURITY TOWER.
THERE'S STILL A **CHANCE** TO SAVE HAN....
?
CLOUD CITY, EAST PLATFORM.
PUT CAPTAIN SOLO IN THE CARGO HOLD.

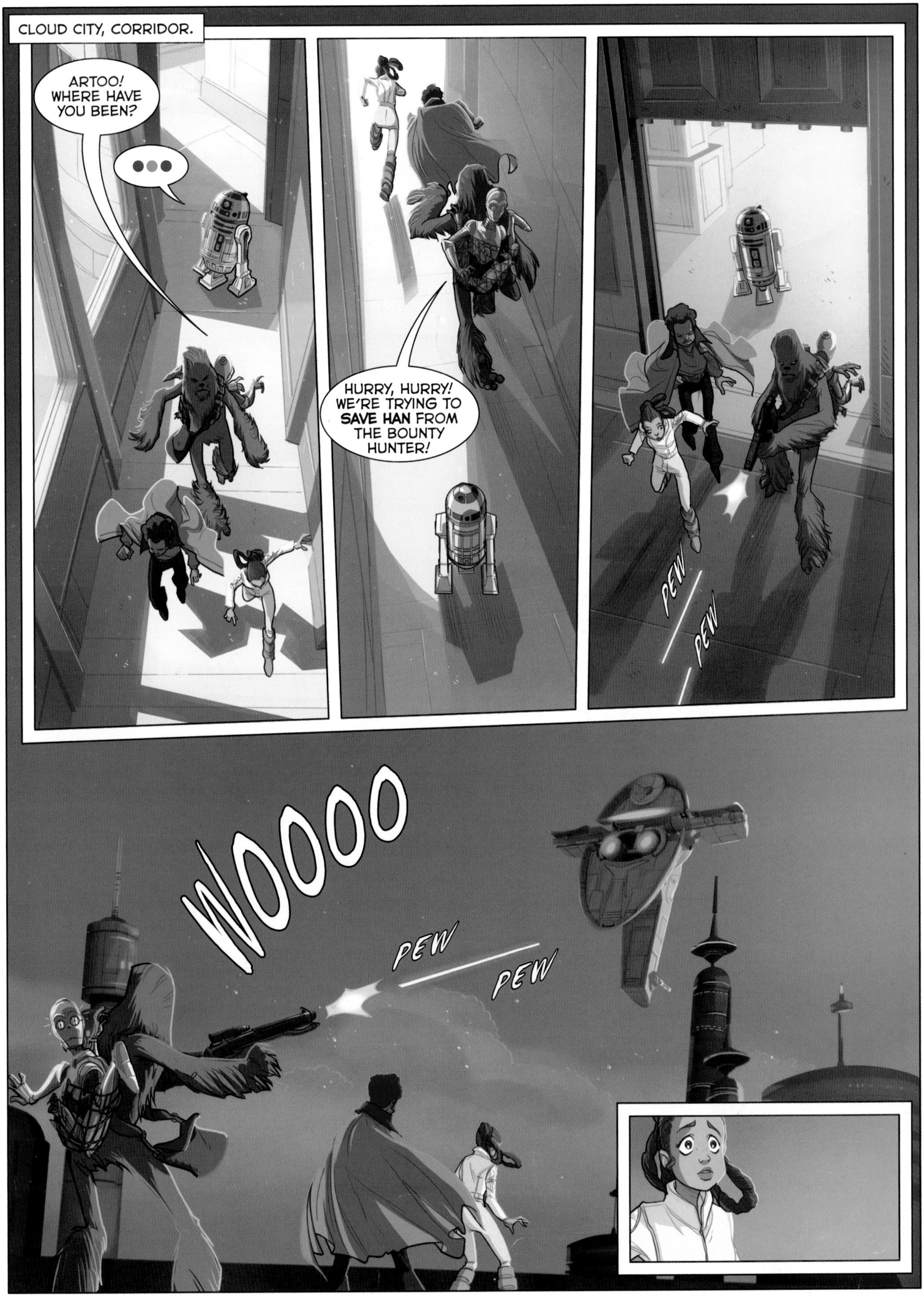
CLOUD CITY, CORRIDOR.
ARTOO! WHERE HAVE YOU BEEN?
HURRY, HURRY! WE'RE TRYING TO **SAVE HAN** FROM THE BOUNTY HUNTER!
PEW
PEW
WOOOO
PEW
PEW

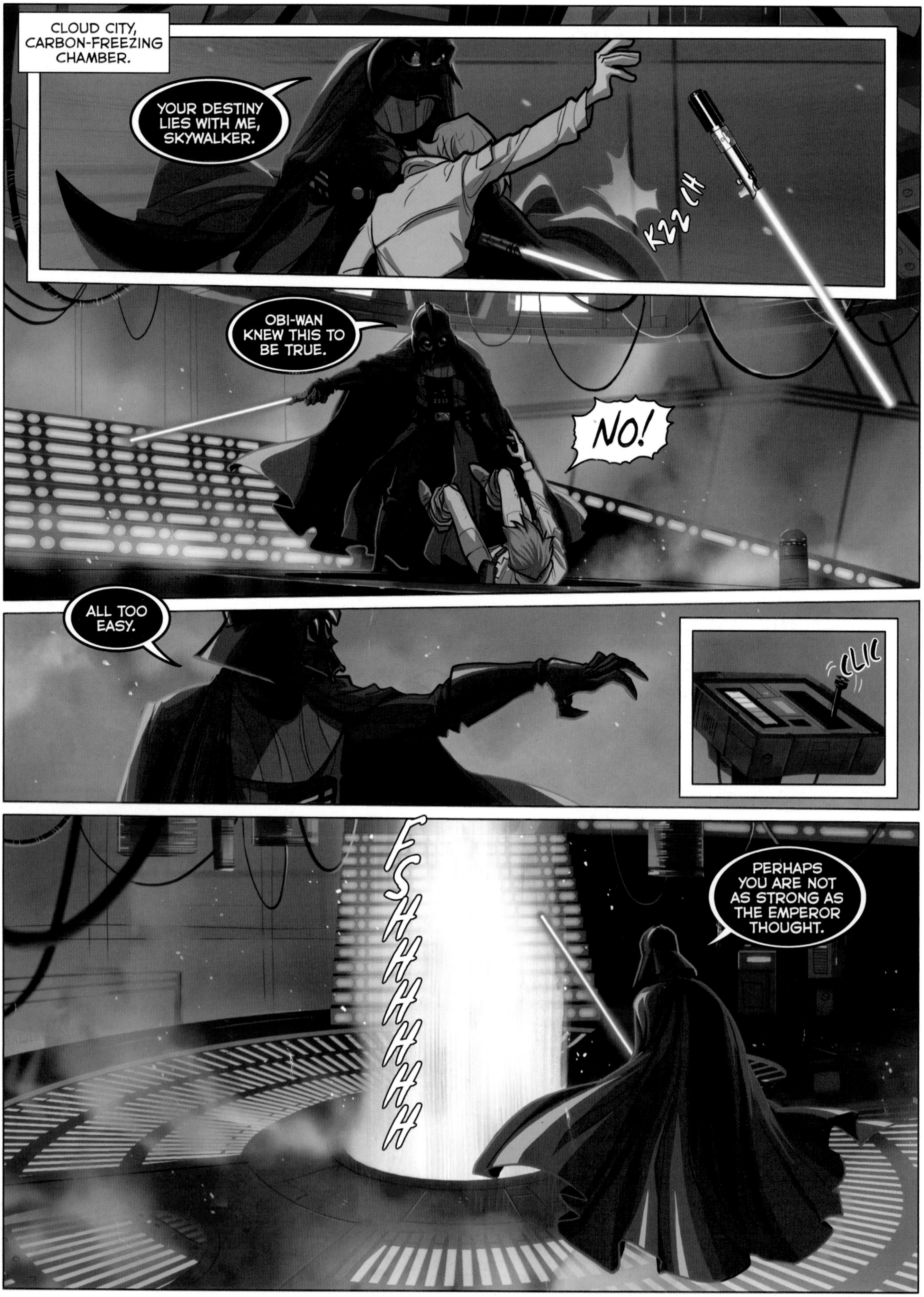
CLOUD CITY, CARBON-FREEZING CHAMBER.
YOUR DESTINY LIES WITH ME, SKYWALKER.
KZZCH
OBI-WAN KNEW THIS TO BE TRUE.
NO!
ALL TOO EASY.
CLIC
FSHHHHHHHHH
PERHAPS YOU ARE NOT AS STRONG AS THE EMPEROR THOUGHT.

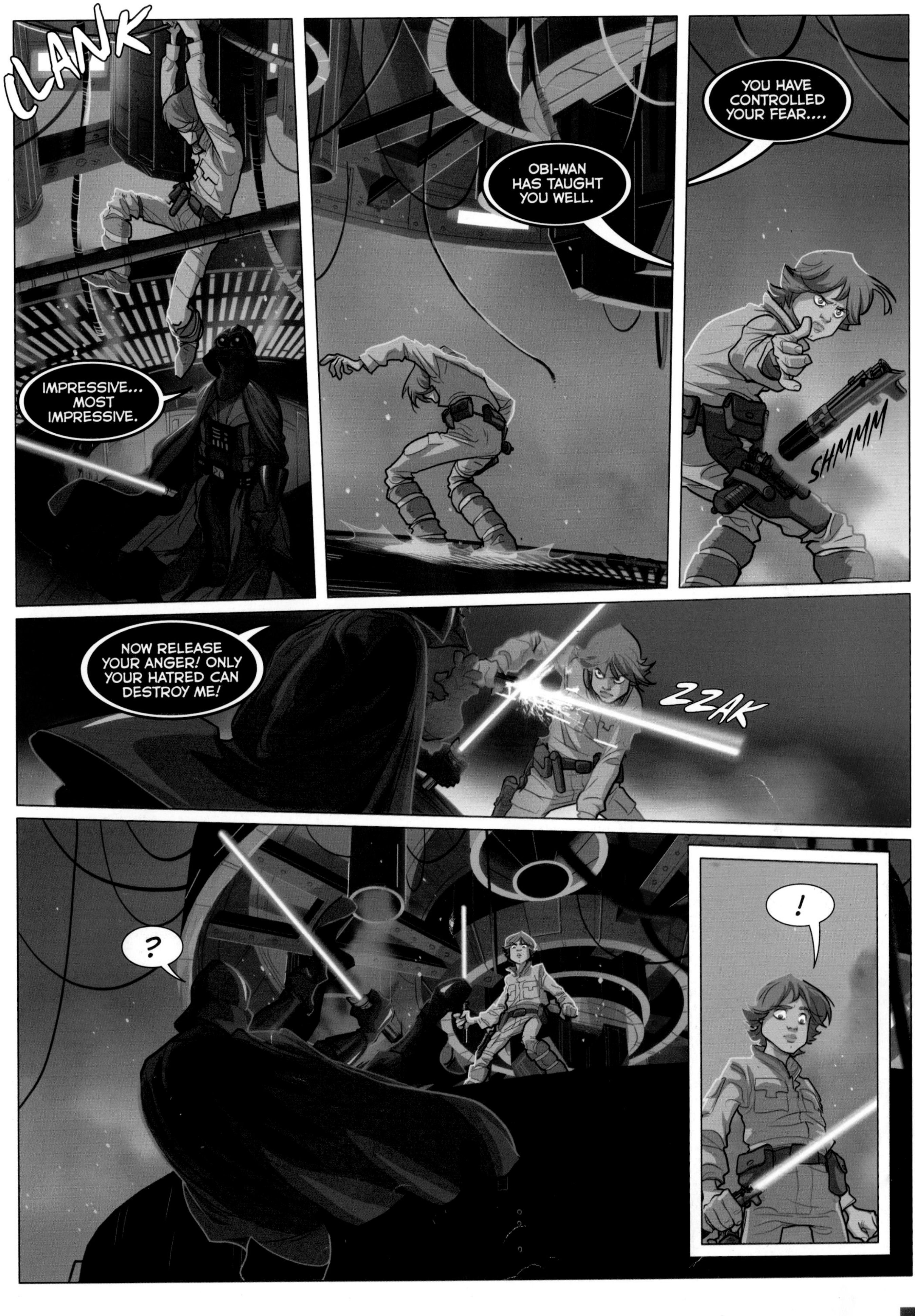
CLANK
IMPRESSIVE... MOST IMPRESSIVE.
OBI-WAN HAS TAUGHT YOU WELL.
YOU HAVE CONTROLLED YOUR FEAR....
SHMMM
NOW RELEASE YOUR ANGER! ONLY YOUR HATRED CAN DESTROY ME!
ZZAK
?
!

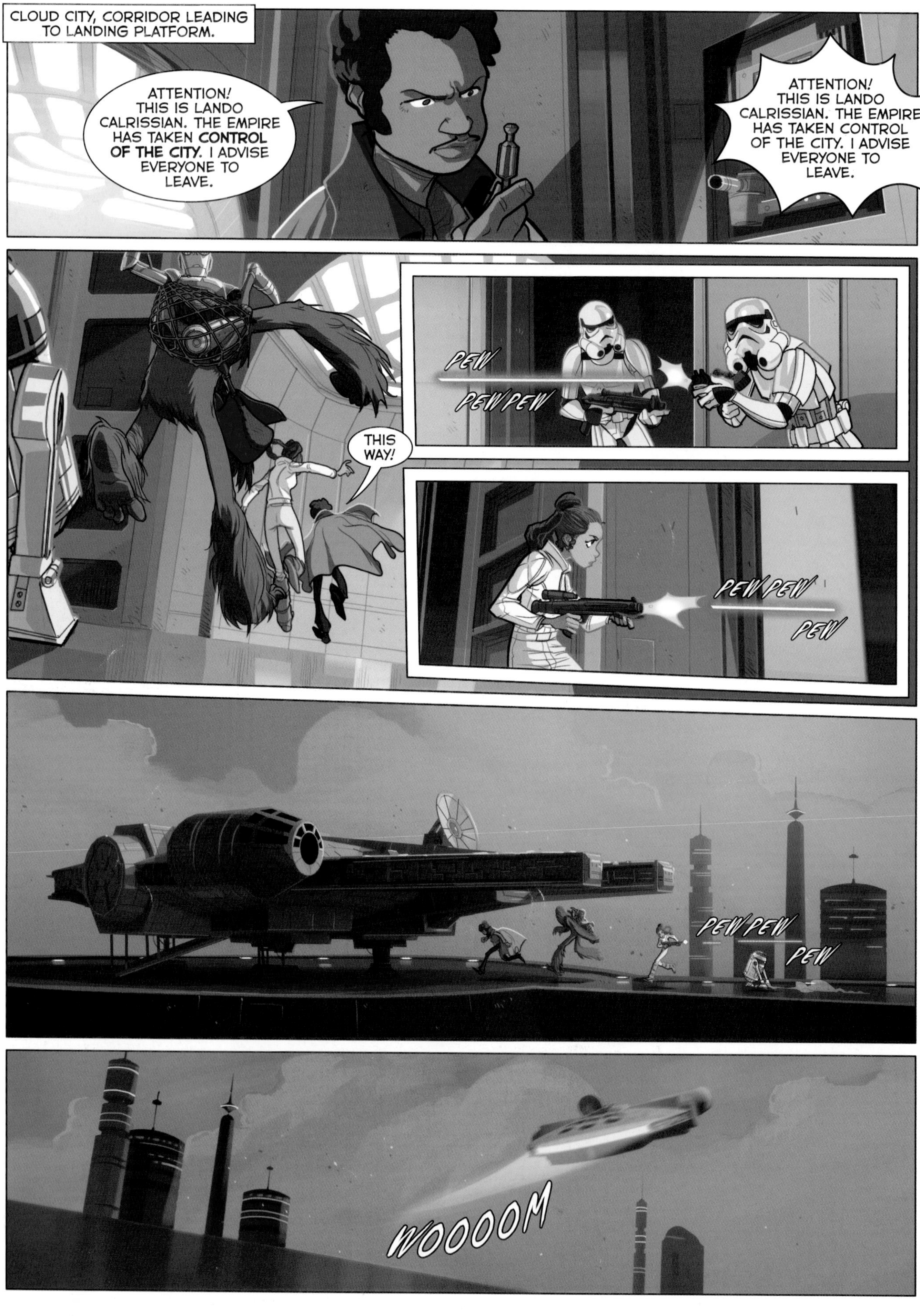
CLOUD CITY, CORRIDOR LEADING TO LANDING PLATFORM.
ATTENTION! THIS IS LANDO CALRISSIAN. THE EMPIRE HAS TAKEN CONTROL OF THE CITY. I ADVISE EVERYONE TO LEAVE.
ATTENTION! THIS IS LANDO CALRISSIAN. THE EMPIRE HAS TAKEN CONTROL OF THE CITY. I ADVISE EVERYONE TO LEAVE.
THIS WAY!
PEW
PEW PEW
PEW PEW
PEW
PEW PEW
PEW
WOOOOM

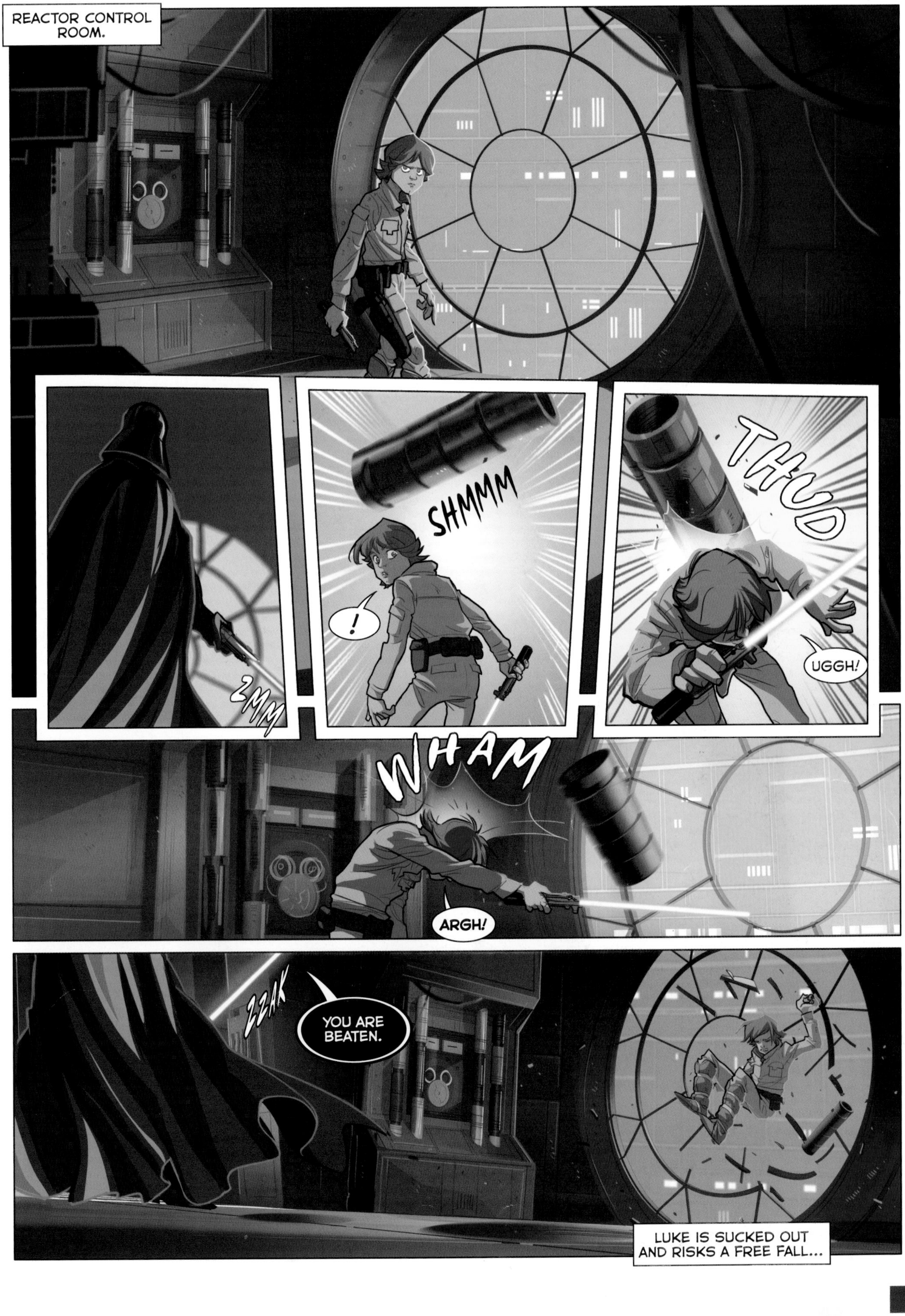
REACTOR CONTROL ROOM.
ZMM
SHMMM
!
THUD
UGGH!
WHAM
ARGH!
ZZAK
YOU ARE BEATEN.
LUKE IS SUCKED OUT AND RISKS A FREE FALL...

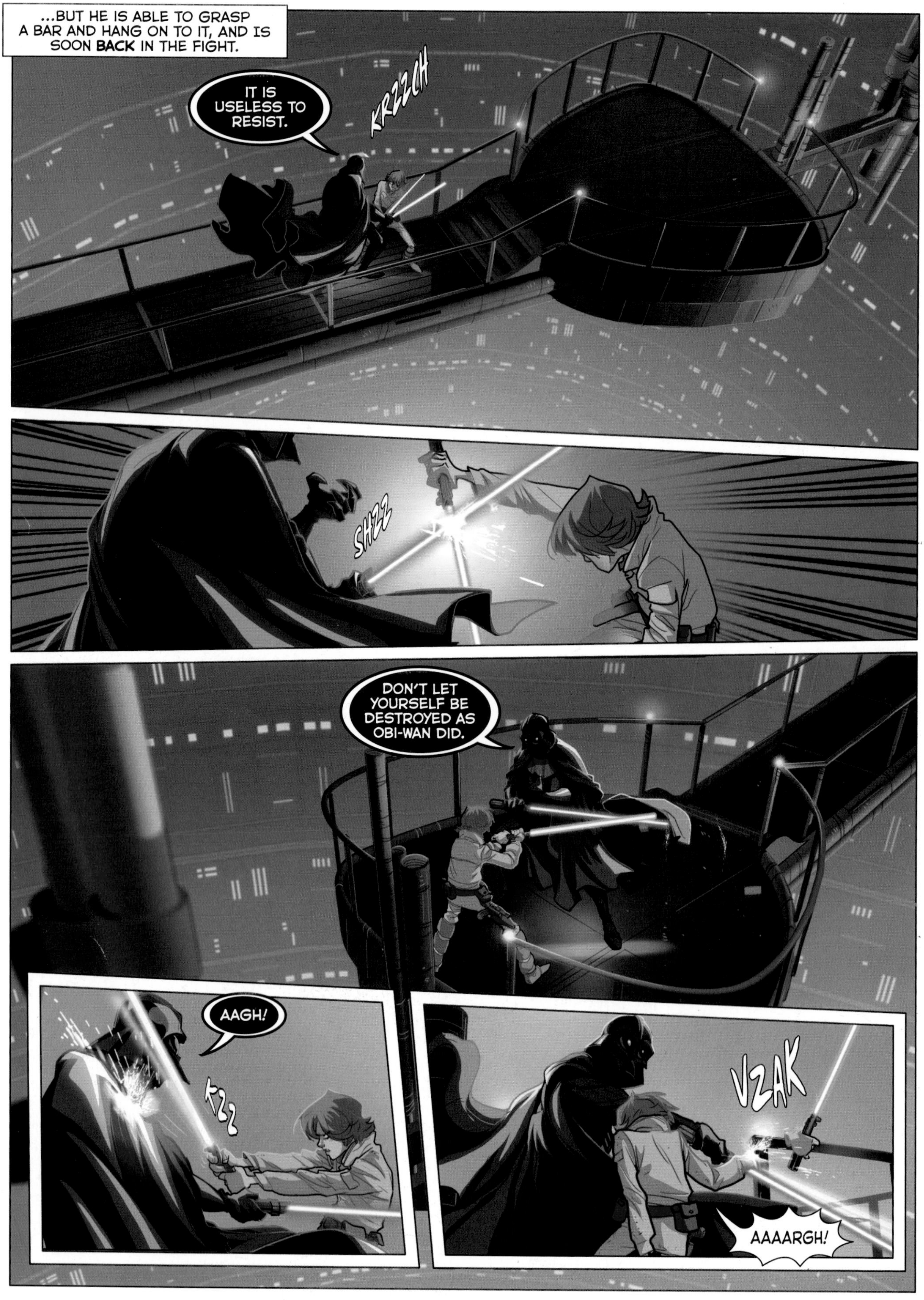
...BUT HE IS ABLE TO GRASP A BAR AND HANG ON TO IT, AND IS SOON BACK IN THE FIGHT.
IT IS USELESS TO RESIST.
KRZZCH
SHZZ
DON'T LET YOURSELF BE DESTROYED AS OBI-WAN DID.
AAGH!
KZZ
VZAK
AAAARGH!

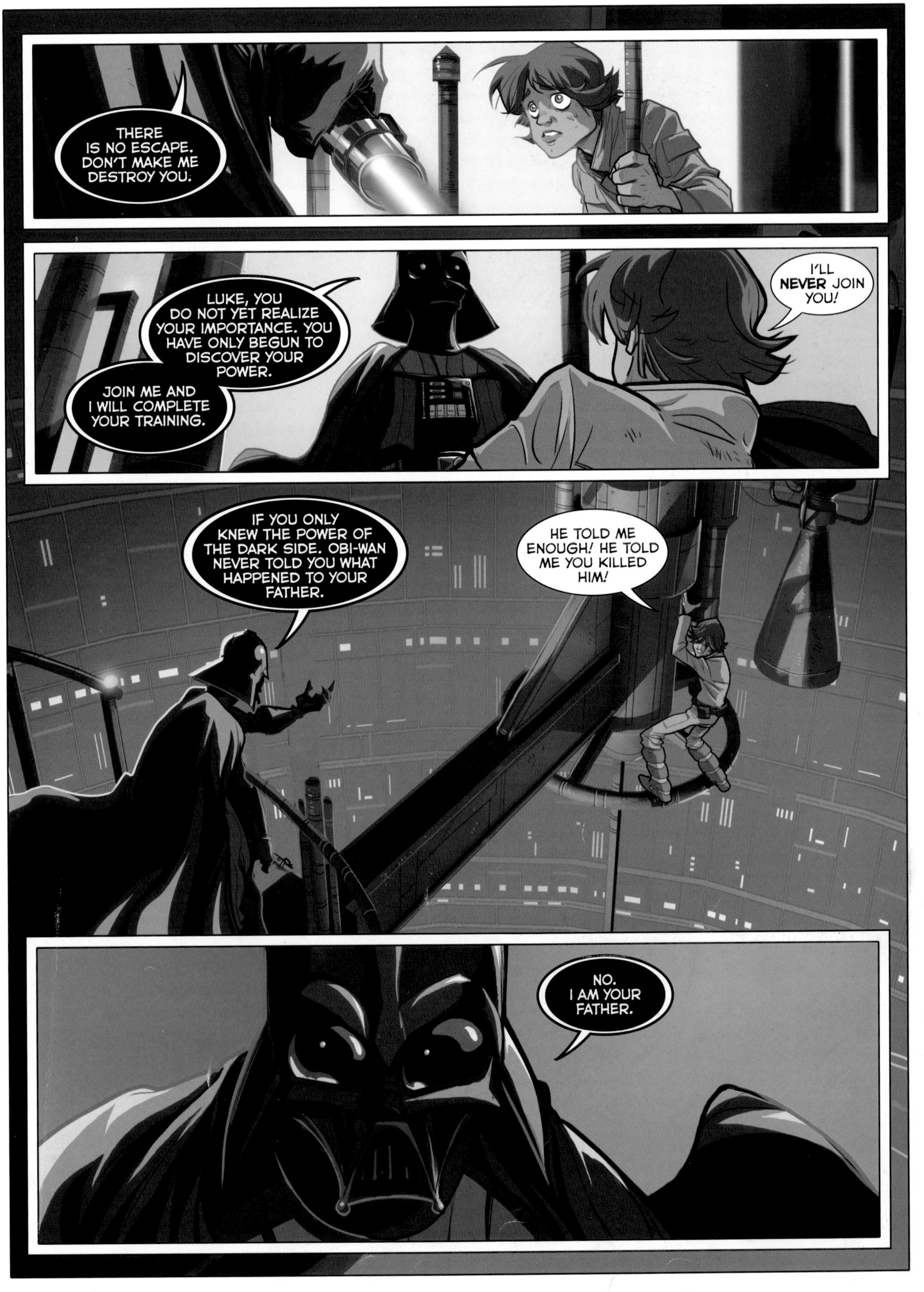
THERE IS NO ESCAPE. DON'T MAKE ME DESTROY YOU.
LUKE, YOU DO NOT YET REALIZE YOUR IMPORTANCE. YOU HAVE ONLY BEGUN TO DISCOVER YOUR POWER.
JOIN ME AND I WILL COMPLETE YOUR TRAINING.
I'LL **NEVER** JOIN YOU!
IF YOU ONLY KNEW THE POWER OF THE DARK SIDE. OBI-WAN NEVER TOLD YOU WHAT HAPPENED TO YOUR FATHER.
HE TOLD ME ENOUGH! HE TOLD ME YOU KILLED HIM!
NO. I AM YOUR FATHER.

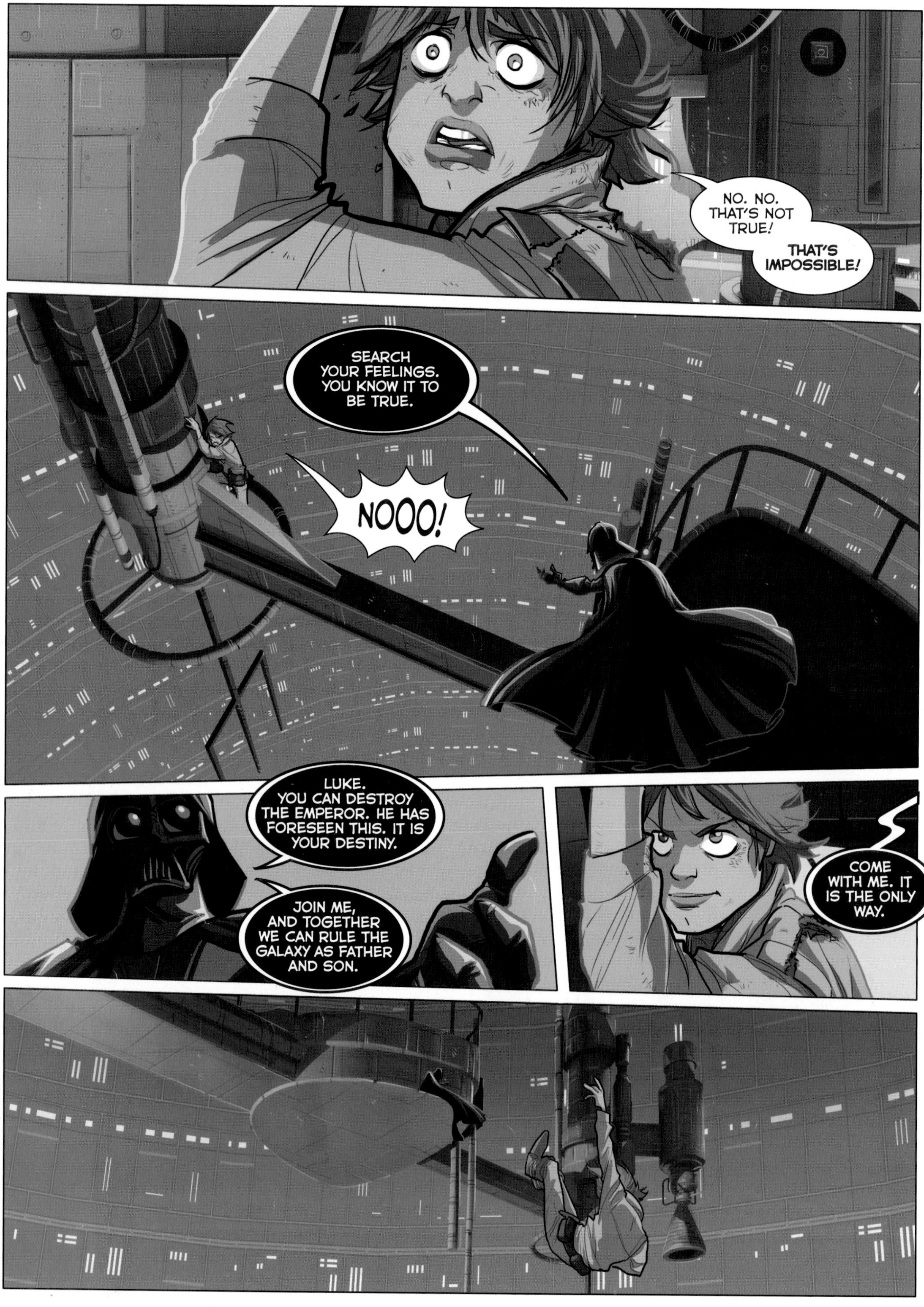

NO. NO. THAT'S NOT TRUE!
THAT'S IMPOSSIBLE!
SEARCH YOUR FEELINGS. YOU KNOW IT TO BE TRUE.
NOOO!
LUKE. YOU CAN DESTROY THE EMPEROR. HE HAS FORESEEN THIS. IT IS YOUR DESTINY.
JOIN ME, AND TOGETHER WE CAN RULE THE GALAXY AS FATHER AND SON.
COME WITH ME. IT IS THE ONLY WAY.

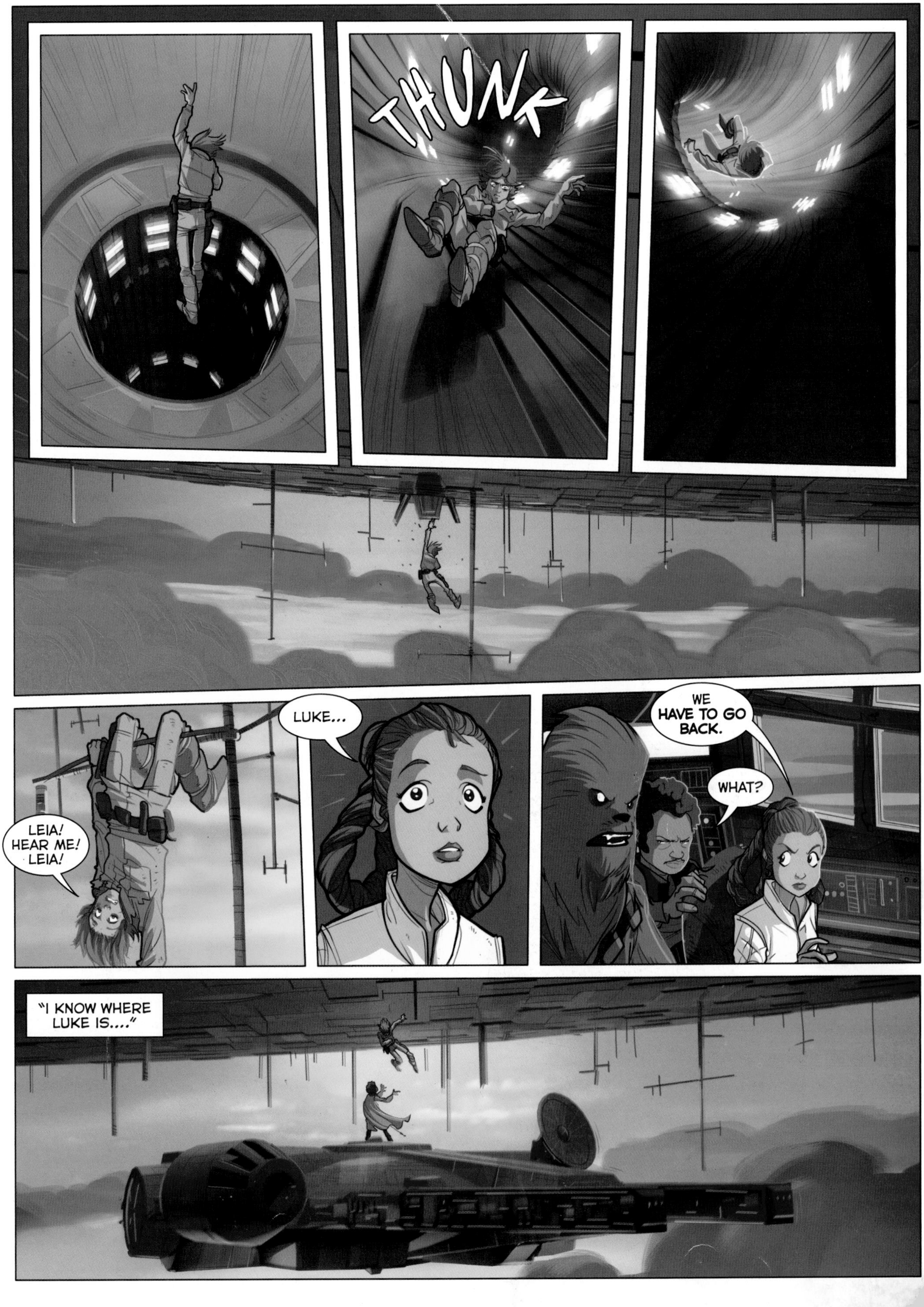
THUNK
LEIA! HEAR ME! LEIA!
LUKE...
WE HAVE TO GO BACK.
WHAT?
"I KNOW WHERE LUKE IS...."

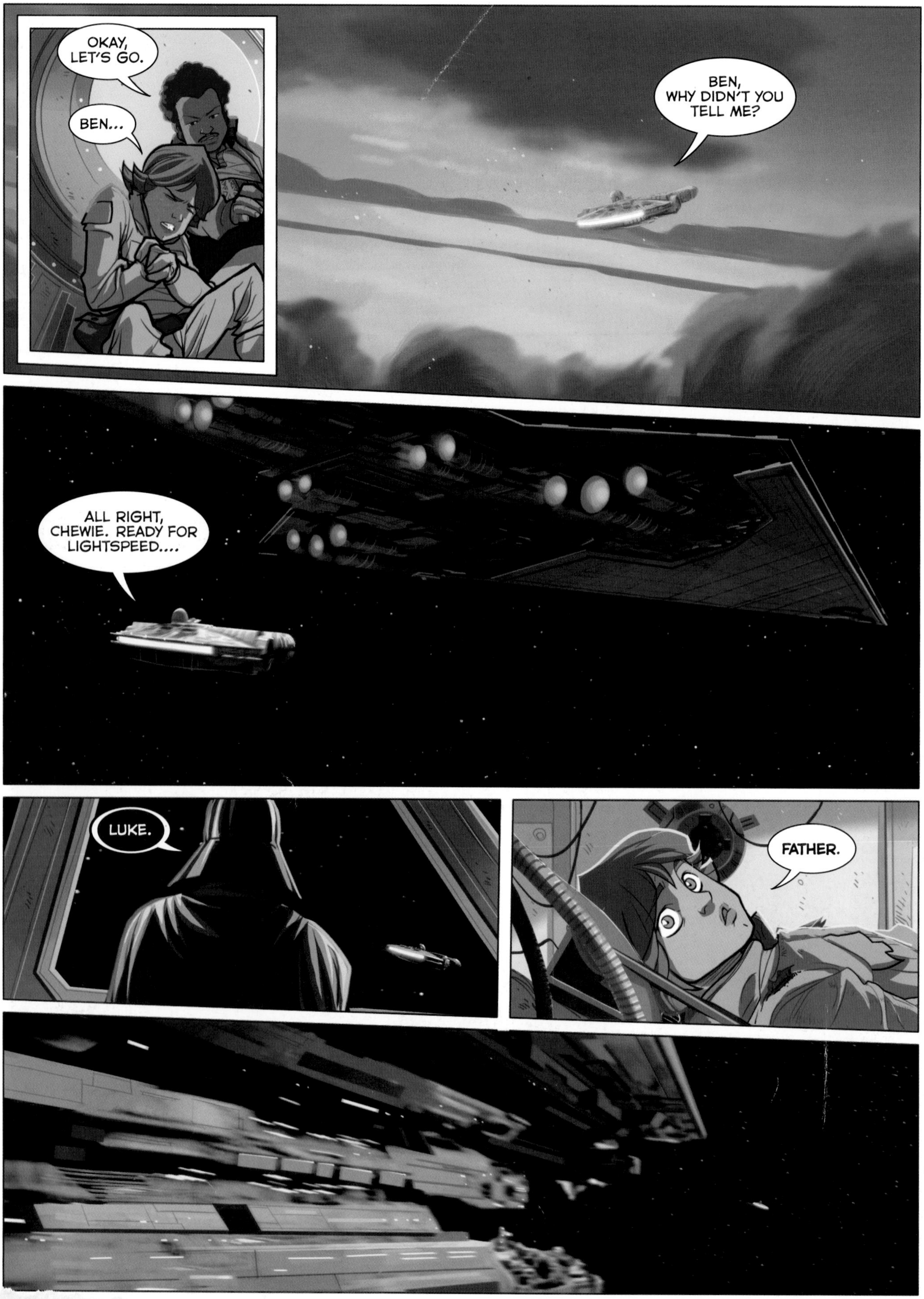
OKAY, LET'S GO.
BEN...
BEN, WHY DIDN'T YOU TELL ME?
ALL RIGHT, CHEWIE. READY FOR LIGHTSPEED....
LUKE.
FATHER.

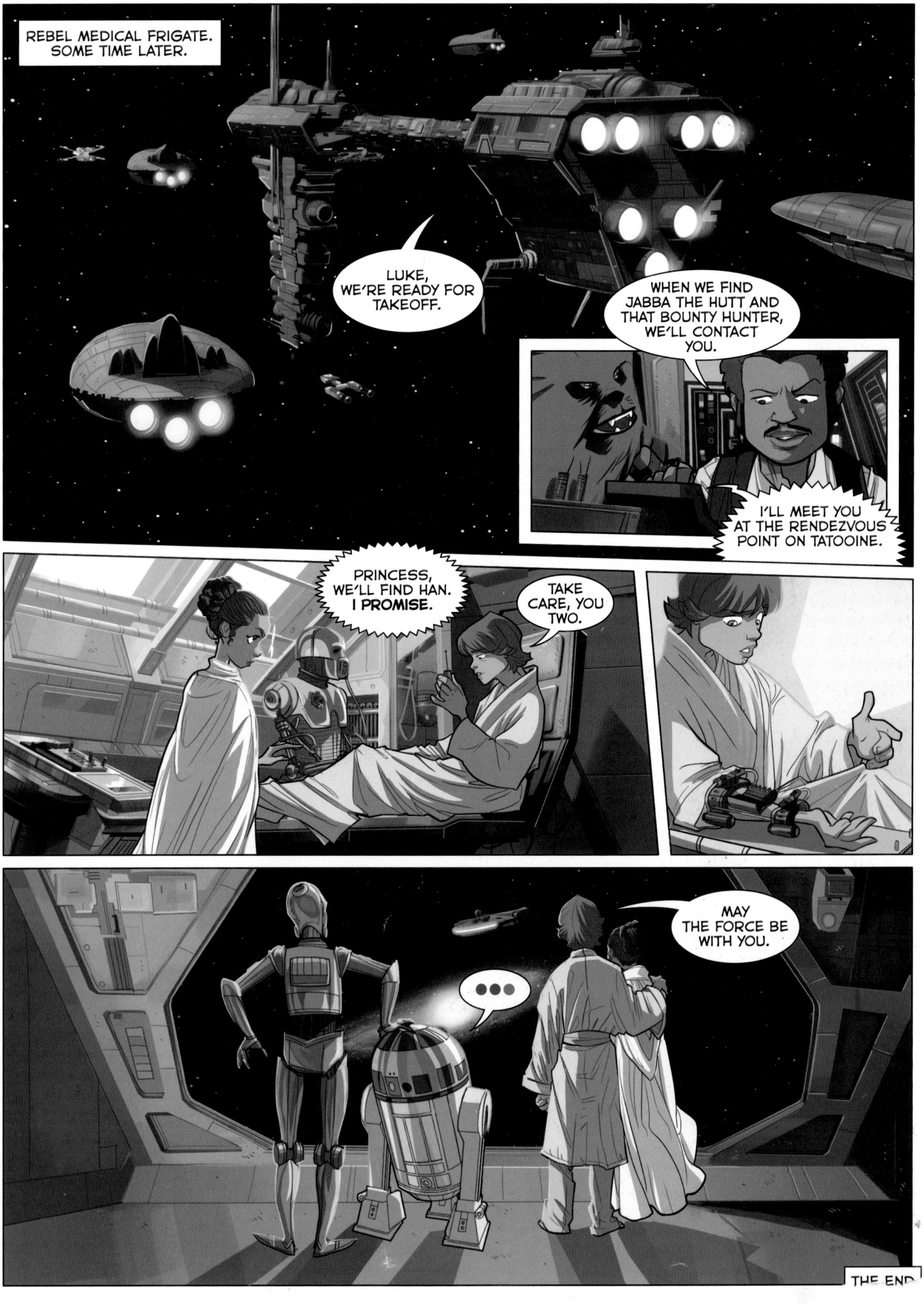
REBEL MEDICAL FRIGATE. SOME TIME LATER.
LUKE, WE'RE READY FOR TAKEOFF.
WHEN WE FIND JABBA THE HUTT AND THAT BOUNTY HUNTER, WE'LL CONTACT YOU.
I'LL MEET YOU AT THE RENDEZVOUS POINT ON TATOOINE.
PRINCESS, WE'LL FIND HAN. **I PROMISE.**
TAKE CARE, YOU TWO.
MAY THE FORCE BE WITH YOU.
•••
THE END

STAR WARS

RETURN OF THE JEDI

*A LONG TIME AGO
IN A GALAXY FAR, FAR AWAY....*

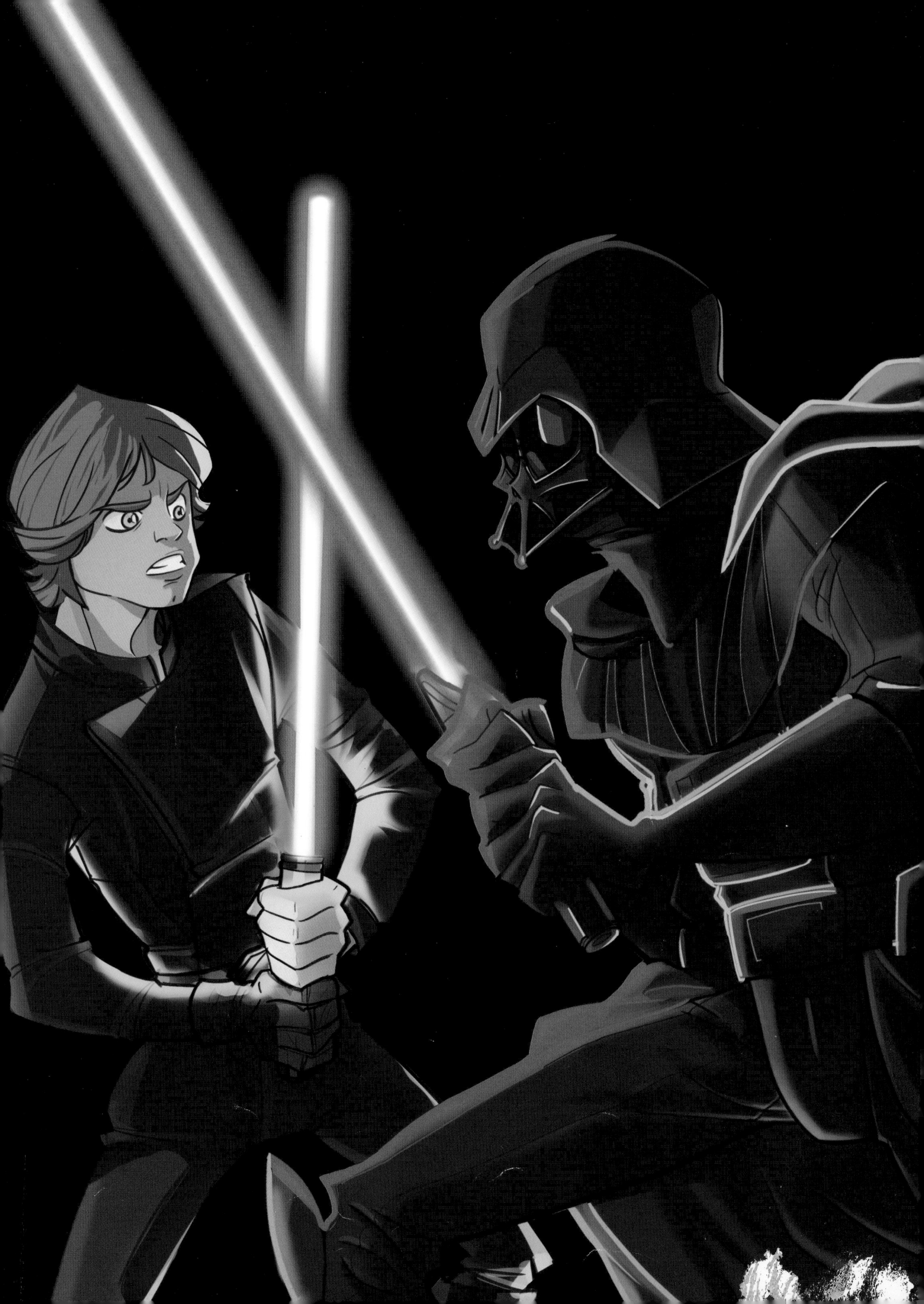

Episode VI
RETURN OF THE JEDI

Luke Skywalker has returned to his home planet of Tatooine in an attempt to rescue his friend Han Solo from the clutches of the vile gangster Jabba the Hutt.

Little does Luke know that the GALACTIC EMPIRE has secretly begun construction on a new armored space station even more powerful than the first dreaded Death Star.

When completed, this ultimate weapon will spell certain doom for the small band of rebels struggling to restore freedom to the galaxy. . . .

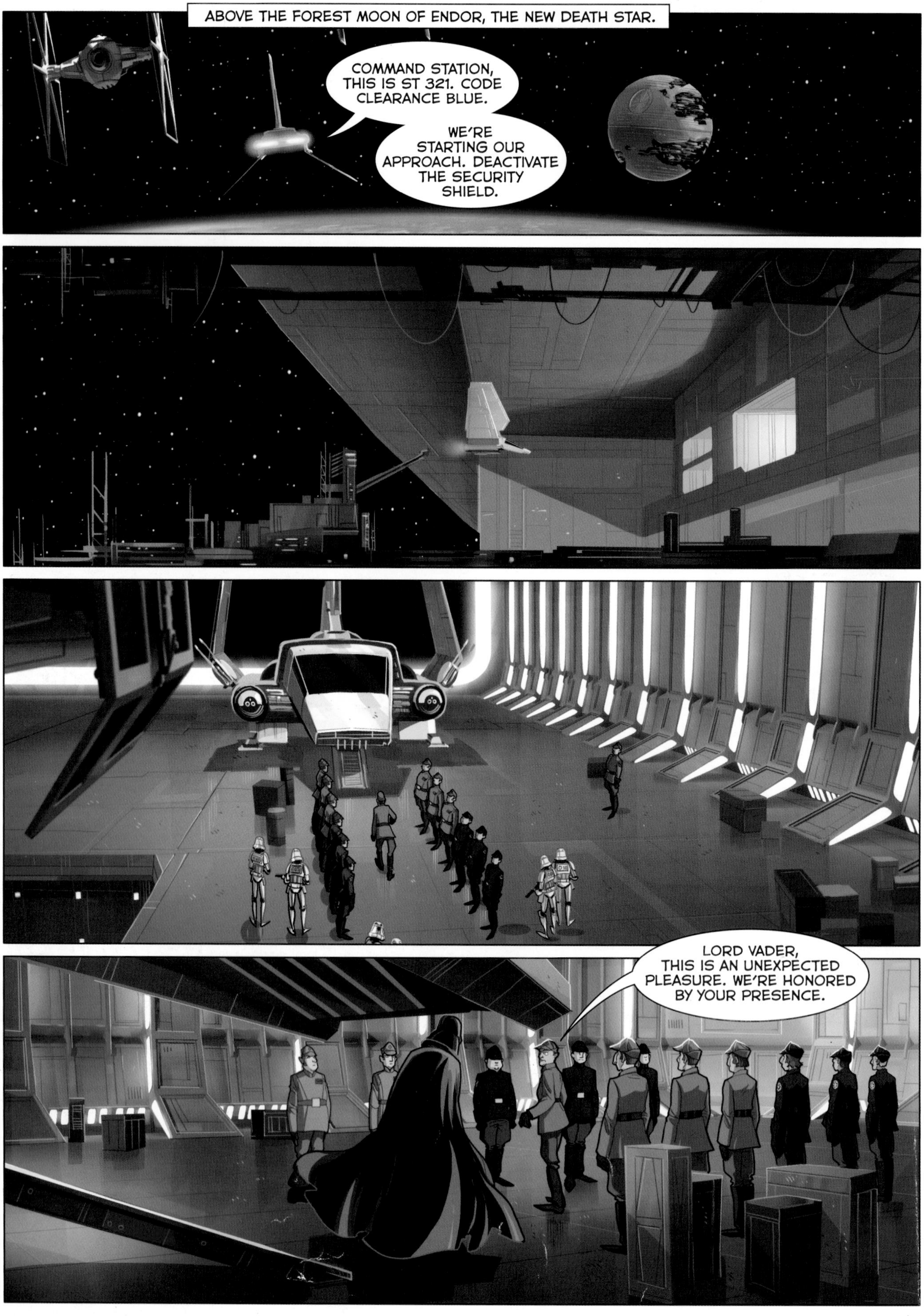
ABOVE THE FOREST MOON OF ENDOR, THE NEW DEATH STAR.
COMMAND STATION, THIS IS ST 321. CODE CLEARANCE BLUE.
WE'RE STARTING OUR APPROACH. DEACTIVATE THE SECURITY SHIELD.
LORD VADER, THIS IS AN UNEXPECTED PLEASURE. WE'RE HONORED BY YOUR PRESENCE.

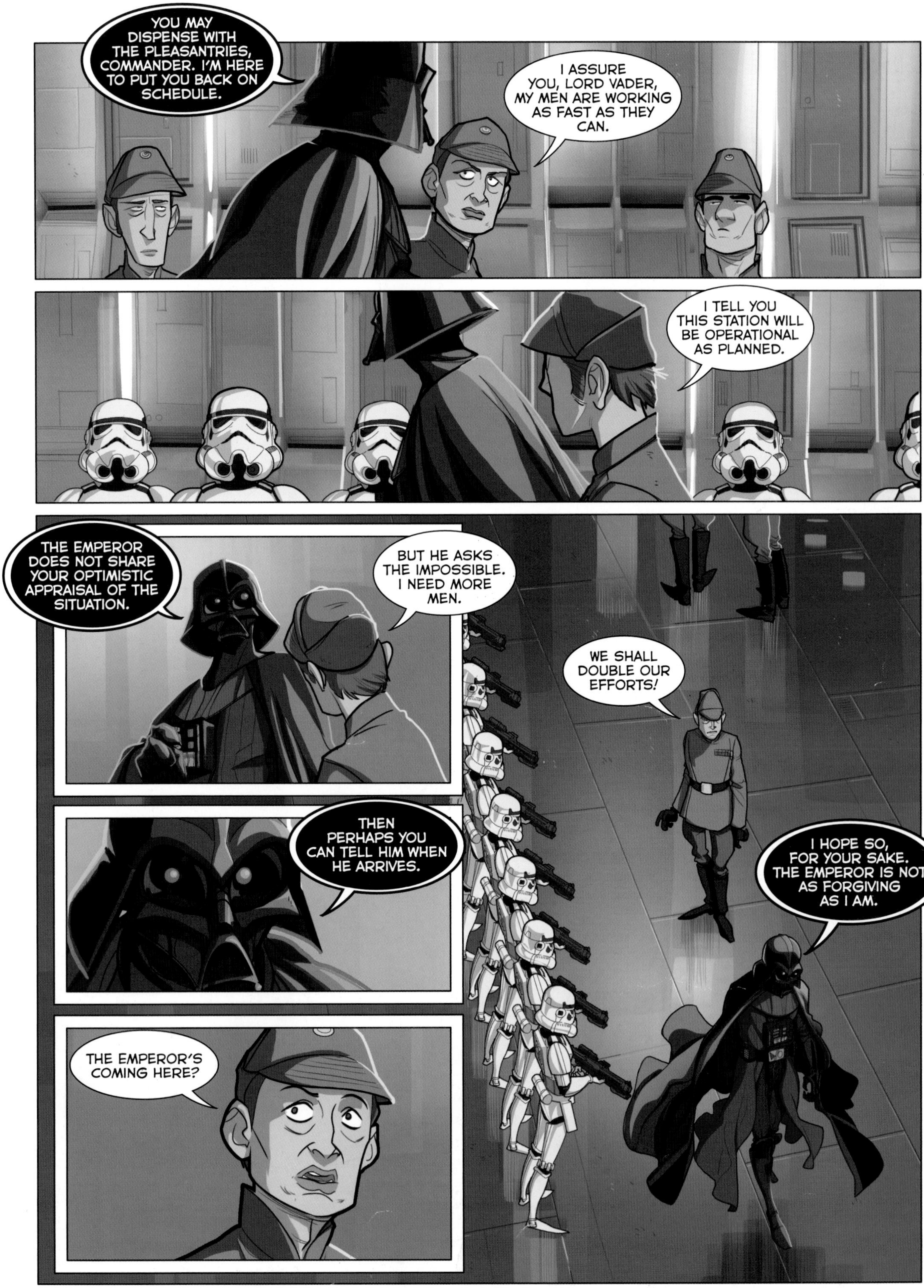
YOU MAY DISPENSE WITH THE PLEASANTRIES, COMMANDER. I'M HERE TO PUT YOU BACK ON SCHEDULE.
I ASSURE YOU, LORD VADER, MY MEN ARE WORKING AS FAST AS THEY CAN.
I TELL YOU THIS STATION WILL BE OPERATIONAL AS PLANNED.
THE EMPEROR DOES NOT SHARE YOUR OPTIMISTIC APPRAISAL OF THE SITUATION.
BUT HE ASKS THE IMPOSSIBLE. I NEED MORE MEN.
THEN PERHAPS YOU CAN TELL HIM WHEN HE ARRIVES.
THE EMPEROR'S COMING HERE?
WE SHALL DOUBLE OUR EFFORTS!
I HOPE SO, FOR YOUR SAKE. THE EMPEROR IS NOT AS FORGIVING AS I AM.

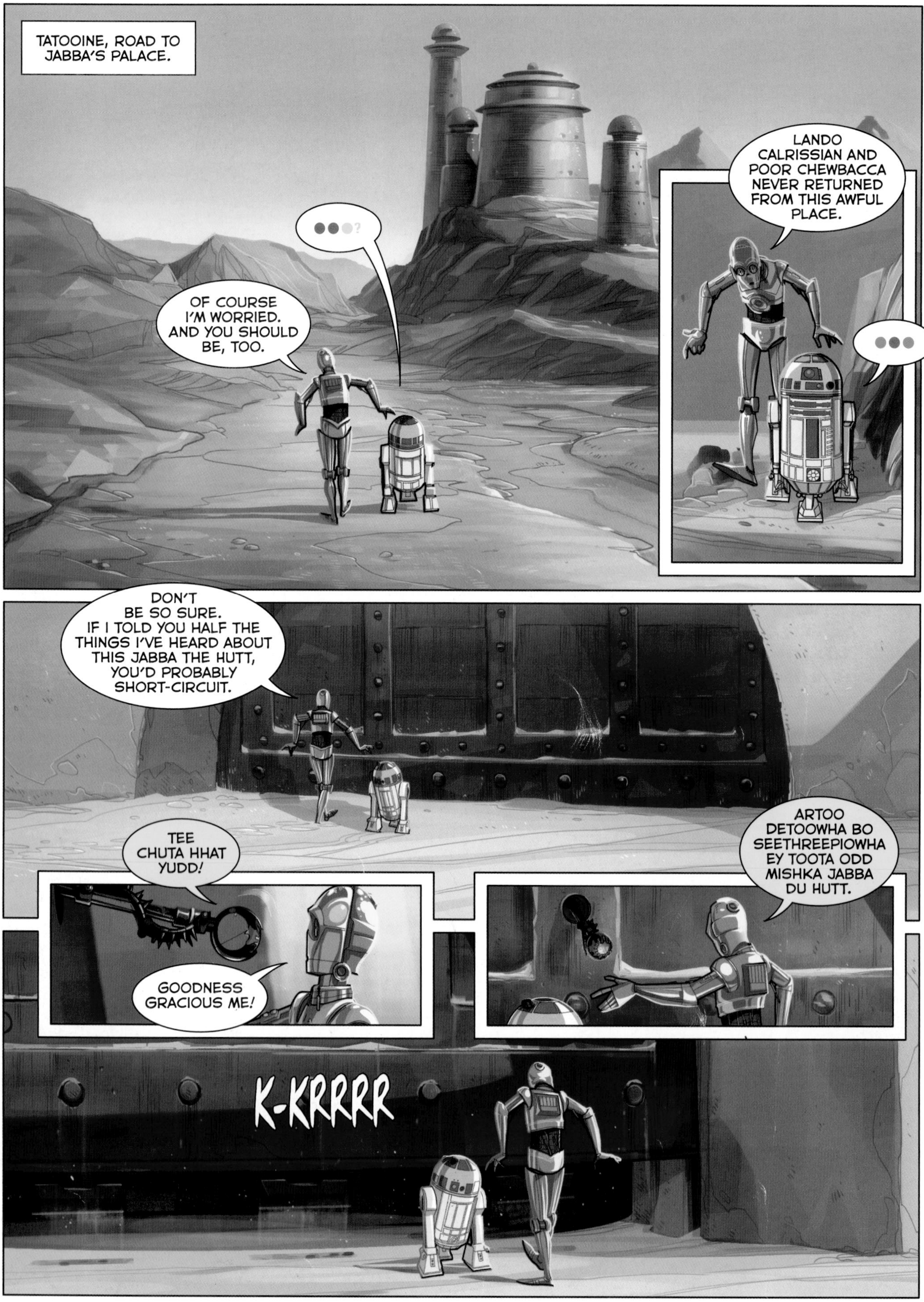
TATOOINE, ROAD TO JABBA'S PALACE.
OF COURSE I'M WORRIED. AND YOU SHOULD BE, TOO.
LANDO CALRISSIAN AND POOR CHEWBACCA NEVER RETURNED FROM THIS AWFUL PLACE.
DON'T BE SO SURE. IF I TOLD YOU HALF THE THINGS I'VE HEARD ABOUT THIS JABBA THE HUTT, YOU'D PROBABLY SHORT-CIRCUIT.
TEE CHUTA HHAT YUDD!
GOODNESS GRACIOUS ME!
ARTOO DETOOWHA BO SEETHREEPIOWHA EY TOOTA ODD MISHKA JABBA DU HUTT.
K-KRRRR

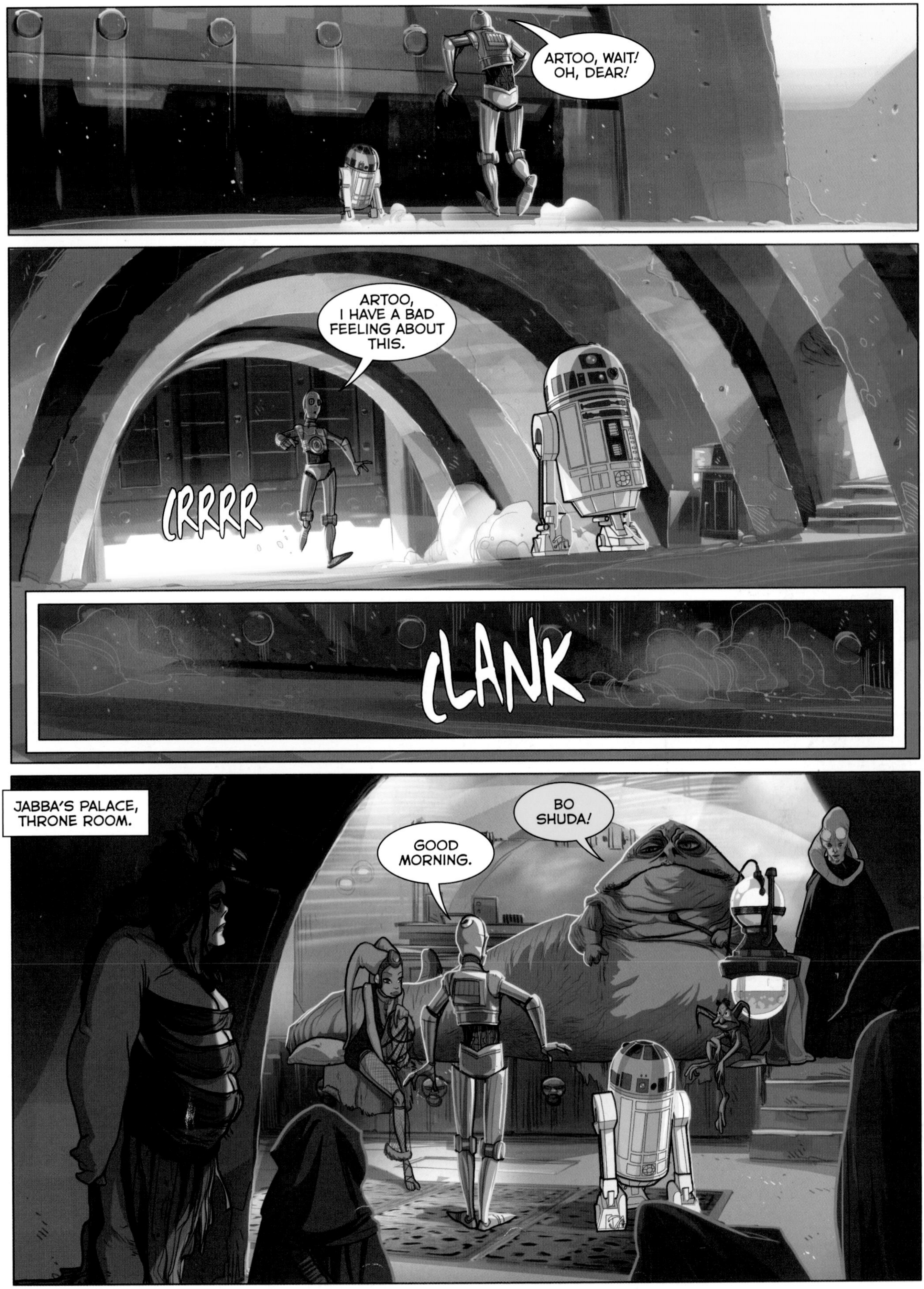
ARTOO, WAIT! OH, DEAR!
ARTOO, I HAVE A BAD FEELING ABOUT THIS.
CRRRR
CLANK
JABBA'S PALACE, THRONE ROOM.
GOOD MORNING.
BO SHUDA!

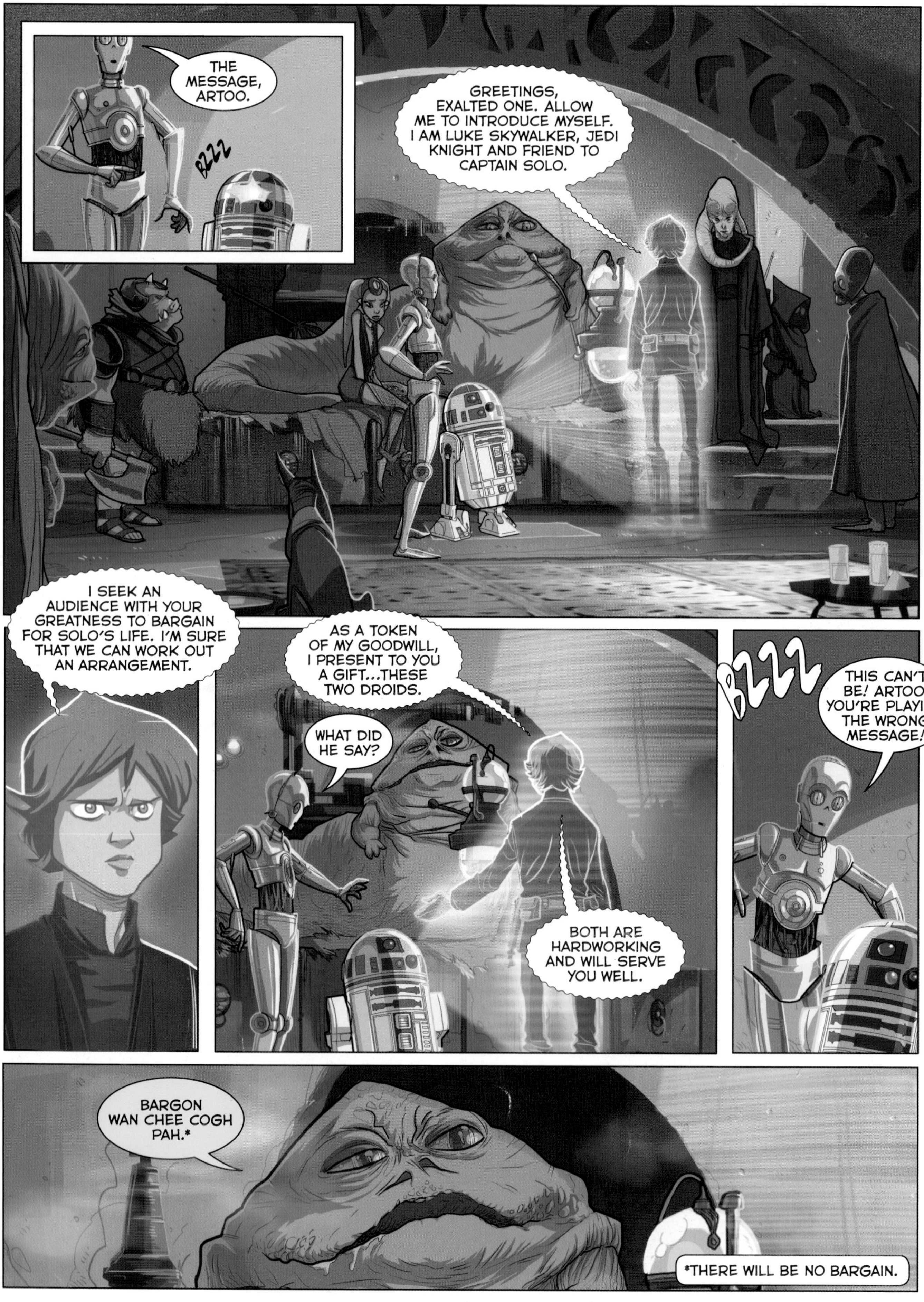
THE MESSAGE, ARTOO.
BZZZ
GREETINGS, EXALTED ONE. ALLOW ME TO INTRODUCE MYSELF. I AM LUKE SKYWALKER, JEDI KNIGHT AND FRIEND TO CAPTAIN SOLO.
I SEEK AN AUDIENCE WITH YOUR GREATNESS TO BARGAIN FOR SOLO'S LIFE. I'M SURE THAT WE CAN WORK OUT AN ARRANGEMENT.
AS A TOKEN OF MY GOODWILL, I PRESENT TO YOU A GIFT…THESE TWO DROIDS.
WHAT DID HE SAY?
BOTH ARE HARDWORKING AND WILL SERVE YOU WELL.
BZZZ
THIS CAN'T BE! ARTOO, YOU'RE PLAYING THE WRONG MESSAGE!
BARGON WAN CHEE COGH PAH.*
*THERE WILL BE NO BARGAIN.

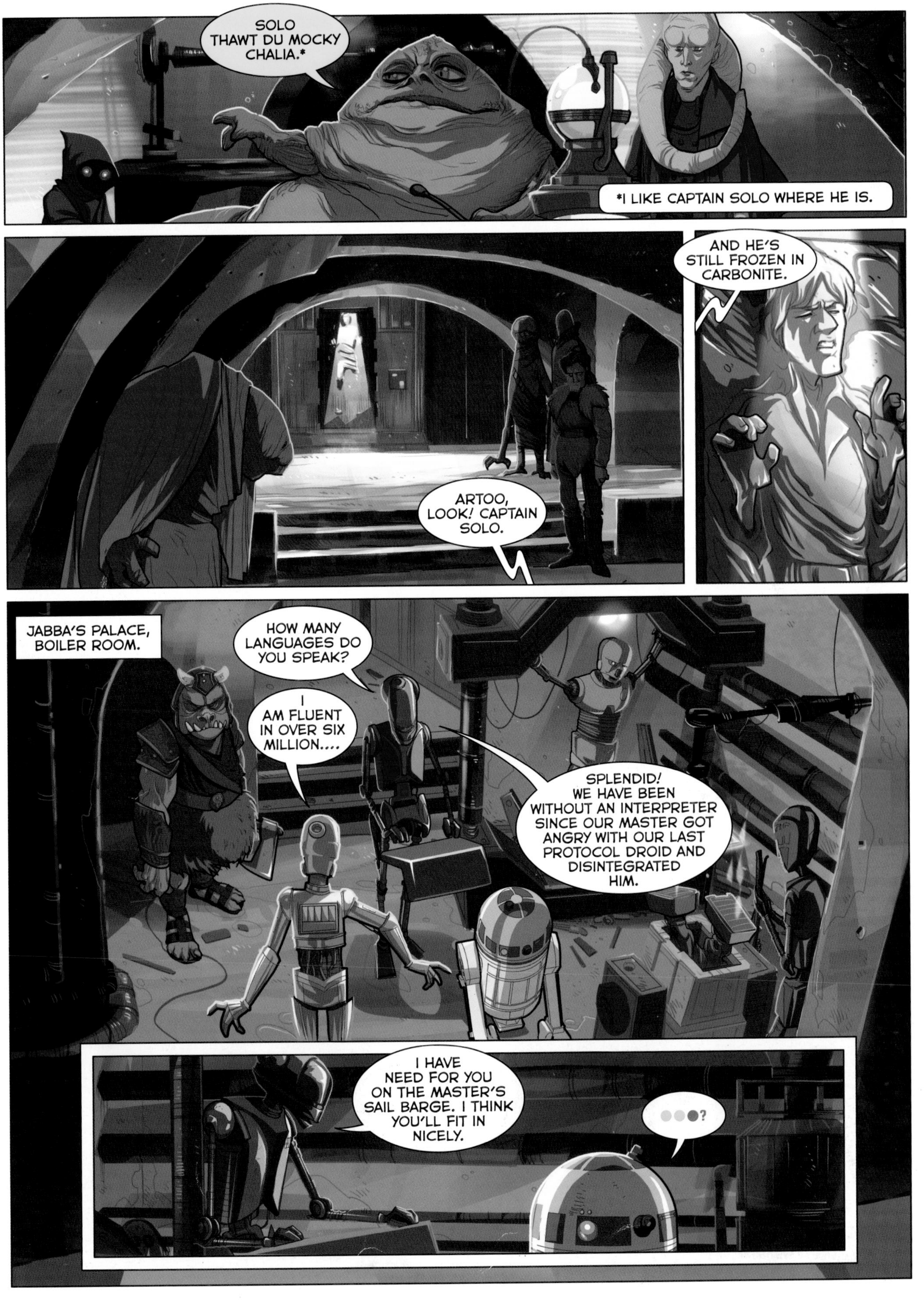
SOLO THAWT DU MOCKY CHALIA.*
*I LIKE CAPTAIN SOLO WHERE HE IS.
ARTOO, LOOK! CAPTAIN SOLO.
AND HE'S STILL FROZEN IN CARBONITE.
JABBA'S PALACE, BOILER ROOM.
HOW MANY LANGUAGES DO YOU SPEAK?
I AM FLUENT IN OVER SIX MILLION....
SPLENDID! WE HAVE BEEN WITHOUT AN INTERPRETER SINCE OUR MASTER GOT ANGRY WITH OUR LAST PROTOCOL DROID AND DISINTEGRATED HIM.
I HAVE NEED FOR YOU ON THE MASTER'S SAIL BARGE. I THINK YOU'LL FIT IN NICELY.
?

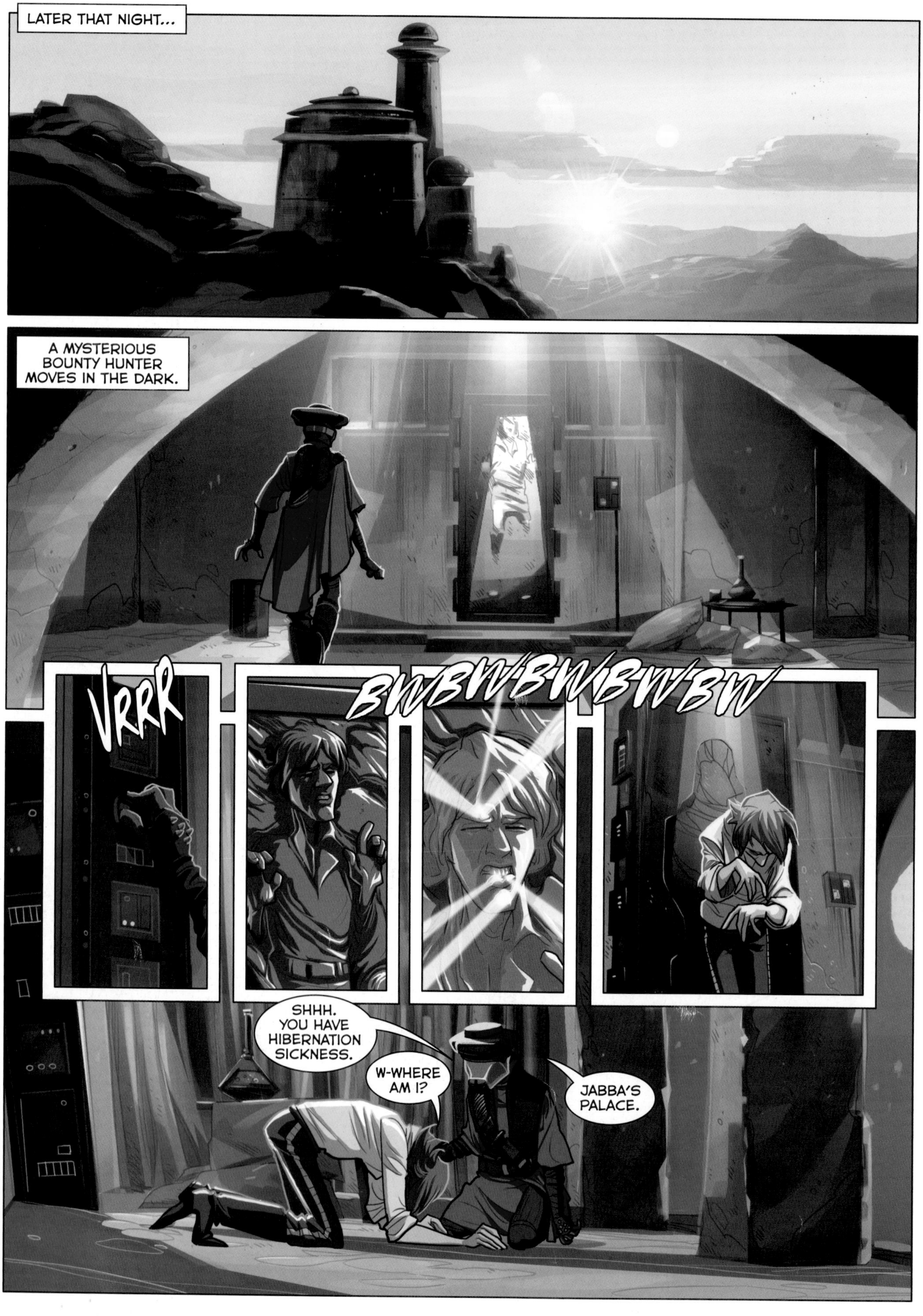

LATER THAT NIGHT...
A MYSTERIOUS BOUNTY HUNTER MOVES IN THE DARK.
VRRR
BWBWBWBWBWBW
SHHH. YOU HAVE HIBERNATION SICKNESS.
W-WHERE AM I?
JABBA'S PALACE.

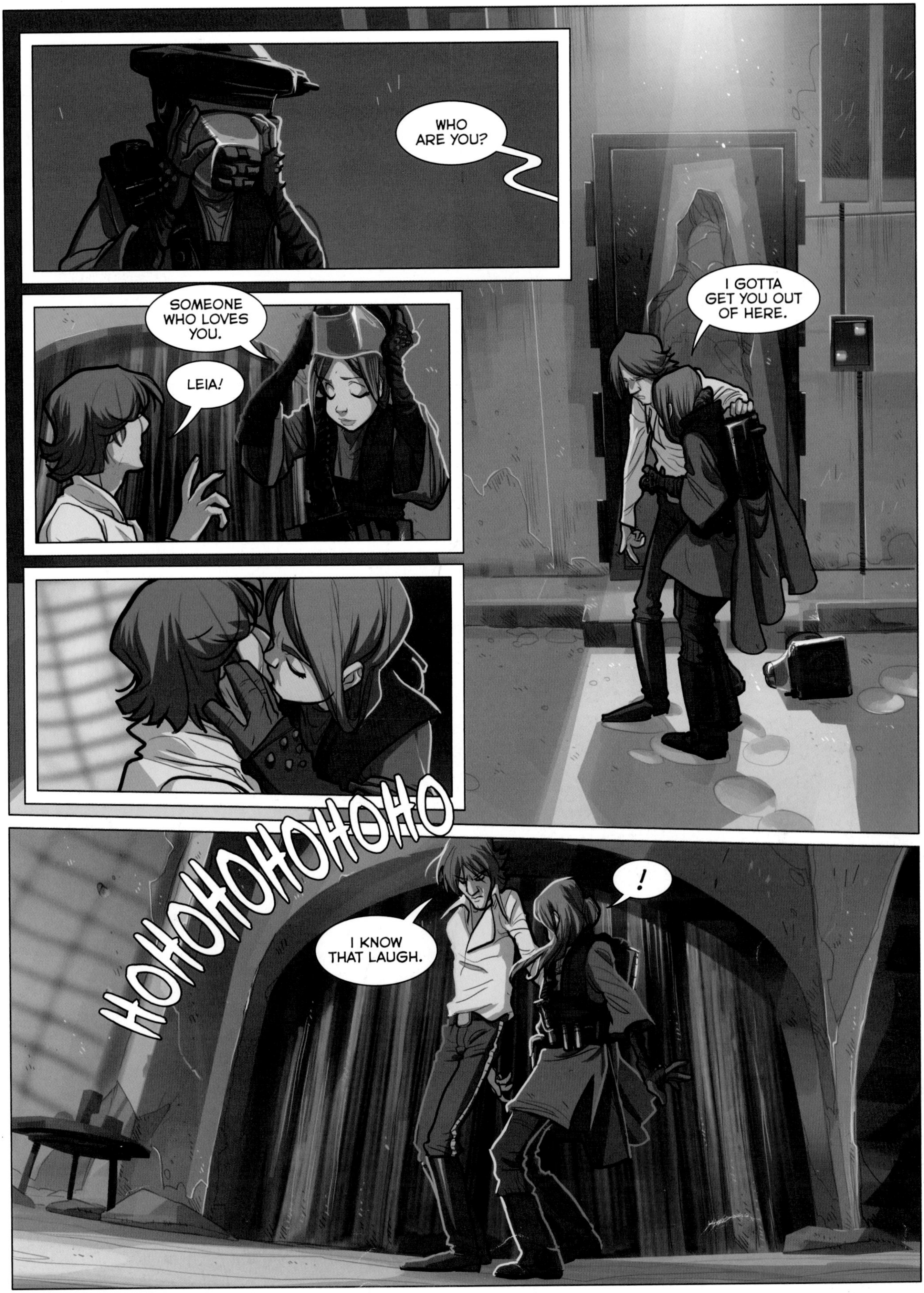
WHO ARE YOU?
SOMEONE WHO LOVES YOU.
LEIA!
I GOTTA GET YOU OUT OF HERE.
HOHOHOHOHOHOHO
I KNOW THAT LAUGH.
!

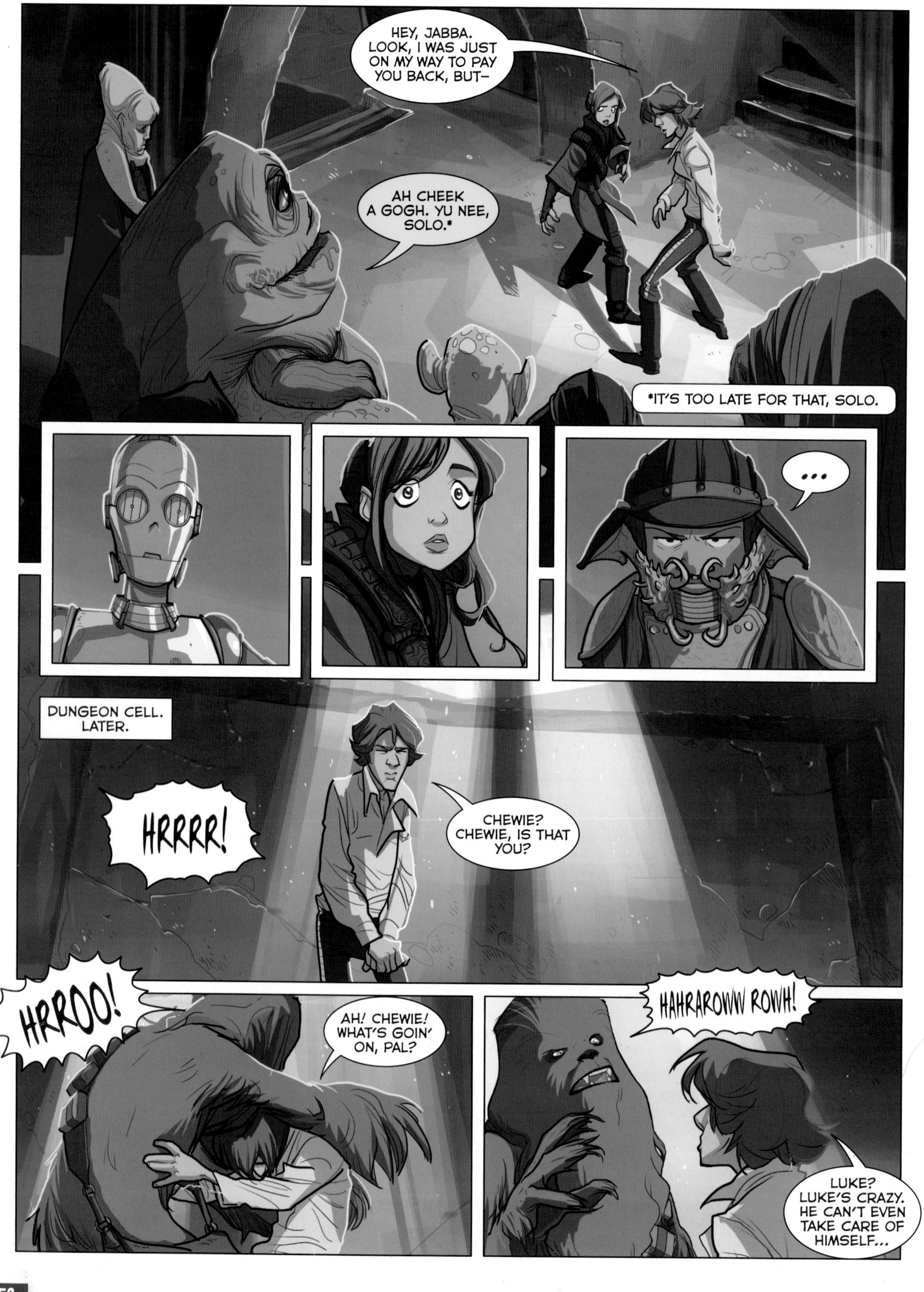
HEY, JABBA. LOOK, I WAS JUST ON MY WAY TO PAY YOU BACK, BUT–
AH CHEEK A GOGH. YU NEE, SOLO.*
*IT'S TOO LATE FOR THAT, SOLO.
...
DUNGEON CELL. LATER.
HRRRR!
CHEWIE? CHEWIE, IS THAT YOU?
HRROO!
AH! CHEWIE! WHAT'S GOIN' ON, PAL?
HAHRAROWW ROWH!
LUKE? LUKE'S CRAZY. HE CAN'T EVEN TAKE CARE OF HIMSELF...

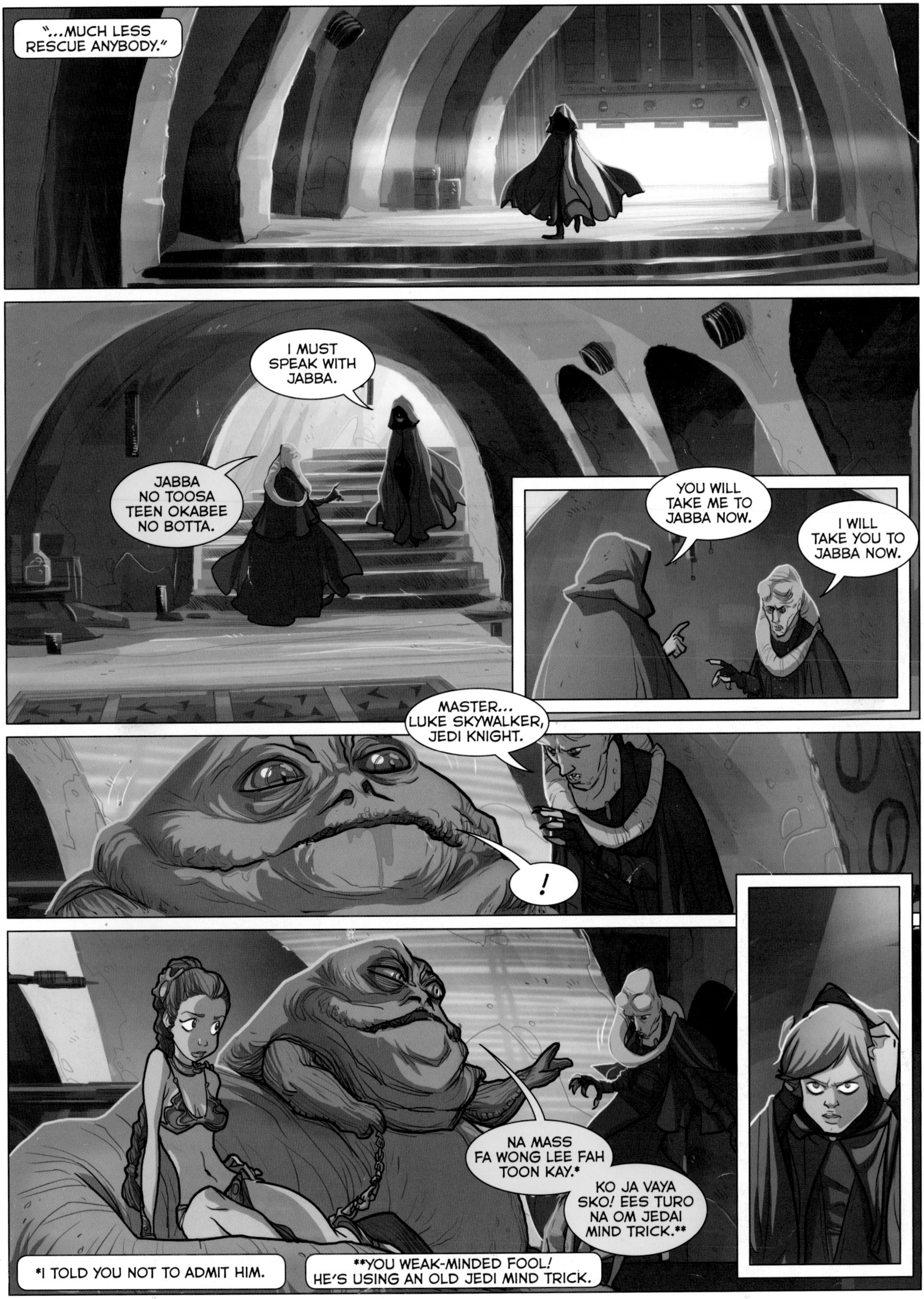
"...MUCH LESS RESCUE ANYBODY."
I MUST SPEAK WITH JABBA.
JABBA NO TOOSA TEEN OKABEE NO BOTTA.
YOU WILL TAKE ME TO JABBA NOW.
I WILL TAKE YOU TO JABBA NOW.
MASTER... LUKE SKYWALKER, JEDI KNIGHT.
!
NA MASS FA WONG LEE FAH TOON KAY.*
KO JA VAYA SKO! EES TURO NA OM JEDAI MIND TRICK.**
*I TOLD YOU NOT TO ADMIT HIM.
**YOU WEAK-MINDED FOOL! HE'S USING AN OLD JEDI MIND TRICK.

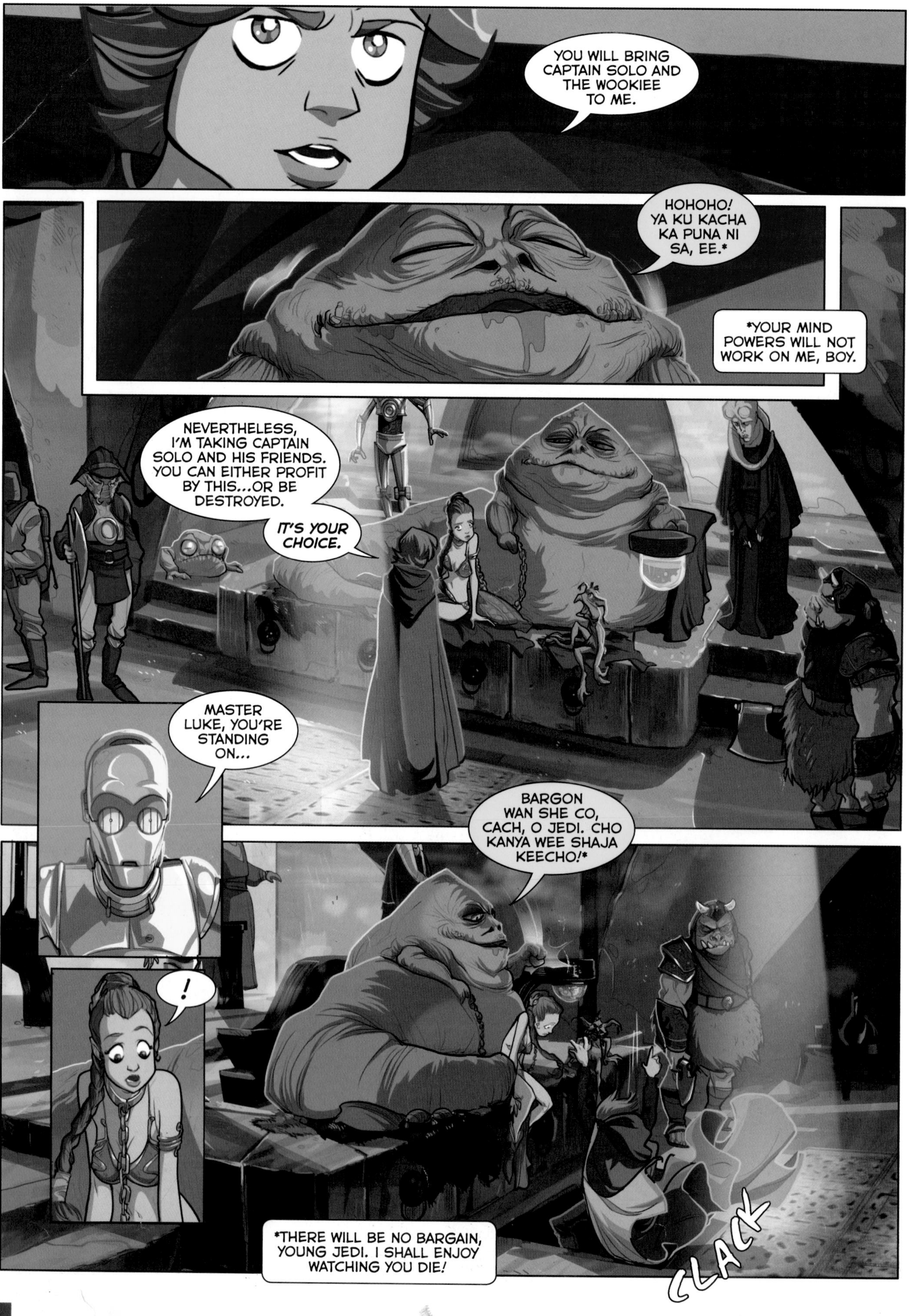

YOU WILL BRING CAPTAIN SOLO AND THE WOOKIEE TO ME.
HOHOHO! YA KU KACHA KA PUNA NI SA, EE.*
*YOUR MIND POWERS WILL NOT WORK ON ME, BOY.
NEVERTHELESS, I'M TAKING CAPTAIN SOLO AND HIS FRIENDS. YOU CAN EITHER PROFIT BY THIS...OR BE DESTROYED.
IT'S YOUR CHOICE.
MASTER LUKE, YOU'RE STANDING ON...
BARGON WAN SHE CO, CACH, O JEDI. CHO KANYA WEE SHAJA KEECHO!*
!
*THERE WILL BE NO BARGAIN, YOUNG JEDI. I SHALL ENJOY WATCHING YOU DIE!
CLACK

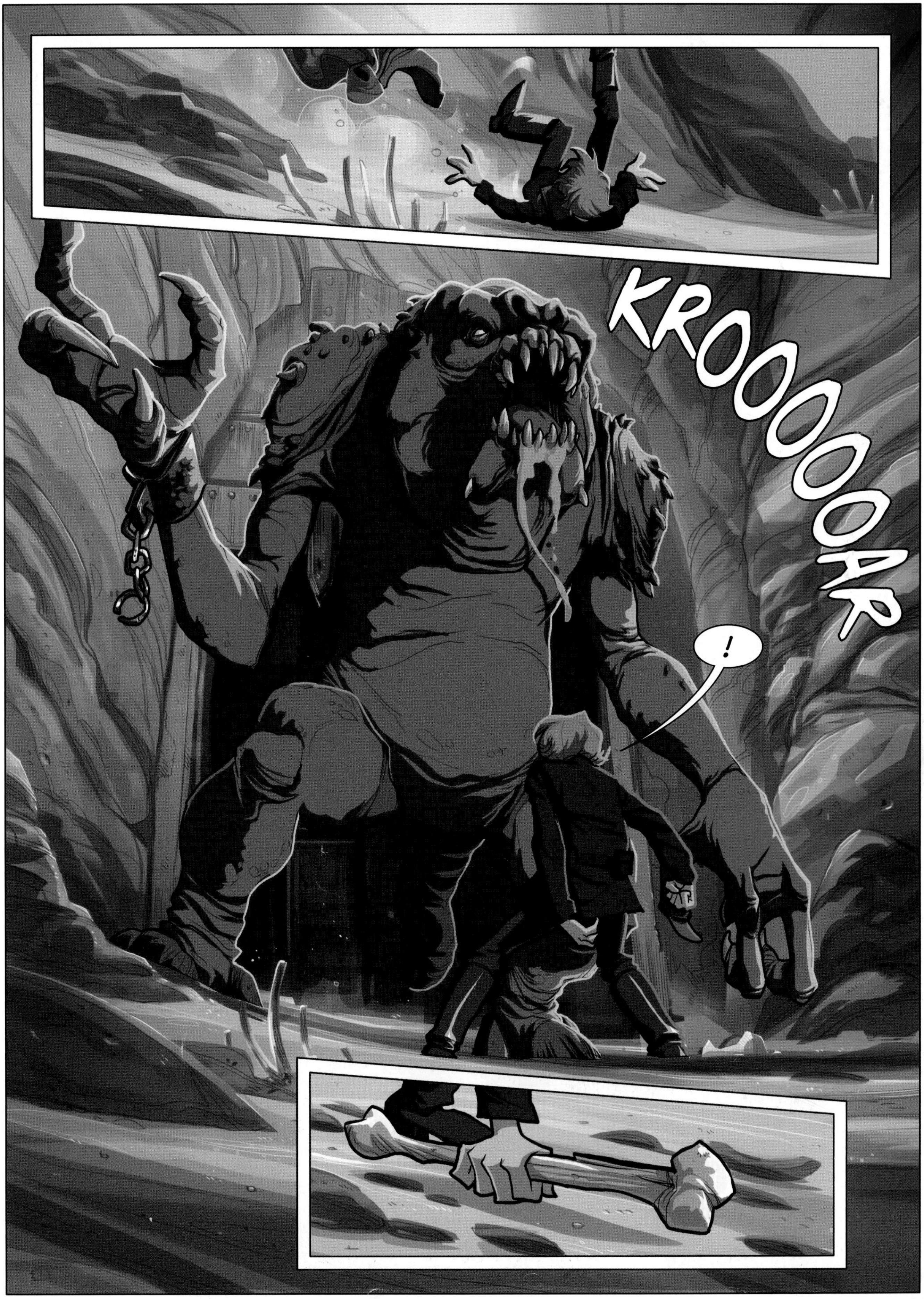
KROOOOOAR
!

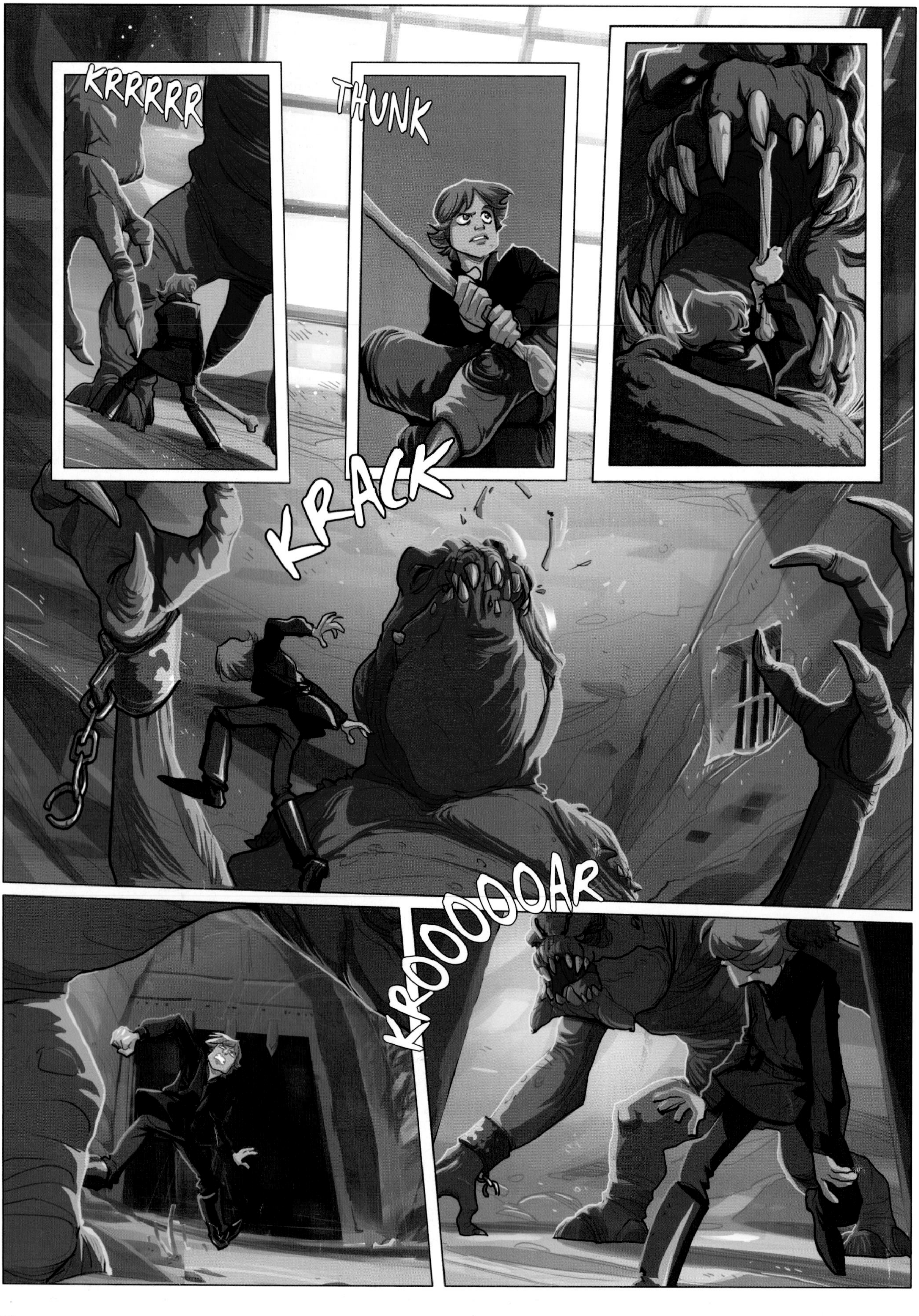
KRRRRR
THUNK
KRACK
KROOOOOAR

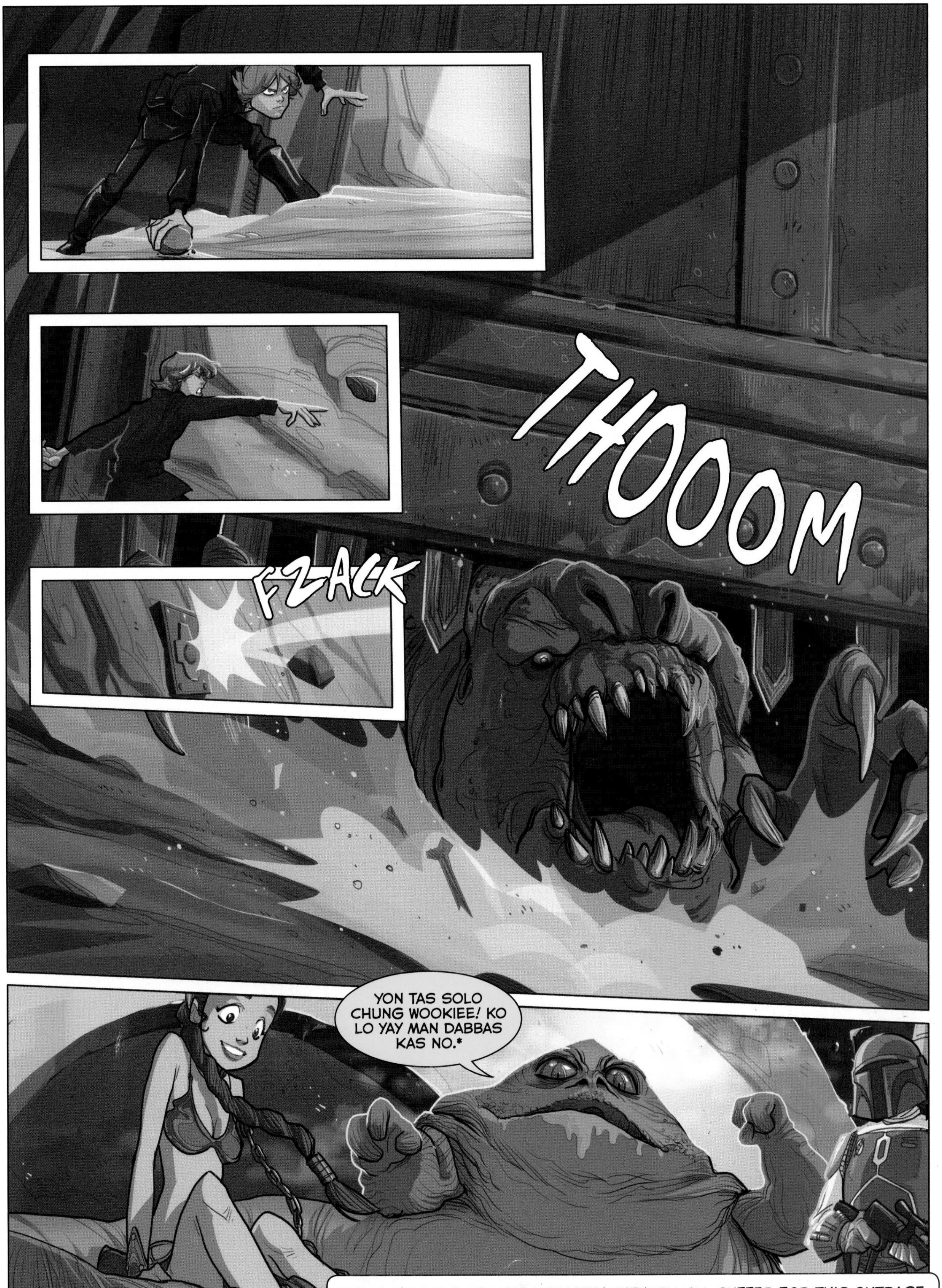
FZACK
THOOOM
YON TAS SOLO CHUNG WOOKIEE! KO LO YAY MAN DABBAS KAS NO.*
*BRING ME SOLO AND THE WOOKIEE! THEY WILL ALL SUFFER FOR THIS OUTRAGE.

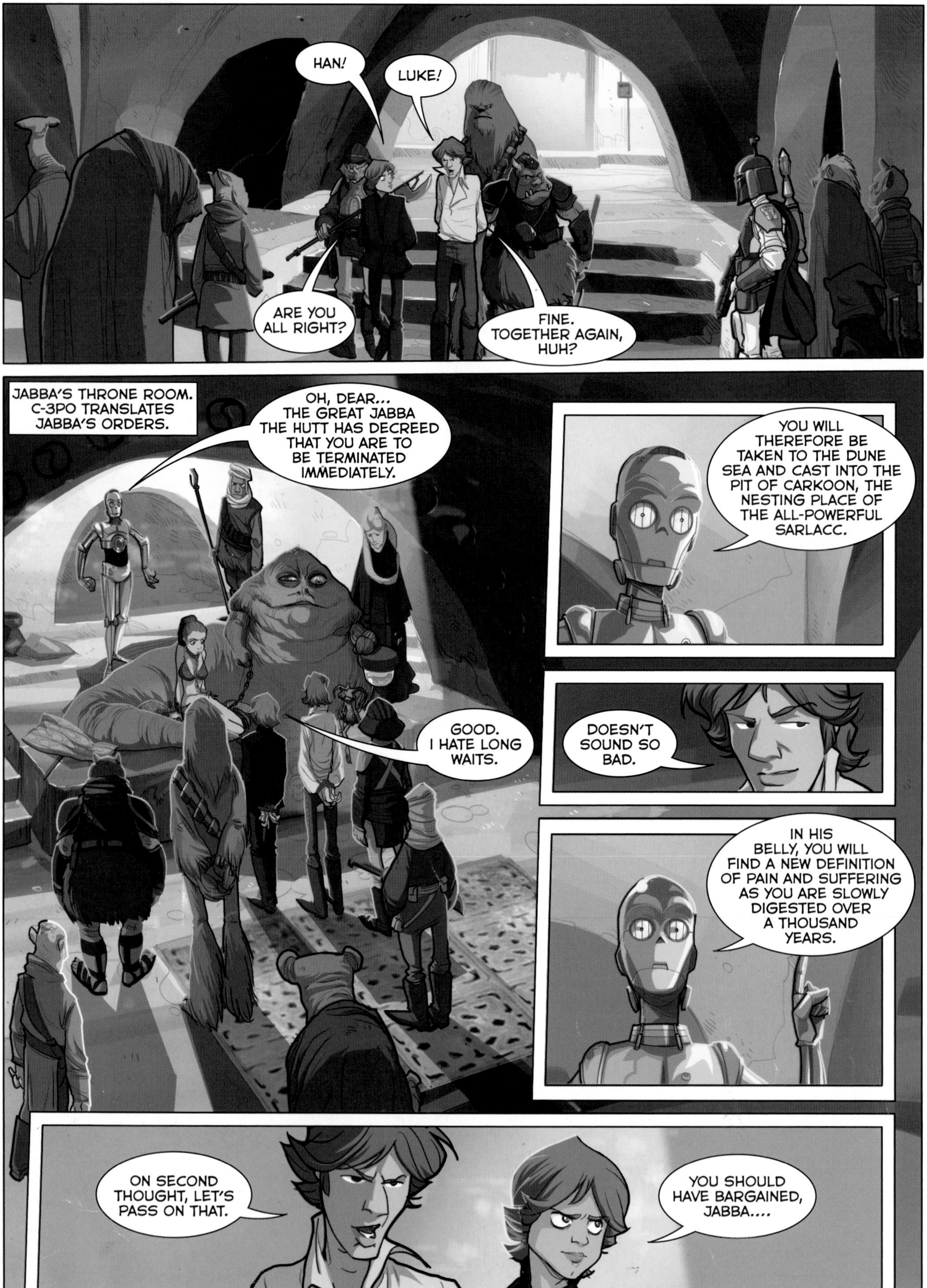
HAN!
LUKE!
ARE YOU ALL RIGHT?
FINE. TOGETHER AGAIN, HUH?
JABBA'S THRONE ROOM. C-3PO TRANSLATES JABBA'S ORDERS.
OH, DEAR... THE GREAT JABBA THE HUTT HAS DECREED THAT YOU ARE TO BE TERMINATED IMMEDIATELY.
GOOD. I HATE LONG WAITS.
YOU WILL THEREFORE BE TAKEN TO THE DUNE SEA AND CAST INTO THE PIT OF CARKOON, THE NESTING PLACE OF THE ALL-POWERFUL SARLACC.
DOESN'T SOUND SO BAD.
IN HIS BELLY, YOU WILL FIND A NEW DEFINITION OF PAIN AND SUFFERING AS YOU ARE SLOWLY DIGESTED OVER A THOUSAND YEARS.
ON SECOND THOUGHT, LET'S PASS ON THAT.
YOU SHOULD HAVE BARGAINED, JABBA....

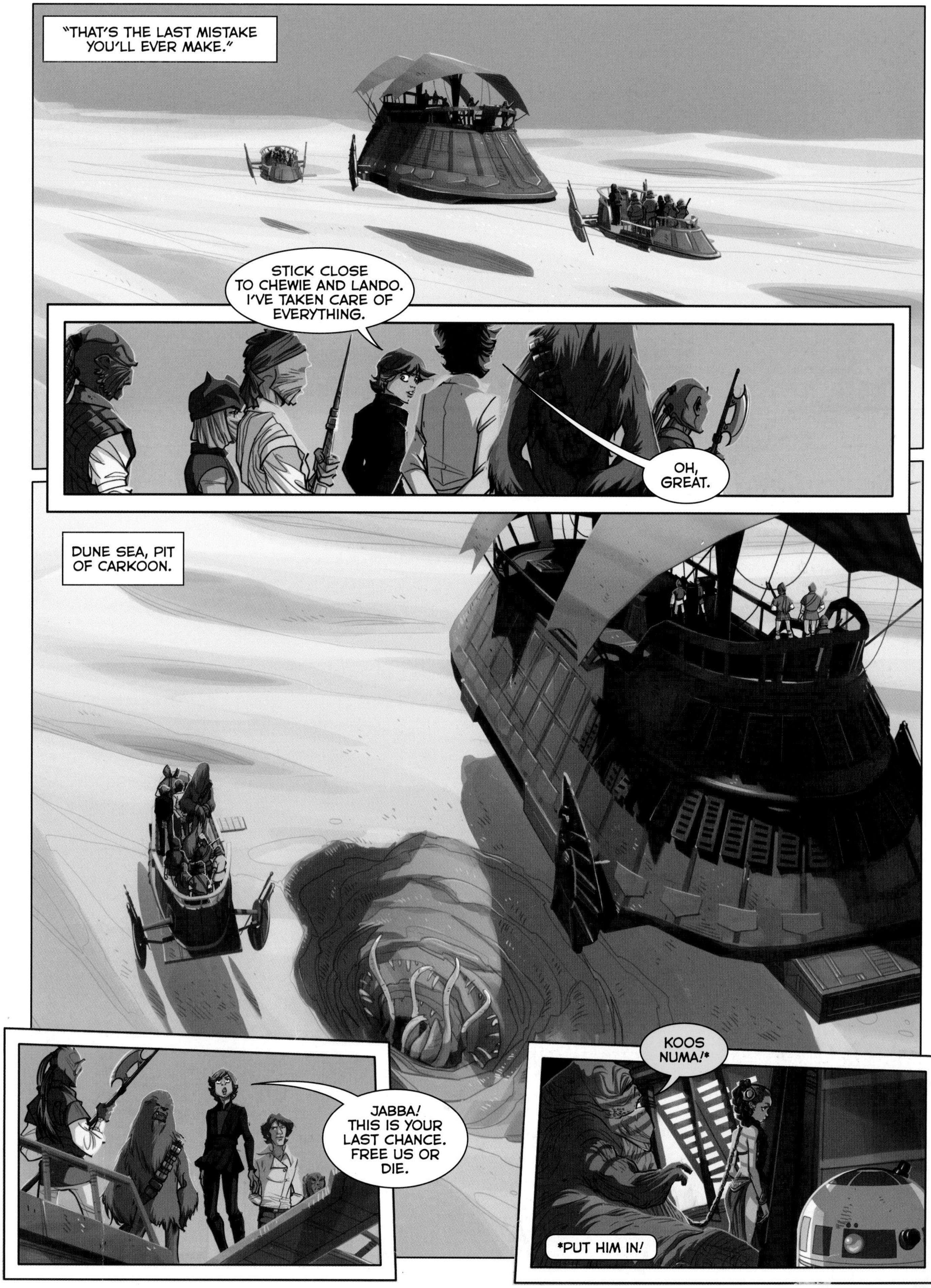

"THAT'S THE LAST MISTAKE YOU'LL EVER MAKE."
STICK CLOSE TO CHEWIE AND LANDO. I'VE TAKEN CARE OF EVERYTHING.
OH, GREAT.
DUNE SEA, PIT OF CARKOON.
JABBA! THIS IS YOUR LAST CHANCE. FREE US OR DIE.
KOOS NUMA!*
*PUT HIM IN!

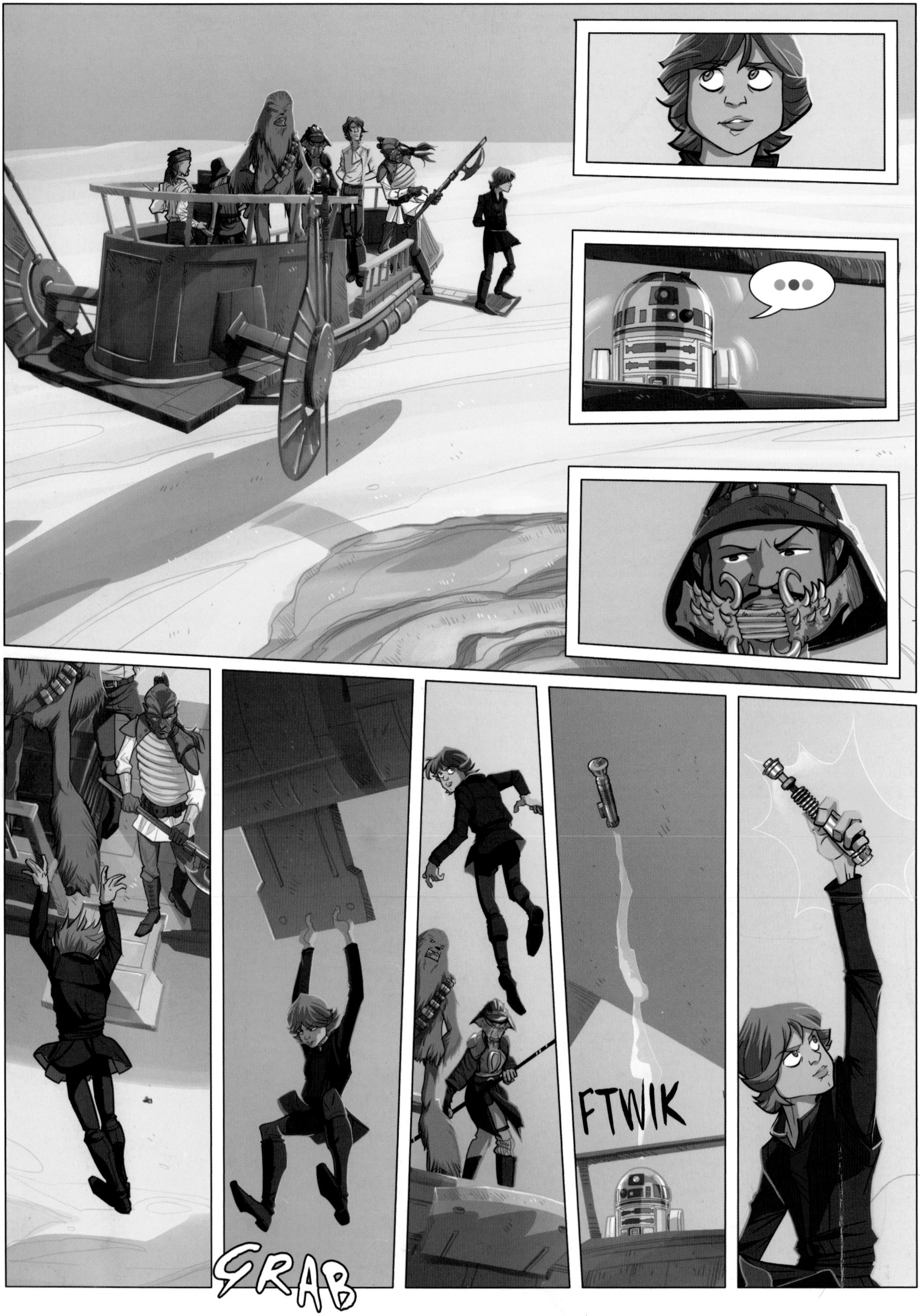
GRAB
FTWIK

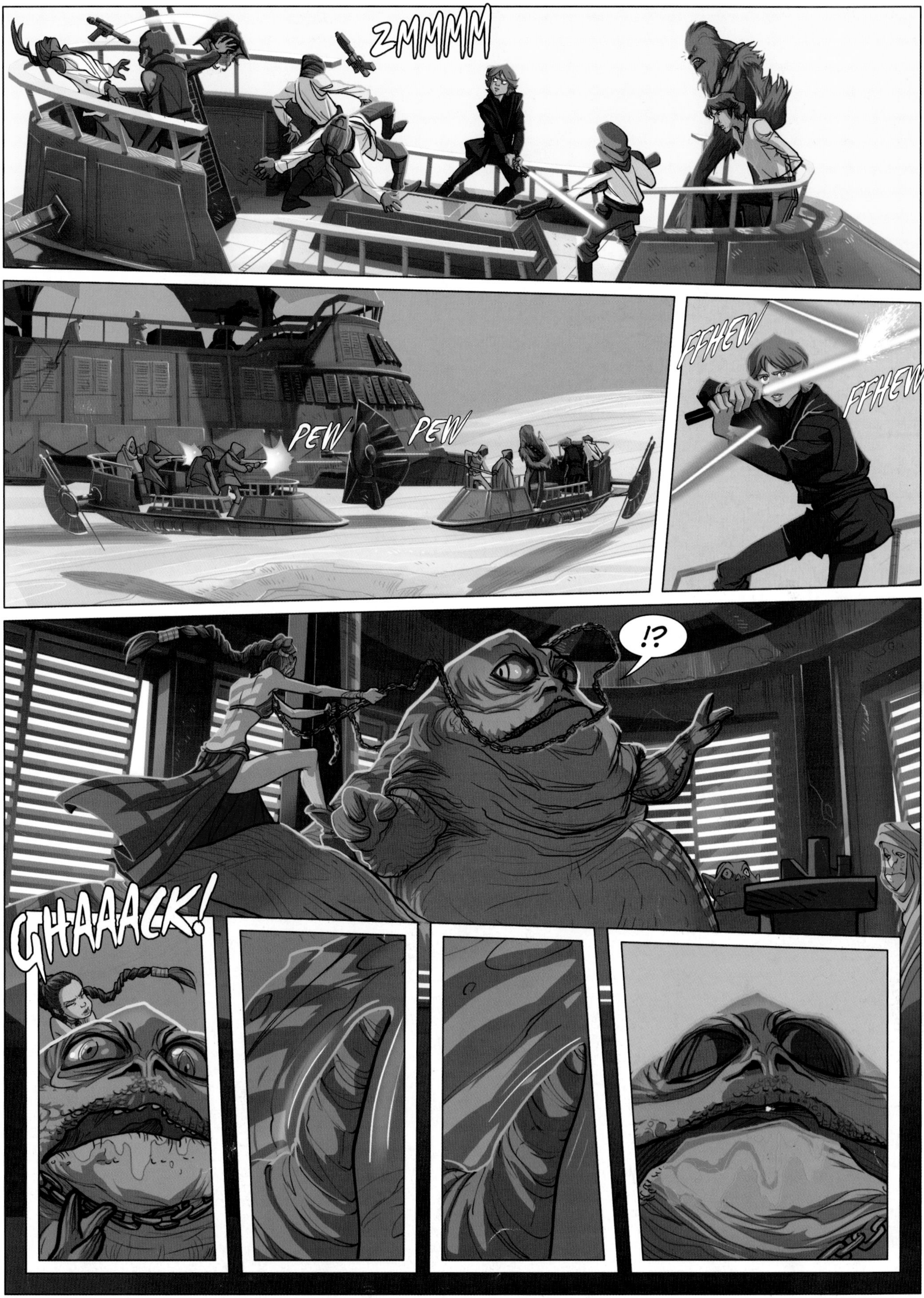
ZMMMM
PEW
PEW
FFHEW
FFHEW
!?
GHAAACK!

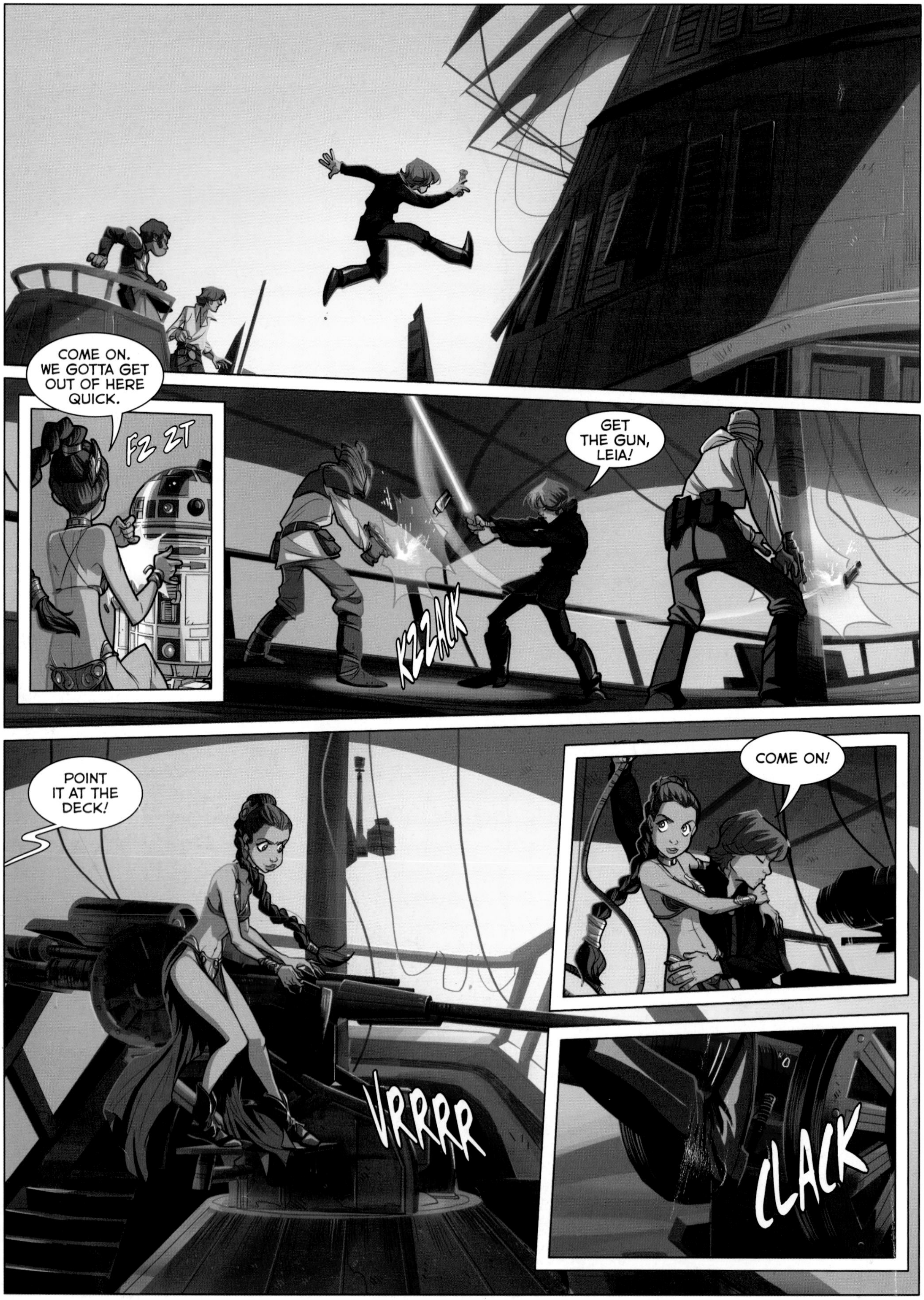
COME ON. WE GOTTA GET OUT OF HERE QUICK.
FZ ZT
GET THE GUN, LEIA!
KZZACK
POINT IT AT THE DECK!
VRRRR
COME ON!
CLACK

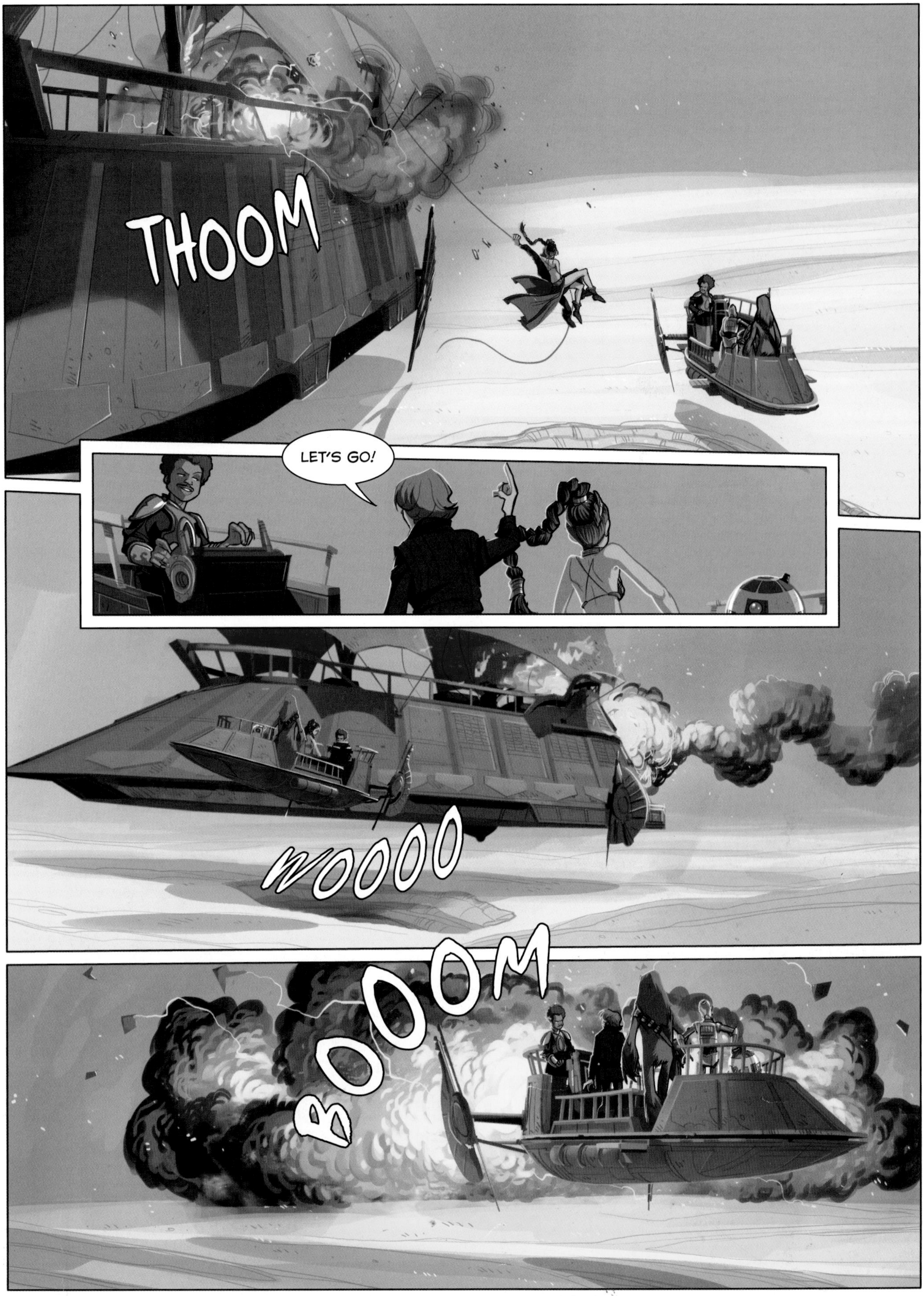
THOOM
LET'S GO!
WOOOO
BOOOOM

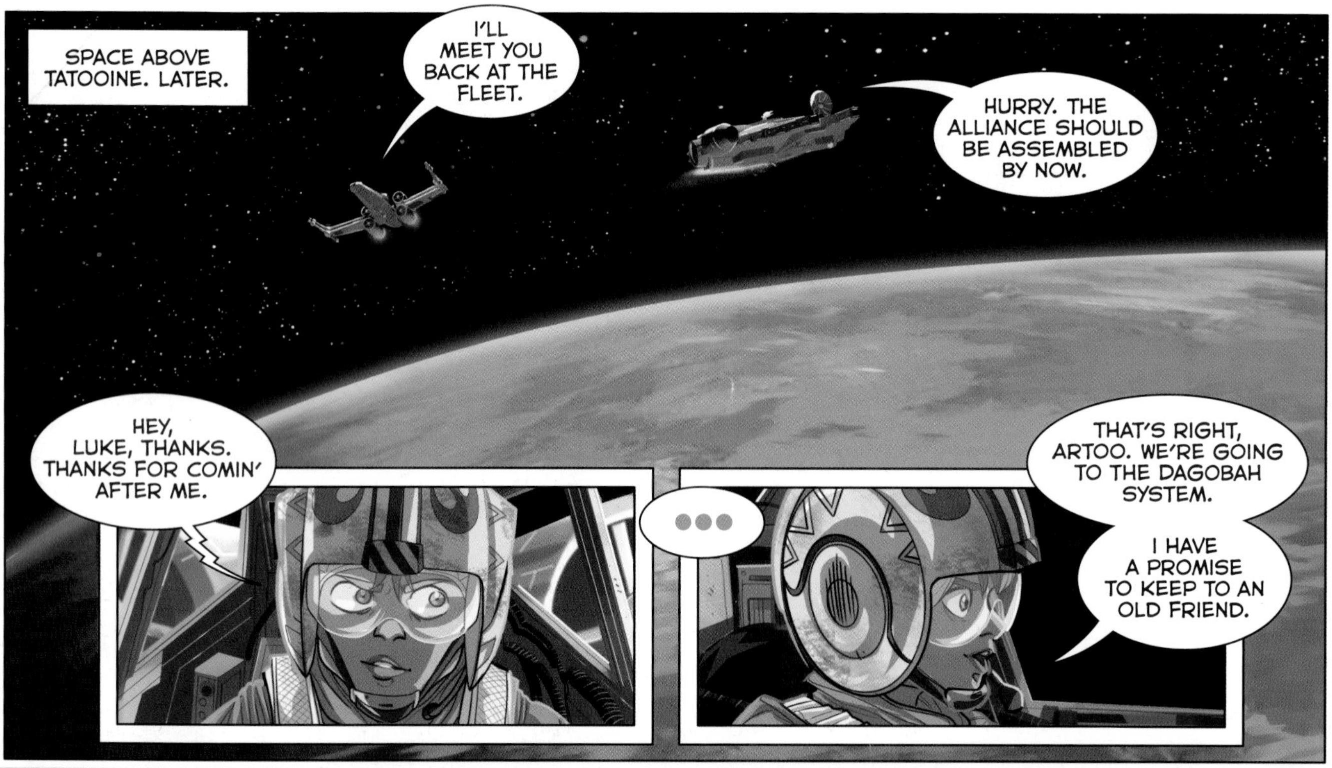
SPACE ABOVE TATOOINE. LATER.
I'LL MEET YOU BACK AT THE FLEET.
HURRY. THE ALLIANCE SHOULD BE ASSEMBLED BY NOW.
HEY, LUKE, THANKS. THANKS FOR COMIN' AFTER ME.
THAT'S RIGHT, ARTOO. WE'RE GOING TO THE DAGOBAH SYSTEM.
I HAVE A PROMISE TO KEEP TO AN OLD FRIEND.

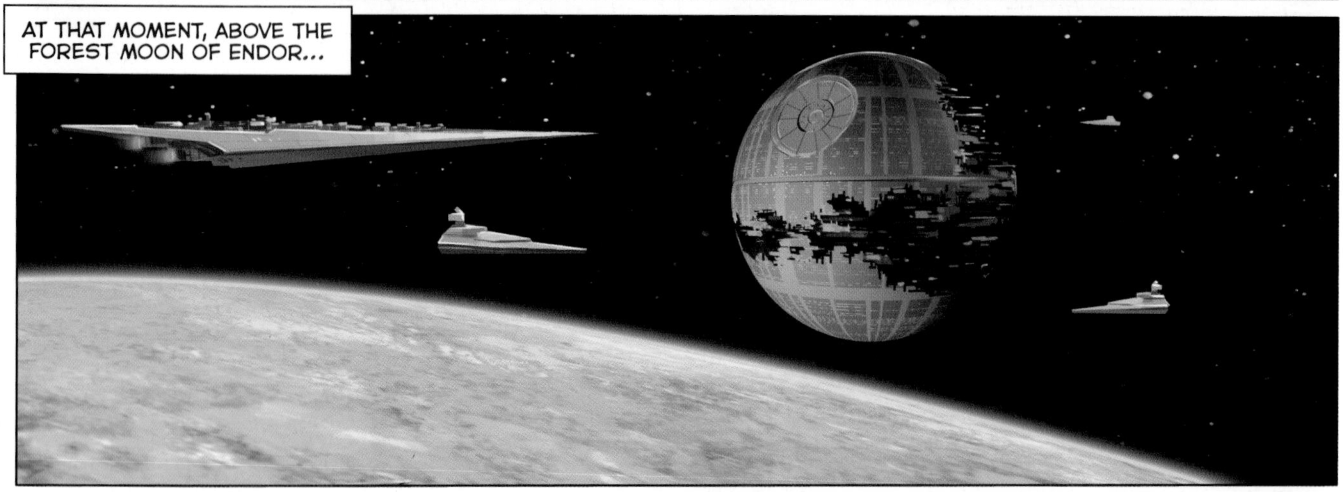
AT THAT MOMENT, ABOVE THE FOREST MOON OF ENDOR...

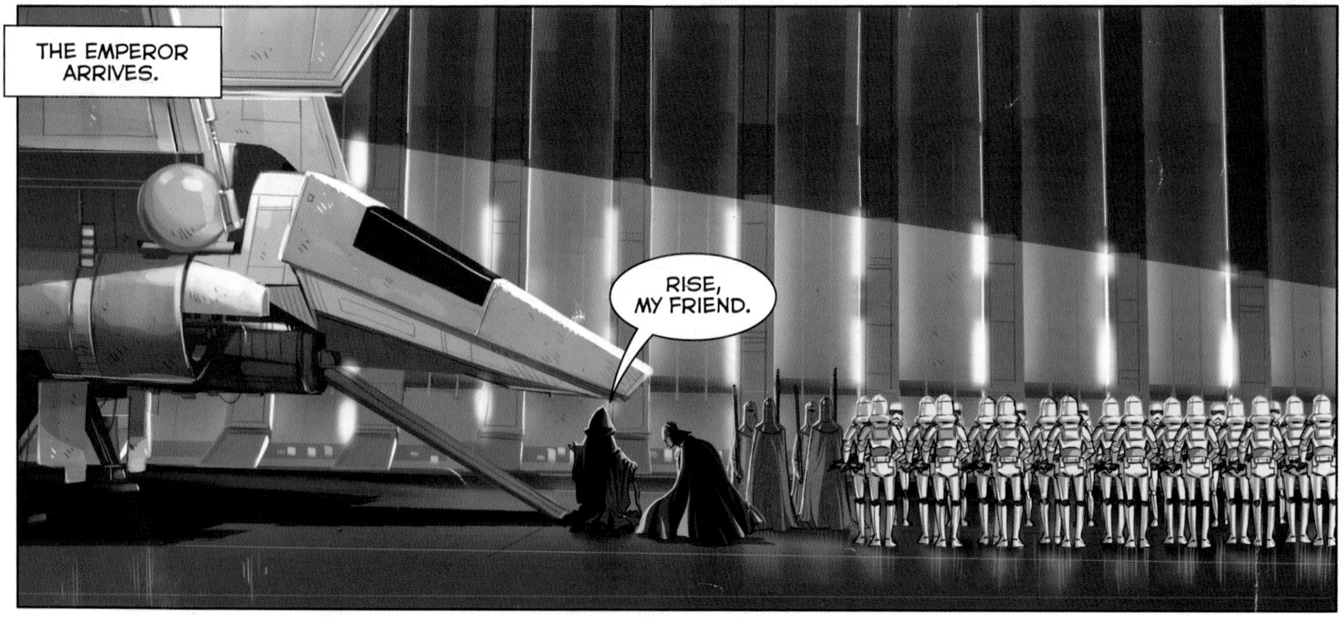
THE EMPEROR ARRIVES.
RISE, MY FRIEND.

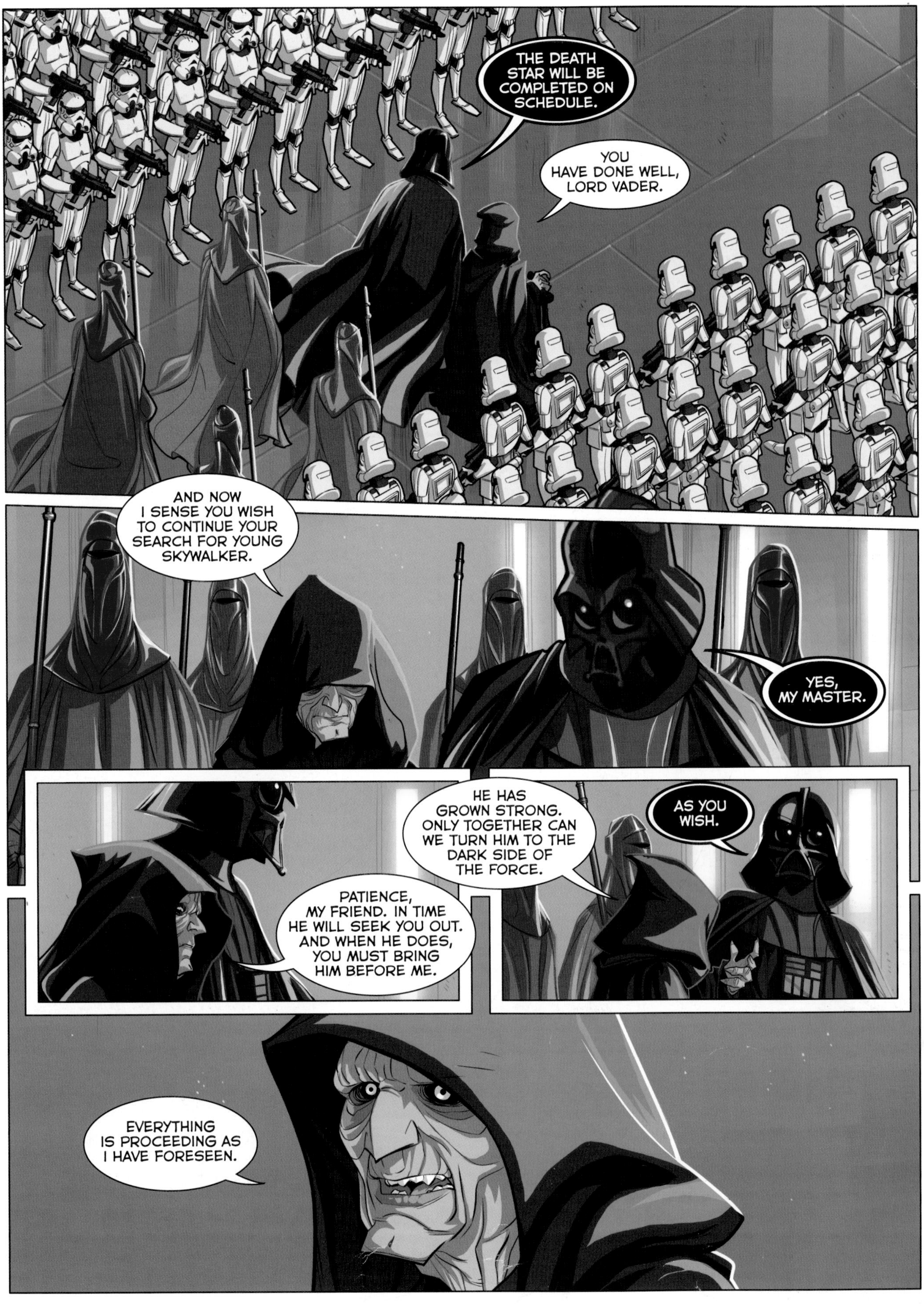
THE DEATH STAR WILL BE COMPLETED ON SCHEDULE.
YOU HAVE DONE WELL, LORD VADER.
AND NOW I SENSE YOU WISH TO CONTINUE YOUR SEARCH FOR YOUNG SKYWALKER.
YES, MY MASTER.
PATIENCE, MY FRIEND. IN TIME HE WILL SEEK YOU OUT. AND WHEN HE DOES, YOU MUST BRING HIM BEFORE ME.
HE HAS GROWN STRONG. ONLY TOGETHER CAN WE TURN HIM TO THE DARK SIDE OF THE FORCE.
AS YOU WISH.
EVERYTHING IS PROCEEDING AS I HAVE FORESEEN.

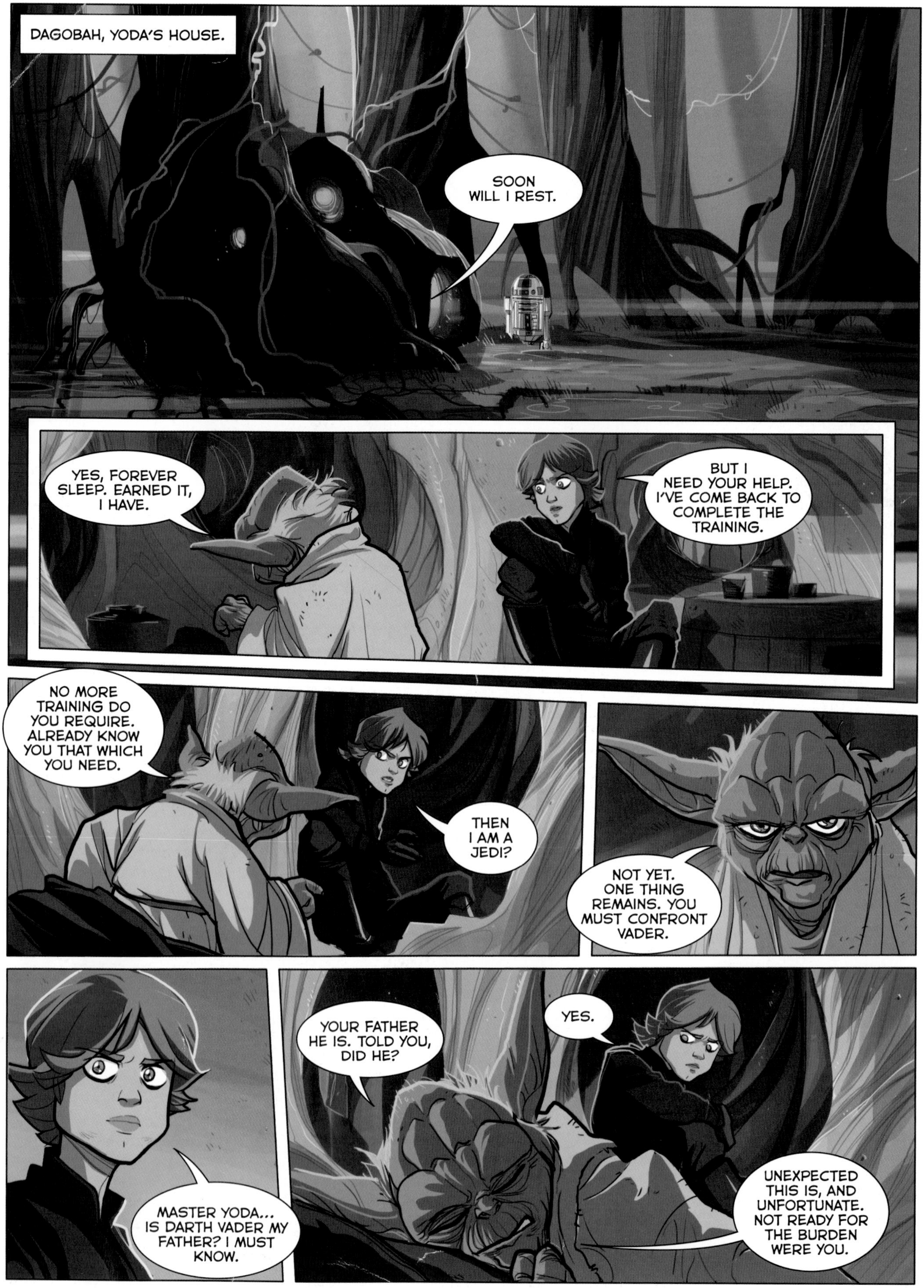
DAGOBAH, YODA'S HOUSE.
SOON WILL I REST.
YES, FOREVER SLEEP. EARNED IT, I HAVE.
BUT I NEED YOUR HELP. I'VE COME BACK TO COMPLETE THE TRAINING.
NO MORE TRAINING DO YOU REQUIRE. ALREADY KNOW YOU THAT WHICH YOU NEED.
THEN I AM A JEDI?
NOT YET. ONE THING REMAINS. YOU MUST CONFRONT VADER.
MASTER YODA... IS DARTH VADER MY FATHER? I MUST KNOW.
YOUR FATHER HE IS. TOLD YOU, DID HE?
YES.
UNEXPECTED THIS IS, AND UNFORTUNATE. NOT READY FOR THE BURDEN WERE YOU.

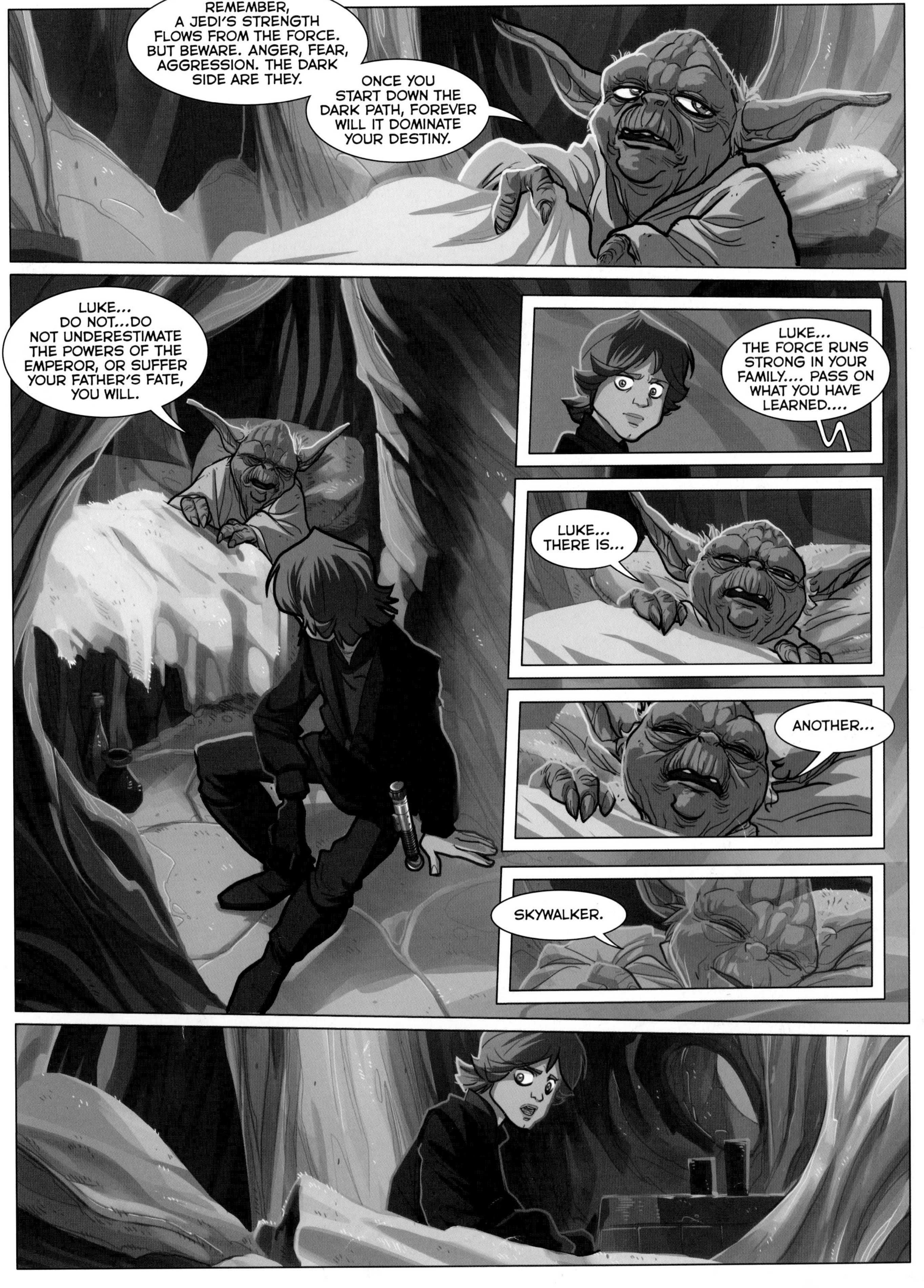
REMEMBER, A JEDI'S STRENGTH FLOWS FROM THE FORCE. BUT BEWARE. ANGER, FEAR, AGGRESSION. THE DARK SIDE ARE THEY.
ONCE YOU START DOWN THE DARK PATH, FOREVER WILL IT DOMINATE YOUR DESTINY.
LUKE... DO NOT...DO NOT UNDERESTIMATE THE POWERS OF THE EMPEROR, OR SUFFER YOUR FATHER'S FATE, YOU WILL.
LUKE... THE FORCE RUNS STRONG IN YOUR FAMILY.... PASS ON WHAT YOU HAVE LEARNED....
LUKE... THERE IS...
ANOTHER...
SKYWALKER.

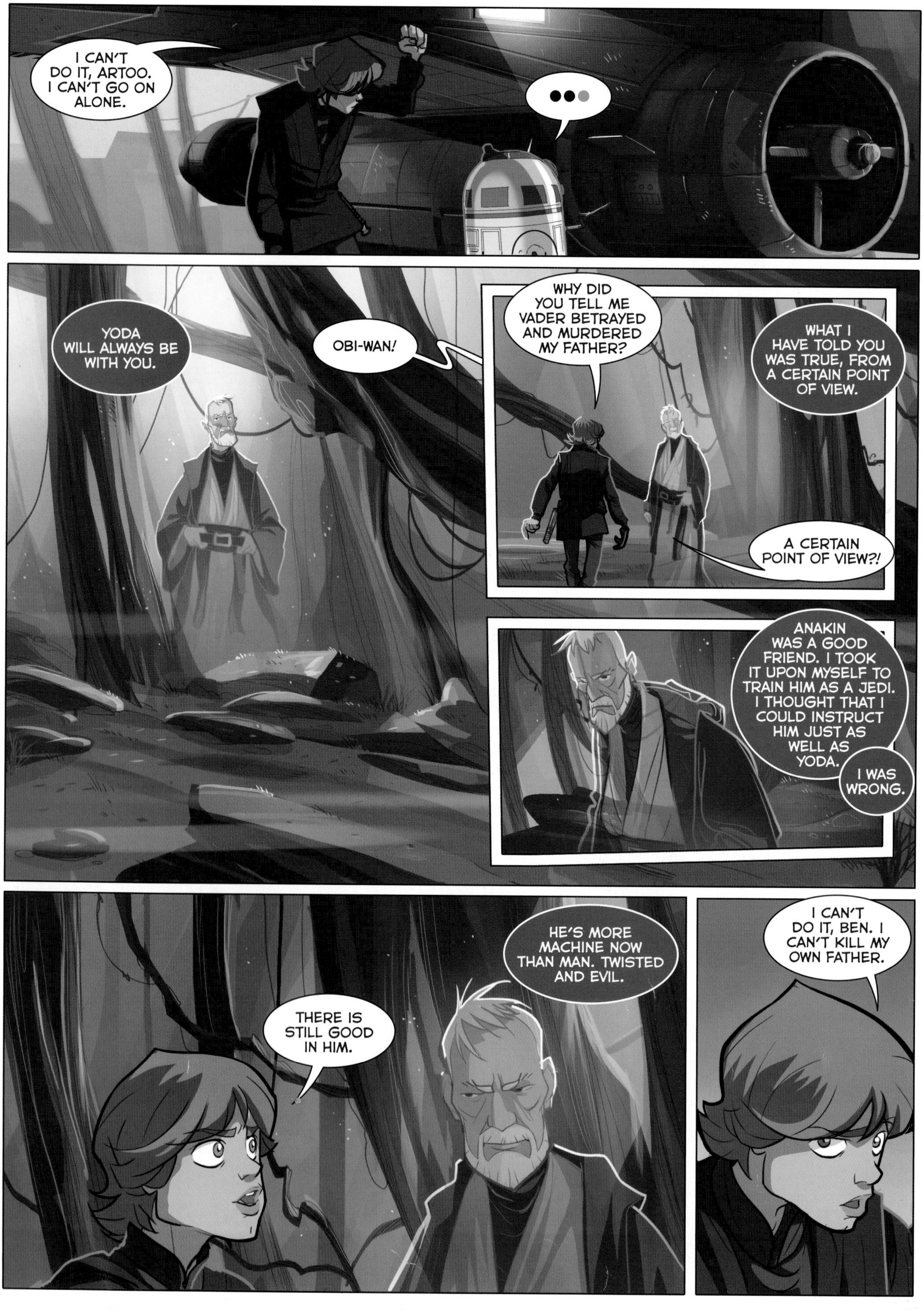
I CAN'T DO IT, ARTOO. I CAN'T GO ON ALONE.
YODA WILL ALWAYS BE WITH YOU.
OBI-WAN!
WHY DID YOU TELL ME VADER BETRAYED AND MURDERED MY FATHER?
WHAT I HAVE TOLD YOU WAS TRUE, FROM A CERTAIN POINT OF VIEW.
A CERTAIN POINT OF VIEW?!
ANAKIN WAS A GOOD FRIEND. I TOOK IT UPON MYSELF TO TRAIN HIM AS A JEDI. I THOUGHT THAT I COULD INSTRUCT HIM JUST AS WELL AS YODA.
I WAS WRONG.
THERE IS STILL GOOD IN HIM.
HE'S MORE MACHINE NOW THAN MAN. TWISTED AND EVIL.
I CAN'T DO IT, BEN. I CAN'T KILL MY OWN FATHER.

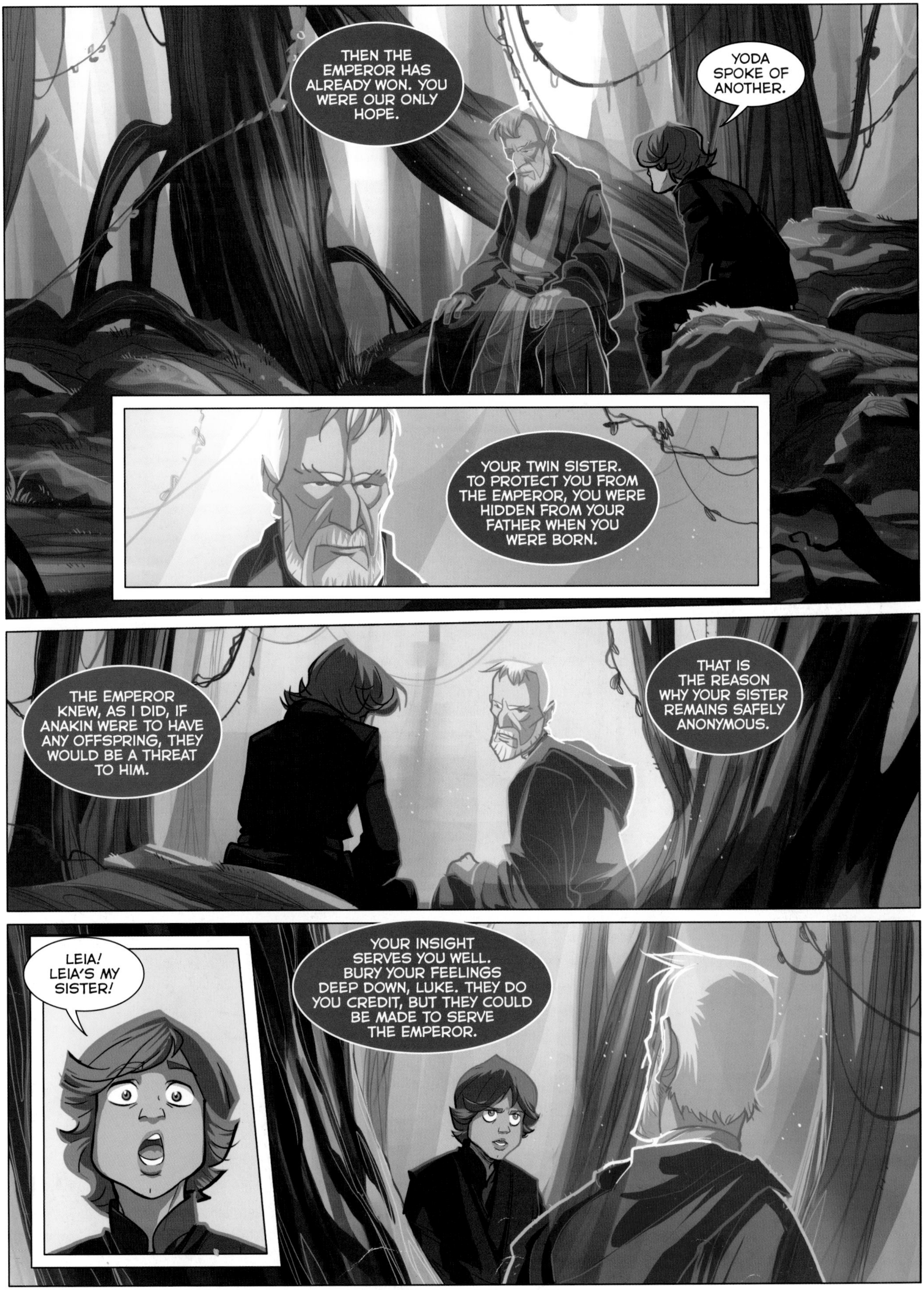
THEN THE EMPEROR HAS ALREADY WON. YOU WERE OUR ONLY HOPE.
YODA SPOKE OF ANOTHER.
YOUR TWIN SISTER. TO PROTECT YOU FROM THE EMPEROR, YOU WERE HIDDEN FROM YOUR FATHER WHEN YOU WERE BORN.
THE EMPEROR KNEW, AS I DID, IF ANAKIN WERE TO HAVE ANY OFFSPRING, THEY WOULD BE A THREAT TO HIM.
THAT IS THE REASON WHY YOUR SISTER REMAINS SAFELY ANONYMOUS.
LEIA! LEIA'S MY SISTER!
YOUR INSIGHT SERVES YOU WELL. BURY YOUR FEELINGS DEEP DOWN, LUKE. THEY DO YOU CREDIT, BUT THEY COULD BE MADE TO SERVE THE EMPEROR.

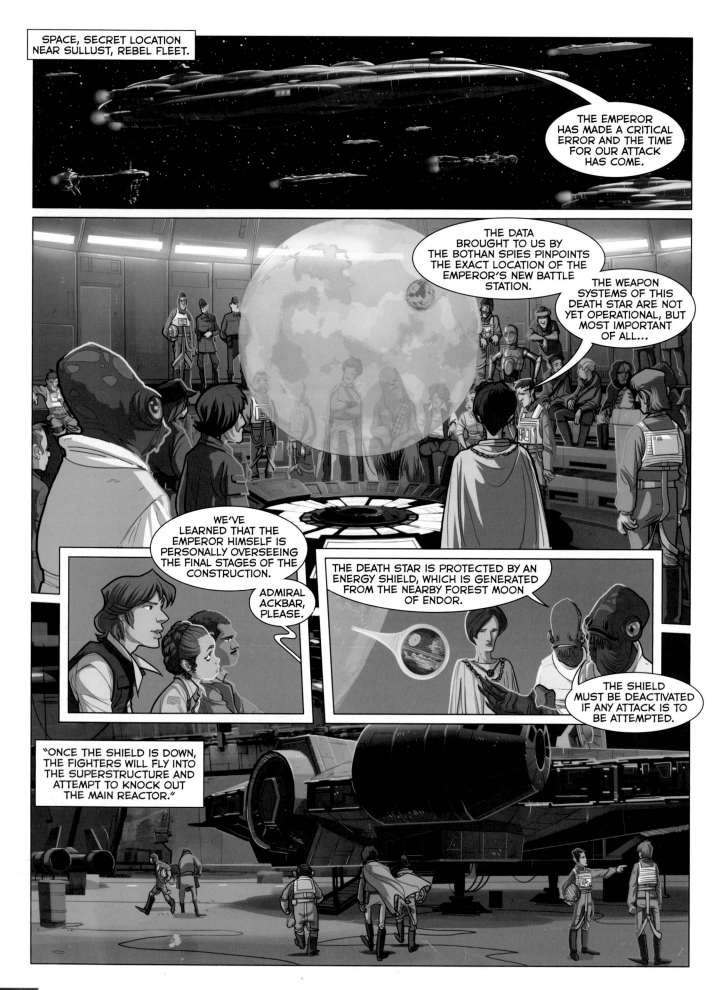

SPACE, SECRET LOCATION NEAR SULLUST, REBEL FLEET.

THE EMPEROR HAS MADE A CRITICAL ERROR AND THE TIME FOR OUR ATTACK HAS COME.

THE DATA BROUGHT TO US BY THE BOTHAN SPIES PINPOINTS THE EXACT LOCATION OF THE EMPEROR'S NEW BATTLE STATION.

THE WEAPON SYSTEMS OF THIS DEATH STAR ARE NOT YET OPERATIONAL, BUT MOST IMPORTANT OF ALL...

WE'VE LEARNED THAT THE EMPEROR HIMSELF IS PERSONALLY OVERSEEING THE FINAL STAGES OF THE CONSTRUCTION.

ADMIRAL ACKBAR, PLEASE.

THE DEATH STAR IS PROTECTED BY AN ENERGY SHIELD, WHICH IS GENERATED FROM THE NEARBY FOREST MOON OF ENDOR.

THE SHIELD MUST BE DEACTIVATED IF ANY ATTACK IS TO BE ATTEMPTED.

"ONCE THE SHIELD IS DOWN, THE FIGHTERS WILL FLY INTO THE SUPERSTRUCTURE AND ATTEMPT TO KNOCK OUT THE MAIN REACTOR."

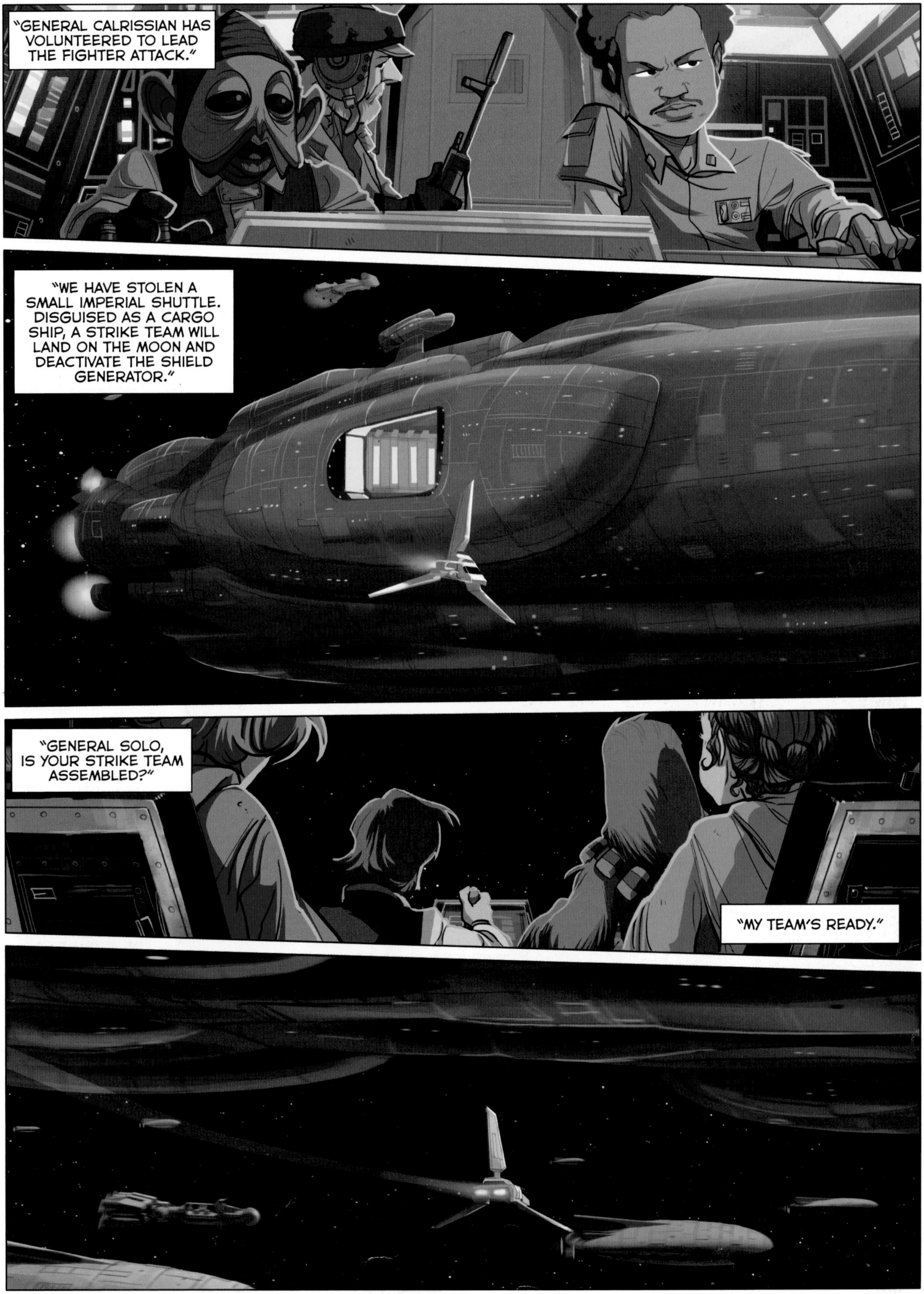
"GENERAL CALRISSIAN HAS VOLUNTEERED TO LEAD THE FIGHTER ATTACK."
"WE HAVE STOLEN A SMALL IMPERIAL SHUTTLE. DISGUISED AS A CARGO SHIP, A STRIKE TEAM WILL LAND ON THE MOON AND DEACTIVATE THE SHIELD GENERATOR."
"GENERAL SOLO, IS YOUR STRIKE TEAM ASSEMBLED?"
"MY TEAM'S READY."

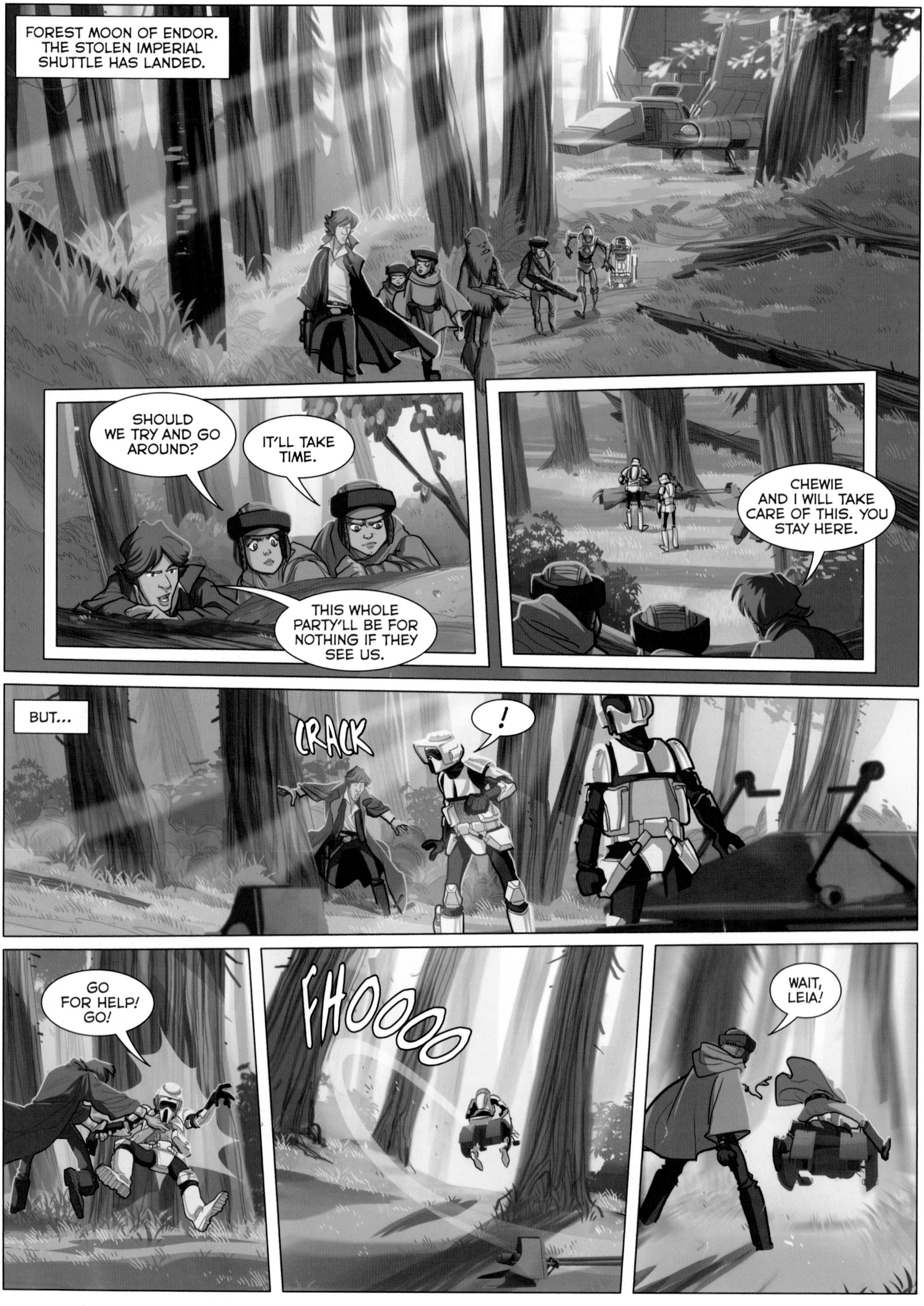

FOREST MOON OF ENDOR. THE STOLEN IMPERIAL SHUTTLE HAS LANDED.
SHOULD WE TRY AND GO AROUND?
IT'LL TAKE TIME.
THIS WHOLE PARTY'LL BE FOR NOTHING IF THEY SEE US.
CHEWIE AND I WILL TAKE CARE OF THIS. YOU STAY HERE.
BUT...
CRACK
!
GO FOR HELP! GO!
FHOOOO
WAIT, LEIA!

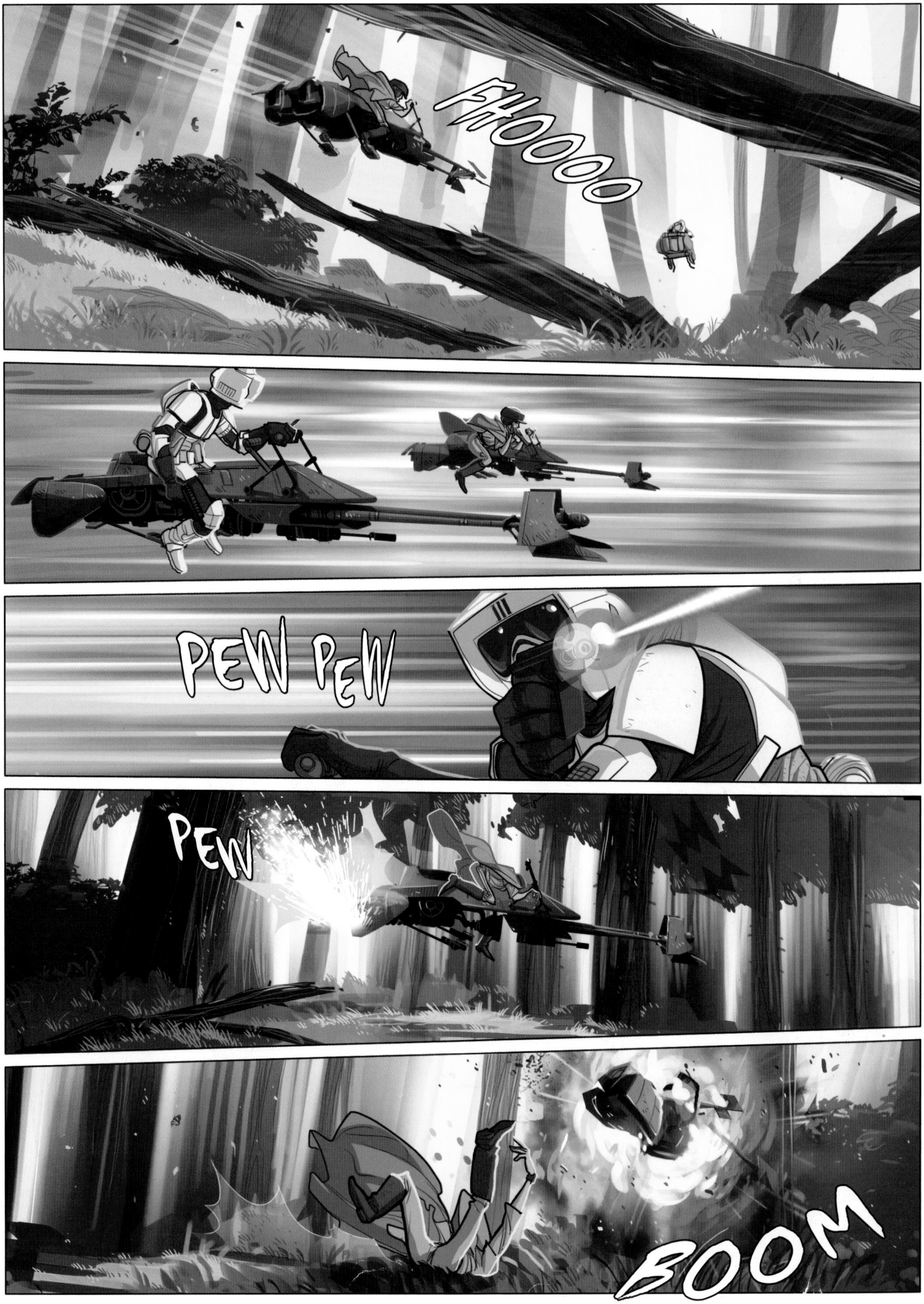
FHOOOO
PEW PEW
PEW
BOOM

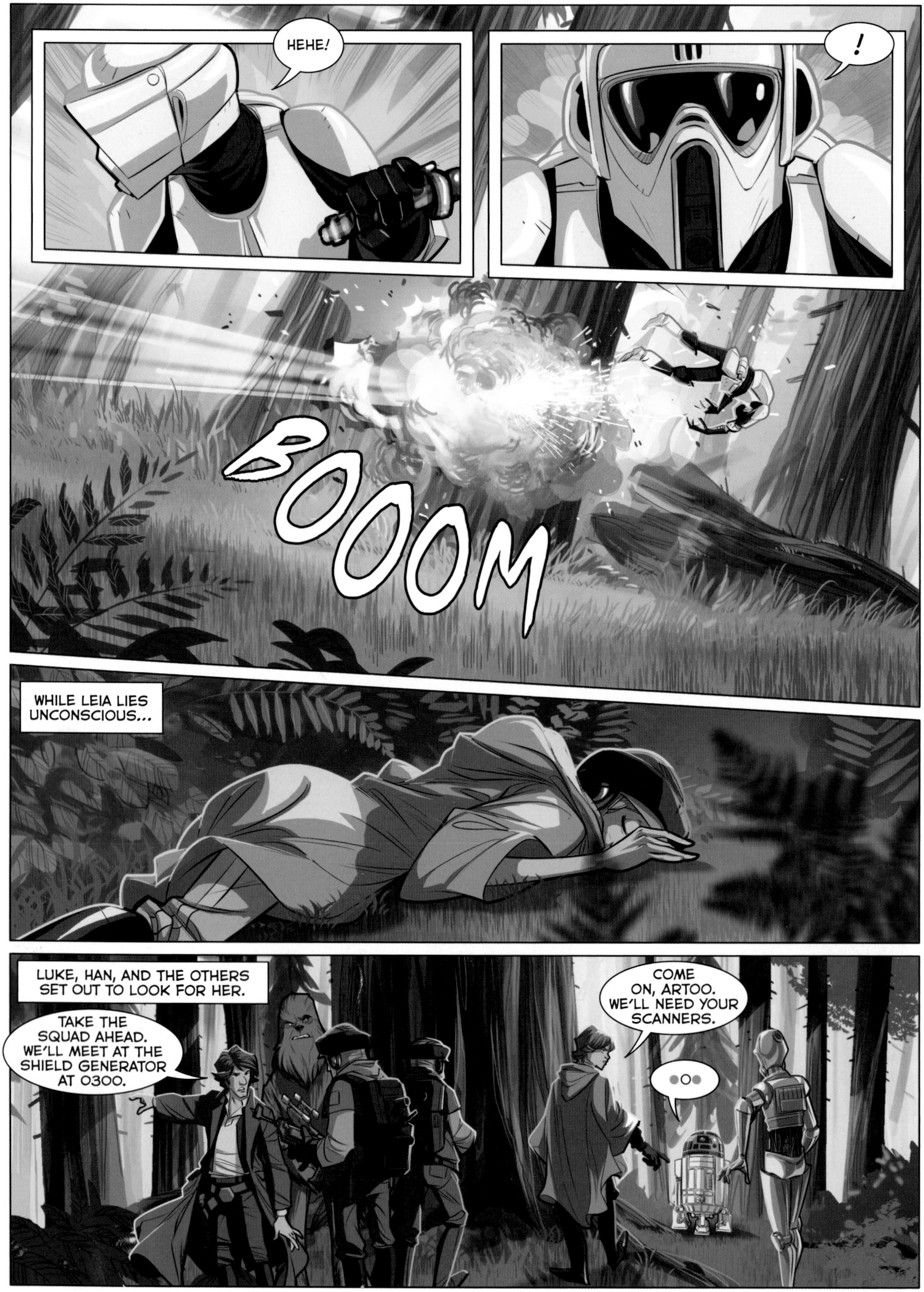

HEHE!
!
BOOOM
WHILE LEIA LIES UNCONSCIOUS...
LUKE, HAN, AND THE OTHERS SET OUT TO LOOK FOR HER.
TAKE THE SQUAD AHEAD. WE'LL MEET AT THE SHIELD GENERATOR AT 0300.
COME ON, ARTOO. WE'LL NEED YOUR SCANNERS.

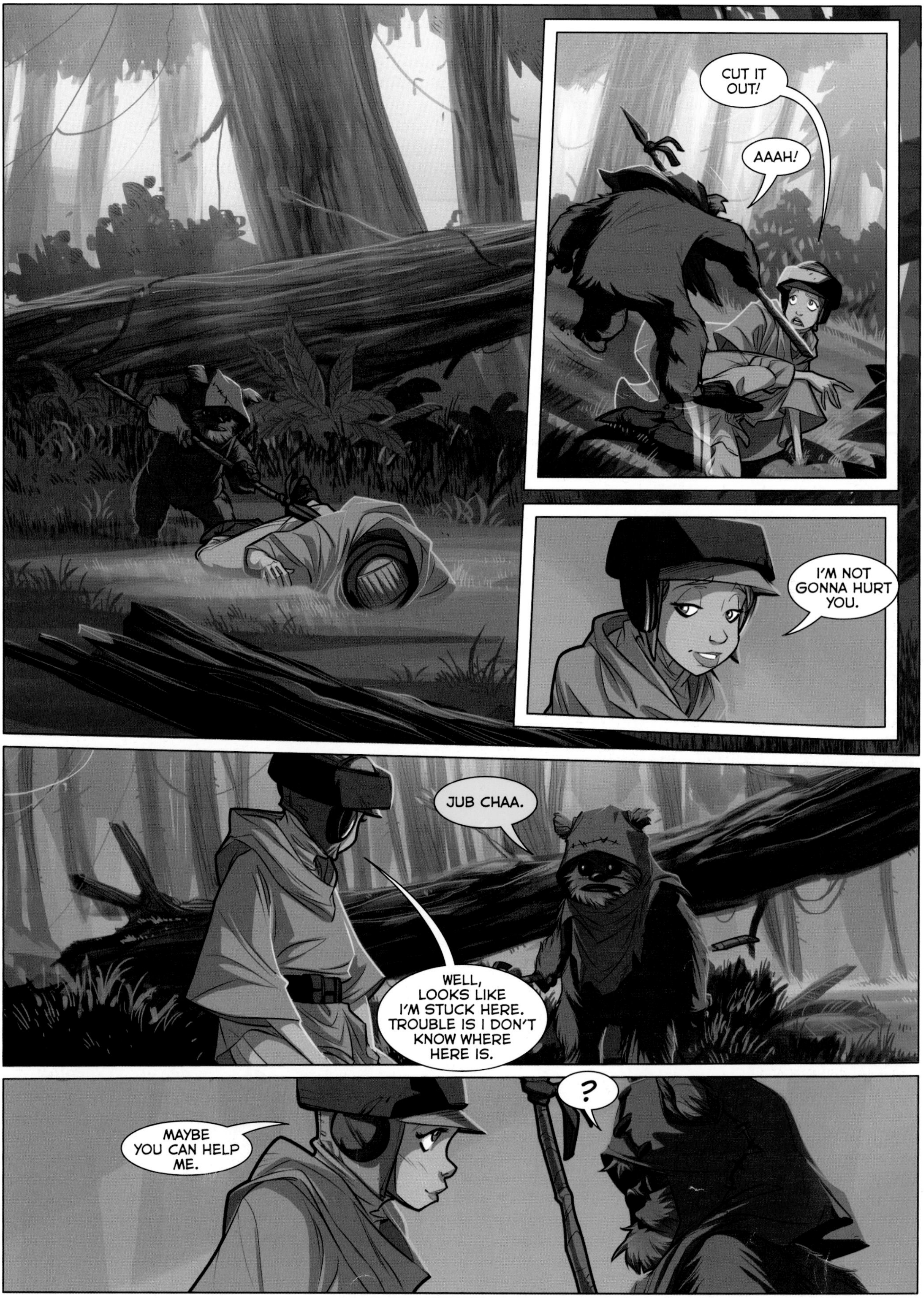
CUT IT OUT!
AAAH!
I'M NOT GONNA HURT YOU.
JUB CHAA.
WELL, LOOKS LIKE I'M STUCK HERE. TROUBLE IS I DON'T KNOW WHERE HERE IS.
?
MAYBE YOU CAN HELP ME.

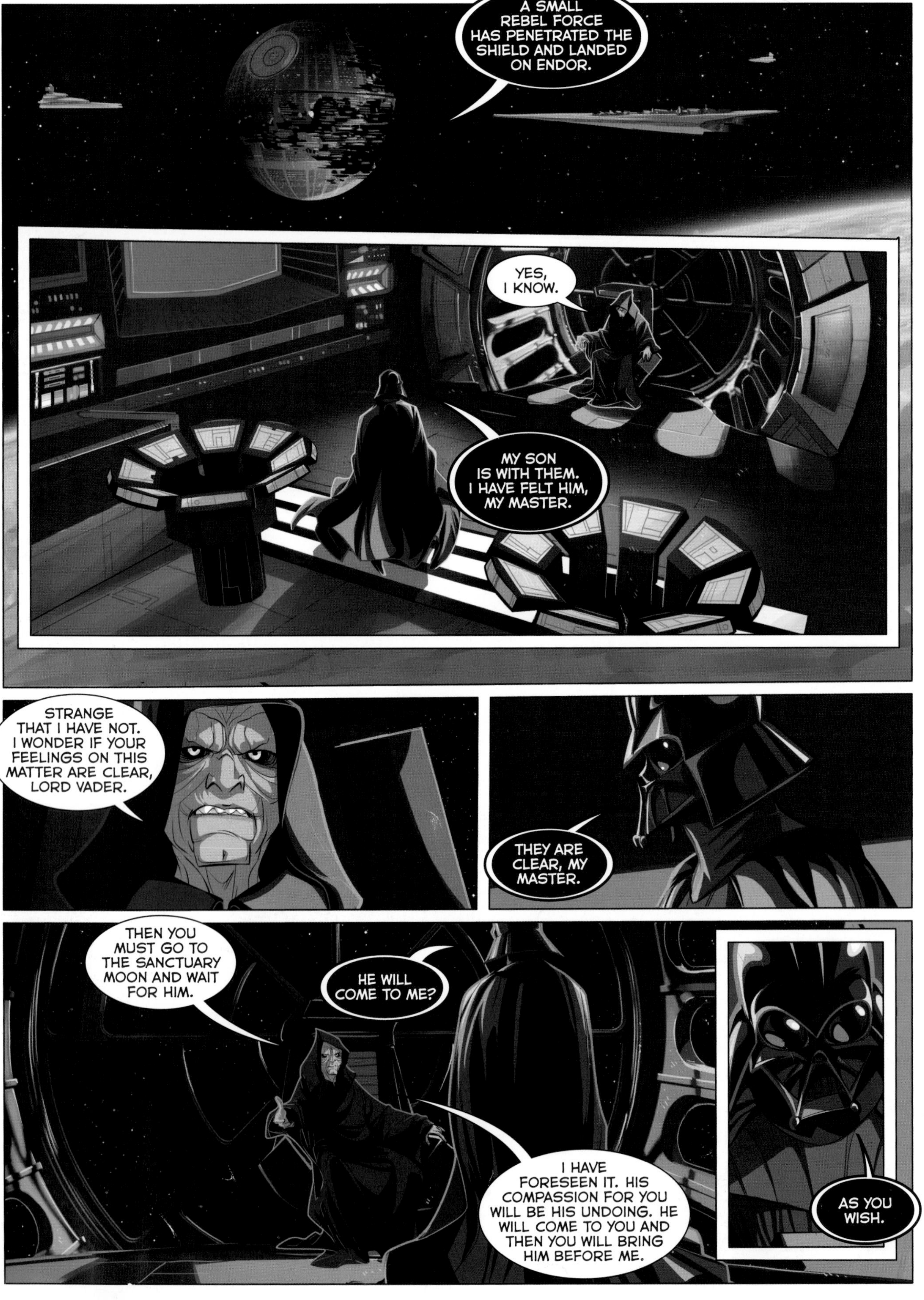
A SMALL REBEL FORCE HAS PENETRATED THE SHIELD AND LANDED ON ENDOR.
YES, I KNOW.
MY SON IS WITH THEM. I HAVE FELT HIM, MY MASTER.
STRANGE THAT I HAVE NOT. I WONDER IF YOUR FEELINGS ON THIS MATTER ARE CLEAR, LORD VADER.
THEY ARE CLEAR, MY MASTER.
THEN YOU MUST GO TO THE SANCTUARY MOON AND WAIT FOR HIM.
HE WILL COME TO ME?
I HAVE FORESEEN IT. HIS COMPASSION FOR YOU WILL BE HIS UNDOING. HE WILL COME TO YOU AND THEN YOU WILL BRING HIM BEFORE ME.
AS YOU WISH.

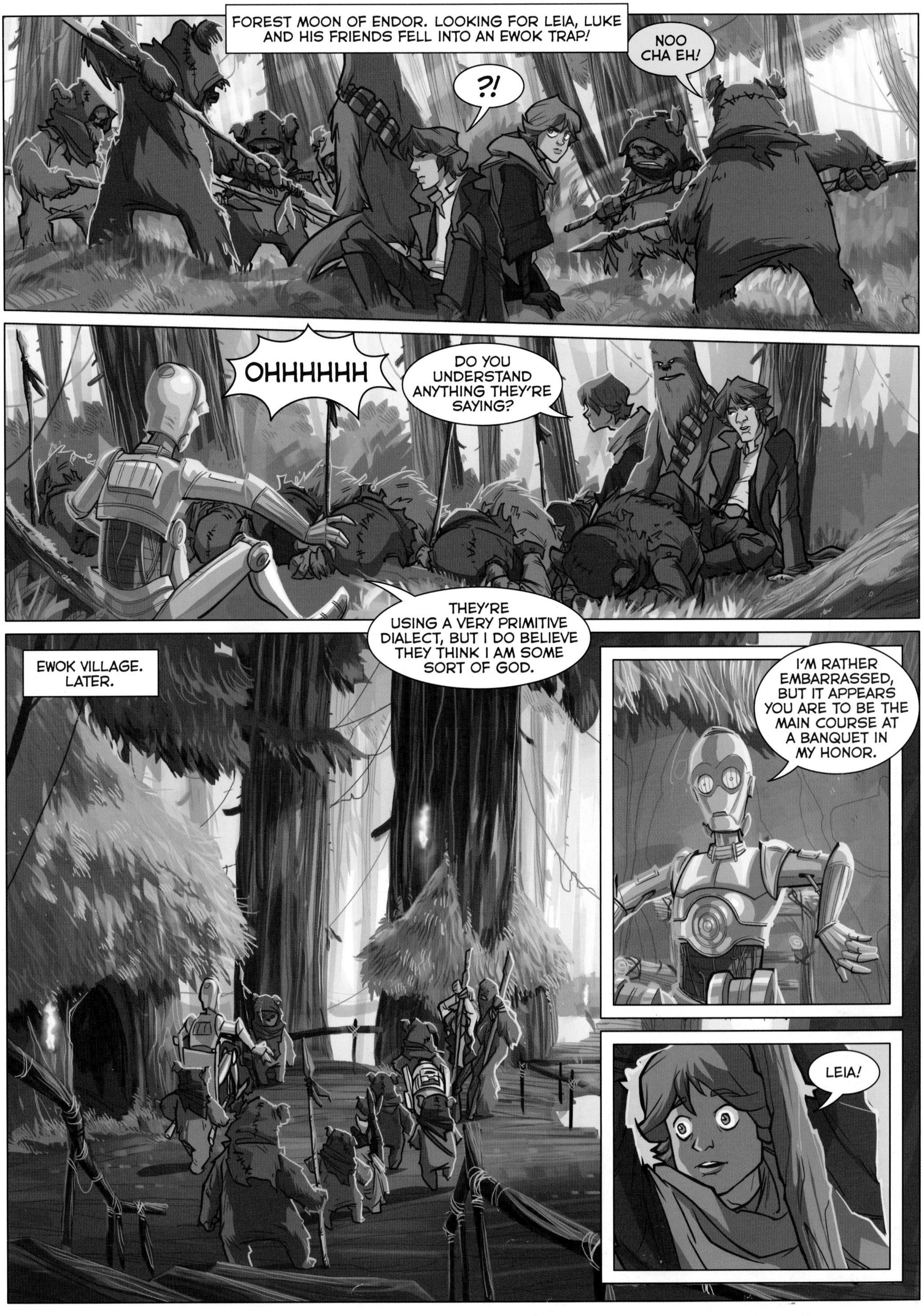
FOREST MOON OF ENDOR. LOOKING FOR LEIA, LUKE AND HIS FRIENDS FELL INTO AN EWOK TRAP!
?!
NOO CHA EH!
OHHHHHH
DO YOU UNDERSTAND ANYTHING THEY'RE SAYING?
THEY'RE USING A VERY PRIMITIVE DIALECT, BUT I DO BELIEVE THEY THINK I AM SOME SORT OF GOD.
EWOK VILLAGE. LATER.
I'M RATHER EMBARRASSED, BUT IT APPEARS YOU ARE TO BE THE MAIN COURSE AT A BANQUET IN MY HONOR.
LEIA!

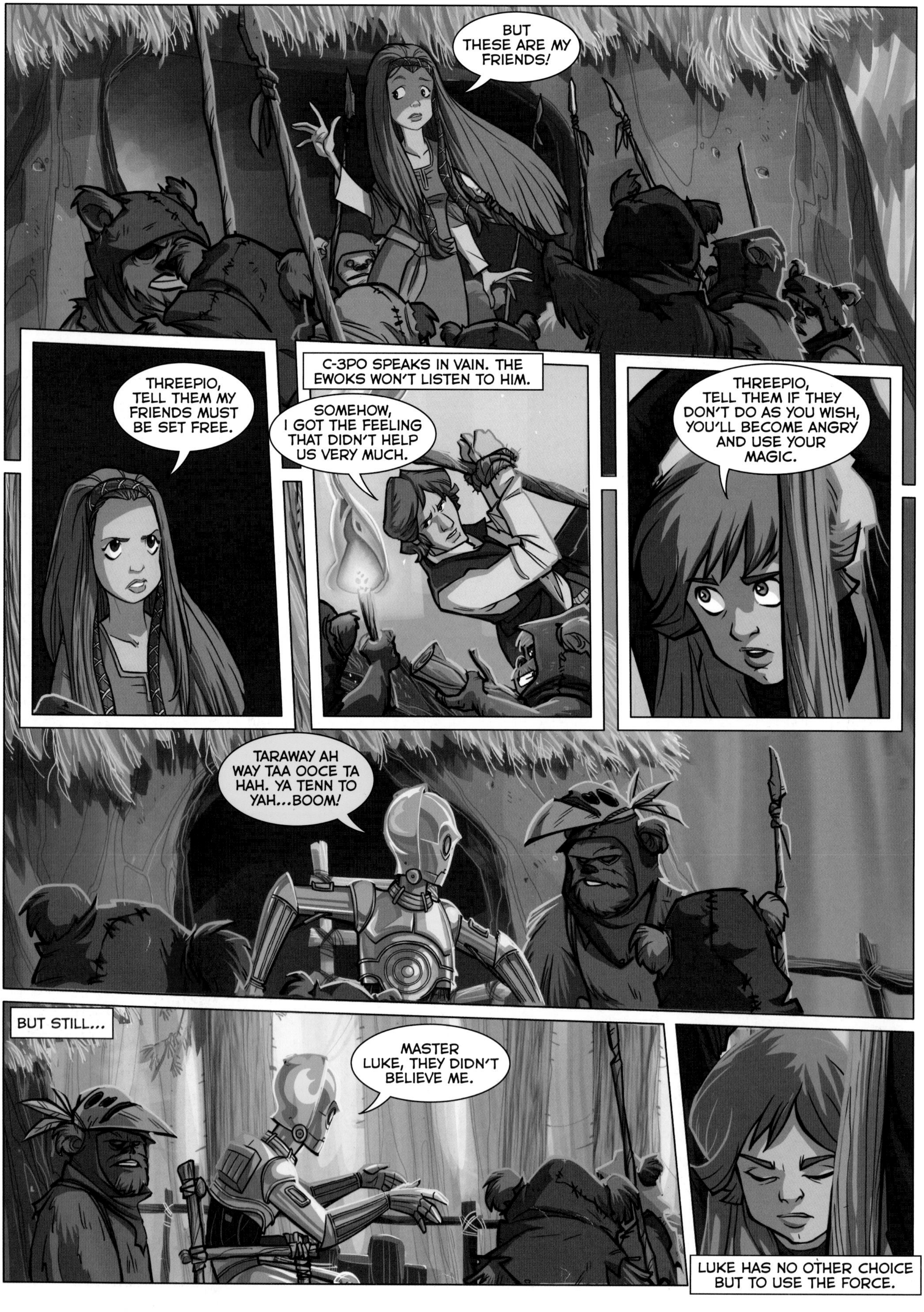
BUT THESE ARE MY FRIENDS!
THREEPIO, TELL THEM MY FRIENDS MUST BE SET FREE.
C-3PO SPEAKS IN VAIN. THE EWOKS WON'T LISTEN TO HIM.
SOMEHOW, I GOT THE FEELING THAT DIDN'T HELP US VERY MUCH.
THREEPIO, TELL THEM IF THEY DON'T DO AS YOU WISH, YOU'LL BECOME ANGRY AND USE YOUR MAGIC.
TARAWAY AH WAY TAA OOCE TA HAH. YA TENN TO YAH...BOOM!
BUT STILL...
MASTER LUKE, THEY DIDN'T BELIEVE ME.
LUKE HAS NO OTHER CHOICE BUT TO USE THE FORCE.

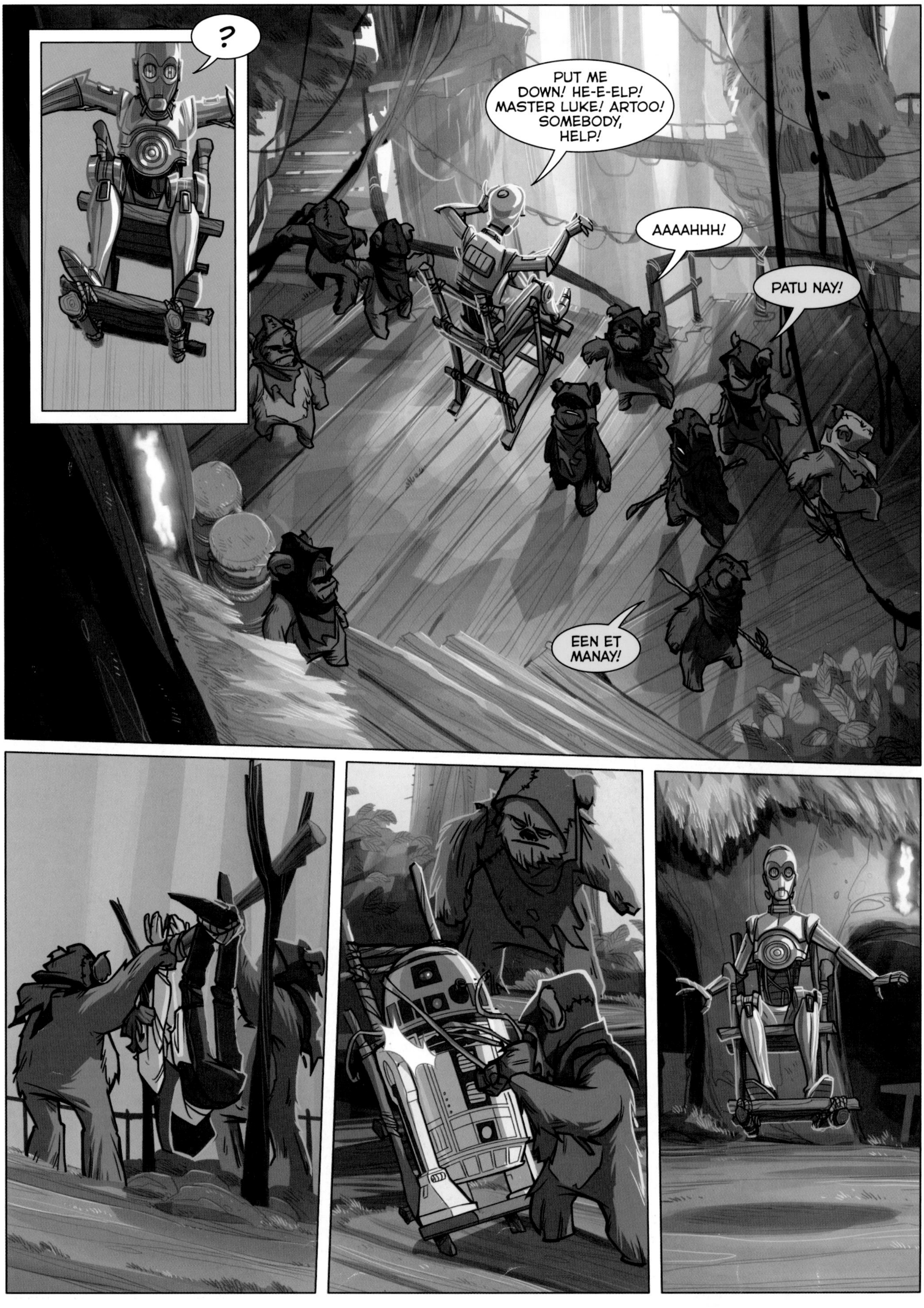
?
PUT ME DOWN! HE-E-ELP! MASTER LUKE! ARTOO! SOMEBODY, HELP!
AAAAHHH!
PATU NAY!
EEN ET MANAY!

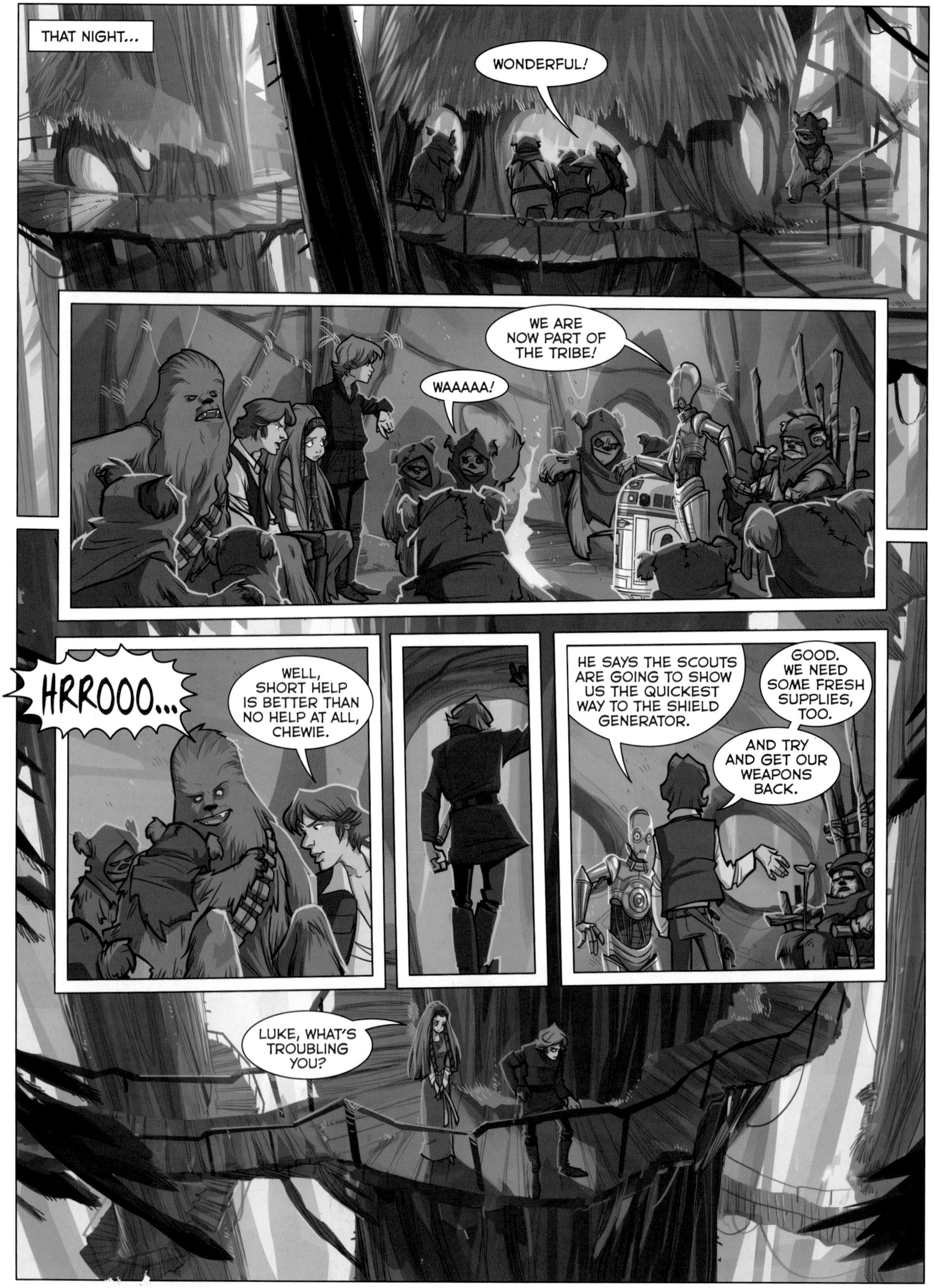
THAT NIGHT...
WONDERFUL!
WE ARE NOW PART OF THE TRIBE!
WAAAAA!
HRROOO...
WELL, SHORT HELP IS BETTER THAN NO HELP AT ALL, CHEWIE.
HE SAYS THE SCOUTS ARE GOING TO SHOW US THE QUICKEST WAY TO THE SHIELD GENERATOR.
GOOD. WE NEED SOME FRESH SUPPLIES, TOO.
AND TRY AND GET OUR WEAPONS BACK.
LUKE, WHAT'S TROUBLING YOU?

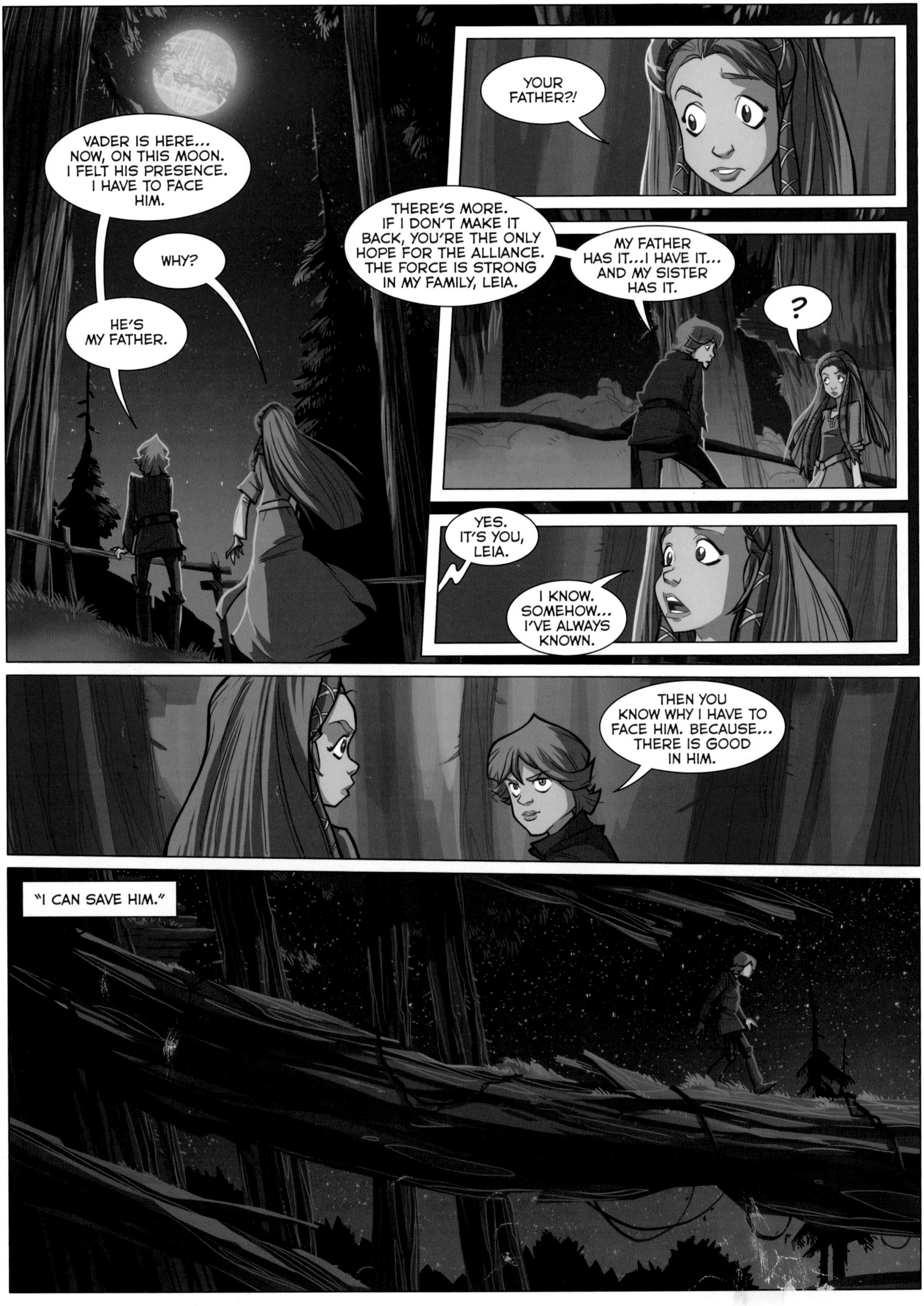
VADER IS HERE... NOW, ON THIS MOON. I FELT HIS PRESENCE. I HAVE TO FACE HIM.
WHY?
HE'S MY FATHER.
YOUR FATHER?!
THERE'S MORE. IF I DON'T MAKE IT BACK, YOU'RE THE ONLY HOPE FOR THE ALLIANCE. THE FORCE IS STRONG IN MY FAMILY, LEIA.
MY FATHER HAS IT...I HAVE IT... AND MY SISTER HAS IT.
?
YES. IT'S YOU, LEIA.
I KNOW. SOMEHOW... I'VE ALWAYS KNOWN.
THEN YOU KNOW WHY I HAVE TO FACE HIM. BECAUSE... THERE IS GOOD IN HIM.
"I CAN SAVE HIM."

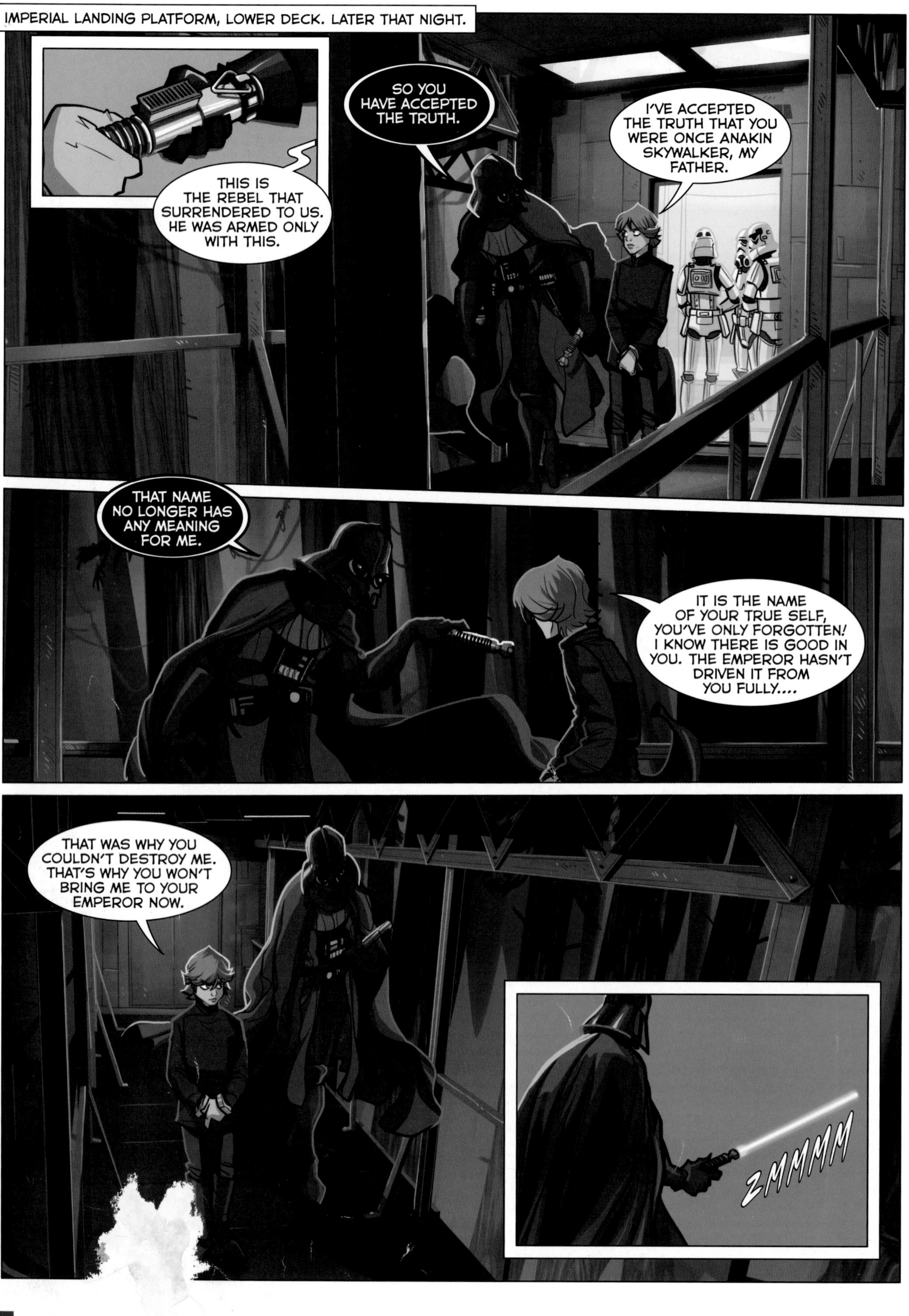
IMPERIAL LANDING PLATFORM, LOWER DECK. LATER THAT NIGHT.
THIS IS THE REBEL THAT SURRENDERED TO US. HE WAS ARMED ONLY WITH THIS.
SO YOU HAVE ACCEPTED THE TRUTH.
I'VE ACCEPTED THE TRUTH THAT YOU WERE ONCE ANAKIN SKYWALKER, MY FATHER.
THAT NAME NO LONGER HAS ANY MEANING FOR ME.
IT IS THE NAME OF YOUR TRUE SELF, YOU'VE ONLY FORGOTTEN! I KNOW THERE IS GOOD IN YOU. THE EMPEROR HASN'T DRIVEN IT FROM YOU FULLY....
THAT WAS WHY YOU COULDN'T DESTROY ME. THAT'S WHY YOU WON'T BRING ME TO YOUR EMPEROR NOW.
ZMMMM

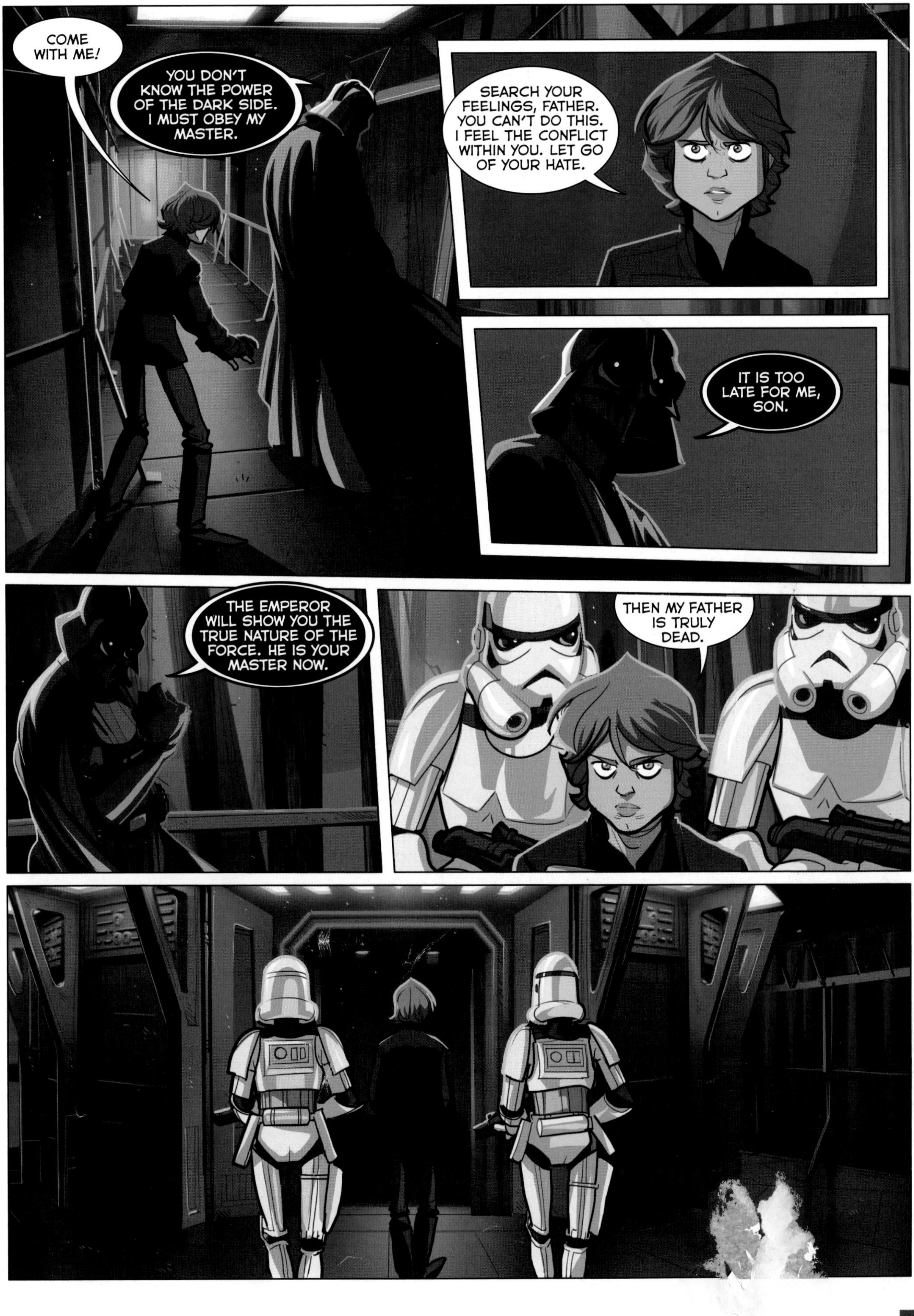
COME WITH ME!
YOU DON'T KNOW THE POWER OF THE DARK SIDE. I MUST OBEY MY MASTER.
SEARCH YOUR FEELINGS, FATHER. YOU CAN'T DO THIS. I FEEL THE CONFLICT WITHIN YOU. LET GO OF YOUR HATE.
IT IS TOO LATE FOR ME, SON.
THE EMPEROR WILL SHOW YOU THE TRUE NATURE OF THE FORCE. HE IS YOUR MASTER NOW.
THEN MY FATHER IS TRULY DEAD.

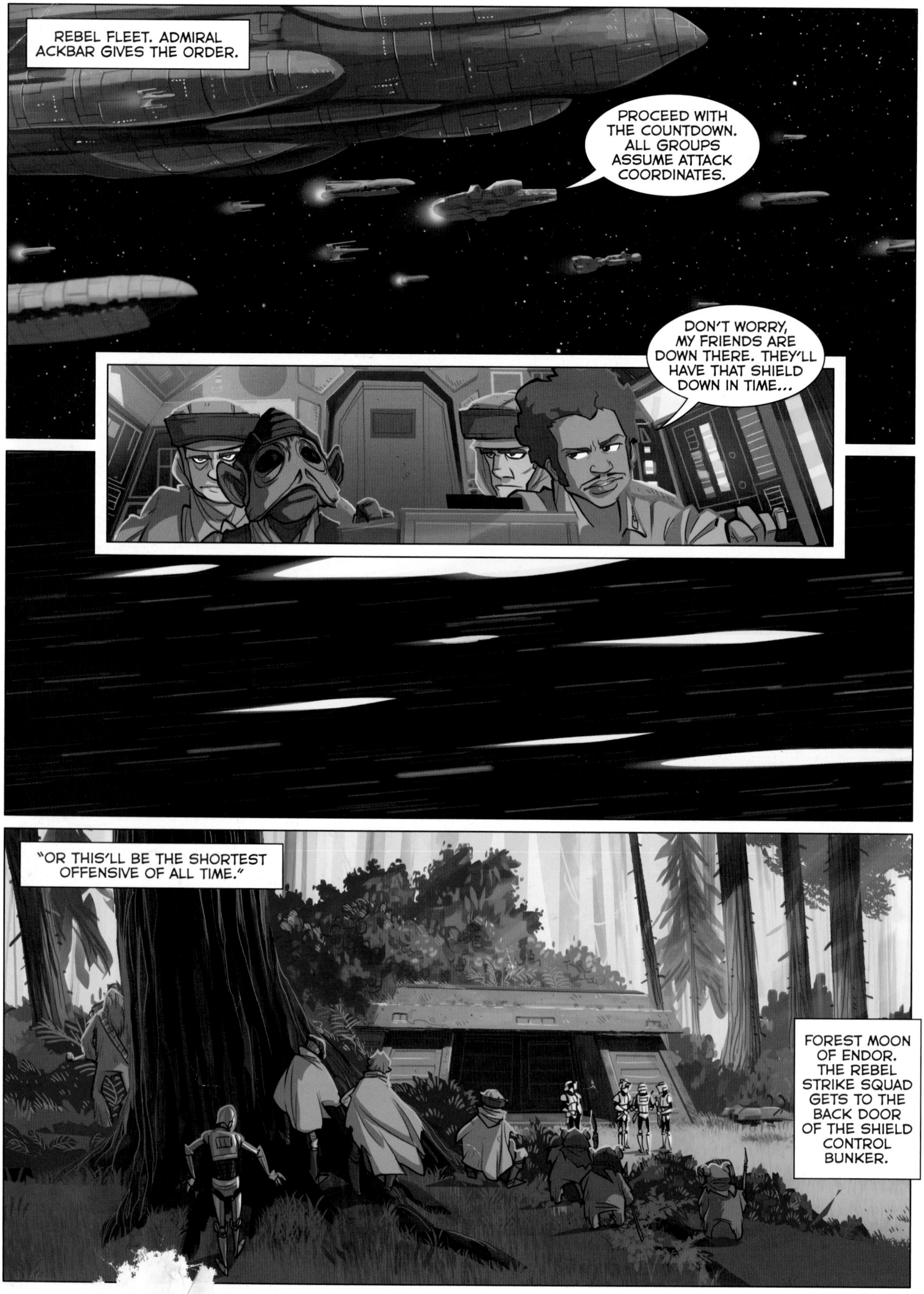

REBEL FLEET. ADMIRAL ACKBAR GIVES THE ORDER.
PROCEED WITH THE COUNTDOWN. ALL GROUPS ASSUME ATTACK COORDINATES.
DON'T WORRY, MY FRIENDS ARE DOWN THERE. THEY'LL HAVE THAT SHIELD DOWN IN TIME...
"OR THIS'LL BE THE SHORTEST OFFENSIVE OF ALL TIME."
FOREST MOON OF ENDOR. THE REBEL STRIKE SQUAD GETS TO THE BACK DOOR OF THE SHIELD CONTROL BUNKER.

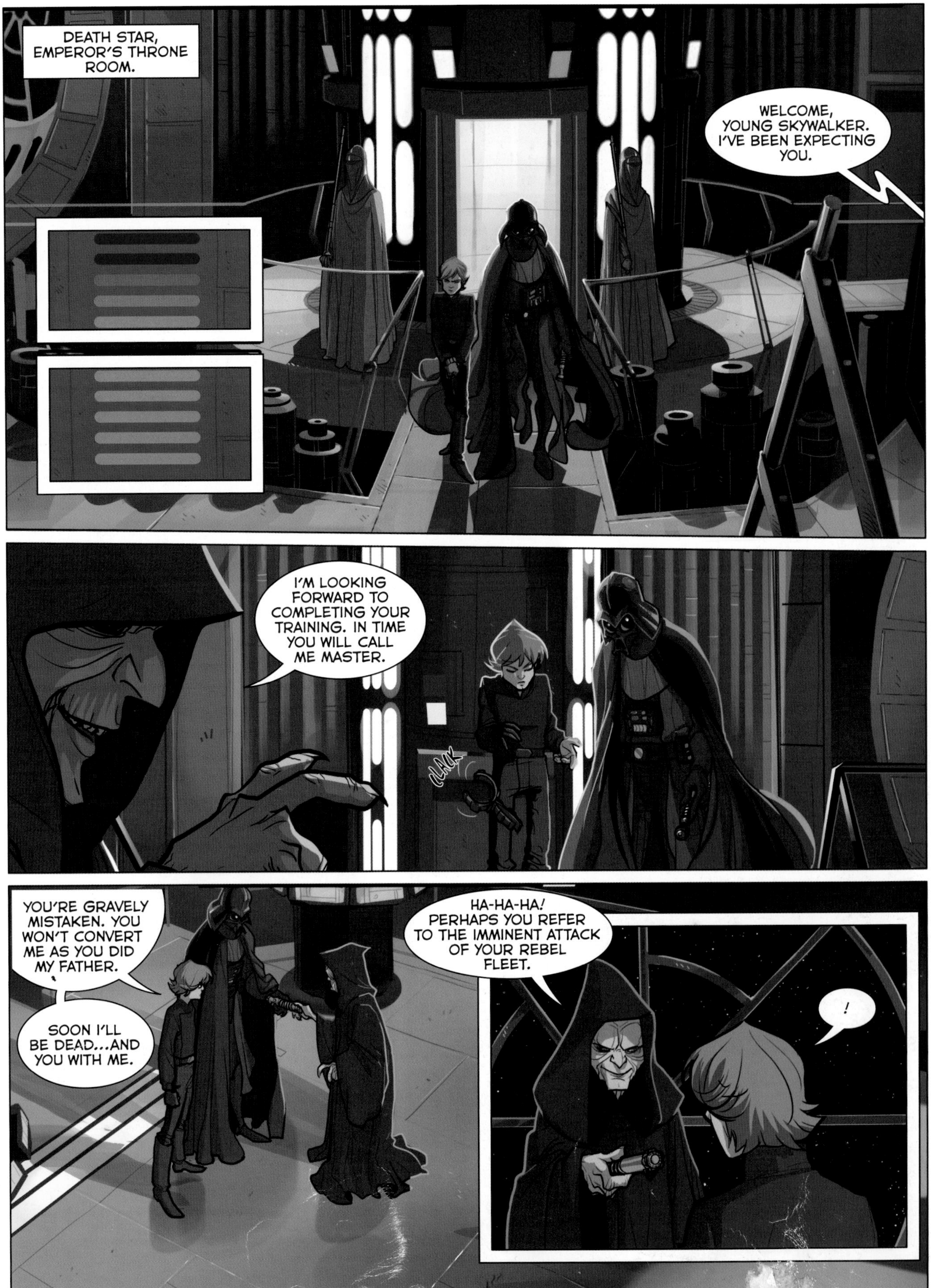
DEATH STAR, EMPEROR'S THRONE ROOM.
WELCOME, YOUNG SKYWALKER. I'VE BEEN EXPECTING YOU.
I'M LOOKING FORWARD TO COMPLETING YOUR TRAINING. IN TIME YOU WILL CALL ME MASTER.
CLACK
YOU'RE GRAVELY MISTAKEN. YOU WON'T CONVERT ME AS YOU DID MY FATHER.
SOON I'LL BE DEAD...AND YOU WITH ME.
HA-HA-HA! PERHAPS YOU REFER TO THE IMMINENT ATTACK OF YOUR REBEL FLEET.
!

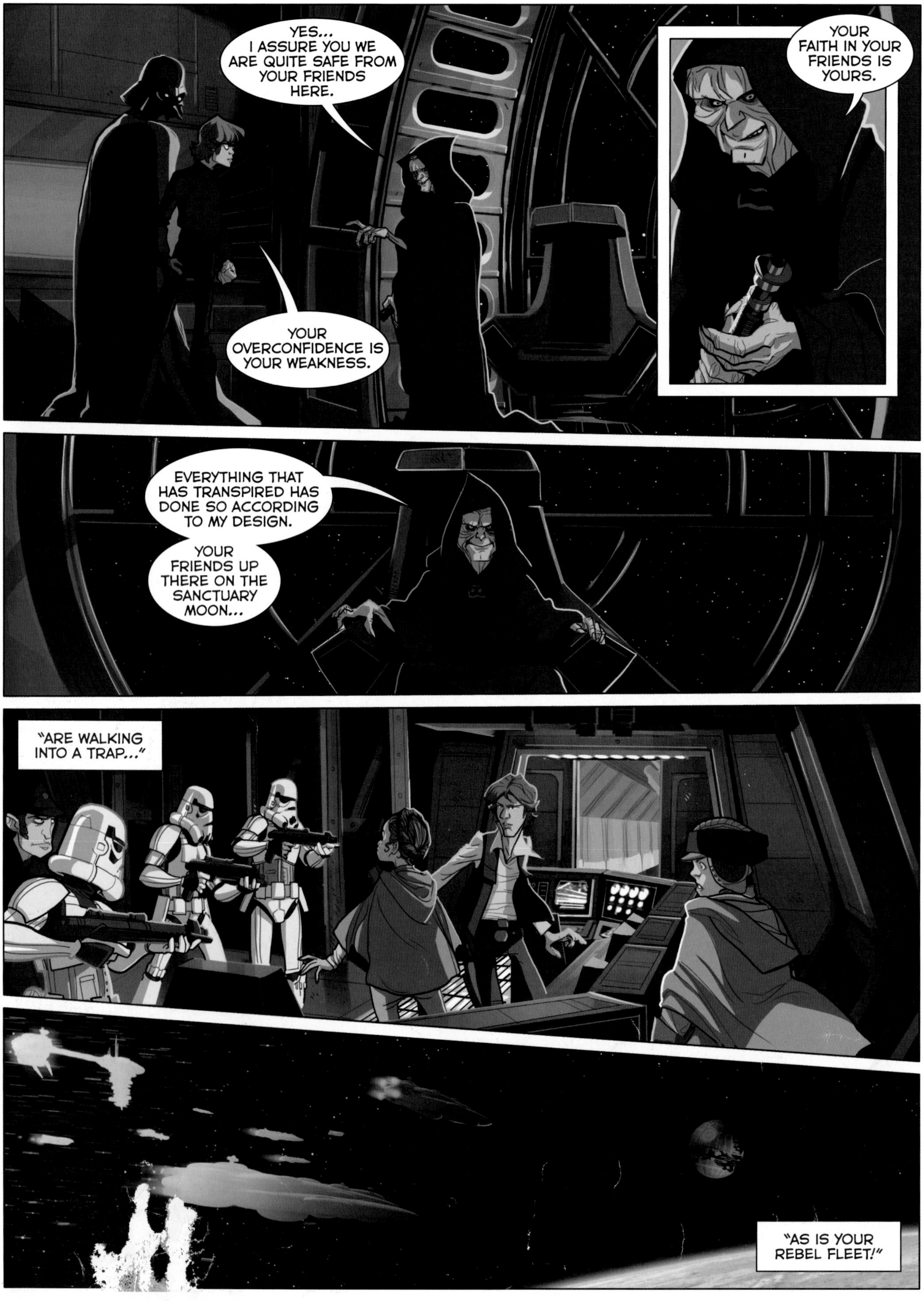
YES... I ASSURE YOU WE ARE QUITE SAFE FROM YOUR FRIENDS HERE.
YOUR OVERCONFIDENCE IS YOUR WEAKNESS.
YOUR FAITH IN YOUR FRIENDS IS YOURS.
EVERYTHING THAT HAS TRANSPIRED HAS DONE SO ACCORDING TO MY DESIGN.
YOUR FRIENDS UP THERE ON THE SANCTUARY MOON...
"ARE WALKING INTO A TRAP..."
"AS IS YOUR REBEL FLEET!"

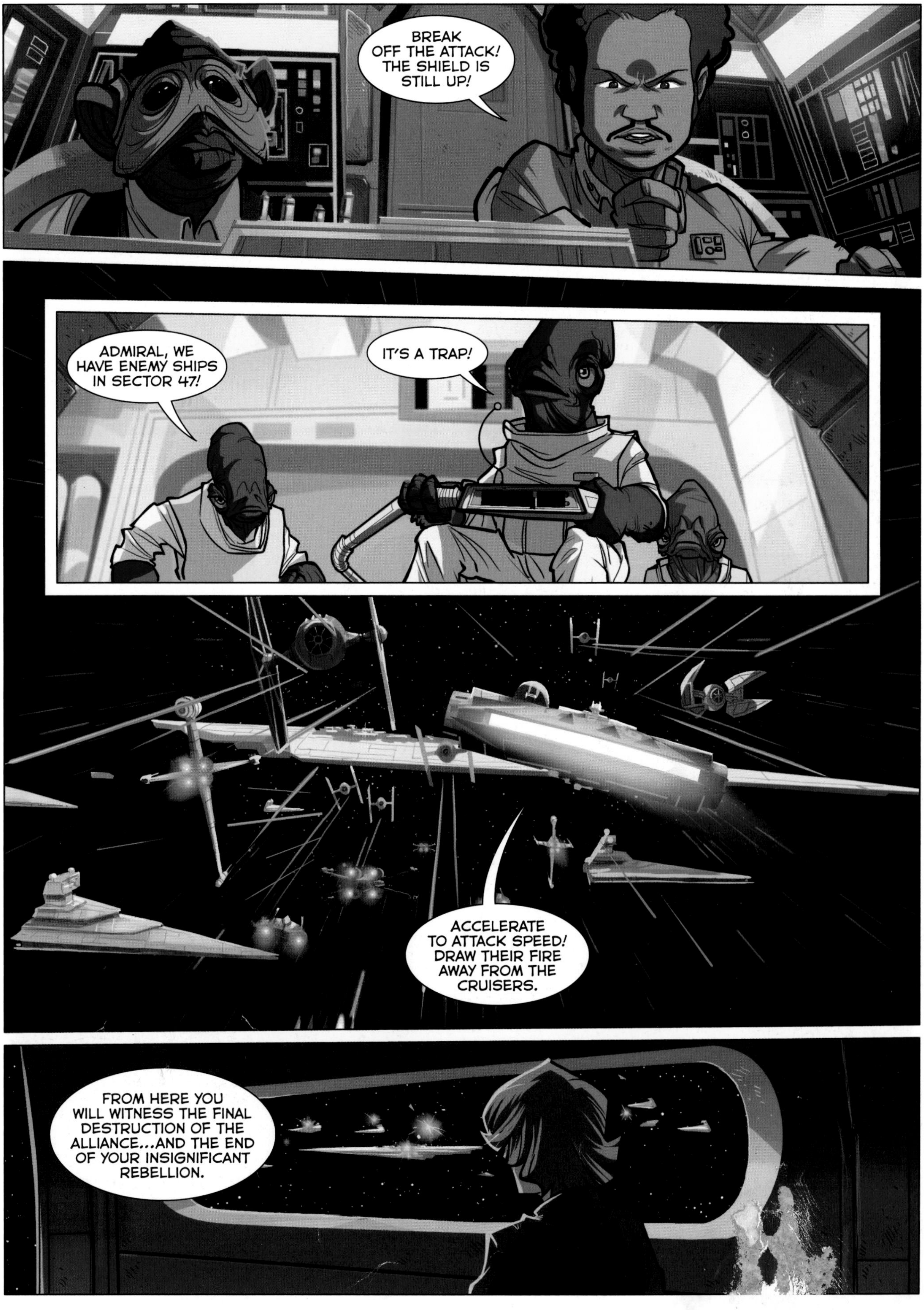
BREAK OFF THE ATTACK! THE SHIELD IS STILL UP!
ADMIRAL, WE HAVE ENEMY SHIPS IN SECTOR 47!
IT'S A TRAP!
ACCELERATE TO ATTACK SPEED! DRAW THEIR FIRE AWAY FROM THE CRUISERS.
FROM HERE YOU WILL WITNESS THE FINAL DESTRUCTION OF THE ALLIANCE...AND THE END OF YOUR INSIGNIFICANT REBELLION.

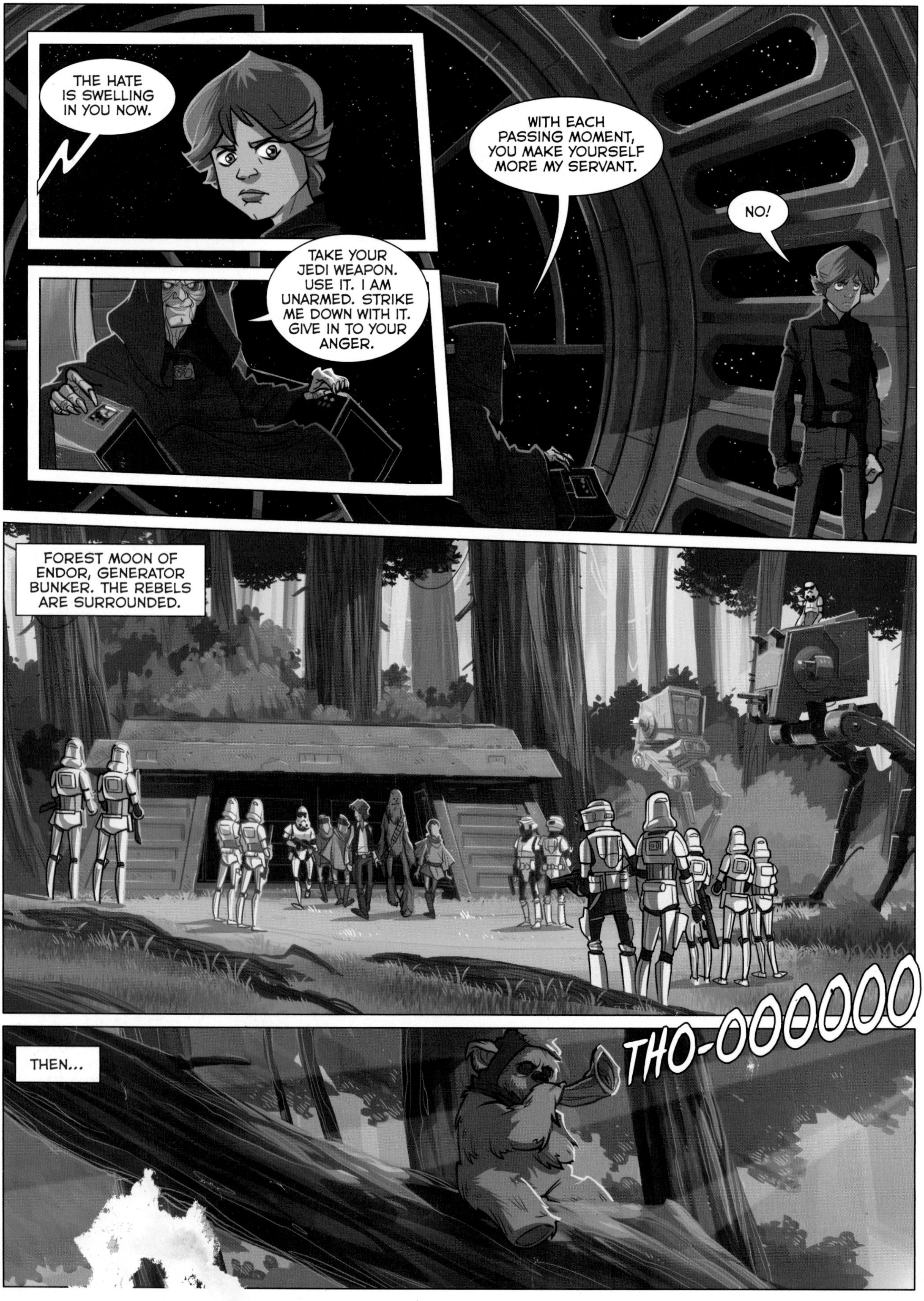
THE HATE IS SWELLING IN YOU NOW.
TAKE YOUR JEDI WEAPON. USE IT. I AM UNARMED. STRIKE ME DOWN WITH IT. GIVE IN TO YOUR ANGER.
WITH EACH PASSING MOMENT, YOU MAKE YOURSELF MORE MY SERVANT.
NO!
FOREST MOON OF ENDOR, GENERATOR BUNKER. THE REBELS ARE SURROUNDED.
THEN...
THO-OOOOOO

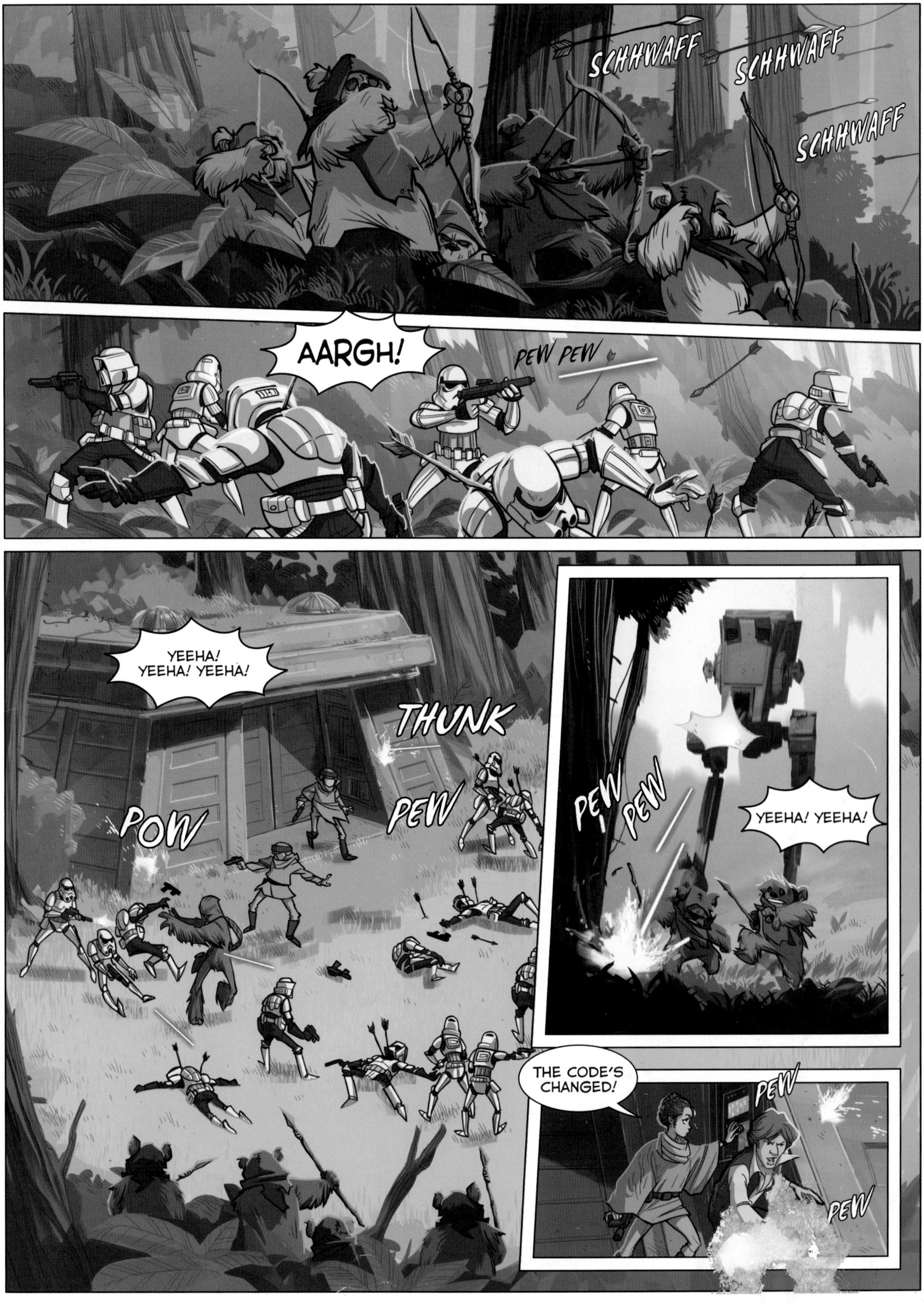
SCHHWAFF
SCHHWAFF
SCHHWAFF
AARGH!
PEW PEW
YEEHA! YEEHA! YEEHA!
THUNK
POW
PEW
PEW
PEW
YEEHA! YEEHA!
THE CODE'S CHANGED!
PEW
PEW

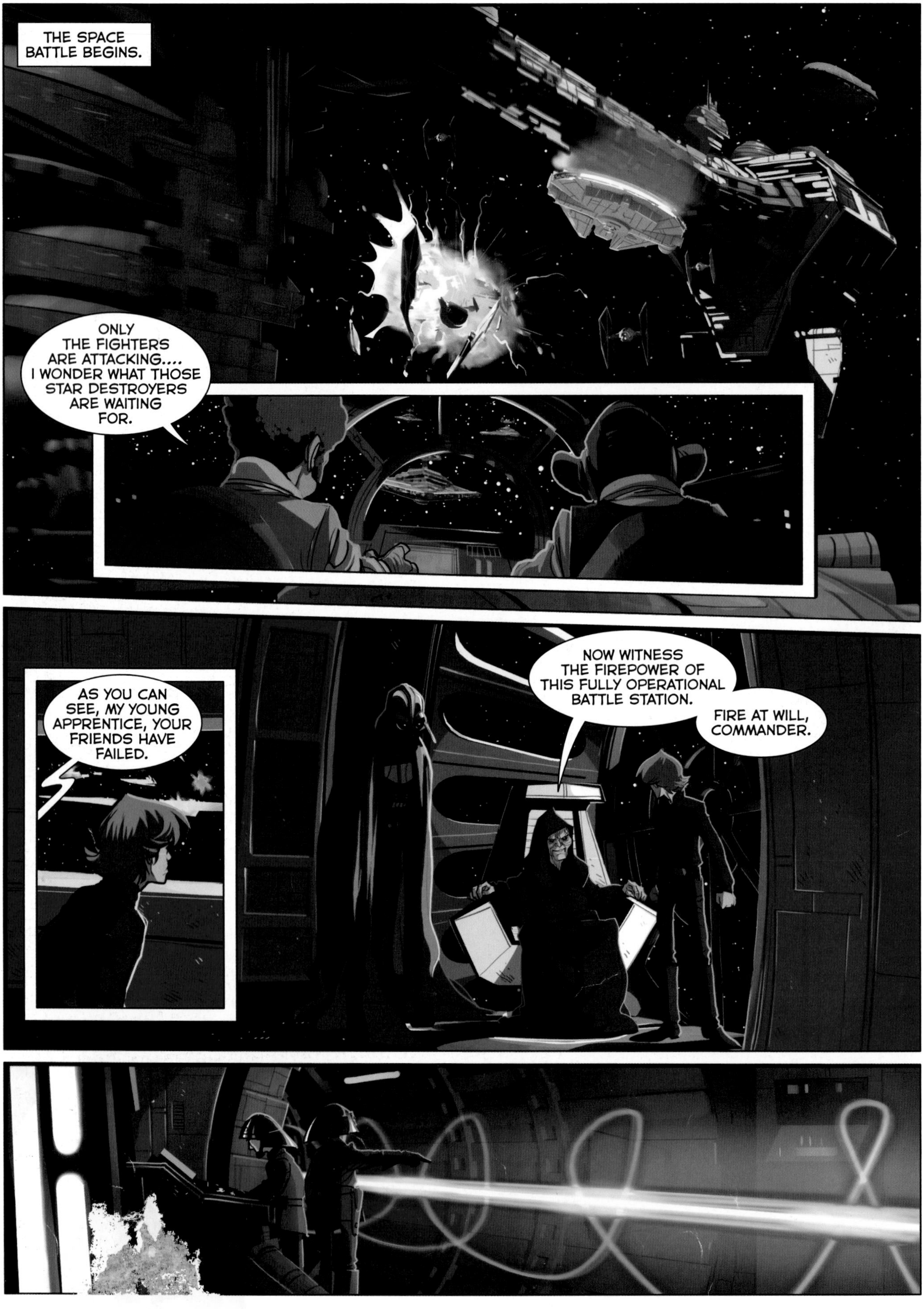

THE SPACE BATTLE BEGINS.
ONLY THE FIGHTERS ARE ATTACKING.... I WONDER WHAT THOSE STAR DESTROYERS ARE WAITING FOR.
AS YOU CAN SEE, MY YOUNG APPRENTICE, YOUR FRIENDS HAVE FAILED.
NOW WITNESS THE FIREPOWER OF THIS FULLY OPERATIONAL BATTLE STATION.
FIRE AT WILL, COMMANDER.

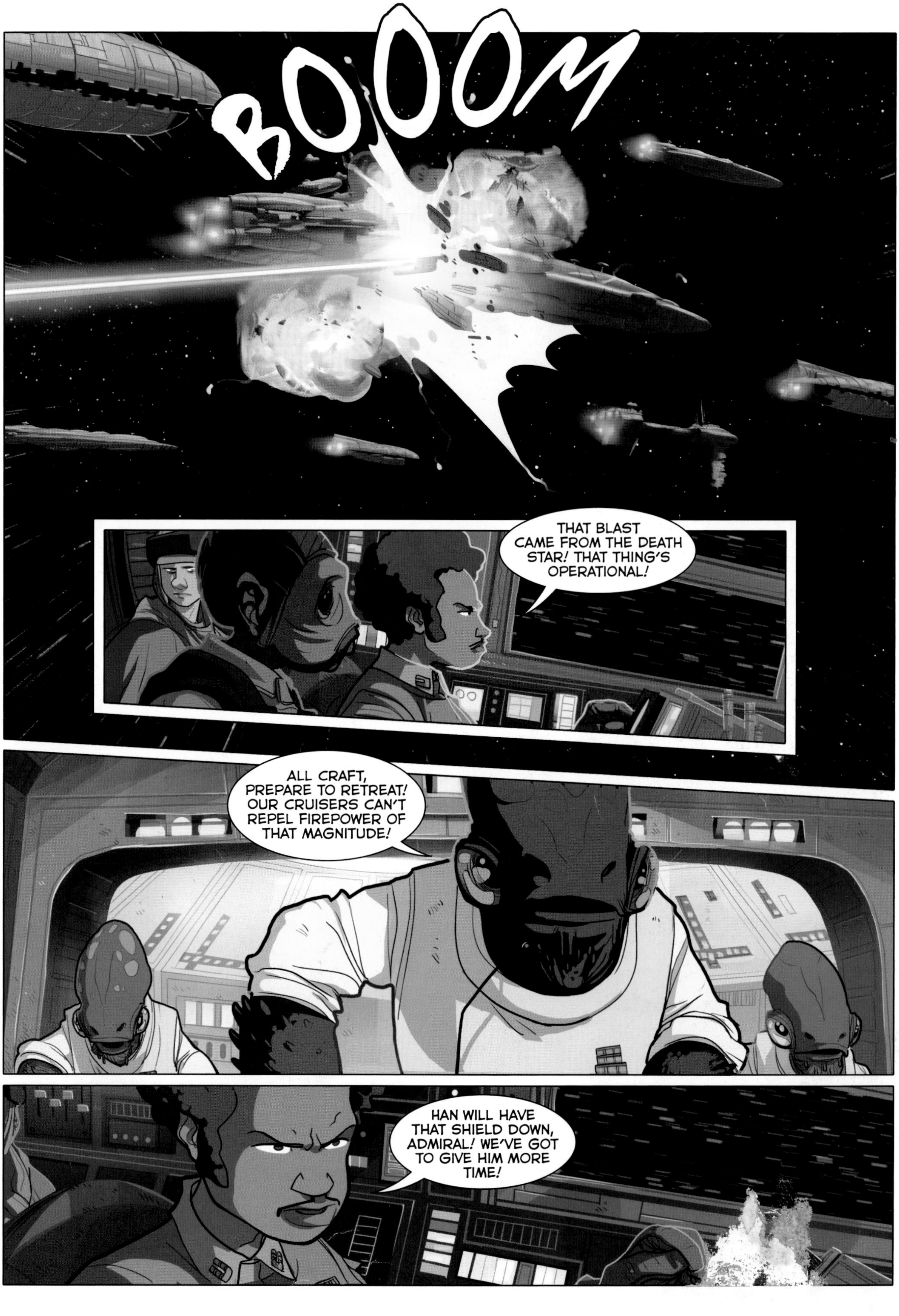
BOOOM
THAT BLAST CAME FROM THE DEATH STAR! THAT THING'S OPERATIONAL!
ALL CRAFT, PREPARE TO RETREAT! OUR CRUISERS CAN'T REPEL FIREPOWER OF THAT MAGNITUDE!
HAN WILL HAVE THAT SHIELD DOWN, ADMIRAL! WE'VE GOT TO GIVE HIM MORE TIME!

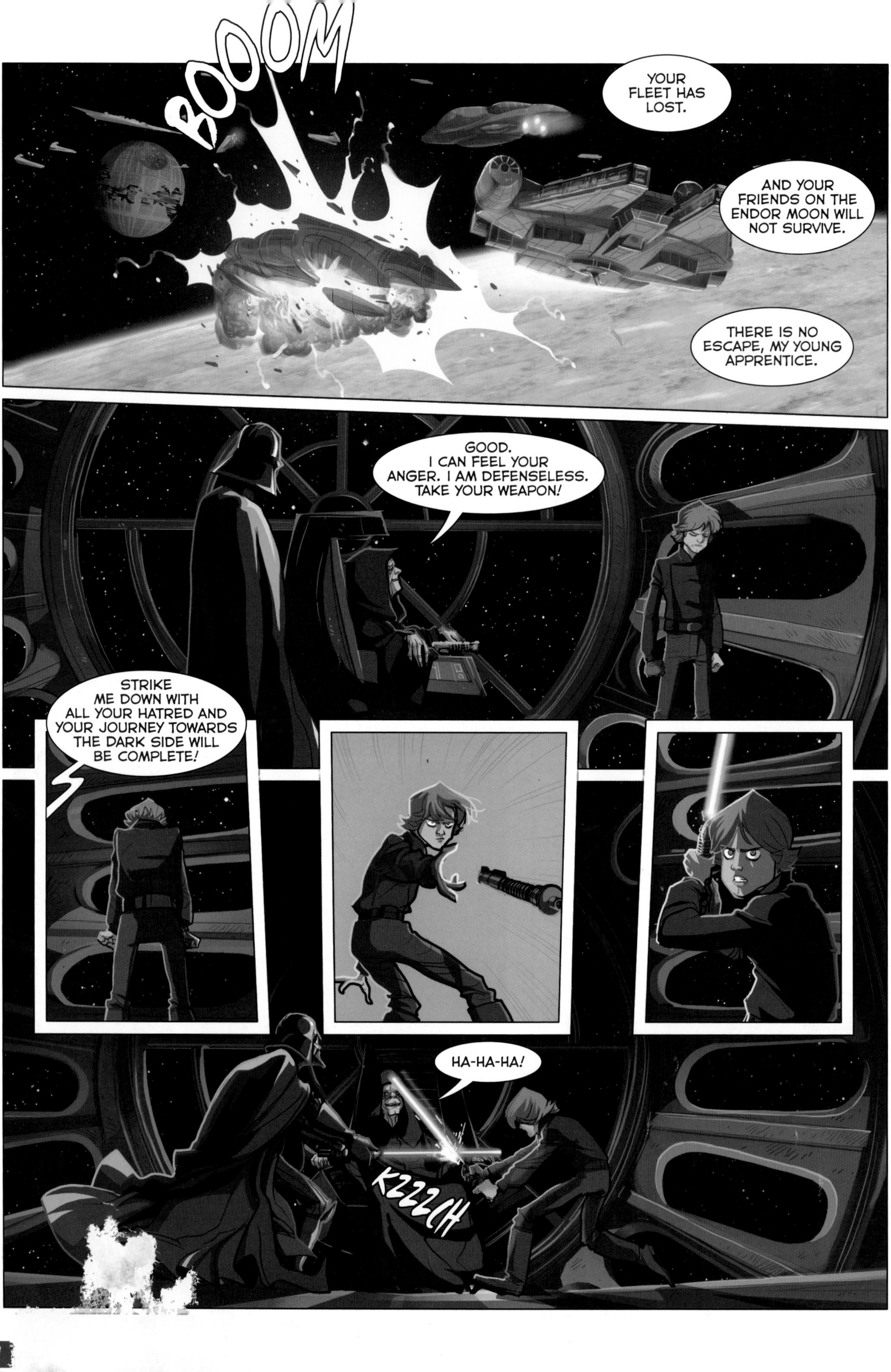
BOOOM
YOUR FLEET HAS LOST.
AND YOUR FRIENDS ON THE ENDOR MOON WILL NOT SURVIVE.
THERE IS NO ESCAPE, MY YOUNG APPRENTICE.
GOOD. I CAN FEEL YOUR ANGER. I AM DEFENSELESS. TAKE YOUR WEAPON!
STRIKE ME DOWN WITH ALL YOUR HATRED AND YOUR JOURNEY TOWARDS THE DARK SIDE WILL BE COMPLETE!
HA-HA-HA!
KZZZCH

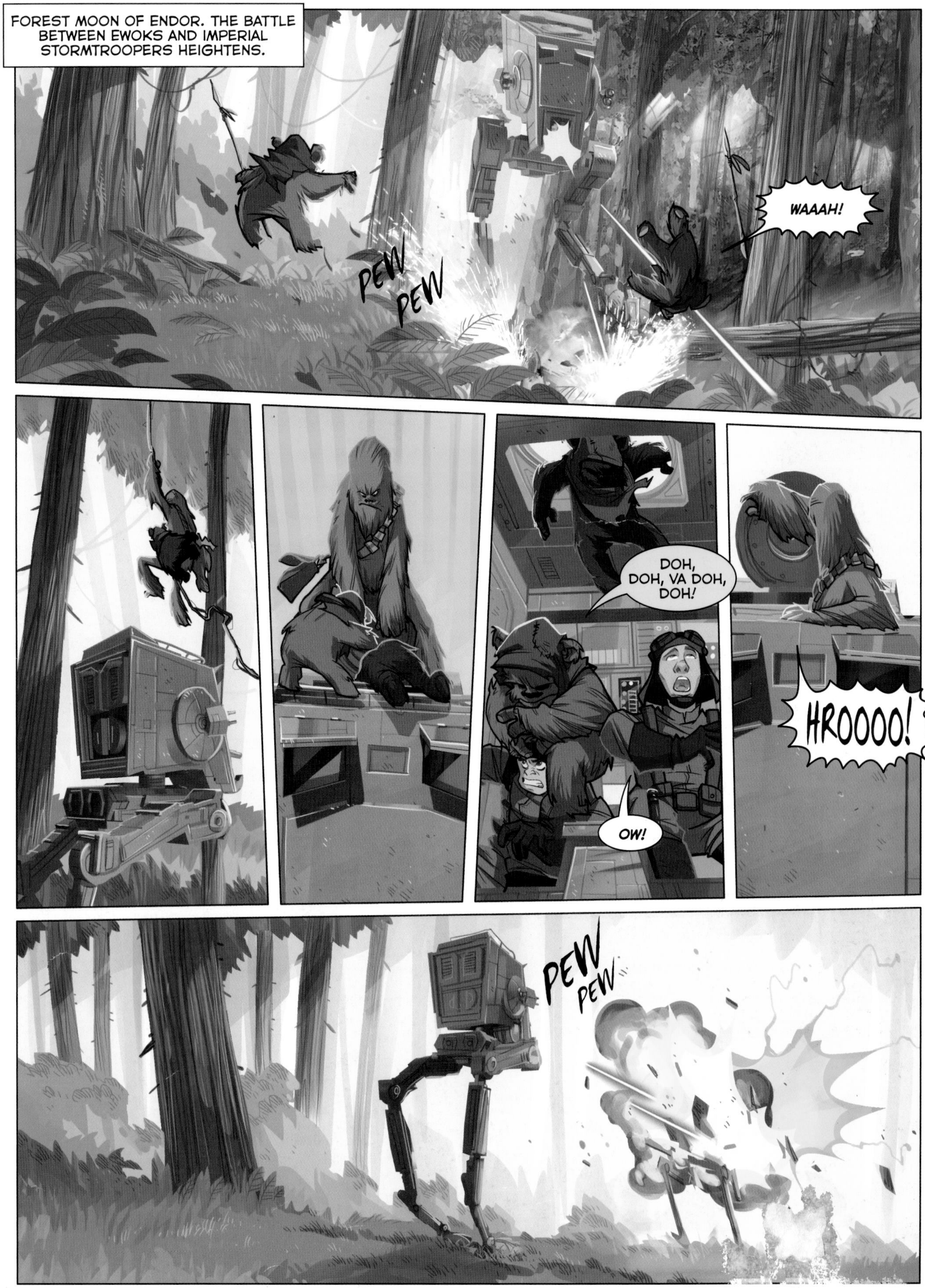
FOREST MOON OF ENDOR. THE BATTLE BETWEEN EWOKS AND IMPERIAL STORMTROOPERS HEIGHTENS.
WAAAH!
PEW PEW
DOH, DOH, VA DOH, DOH!
OW!
HROOOO!
PEW PEW

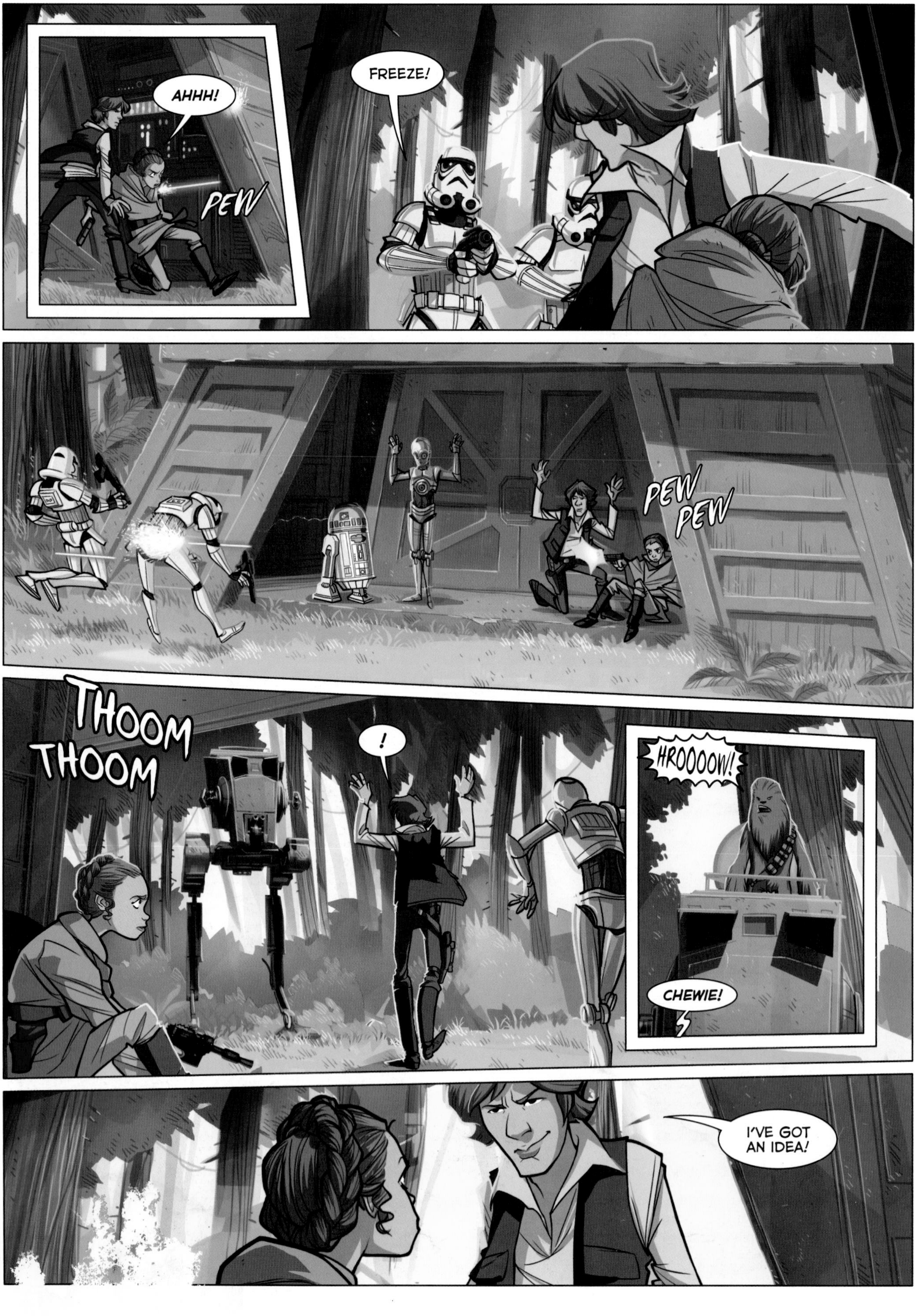
AHHH!
PEW
FREEZE!
PEW
PEW
THOOM
THOOM
!
HROOOOW!
CHEWIE!
I'VE GOT AN IDEA!

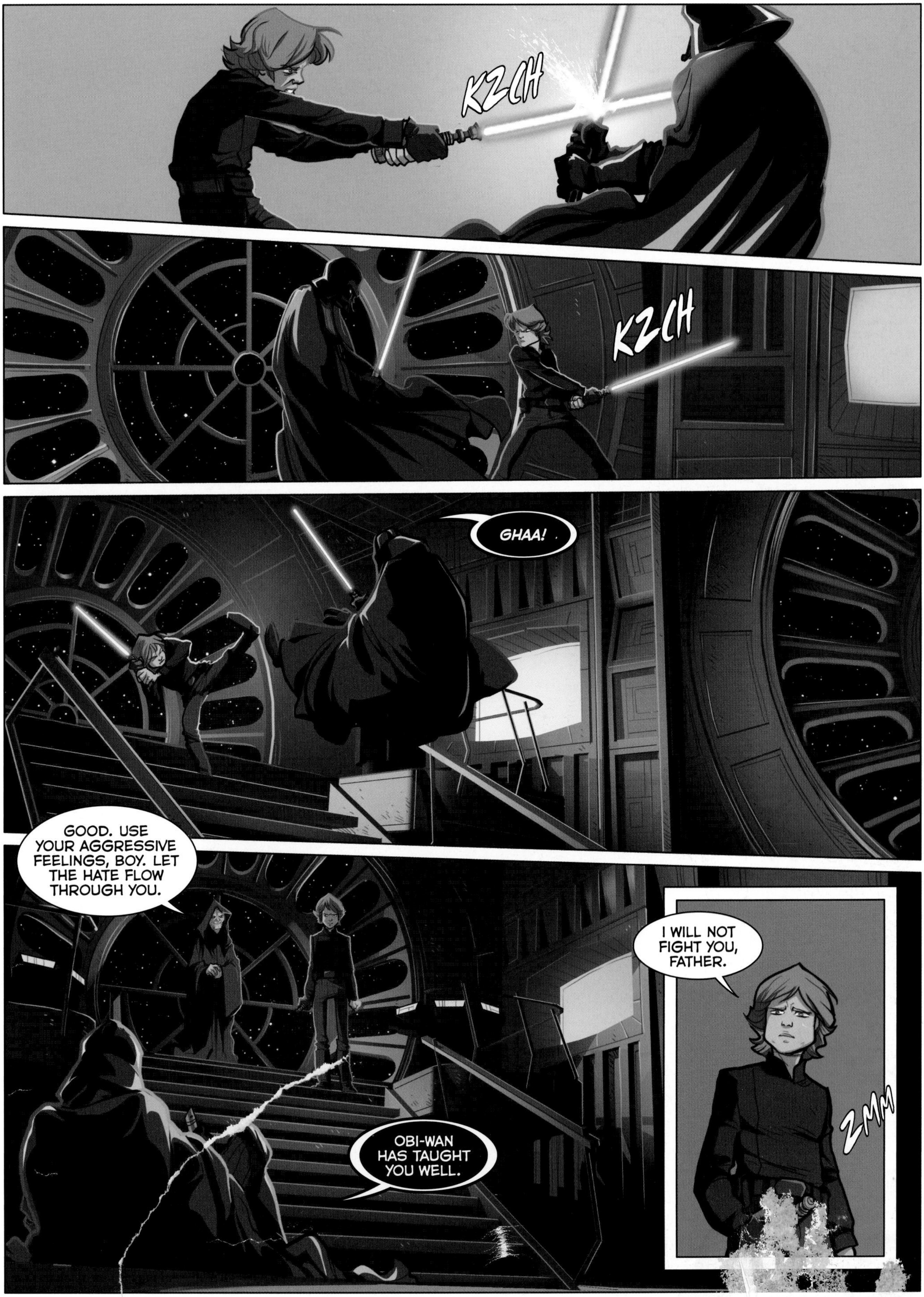
KZCH
KZCH
GHAA!
GOOD. USE YOUR AGGRESSIVE FEELINGS, BOY. LET THE HATE FLOW THROUGH YOU.
OBI-WAN HAS TAUGHT YOU WELL.
I WILL NOT FIGHT YOU, FATHER.
ZMM

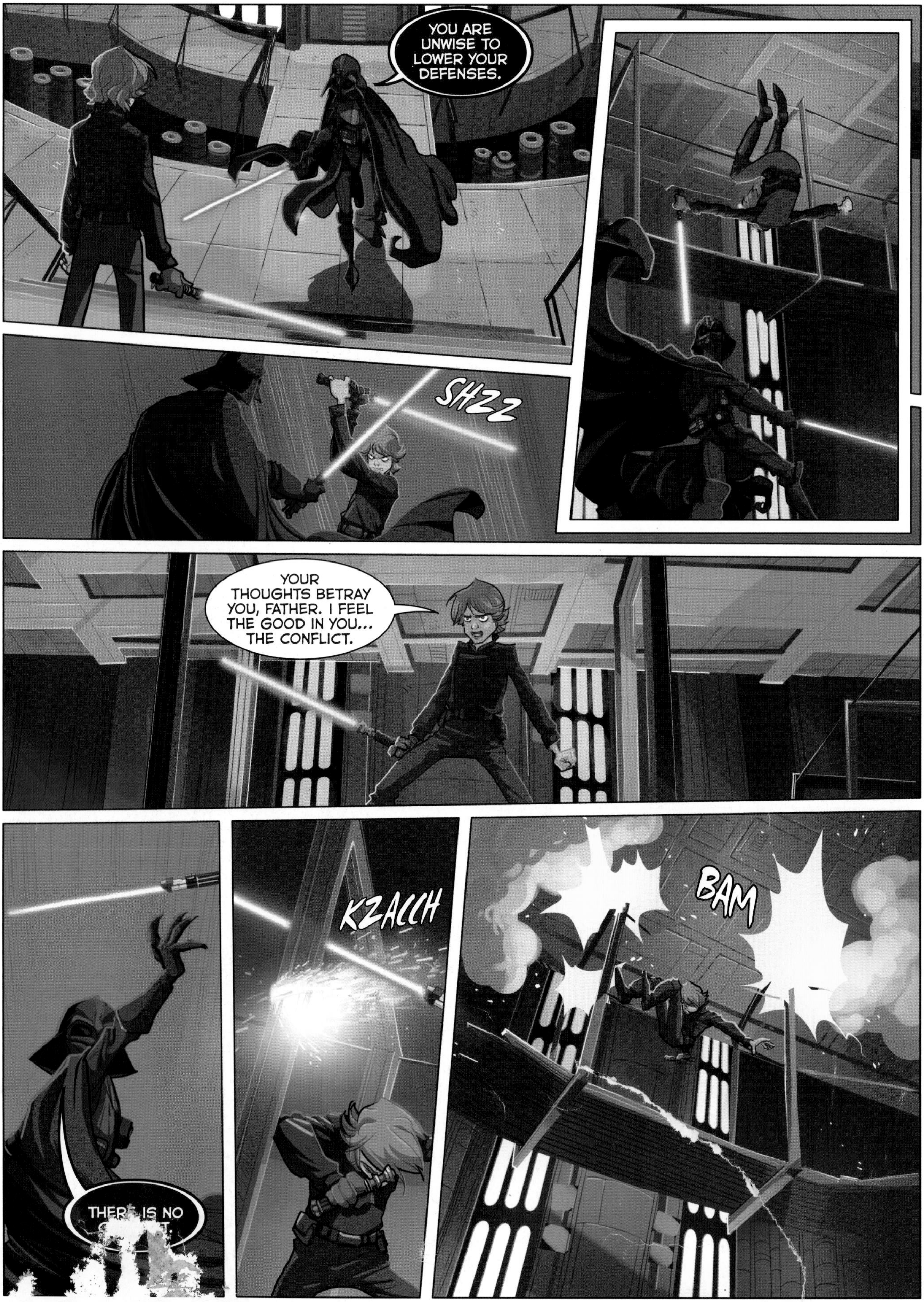
YOU ARE UNWISE TO LOWER YOUR DEFENSES.
SHZZ
YOUR THOUGHTS BETRAY YOU, FATHER. I FEEL THE GOOD IN YOU... THE CONFLICT.
THERE IS NO
KZACCH
BAM

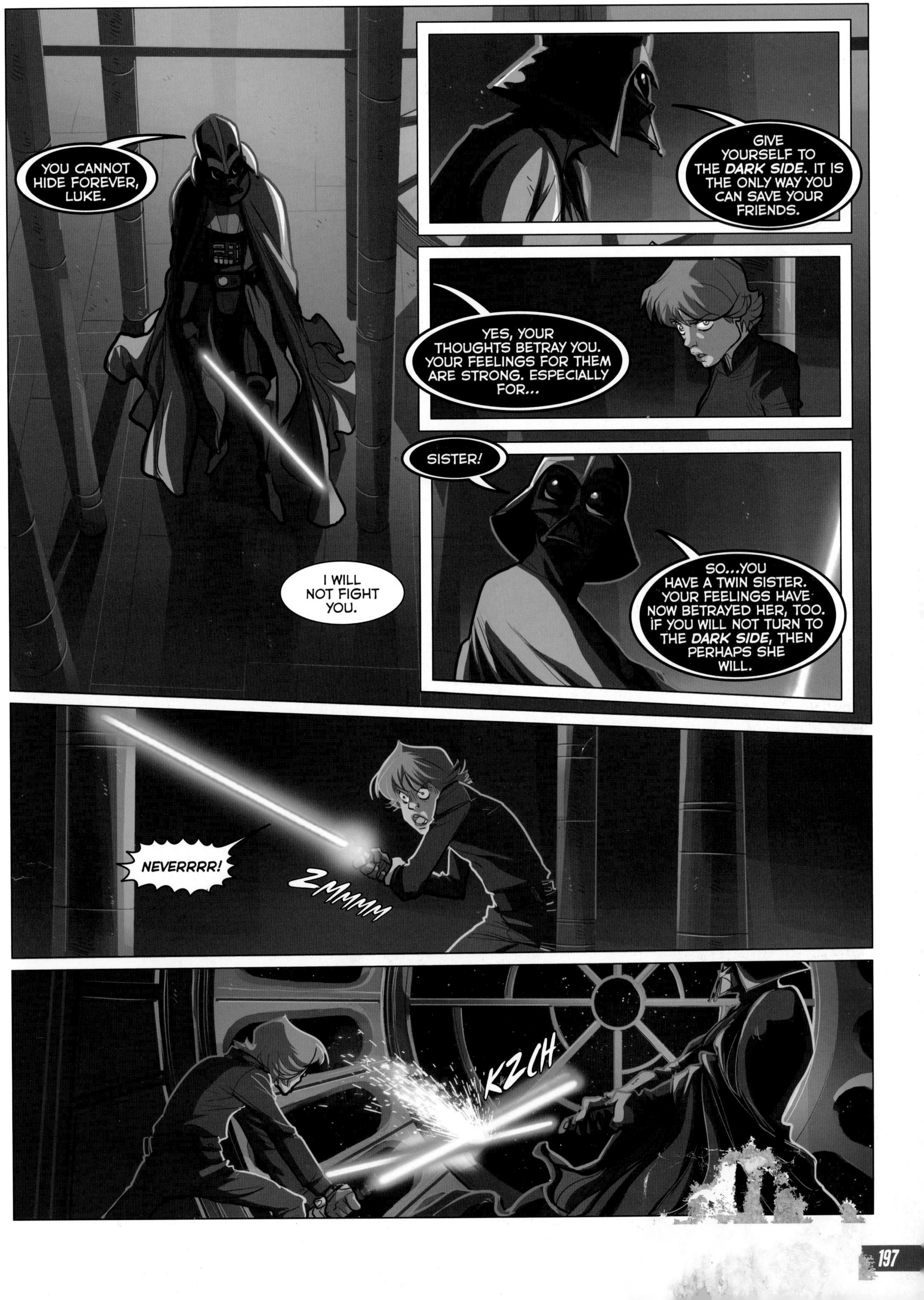

YOU CANNOT HIDE FOREVER, LUKE.
GIVE YOURSELF TO THE DARK SIDE. IT IS THE ONLY WAY YOU CAN SAVE YOUR FRIENDS.
YES, YOUR THOUGHTS BETRAY YOU. YOUR FEELINGS FOR THEM ARE STRONG. ESPECIALLY FOR...
SISTER!
SO...YOU HAVE A TWIN SISTER. YOUR FEELINGS HAVE NOW BETRAYED HER, TOO. IF YOU WILL NOT TURN TO THE DARK SIDE, THEN PERHAPS SHE WILL.
I WILL NOT FIGHT YOU.
NEVERRRR!
ZMMMMM
KZCH

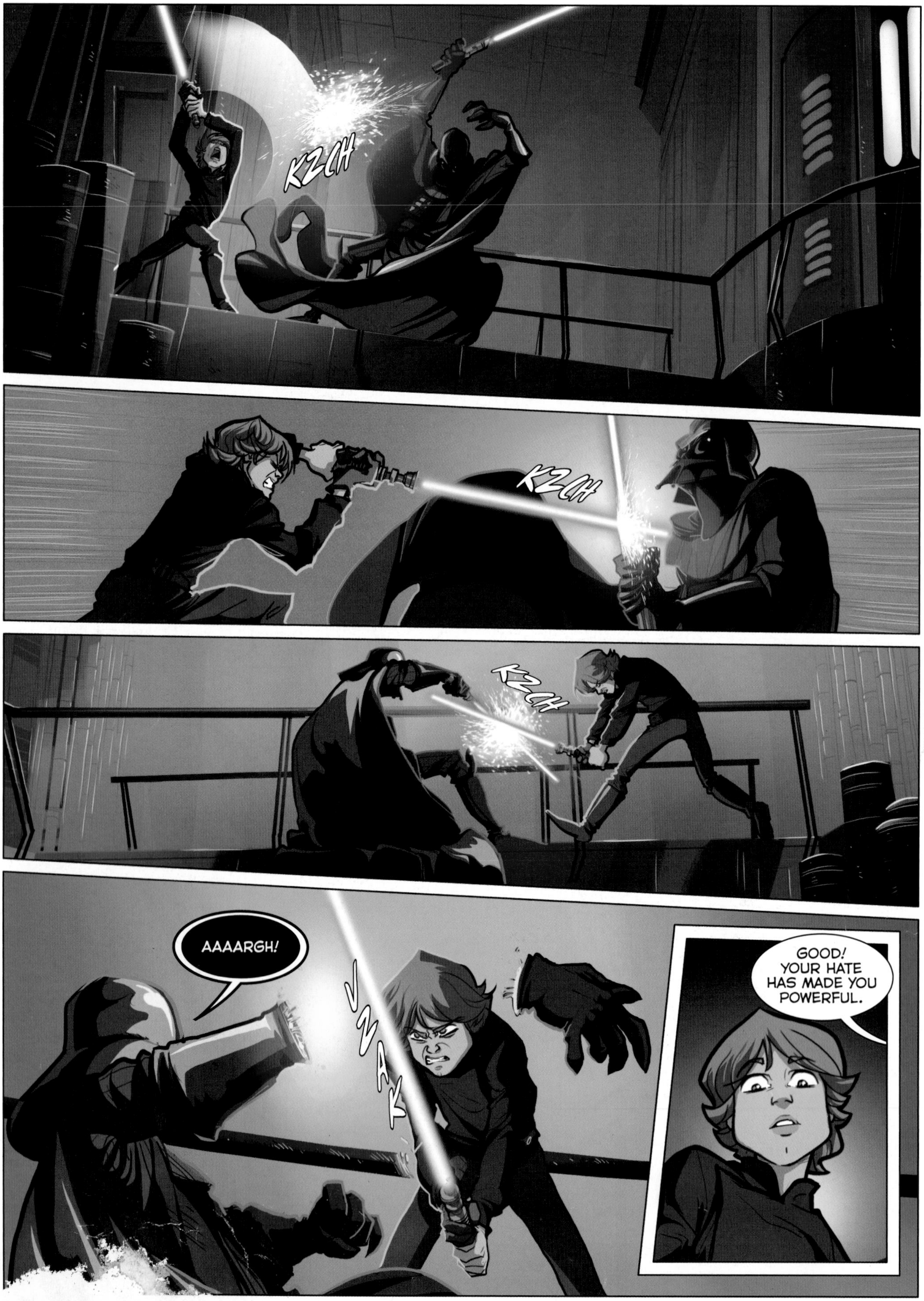
KZCH
KZCH
KZCH
AAAARGH!
SNAK
GOOD! YOUR HATE HAS MADE YOU POWERFUL.

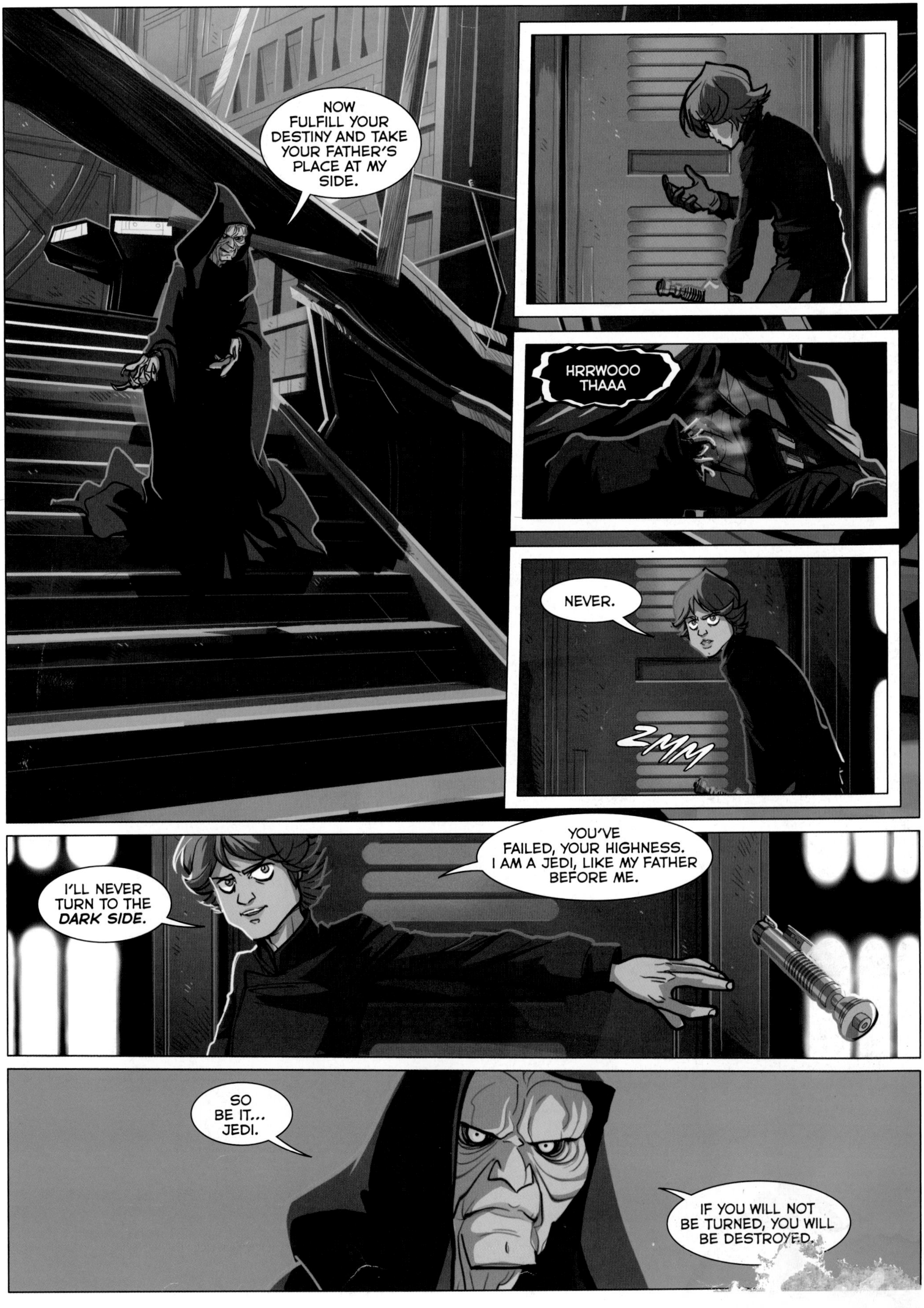
NOW FULFILL YOUR DESTINY AND TAKE YOUR FATHER'S PLACE AT MY SIDE.
HRRWOOO THAAA
NEVER.
ZMM
I'LL NEVER TURN TO THE *DARK SIDE*.
YOU'VE FAILED, YOUR HIGHNESS. I AM A JEDI, LIKE MY FATHER BEFORE ME.
SO BE IT... JEDI.
IF YOU WILL NOT BE TURNED, YOU WILL BE DESTROYED.

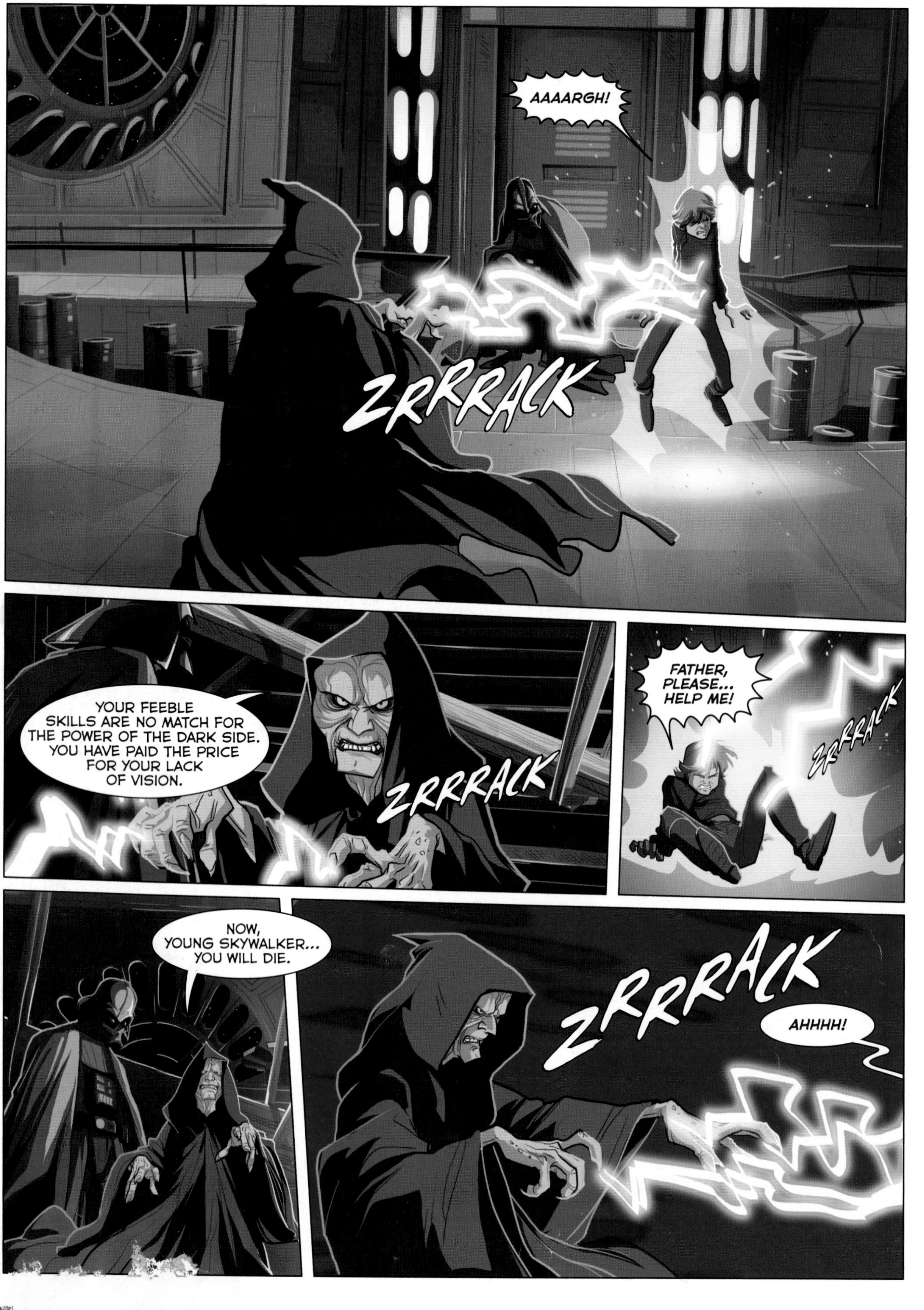
AAAARGH!
ZRRRACK
YOUR FEEBLE SKILLS ARE NO MATCH FOR THE POWER OF THE DARK SIDE. YOU HAVE PAID THE PRICE FOR YOUR LACK OF VISION.
ZRRRACK
FATHER, PLEASE... HELP ME!
ZRRRACK
NOW, YOUNG SKYWALKER... YOU WILL DIE.
ZRRRACK
AHHHH!

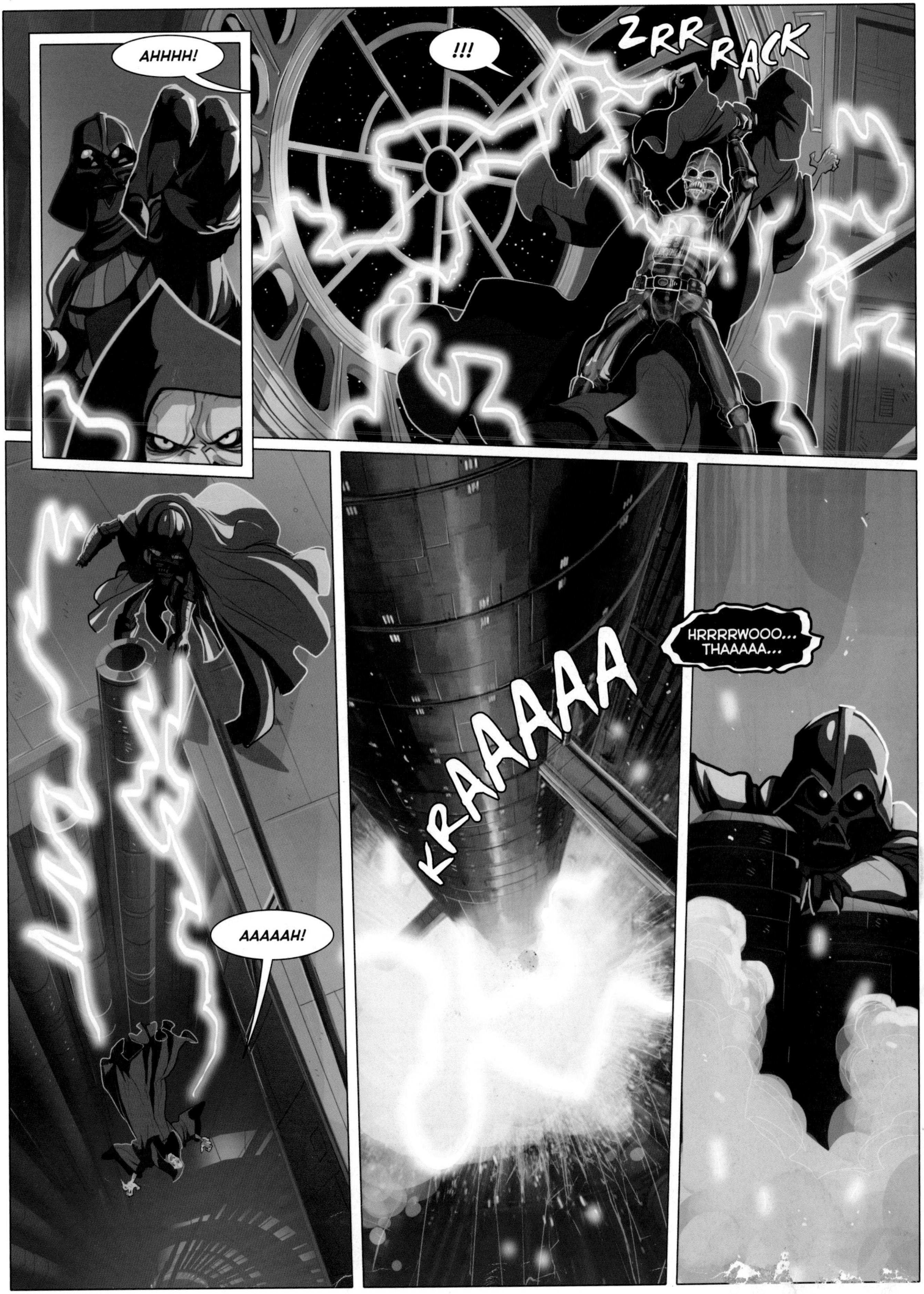
AHHHH!
!!!
ZRR RACK
AAAAAH!
KRAAAAAA
HRRRRWOOO... THAAAAA...

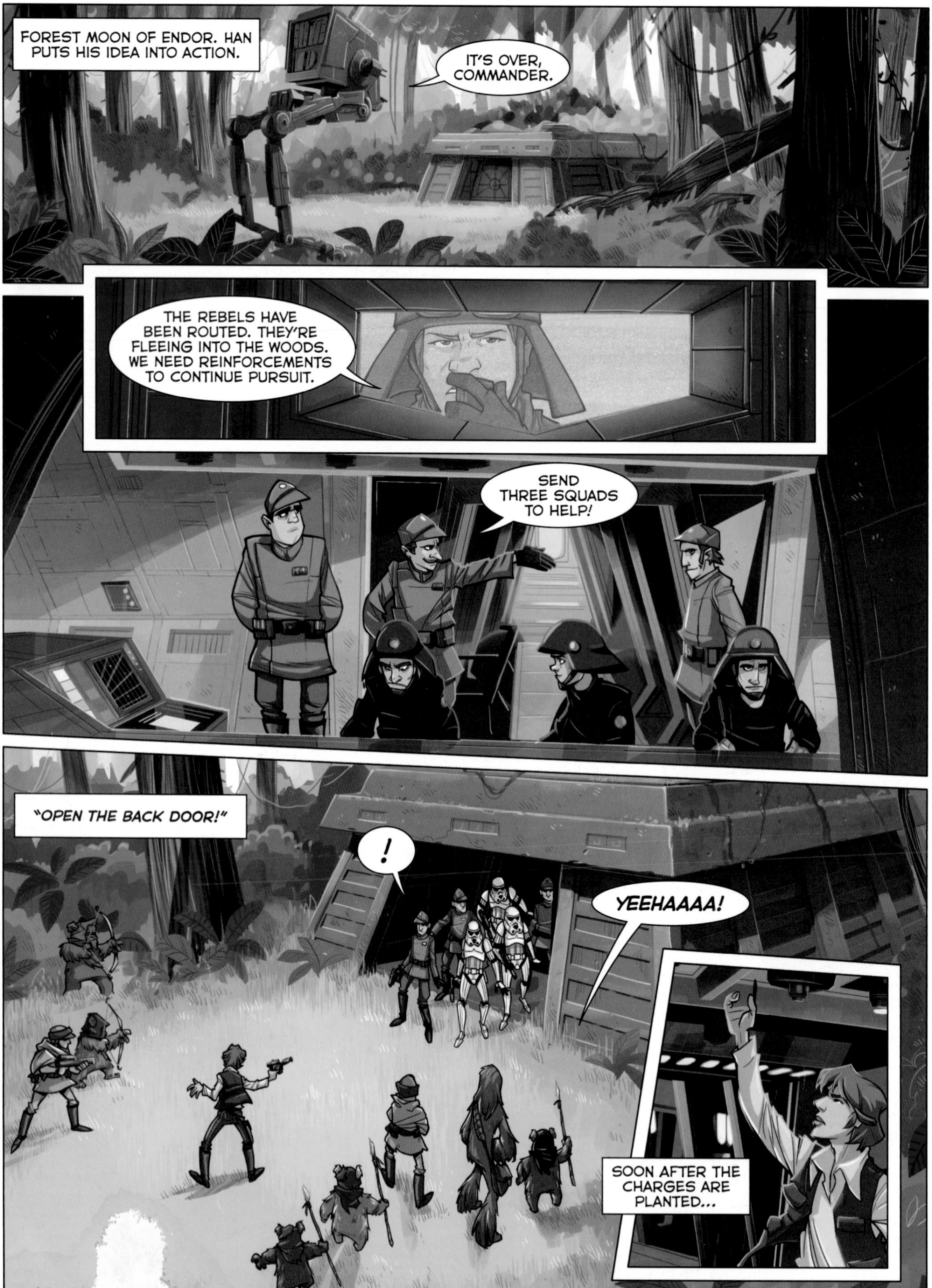
FOREST MOON OF ENDOR. HAN PUTS HIS IDEA INTO ACTION.
IT'S OVER, COMMANDER.
THE REBELS HAVE BEEN ROUTED. THEY'RE FLEEING INTO THE WOODS. WE NEED REINFORCEMENTS TO CONTINUE PURSUIT.
SEND THREE SQUADS TO HELP!
"OPEN THE BACK DOOR!"
!
YEEHAAAA!
SOON AFTER THE CHARGES ARE PLANTED...

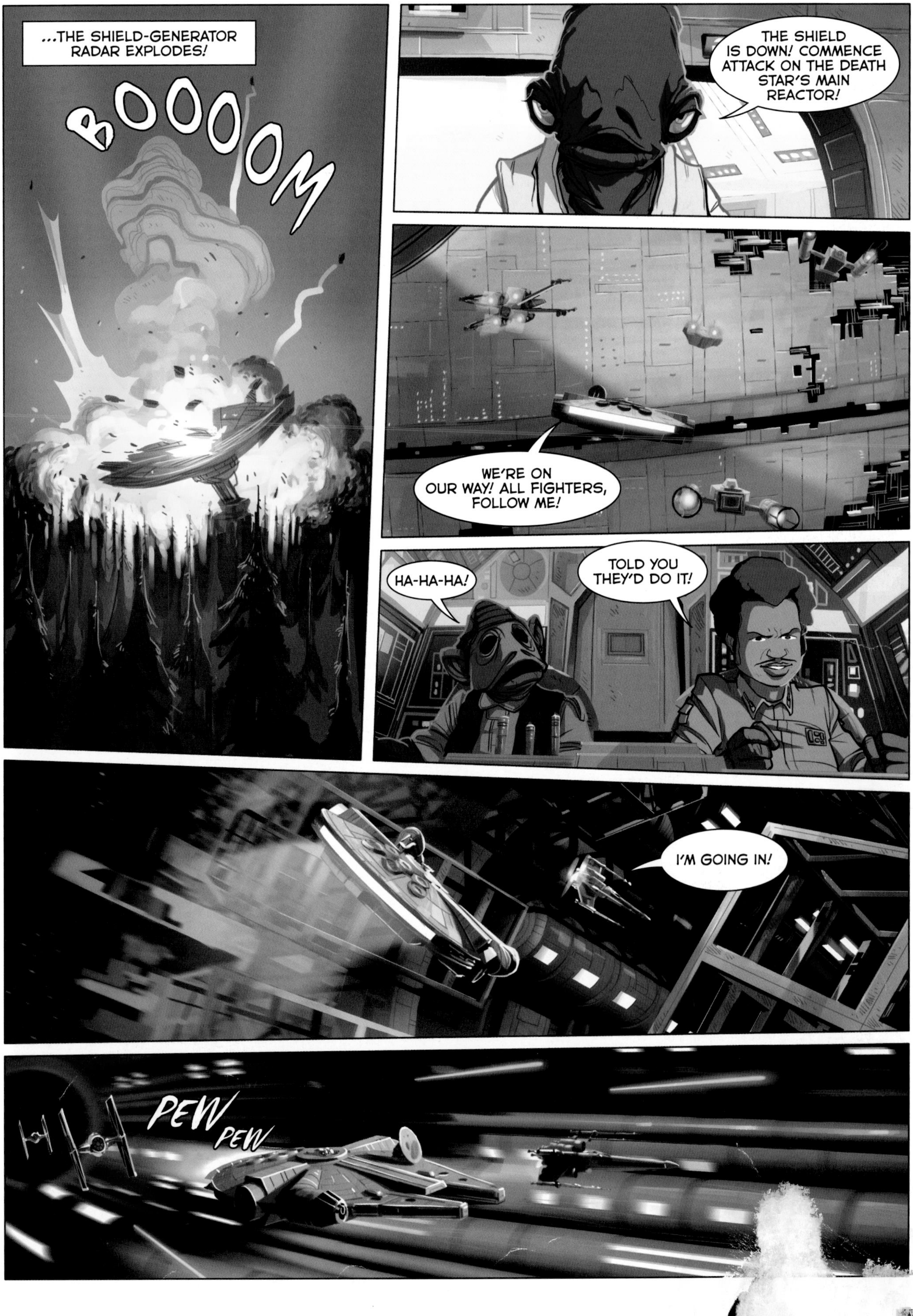
...THE SHIELD-GENERATOR RADAR EXPLODES!
BOOOOM
THE SHIELD IS DOWN! COMMENCE ATTACK ON THE DEATH STAR'S MAIN REACTOR!
WE'RE ON OUR WAY! ALL FIGHTERS, FOLLOW ME!
HA-HA-HA!
TOLD YOU THEY'D DO IT!
I'M GOING IN!
PEW
PEW

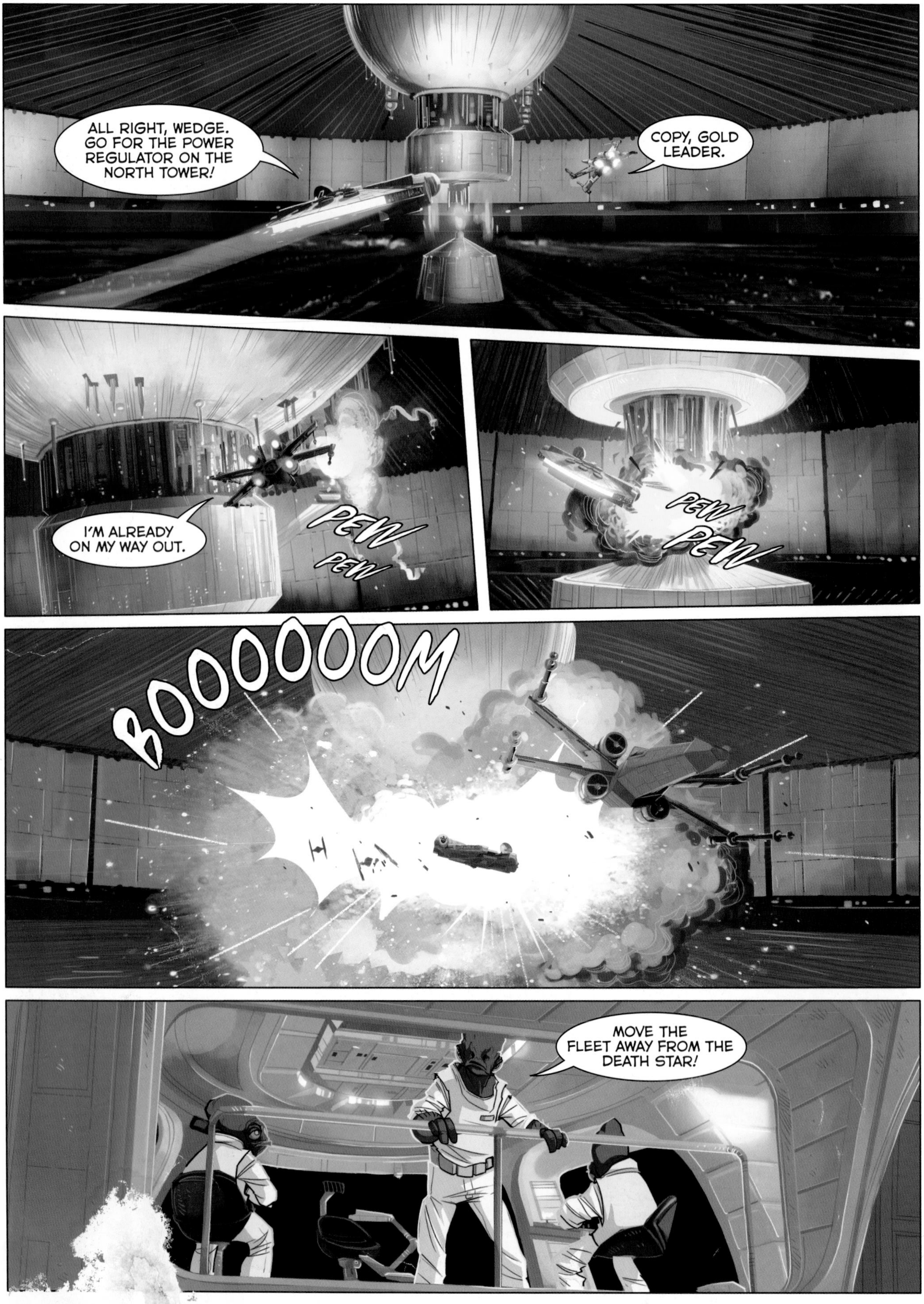
ALL RIGHT, WEDGE. GO FOR THE POWER REGULATOR ON THE NORTH TOWER!
COPY, GOLD LEADER.
I'M ALREADY ON MY WAY OUT.
PEW
PEW
PEW
PEW
BOOOOOOM
MOVE THE FLEET AWAY FROM THE DEATH STAR!

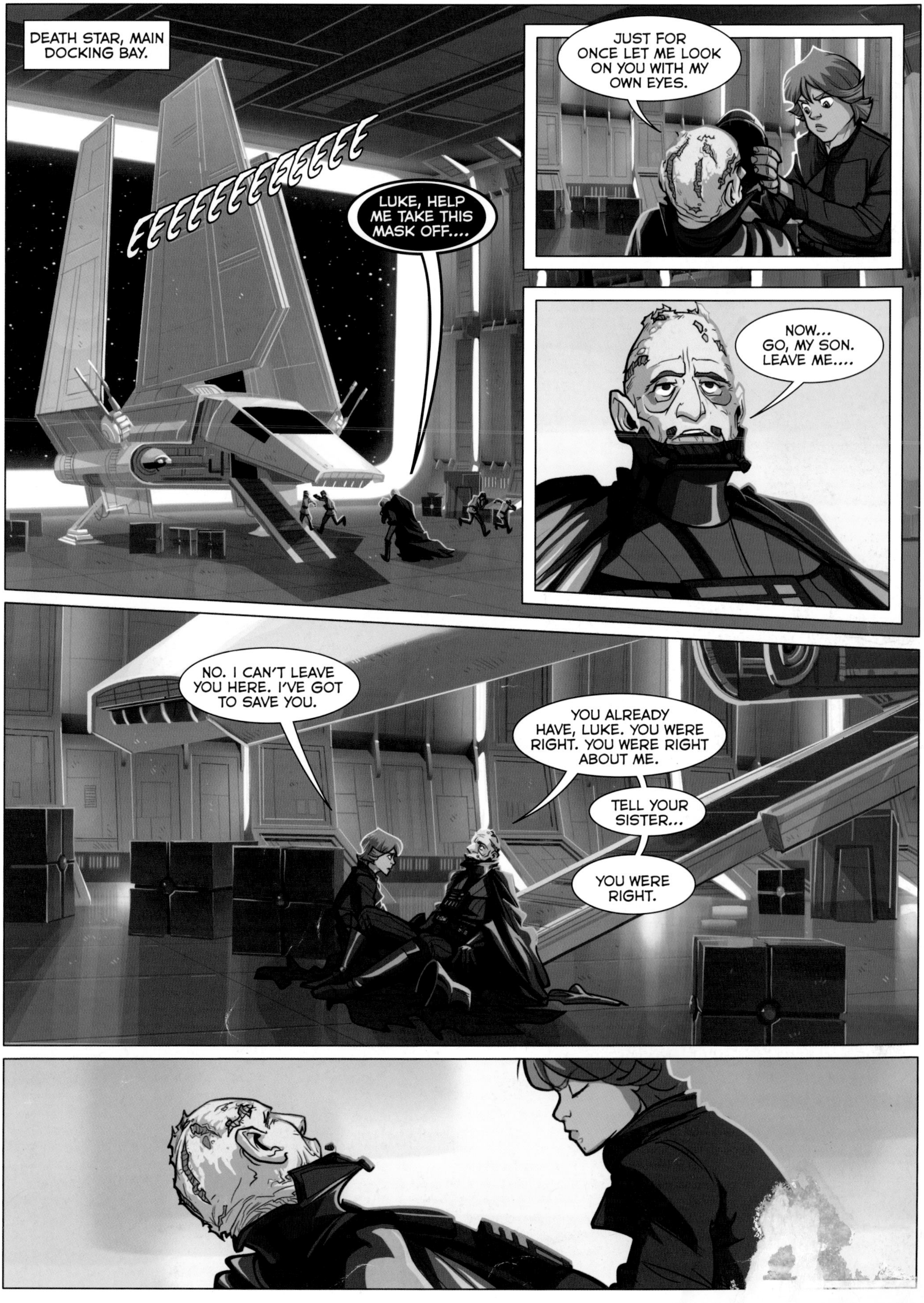
DEATH STAR, MAIN DOCKING BAY.
EEEEEEEEEEEEEEEE
LUKE, HELP ME TAKE THIS MASK OFF....
JUST FOR ONCE LET ME LOOK ON YOU WITH MY OWN EYES.
NOW... GO, MY SON. LEAVE ME....
NO. I CAN'T LEAVE YOU HERE. I'VE GOT TO SAVE YOU.
YOU ALREADY HAVE, LUKE. YOU WERE RIGHT. YOU WERE RIGHT ABOUT ME.
TELL YOUR SISTER...
YOU WERE RIGHT.

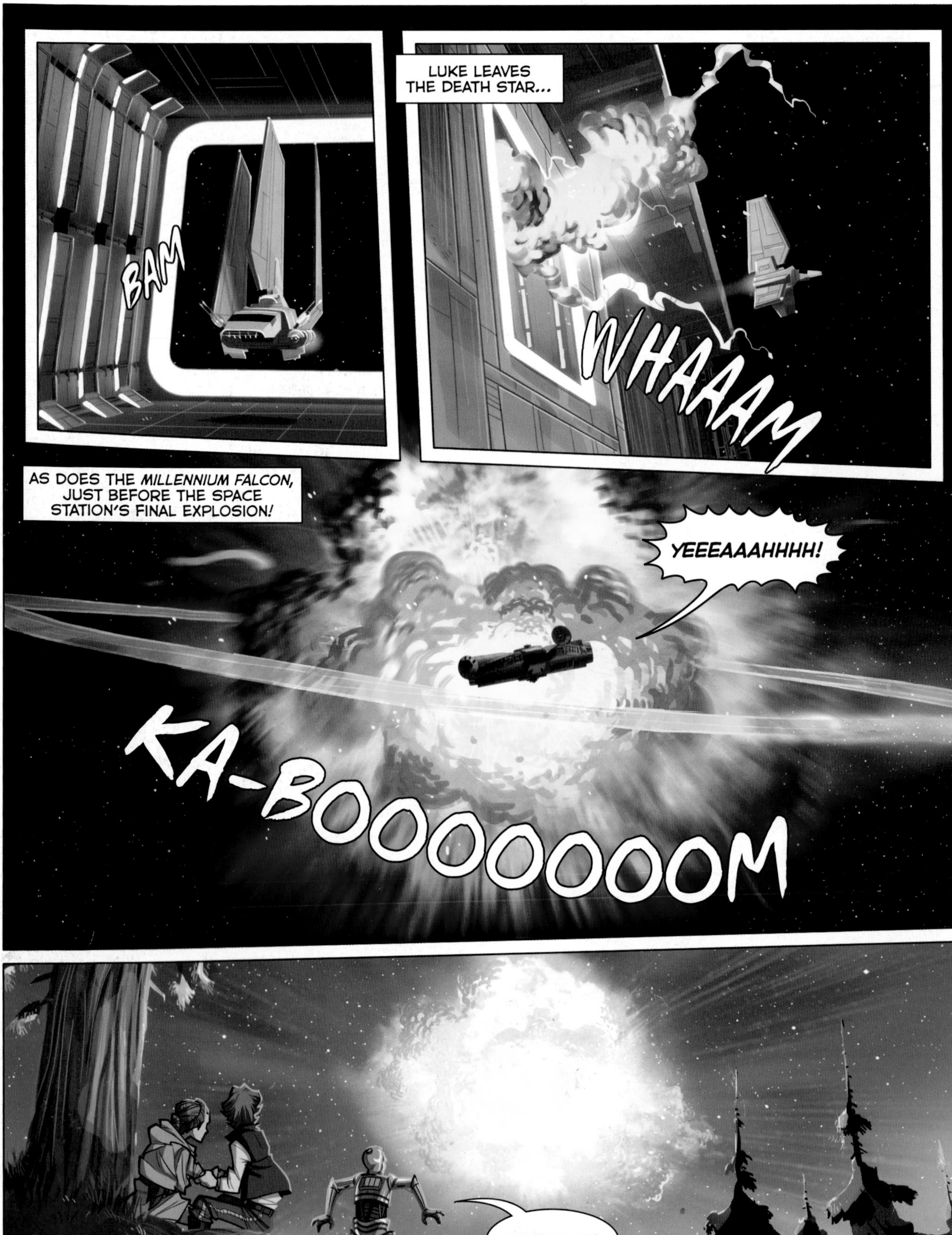
BAM
LUKE LEAVES THE DEATH STAR...
WHAAAM
AS DOES THE *MILLENNIUM FALCON*, JUST BEFORE THE SPACE STATION'S FINAL EXPLOSION!
YEEEAAAHHHH!
KA-BOOOOOOOM
THEY DID IT!

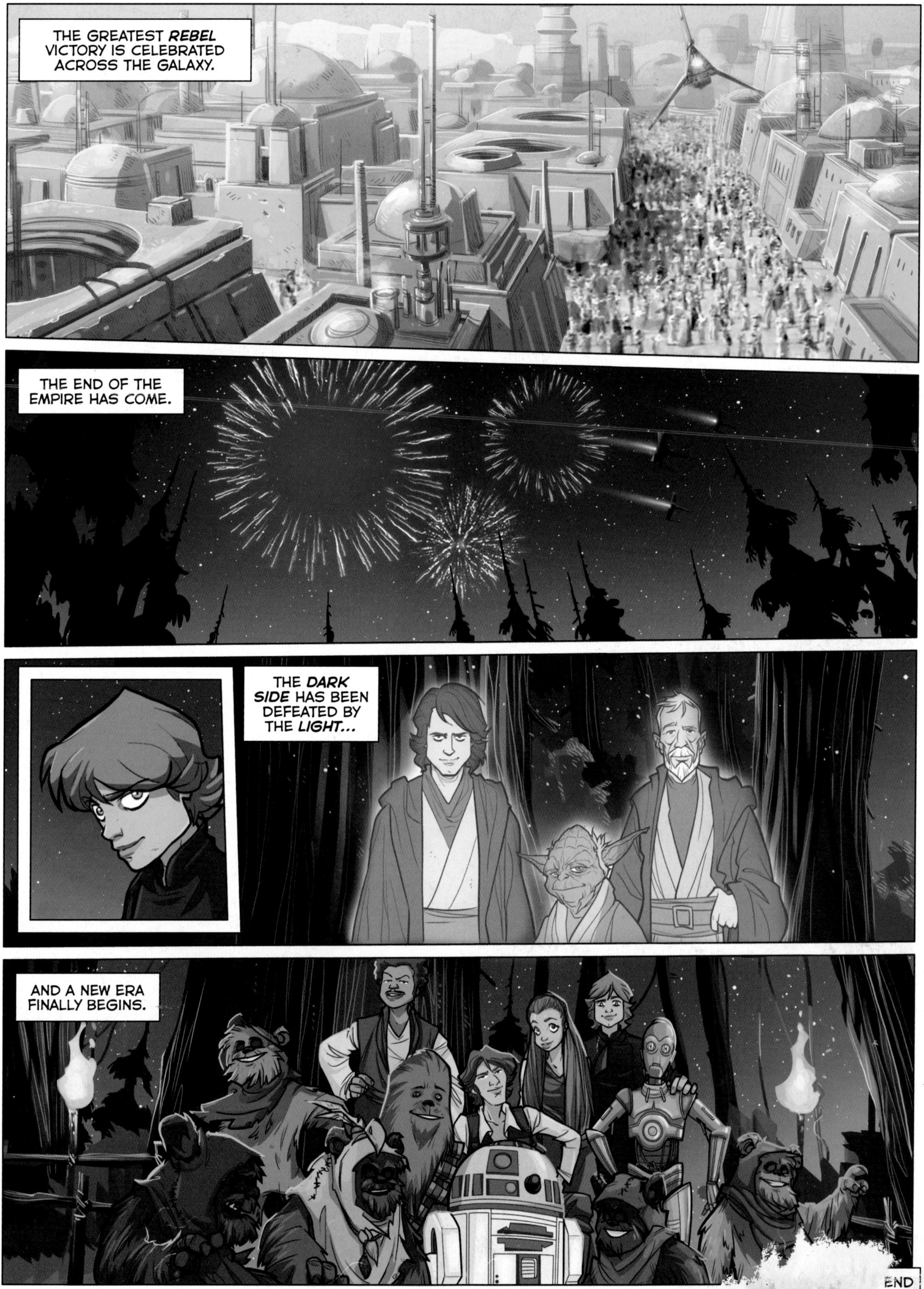
THE GREATEST REBEL VICTORY IS CELEBRATED ACROSS THE GALAXY.
THE END OF THE EMPIRE HAS COME.
THE DARK SIDE HAS BEEN DEFEATED BY THE LIGHT...
AND A NEW ERA FINALLY BEGINS.
END

CREDITS

Manuscript Adaptation
Alessandro Ferrari

Layout and Cleanup
Matteo Piana, Igor Chimisso

Ink
Igor Chimisso, Alessandro Pastrovicchio,
Matteo Piana

Paint (background and settings)
Davide Turotti

Paint (characters)
Kawaii Creative Studio

Special Thanks To
Michael Siglain, Jennifer Heddle,
Rayne Roberts, Pablo Hidalgo,
Leland Chee

Adapted from the films by George Lucas

DISNEY PUBLISHING WORLDWIDE
Global Magazines, Comics,
and Partworks
Publisher
Gianfranco Cordara
*(Vice President, Global Magazines
and New IP)*

Editorial Director
Bianca Coletti

Editorial Team
Guido Frazzini *(Director, Comics)*
Stefano Ambrosio *(Executive Editor, New IP)*
Carlotta Quattrocolo *(Executive Editor, Franchise)*
Camilla Vedove *(Senior Manager, Editorial
Development)*
Behnoosh Khalili *(Senior Editor)*
Julie Dorris *(Senior Editor)*

Design
Enrico Soave *(Senior Designer)*

Art
Ken Shue *(Vice President, Global Art)*
Roberto Santillo *(Creative Director)*
Marco Ghiglione *(Creative Manager)*
Stefano Attardi *(Computer Art Designer)*

Portfolio Management
Olivia Ciancarelli *(Director)*

Business and Marketing
Mariantonietta Galla *(Marketing Manager)*
Virpi Korhonen *(Editorial Manager)*
Kristen Ginter *(Publishing Coordinator)*

Editing – Graphic Design
Absink, Edizioni BD, Lito milano S.r.l.

Contributor
Carlo Resca

COMING SOON IN THE SAME SERIES, ALL THE OTHER EPISODES OF THE EPIC SAGA!